RICK MOFINA

THE BURNING EDGE

MIRA®

MIRA®

Recycling programs
for this product may
not exist in your area.

ISBN-13: 978-0-7783-1301-4

THE BURNING EDGE

Copyright © 2012 by Highway Nine, Inc.

For questions and comments about the quality of this book please contact us at Customer_eCare@Harlequin.ca.

www.Harlequin.com

Printed in U.S.A.

This book is for
Mildred Marmur

Give sorrow words: the grief that does not speak
Whispers the o'er-fraught heart and bids it break.
—*Macbeth,* Act iv, Scene iii
William Shakespeare

1

Maybe the worst was really over, Lisa Palmer thought, driving home alone to Queens from Upstate New York.

Her fingers tightened on the wheel. She was trying to get a grip on her life, trying to regain control, but it was hard, so hard. It had been nearly two years since her husband, Bobby, had died, but now, for the first time, Lisa believed that she and her kids would endure.

They had to.

They needed to move on with their lives. Selling the cabin in the Adirondacks was the first big step Lisa had taken.

But was it the right thing to do?

She glanced at the passenger seat and the slim briefcase holding all the paperwork. A few hours ago she'd closed the sale at the Realtor's office. The new owners, a retired chef and his wife, a florist, from Newark, would take possession in thirty days.

The cabin was still Lisa's until then.

She had promised Ethan and Taylor one last visit to the lake. It was important for all of them to say goodbye to this part of their lives. They'd go up to the cabin together in a few weeks. Lisa brushed a tear from her eye. God, the kids loved it there. She did, too. It was on Lake George and so pretty. It had been in Bobby's family since his great-grandfather bought it in 1957.

Bobby had treasured the place. Lisa's hand shook when she'd signed the papers and all the way down I-87 she'd begged Bobby to forgive her.

I had to do it. The insurance is still a mess. The bills keep coming. I can't make ends meet anymore, not on my pay. The cabin was our only asset. I'm so sorry. I have to think of the future; of going on without you.

She would always love Bobby. But while her aching for him would never stop, she found hope in the thick forests that swept down the hills and rock cuts of the region.

Suddenly, she felt he was near.

He was a mechanic who'd quit school to work in a garage in Corona. A kind, good-looking guy who was good with cars. He loved history, always had his nose in a book. It was at this point of the cabin drive that he would say that the lumber and iron from these hills helped build New York City. Then he would tell her how George Washington had climbed one of the rocks out there and watched for British ships down by Sandy Hook.

Lisa smiled at the memory as her Ford Focus glided down the New York Thruway. After drinking the last of her bottled water, she decided she'd take a break at the new truck stop coming up at the exit for Ramapo, which would put her about an hour or so from home.

This trip to sell the cabin had overwhelmed her. Along the drive, she thought of her best friend from the old neighborhood, Sophia Gretto. They'd grown up together and were like sisters. Even after Sophia had left Queens for college in California they'd kept in touch. Now Sophia was an executive with a public relations firm. Her husband, Ted, was an entertainment lawyer. No children, two Mercedes and a house on Mulholland Drive. Lisa was a supermarket cashier in Queens who never made it to college.

When Bobby died, Sophia and Ted flew to New York to be with Lisa and the kids. Ted had been a saint. They'd both been so good to her.

In the months after Bobby's death, Sophia had visited a few times and called almost every day.

"Why don't you think about moving to Los Angeles," Sophia suggested a few months ago, during one of their calls.

"I couldn't."

"Ted and I could get you a job in one of our offices. You could take courses and get your real estate license like we talked about. We could help you, Ethan and Taylor. Think it over."

"I don't know, Sophia. It could be too much change for the kids."

"Promise me you'll just think about it, honey, okay?"

Lisa did.

In fact, it was all she could think about.

Being a cashier was a good job, but it was not what she wanted to do for the rest of her life. Before she'd met Bobby and got pregnant, Lisa had dreamed of going to college to study interior decorating and start her own business. It didn't happen. After high school she had to work to help take care of her mother. Lisa loved Bobby and her life with the kids, but in a far corner of her heart her dream still flickered.

Should she go after it?

Could she leave everything here and move to Los Angeles?

"It would be like walking away from him, from the life we had here," Lisa had told Sophia.

"Lisa, before all this, you were the fiercest, toughest person I've ever known. You could handle anything without anyone's help. So whatever you decide to do, you'll make it work. You just need to get your strength back." Then Sophia said, "You did not die with him."

"Part of me did."

"Not all of you. You have a life to live. You have to go on."

Everything Sophia had said made sense.

Lisa was about to arrive at a decision as she left the thruway and wheeled into the big, new Freedom Freeway Service Center at Ramapo. She parked some distance from the rigs easing in and out of the lot. Diesel engines growled, air brakes hissed. She was enveloped by humid air as she walked across the hot pavement.

After driving nearly two hundred miles, stretching her legs was a luxury.

The interstate traffic droned.

The building was landscaped with clipped shrubs. Its neo-deco facade had huge windows. New York State flags and the Stars and Stripes flapped on gold-tipped poles above the mammoth entrance.

Inside, the air-conditioning was soothing. After using the restroom, Lisa went to the snack shop for bottled water, a candy bar, a comic for Ethan and a magazine for Taylor. She knew she shouldn't be spending the money, but she missed her kids and wanted to give them something.

A few people stood ahead of her to pay.

As the line advanced, all the lights went off. The ventilation fans stopped and the building lost power. People glanced at each other for an answer. A moment later, the lights came back on and the fans restarted.

Keys jingled and a man in a business jacket loosened his tie, hurried from a rear office toward the restaurant, grumbling to the woman accompanying him. "Call them and tell them it's another false alarm."

Lisa saw the man go to a control panel at the far end of the restaurant. The panel's lights stopped flashing after he inserted a key and turned it.

Must be this hot weather straining the air-conditioning. Come on, please.

This was taking longer than she'd expected and she still faced New York traffic. She wanted to get back on the road.

Lisa looked outside as an American Centurion armored truck stopped in front of the lobby, which had three ATMs. One guard started loading a cart while another stood by, scanning the lot and the building.

The guards started for the entrance as Lisa stepped to the counter. After paying, she slid her items and wallet into her shoulder bag. Then she made a quick search in her bag for her supermarket ID, not certain if she'd left it at home, or if she'd thrust it in her bag after finishing her shift before driving upstate.

She barely noticed the rumble of the four motorcycles that had pulled up alongside the armored truck. Adjusting her bag, she saw several people standing near the ATMs; some were studying the large map of Greater New York City above the machines.

As the armored truck guards entered, Lisa froze.

Two of the motorcycle riders, their faces hidden by their helmets and dark shields, were dressed in full-body riding suits that were bulky around their abdomens. They were wearing gloves and gripping handguns as they came up behind the guards.

Pop!

The first rider shot the first guard. A gout of blood and

fragments of his skull blasted across the floor to a vending machine.

At the same time, the second rider came up on the guard wheeling the money cart and fired into the back of his neck. *Crack!* The impact forced the top of the guard's head to flap open, cranial matter springing out. The money cart clanged to the floor between the dead men, their blood blossoming into widening pools.

Lisa caught her breath.

"Everyone down!" the first shooter yelled, seizing the guards' guns. "Nobody fucking move! Put your phones on the floor beside you now! Put your hands behind your head! Look at the floor! Don't look at us!"

Lisa slid to the floor. Her magazines, water and other items tumbled from her bag around her.

The second rider produced a sack and moved swiftly, collecting cell phones from staff and customers throughout the center.

Outside, the two other riders had sprayed something into the truck's air intake, forcing the driver to exit, double over and vomit. Then they shot him. The two riders entered the truck and quickly unloaded money into backpacks and saddlebags.

In the service center, a woman began wailing.

One of the riders herded all staff and customers from the washroom, the restaurant, the kitchen, the snack shop and gas counter into the center's lobby, forcing them to the floor at gunpoint. The other gunman produced folded nylon bags and commanded the nearest person, a sobbing teenage girl, to help him fill them. The plastic wrapped around some of the cash had torn. Bundles had rolled over the center's floor lobby near Lisa.

The gunman collecting the cash grunted as he snatched the packs that had fallen around her, whizzing them into the nylon bags. His partner eyed the people on the floor for movement.

Please, God, let someone call the police, Lisa thought.

The man on the floor next to Lisa turned his face to her. He looked about thirty, was clean shaven with quick intelligent eyes. He was wearing jeans, a jacket and T-shirt.

"I'm a cop," he whispered, keeping his hands outstretched over his head. "My gun's on my right hip under my shirt."

She nodded.

"You slide closer, lift it out," he said. "Tuck it under me. They're wearing vests, but I can get off head shots."

Lisa could not breathe.

She was motionless until the man's urgent gaze compelled her to move. She worked her way closer to him, carefully extending her left hand, pulling away his jacket, feeling the hardness of his gun. Lisa got it loose. Her sweating face was two feet from his.

He nodded encouragement.

As Lisa pulled, the weapon slipped from her fingers and rattled on the floor. A gunman flew to them, grabbing the gun before the cop could. He patted the man, taking his second gun from his ankle holster. He jerked at the man's jacket, extracting a folding police wallet and examining it.

"Fucking FBI!"

Lisa looked into the young agent's eyes.

The gunman pushed the muzzle against his head.

Lisa's breathing quickened. The agent blinked and said, "Jennifer, I love you," before his skull exploded, propelling brain matter onto Lisa's face.

The killer moved and pressed his gun to her head.

2

The gun drilled into her head with crushing savagery.

As Lisa waited for death, blood pounded against her skull.

She looked into the lifeless eyes of the cop beside her, feeling bits of his brain tissue on her face, her skin prickling with fear, her heart hammering against the floor.

Time stood still. Like a dream.

The smell of lemon floor cleaner mixed with a burning aroma from the gun. She sensed sweet lake air and water lapping on the shore as she saw Taylor and Ethan, then Bobby, their smiles melting in the sun.

As Lisa's pulse thundered, she found her misshapen reflection in the black shield of the killer's helmet, trapped in a dark abyss.

Her mind streaked to her last seconds with Bobby, his stubble brushing her cheek, the hint of his cologne, his soft, *"Love you, babe,"* before he left for work that day and was gone forever.

Ethan. Taylor.

Her last moments with them when she'd dropped them off at Rita's before driving upstate: Taylor in her pink

T-shirt with the kittens and the tiny mustard stain; Ethan, serious and angling for a new computer game.

She'd hugged them so hard.

"You're hurting me, Mom."

"I love you two so much."

"Love you, too, Mom."

Watching them shrink in her rearview mirror, leaving them behind.

Is this the last time? No! You can't do this to them! Oh, Jesus, I need to be with them!

Lisa raised her head, turning so it scraped against the gun. Turning until she looked into the black shield, searching the monstrous darkness, piercing its semitransparency, she found the killer's eyes, two black points of fury, boring into her through the blood splatter.

With every ounce of her strength, Lisa summoned Bobby, Ethan and Taylor, feeling their brilliant faces shining down on her. She seized them, wrapped herself around them. Lisa could feel them now, smelling their skin, their hair, their essence. Her entire life blazed before her like a falling star as she begged heaven not to take her from her children, prayed with such intensity she voiced the words.

"Please, don't. I've got kids. I'm just a cashier. Please, I'm begging you."

All of it had happened in a heartbeat as Lisa waited for the gunman to end her life.

But no shot came.

Another second passed. A shadow crossed over them.

"Did you hear me?" a second gunman shouted at the first. "Let's go!"

The second man gripped a bulging canvas bag and jerked the killer's arm. "Why did you shoot him?"

"Fucking cop went for his gun."

"Okay, forget her! We're done! We're over three minutes! People outside could be making calls—let's go now!"

The pressure of the gun on Lisa's head was gone, along with the four suspects. In their wake, Lisa's ears rang with the shrieking of the victims. They consoled each other. Some huddled over the corpses. Lisa didn't know how much time had passed before the chaos blended with approaching sirens.

The first police officers rushed into the center through every door with handguns and pump-action shotguns drawn and trained in every direction, ordering everyone to kneel and keep their hands up, palms out.

"They're gone! Help us, please! We need ambulances!" a perspiring, overweight man pleaded.

More police arrived, along with paramedics who tried to aid the men who'd been shot, but it was futile.

"Miss, please. Are you in any pain?"

Someone was talking to Lisa.

"Miss, you have to let us help, you have got to let go."

I'm never letting go. I'm alive...

"Miss, please."

Lisa couldn't answer. She blinked several times before realizing she was holding the hand of the dead cop beside her.

"Take care of him," Lisa said. "You have to take care of him. They just shot him."

It's my fault. I dropped the gun. It's my fault.

She was trembling as a paramedic examined her, checking her vital signs, talking to her.

"You're going to be all right. Help is here."

The sirens wouldn't stop. More police cars and ambulances arrived, emergency lights splashing from the lot over the scene.

* * *

Everything was hazy in the aftermath.

All four men were dead.

Sheets were draped over their bodies and the area was cleared, protected; officers moved the survivors to the far end of the center. As they began interviewing each of them, some nodded toward Lisa.

Her heart was racing.

Officer Anita Rowan of the Ramapo Police Department had taken Lisa aside. Rowan had short hair; tiny earrings pierced her lobes. Lisa noticed her polished nails as she wrote in her notebook.

"Now, Lisa, I want you to take a deep breath and tell me what happened."

Lisa recounted everything that she saw. Rowan had a nice tan and a white-toothed smile and touched Lisa's shoulder when she repeated parts of Lisa's account for accuracy. Her utility belt gave little leathery squeaks when she left Lisa to talk to a group of grim-faced men in plain-clothes. From where Lisa was, she could see them in the killing zone. They produced their own clipboards and notebooks, writing down what other uniformed officers reported.

A couple of the plainclothesmen eyed Lisa.

Then the investigators tugged on rubber gloves and slipped on shoe covers and visited the dead as if each were an exhibit on a macabre tour. They raised each sheet, examined each body, took notes and pictures, made sketches and checked identification.

The investigators consulted other investigators and two of them approached Lisa. The first was a few inches over six feet, about forty-five, with thinning hair. A dark mustache accentuated his poker face.

"Lisa Palmer?" he asked.

"Yes."

"Detective Percy Quinn, Ramapo P.D." Quinn's face creased with concern as he took stock of the blood flecks on Lisa's temple, nose, cheeks and chin.

"You want someone to wipe that off her?" Rowan asked.

"That's evidence," Quinn said. "I want a picture first."

Quinn summoned a crime scene tech who took several frames, then got a paramedic to use a medical wipe and swab. The tech preserved the material as evidence. Quinn and the others signed the information.

"Are you okay, Miss Palmer?" Quinn said afterward.

"I don't know."

"You witnessed the shootings?" Quinn asked.

"Yes."

"Lisa, we're going to need your help, but given what's happened, this crime goes beyond our jurisdiction."

She didn't understand.

"I just want to go home."

"We appreciate that," Quinn said. "But we won't be done for some time yet. We're preserving the scene. What we'd like to do is move you into a separate office area here while we wait for the primary investigators."

"I just want to go home to my children."

"We understand, but we really need you to cooperate with us. It's important that you help us. Will you do that for us, Lisa?"

She thought of the man on the floor beside her, how he'd died trying to help.

She nodded and they led her down a hall in the administrative part of the complex to an office. The sign on the wall said, Mac Foyt, Manager. The room was large with blue deep-pile carpet. Photos of cars, trucks and pretty scenes of seasons along the Hudson covered most of the walls. The desk had framed pictures of a boy in a base-ball uniform, a man and woman smiling at Niagara Falls.

Mac and Mrs. Foyt?

Rowan's utility belt squeaked as she set a sweating bottle of water on the desk before Lisa. Sirens continued wailing outside.

"Is there anything else I can get you, Lisa?"

"Can I call home?"

Rowan was sympathetic. "I'm afraid not," she said. "The situation is too serious. I can contact anyone on your behalf."

Lisa's stomach lurched and her head throbbed.

"Lisa?"

As Lisa cupped her hands to her face, she felt the coolness of the medical wipe that removed his blood and brain matter. That's when she realized some of it was still on the backs of her hands.

"I just stopped to go to the bathroom and buy a snack."

Lisa released a long anguished sob.

Rowan held her to keep her from coming apart.

3

New York City

Frank Morrow picked up his line at his desk at the FBI's New York headquarters at 26 Federal Plaza in Lower Manhattan.

He had refused to go to his doctor's office in Greenwich Village today, insisting his specialist deliver the news by phone. After weeks of tests, scans and second opinions, Morrow had braced for this call.

"Frank, it's Art."

"Should I enhance my pension plan or review my will?"

"I wish I had better news. It's worse than we'd feared."

"Is it treatable?"

"Chemo is a long-shot option. You'd have to stop working, and the odds chemo will have any impact are two to three percent, at best."

"Is there any other option?"

"No."

"So I'm terminal?"

"Yes."

"How long?"

"Frank, we can't be sure."

"How long, Art?"

"A year, maybe sixteen months."

Morrow's knuckles whitened as he squeezed his phone.

Silence fell between him and Art Stein, a Johns Hopkins grad who'd interned at Sloan-Kettering. Stein had an excellent bedside manner that he'd taken courtside over the last few months, after agreeing to give Morrow most of his updates during Knicks games at the Garden.

Now, to fill the growing quiet, Stein reached for medical jargon, explaining again about cells, hematology and the stages Morrow faced with this rare form of cancer.

Morrow was no longer listening.

Maybe it was Morrow's private philosophy, forged by his line of work, but for him, death was always near. A view made manifest by the fact that the FBI's New York office was a few blocks from Ground Zero.

As Stein went on, Morrow looked out at Lower Manhattan's skyline and was pulled back to that day, thinking how one moment you are living your life, then fate slams into you the way the planes slammed into the towers.

On that morning, Morrow actually saw the Boeing 767 that was American Airlines flight 11 streak by his twenty-eighth-floor window before it knifed into the North Tower. Within minutes, the New York Division led the investigation. Morrow was immersed in it as the FBI and a spectrum of agencies chased leads, examined the wreckage and collected evidence at Fresh Kills.

Everybody had lost someone in the attacks.

Moments of that morning haunted him.

"Frank?" Stein repeated. "Frank, are you with me? To answer your question—" *I asked a question?* "—there won't be any physical pain. Breathing could cease in your sleep. Frank?"

Morrow searched for words worth using.

"I'm lucky, Art."

"Lucky?" Stein paused. "Frank, do you want me to put you in touch with a shrink, to talk things over?"

Morrow found Elizabeth's and Hailey's faces in the framed photographs next to his computer monitor. He smiled to himself.

He was damn lucky. Unlike the people who died in the attacks. To Morrow they were heroes. Especially the jumpers he'd seen.

They had no choice. They had no time.

Morrow was lucky because he had time to get ready.

"Frank? Do you want me to set it up?"

"No, I don't think I'll need that now. I'll just chew this over for a while, you know?"

"I understand. Call me anytime. Hey, I got Lakers tickets. Are you in?"

"I'm in."

Morrow hung up.

Telling Elizabeth and their daughter, Hailey, would be the hardest thing he'd ever have to do. Elizabeth knew nothing about this. He'd kept it to himself for the last three months. That's when he started getting a few stomach cramps in his sleep, his skin started itching, his piss and crap turned weird colors and he'd lost a bit of weight. He told her he'd cut out the fries at work and used the stairs more.

"That's good." Elizabeth smiled, but her eyes held a degree of suspicion.

Of course, he was a bastard for not telling her and she'd have every right to kill him. But she'd lost her mother last year and he was not going to put more worry on her if there was a chance it was nothing.

All that changed now.

In the back of his mind, Morrow had figured that his number had come up. Somehow he just knew. He was grateful for the good life he'd had, for the time he had left. What tore him up was that it was going to be hard on Elizabeth and Hailey.

At least we have time to prepare.

He'd talk to his boss, get some time off. Maybe drive along the coast with Elizabeth and Hailey, watch the ocean and talk.

Burial or cremation?

He didn't have to decide today.

One thing was certain: he was not going to curl up. To hell with chemo. As long as he could do the job, he would do the job. He'd seize control of every minute he had left. He was not going to eat his gun, or fall in front of a subway train.

Frank Morrow would rage against his impending death.

"Frank—" Agent Rutto rushed by his doorway "—meeting in the boardroom, now!"

About thirty people had gathered quickly around the room's huge cherry-wood table, the venetian blinds opened to a view of the Brooklyn Bridge. Assistant Special Agent in Charge Glenda Stark had called the briefing and, in typical Stark style, cut to the point.

"Listen up, people. We've just received confirmation of four homicides in the robbery of an armored courier, American Centurion, which was servicing ATMs at the Freedom Freeway Service Center at Ramapo."

Stark surveyed the room over her bifocals. She had everyone's attention.

"Three of the victims were Centurion guards. The fourth—" Stark cleared her throat. "The fourth is Special Agent Gregory Scott Dutton, with our Bridgeport office."

Cursing rippled round the room.

"According to preliminary witness accounts, Ramapo P.D. indicates this was a highly organized hit. Dutton was among the hostages and was going for his weapon when he was killed."

Reaction in the room rose. Stark shut it down.

"This one is ours. ERT is en route. Ramapo, Rockland Sheriff and New York State are on scene. We're pulling from New Jersey, Hudson Valley and New Rochelle RAs. And Connecticut is sending agents. I want as many of our people to get up there now to interview witnesses. NHQ has been briefed and the director says this is a priority. Agent Morrow?"

"Yes."

"You're the case agent. That's it. Let's move, people."

4

New York City

The man in the town house apartment was going to kill his neighbor.

The NYPD had sealed his street in Manhattan's Lower East Side, near Stuyvesant Town. News crews had gathered at the east and west cordons. Jack Gannon watched from the east end of the block as a hostage negotiator tried talking the man down.

Gannon, a reporter with the World Press Alliance news service, was with Angelo Dixon, a WPA photographer. Dixon had been using the earpiece on his portable scanner to monitor NYPD radio dispatches.

So far, Gannon knew that the suspect, Sylvester Jerome Nada, was an unemployed carpenter facing eviction, divorce and a mountain of debt. He'd claimed his neighbor, Gustav Trodder, had stolen his antique pistol, which had once belonged to Napoleon Bonaparte. Nada had taken Trodder hostage with his semiautomatic Smith & Wesson, vowing to "blow his freakin' head off."

Nothing was happening.

This standoff is going to turn out to be a supreme waste of time.

Gannon had been here nearly two hours and his gut told him the real story was the tip he'd been working on back in the newsroom.

It came in last week, a call about an impending threat.

"It involves an operation, a mission, an attack on America," the caller had said.

Gannon often got nut-job calls like that and had first considered this one useless. It was short on details, anything he could use for confirmation.

But something about the tipster had gnawed at him.

"This is big! I swear to God, what I'm telling you is true!" the caller had said.

The guy had a nervous air of authenticity. He was scared. He'd called Gannon several times from public phones, refusing to give his name, occupation, address, anything. But he'd grown comfortable with Gannon and finally agreed to meet at a diner near Times Square.

"I'll bring the confirmation you need."

But Mr. Anonymous never showed and his calls stopped.

That was three days ago.

Gannon had told no one about it, adhering to his rules on tips.

Never tell an editor what you've got until you have it nailed. Editors either forced you to push your source until you lost them, or dismissed your tip outright. And with the way things were going at the WPA these days, he was not going to tell anybody what he had until he had it locked. It was the only way he'd guarantee support from the desk.

Instinct told him to pursue the tip, to find out what had happened to his source. Gannon secretly worked on it between other assignments. That's what he'd been doing before he was punted to cover this waste of time.

Normally, the WPA, a worldwide newswire, wouldn't

staff a story like this; it was too local. But things hadn't been normal at the WPA since Melody Lyon, the news-wire's most respected news editor, took a one-year leave three months ago to teach English in Africa.

Lyon was replaced by Dolf Lisker, a man who'd headed the WPA's business coverage. Lisker had little experience leading news teams. He was a heartless slab of misery who loathed the world and everyone in it. He was obsessed with WPA's slipping revenues.

Numbers—*good* numbers—were Lisker's friends.

The WPA was headquartered in Midtown Manhattan where it oversaw bureaus in every major U.S. city and ninety countries, providing a 24/7 flow of fast, accurate information to thousands of newspaper, radio, TV, corporate and online subscribers everywhere.

Gannon was devoted to the WPA. Its reputation for excellence had resulted in twenty-five Pulitzer Prizes. But Lisker was wary of increasing competition from the Associated Press, Bloomberg, Reuters, Agence France-Presse, Deutsche Presse-Agentur, China's Xinhua News Agency and Russia's fast-rising Interfax News Agency.

"Each time subscribers take a competitor's content over WPA content, we bleed," Lisker wrote in his assume-command memo to the staff. "Treat every news organization as the enemy. Regard exclusives as our oxygen. We need to break stories and offer better ones than our competition. This is how we will fortify our numbers."

Rumors flew that Lisker had presented the WPA executive with a "personnel efficiency model"—translation: "editorial cutback plan"—linking story pick-up rates to performance assessments of every WPA reporter.

The pressure was straining morale.

Gannon had felt Lisker's sting a few hours ago. Lisker had walked by the news desk and overheard the call about a hostage taking in the Lower East Side. It had come from a WPA intern posted at the shack in NYPD headquarters at One Police Plaza.

"It's got something to do with a dispute about an antique flintlock pistol that belonged to Napoleon." When Lisker heard that, he stopped cold.

"Napoleon?" Lisker said to the assignment editor on the line with the intern. "That gives this a global hook. We should jump on it."

"I'll send the intern," the assignment editor said.

"No." Lisker looked at Jack. "Send Gannon."

Gannon lifted his head from his keyboard. He'd been working on ways to find his anonymous caller. His monitor displayed his notes on his tip.

"But the intern's closer," Gannon said, closing his file.

Lisker approached, jabbing his finger at him.

"Listen up, hotshot! You've shown us zero since Phoenix, so get your ass down there now and get us a story on Napoleon's pistol!"

Gannon grabbed his jacket, phone, notebook and recorder.

"Jack—" the assignment editor had his hand clasped over a phone "—Angelo Dixon is heading down in his car. He'll pick you up out front."

So now here he was with Dixon, waiting for this thing with Sylvester, Gustav and Napoleon's pistol to wind down.

Dixon had one eye clenched behind his digital camera. Gently rolling his long lens, he shot several frames of a disheveled man crouched near a police car and talking to cops.

"This is crazy." Dixon concentrated on the police chatter flowing into his ear. "You won't believe who that is."

Gannon squinted down the street. "Who?"

Dixon absorbed more from the scanner, then said, "It's Gustav."

"What?"

Dixon held up a finger, listening to his scanner.

"All this time—" Dixon smiled "—he's been at the deli around the block. He heard the commotion, then started asking cops when he can get back into his apartment. Wait. He says Sylvester has no guns, hates guns, is going through tough times, is emotionally unstable and makes stuff up."

"He makes stuff up?"

Gannon saw a uniformed cop enter Nada's building with a large brown bag. "Now what?"

Ten minutes passed and nothing.

Gannon's phone buzzed and he received a photo of himself at the cordon taken from the cordon at the opposite end of the street.

The message with it said Hey.

Gannon studied the press pack at the west cordon. A woman gave him a small wave. Katrina Kisko, a reporter with the *New York Signal*, the new online newspaper.

Seeing her gave him pause.

They'd met at a double homicide in the Bronx and started dating. It was good—better than good. He'd fallen hard for her, thought they had something strong. For the first time in his life, he was no longer alone. Until Katrina broke it off, telling him that being in the same business made things "too complicated" for her.

Too complicated?

He was stunned. He didn't understand. It was like a kick in the teeth.

That was a few months ago and Gannon hadn't seen her until now.

He returned her wave.

Then NYPD radios crackled. The cordon tape was lifted; Dixon and other news photographers rushed toward the building, recording Nada being escorted shirtless and cuffed into a waiting car.

It was over.

Twenty minutes later, the NYPD press officer told reporters that there was never a hostage or guns involved. Nada was going to Bellevue for a psych evaluation.

Reporters fired a barrage of questions. Gannon had to repeat his three times before the officer got to it.

"What about the Napoleon gun?" Gannon asked.

"A fabrication."

More questions and Katrina Kisko weighed in.

"How did you get Nada to surrender?" she asked.

"He asked for food and we gave it to him."

"What kind of food?" Katrina asked.

"A cheeseburger, fries and a milk shake."

"What flavor was the shake?" Katrina asked.

"Cripes." The press officer repeated her question into his radio.

The answer crackled back. "Strawberry."

Katrina smiled and resumed typing on her BlackBerry.

At that point Gannon's phone rang.

"This is Lisker."

"It's over. There's no gun, no hostage, no story."

"Yeah, we've got something else. One of our stringers just picked this up on his police scanners—four murders in an armored car hit at an I-87 truck stop."

"Where?"

"Ramapo. We're breaking it. We'll work the phones here but I want you and Dixon to get up there now. You're the lead. We have to own this story, Gannon."

"On my way."

Gannon turned to face Katrina.

"On your way where?" she asked.

"Really, Katrina? You've got to be kidding." Gannon saw Dixon signaling to hustle to his parked car.

"I thought we were friends, we could help each other," she said.

"Friends? Give me a break."

"Maybe I handled things wrong. I'm sorry if I hurt you, Jack."

"I've got to go."

"You're seriously not going to tell me?"

Gannon left her standing there and rushed to Dixon's Dodge Journey. Ten minutes later, he watched Lower Manhattan and the East River rush by as Dixon accelerated on FDR Drive, weaving through northbound traffic. As they passed the United Nations and the span of the Queensboro Bridge, Dixon estimated they'd get to Ramapo in an hour.

"By the way, what was that with your extremely hot girlfriend?"

"Ex."

"All right, your extremely hot ex-girlfriend."

"Nothing, Angelo."

"Right." Dixon laughed.

Gannon's thoughts of Katrina were eclipsed by the knot tightening in his stomach.

Four homicides awaited him.

5

Ramapo, Metropolitan New York City

*W*homp-whomp-whomp...

A few miles south of Ramapo police roadblocks halted traffic in the south- and northbound lanes of the thruway while a New York State Police helicopter cut across the sky above Gannon and Dixon.

After showing press ID at the roadblock, they were waved through.

Maneuvering through the traffic, Dixon got them down to the exit for the service center, then to the first entrance, but no farther. It was blocked by patrol units with Rockland County.

An officer stepped up to Dixon's SUV.

"You're going to have to turn around, sir. You can't go any farther."

"We're press."

"Who are you with?"

"WPA." Dixon and Gannon held up plastic IDs from their neck chains.

"All right. Park with the others and stay outside the tape." The officer pointed to the distant landscaped island with the service center's sign.

Gannon took stock of the knot of news trucks and cars emblazoned with station call letters. But no media people were around. Dixon grabbed his gear and they walked quickly, keeping outside the yellow tape that stretched around the perimeter of the huge lot. Along the way, they came to clusters of onlookers at the tape and stopped to talk to them.

"All I know is my sister's a waitress in the restaurant and nobody can tell me anything," said Reeve Torbey, a man in his twenties wearing a faded Guns & Roses T-shirt. "I texted her, tried calling her cell, the restaurant. I can't get through."

Gannon quoted him, got his cell number and left his card, urging him to call and promising to share information.

Agnes Slade, a woman with silver hair pulled up in a bun, shielded her eyes as she stared at the center, a phone clutched in one hand.

"My son's in town and just called me. He said police are searching everywhere," she told Gannon. "Things like this just don't happen here."

As Gannon and Dixon moved on, the sound of approaching sirens underscored the drama. Gannon heard the deep rumble of a Cessna.

Could be TV news, or police searching for suspects, he figured.

"Here we go," Dixon said.

Amid the gaps in the lake of rigs, cars and emergency vehicles parked in the lot, Dixon glimpsed the armored truck and crime scene techs working around it. He steadied himself and focused his long lens.

Gannon moved on, exploring farther. Over his years as a crime reporter with the *Buffalo Sentinel,* he knew what to glean from a scene to give his work depth and accuracy.

He'd studied the same textbooks detectives studied to pass their exams. And he'd researched and reported on enough homicides and murder trials to know the anatomy of an investigation.

It had earned him the respect of the seasoned detectives he knew.

Forty yards from Dixon, Gannon stopped and signaled him to the spot.

"Have a look through there."

They still saw the armored car, but from this different perspective they could now see the sheet on the pavement covering the victim near it. Dixon took more pictures.

"Look through the entrance doors," Gannon said.

A cloud passed, dimming the sun's reflection on the glass doors, allowing Dixon to see inside and make out two more sheets covering victims on the lobby floor. In one case, a boot extended from under the sheet. Keeping beyond the tape, Dixon took more pictures, framing them with the outside victim and armored truck in the foreground and the two victims inside in the background with investigators bent over them.

It was a powerful news photo.

A uniformed cop yelled at them to keep moving and pointed toward the flagpoles farther along. As they walked away, Gannon glanced around the scene, feeling the clock ticking down. He had to find a way into the heart of what had happened here and why.

His BlackBerry vibrated with a text. The WPA's news desk advised him that their stringer was having car trouble and would be late. Gannon was not concerned the WPA had dispatched more staff from headquarters.

Gannon and Dixon could handle the early work.

About a dozen news types were gathered at the flag-poles in what was an impromptu press area. Four TV news cameras topped tripods and a couple of photographers chatted with people holding notebooks, recorders and microphones with station flags.

Gannon checked his BlackBerry again. The WPA had already moved another short news hit out of headquarters. The latest read:

Four people are dead after the brazen robbery of an American Centurion armored truck at the Freedom Freeway Service Center in Ramapo, at New York City's northern edge, according to local authorities.

The suspects remain at large.

"Carrie Carter, WRCX Radio 5 News." A woman in her mid-twenties smiled at Gannon. "Who are you with?"

"WPA." Given the size of the group, Gannon figured not all the press from the city had arrived yet. "So what's going on here?"

"You tell us. The WPA beat everybody with that first wire story."

"What have they told you here so far? Looks like you're set up for a briefing. They talk to you yet?" Gannon asked.

"Not yet. Ramapo P.D. promised us a press briefing in ten minutes," Carrie said, "but that was twenty-five minutes ago."

Gannon knew armored car robberies fell to FBI jurisdiction and figured the local cops were likely sorting out just who was going to say what. Glancing to the parking area, he saw satellite trucks from the networks and other news cars arriving.

"What's on the other side of the complex?"

"Nothing, just administrative offices," Carrie said. "There's nothing going on. The entire property is taped off. Police are everywhere. I've never seen so many."

Gannon had to make a choice: stay and be spoon-fed information, or go digging. Figuring he didn't have much time, he jotted his cell number on his business card and passed it to Carrie Carter.

"Will you do me a favor, Carrie? Call me the moment it looks like they'll start?"

"Sure." She glanced at his card. "Jack Gannon? I've heard of you. You broke that big story about the scientist who stole the old CIA experiment."

Gannon nodded, then advised Dixon, who was gossiping with a photographer, that he was going off alone to check a few things out. They'd alert each other if something came up.

He walked quickly along the tape, scrutinizing every window of the center, every movement, every RV, car, truck, ambulance, patrol car and emergency vehicle. He knew that inside the center, police were taking statements from witnesses, getting their accounts while everything was fresh. Crime scene techs would be photographing, tagging and bagging. The county medical examiner would be called in.

As sirens wailed and the activity continued, Gannon searched for something, anything that might help. Maybe a witness would be released and walk to their car or truck? But he saw nothing but police in the lot.

Hold on. Who's that?

Gannon focused on a New York state trooper with a clipboard walking to a patrol car in an isolated area near the tape. It had been a while, but it sure looked like—

"Brad!" Gannon called, careful no one else was close by.

The trooper turned, recognition blossoming on his face.

"Well, I'll be a son of a gun. How the heck are you, Jack?"

He invited Gannon to his car, but Gannon indicated the tape.

"It's okay."

Gannon ducked under and no one saw him hurry to the patrol car.

Brad West had been posted to Troop A at the time Gannon was with the *Buffalo Sentinel*. West did a lot of volunteer work, but after a tough year, his charity for kids with cancer was low on money and on the brink of closing. West approached the paper, Gannon produced a heart-wrenching feature and the donations poured in.

"You got a friend for life here, Jack," West told him.

Now, sitting out of sight in West's patrol car, the two men caught up quickly as the trooper's police radio crackled with dispatches. West said that last year, he transferred to Troop F after he got married to a woman he met at a police function in Syracuse.

"I'll tell you, it's a very small world," West said. "I got called out to help on this and so did my wife. Anita's with Ramapo P.D. She's inside with the victims."

"Really? Can I ask your help on this?"

"Name it."

"You know I protect sources, Brad."

"We're good there."

"What happened?" Gannon nodded to the center.

"It's pretty bad in there. We've got four suspects who carried out the hit. Two of them killed two guards making an ATM delivery inside. Two of them killed the driver waiting in the truck. They got all the cash, could be several million."

"What about the fourth victim?"

"The suspects ordered all the people to get on the floor. Turns out one is an off-duty cop and tries to go for his weapon. They see him and shoot him dead."

"Jesus. Who's he with?"

"He's an FBI agent."

"FBI?"

The story just got larger.

"What about witnesses? Got any?"

"I don't know much about that."

"What about the suspects?"

"I don't think we have much. Faces were covered, they fled on motorcycles. We're searching. FBI's got this one, and with one of their own among the dead… Well, I think this one's personal for the feds."

"Who's the case agent?"

"Somebody named Morrow."

"Is he on-site?"

"He's inside."

"Any idea where? I might try to grab him."

West nodded to the administrative section of the complex.

Gannon thanked West and, before leaving, exchanged cards with him. He returned to walking outside the tape until he came to the far side of the center and the administrative arm, which was circular, with floor-to-ceiling windows.

Gannon's pulse quickened.

There were people and movement inside. Gannon inventoried his immediate area. A few patrol cars among the dozen or so parked vehicles. No cops and no other press.

He estimated that he was one hundred feet or more away. It took time for his eyes to adjust to the light and shadows before he could distinguish a desk and a man standing near it. The man had on a soft blue shirt and tie, sleeves rolled. There was movement. Other people were in the office with him. Gannon saw a cop's uniform. Okay, a female officer.

Could this be it? The FBI talking to a witness?

Gannon ached to slip under the tape and approach the office.

He didn't. He pulled out his phone and called Dixon.

"Angelo, say nothing. Don't react. But take a second to excuse yourself, then head counterclockwise along the tape until you find me on the other side."

"What's up?"

"I think we've got something here."

"Okay, give me a minute."

Hanging up, Gannon nearly dropped his phone.

In the movement he saw a figure, looked like a woman, seated at the desk. Gannon could not see enough detail to determine her identity, but her actions chilled him. She set her head flat on the desk, raised her right hand and extended her forefinger to it as if it were a gun.

Christ, she's acting out one of the murders.

6

Ramapo, Metropolitan New York City

Lisa Anne Palmer was the name of Morrow's eyewitness.

Age: Thirty-one, widowed, with a ten-year-old son, Ethan, and eight-year-old daughter, Taylor. Gripping his folding clipboard, Morrow studied Lisa's personal information, her preliminary statement and her driver's-license picture. Five foot four, one hundred fifteen pounds. Pretty. Dishwater blonde. Blue eyes.

What exactly did you see?

Morrow's collection of information for the investigation was growing. Upon arriving at the center, he'd interviewed the first responding officers to ensure the scene had been protected and to get an assessment. Then he'd slipped on elasticized shoe covers, tugged on latex gloves and examined the body of each victim before members of the FBI's Evidence Response Team put on their coveralls and began processing the scene.

Other agents, supported by local investigators, were conducting separate interviews of travelers, locals, employees—everyone who was here when the crime happened. Outside, they took note of every plate and vehicle in the lot and they were checking security cameras.

An enormous amount of work lay ahead. But as things stood, Lisa Palmer was the most valuable part of Morrow's investigation.

Now, as he stepped into the center's office and looked at her for the first time, sitting there in the manager's leather chair, he asked himself if he could help this widowed supermarket cashier from Queens to lead him to the killers responsible for this bloodbath.

"Lisa…" Morrow shot a glance to the other agents in the room, along with Rowan, the uniform from Ramapo P.D. "I'm Special Agent Frank Morrow, FBI. I'm the case agent. I've read your information and—"

"Did you find them?"

"Not yet."

"You have to find them!"

"We're doing all we can. Odds are they've left the area. We don't think they'd have any interest in having any contact with the victims again."

"You don't know that! I saw what those monsters did!" Anguish webbed across her face. "Are my kids okay? They took our cell phones! What if they get my home address and go after my kids?"

"Take it easy, Lisa. We located the bag with the cell phones," Morrow said. "The suspects tossed it in a ditch near the lot and set it on fire. We believe they took them to buy time. What remains of the phones is evidence."

"But nobody will let me call my kids. Are my kids okay?"

"They're okay. We've taken care of that."

"How?"

Morrow consulted his notes.

"You told us you left them with your friend, Rita Camino."

"Rita, yes."

"We've requested the NYPD send an unmarked plain-clothes unit to get Rita, Ethan and Taylor. We're making arrangements for you to see them. For now, it's vital that we keep things confidential. Okay?"

Lisa's fingertips caressed two small photos on the desk. Her children, Morrow figured, pegging the pictures as the wallet-size format from the type portrait studios offer at malls.

"How long before I can see them?"

"We're working on that." Morrow nodded to two other agents in the office who'd finished setting up a small video camera, then said, "I'm sorry for what you've been through and I know you've already given us your account, but as the case agent, I need you to talk to me and we need to record it. Okay?"

She continued looking at her children and Morrow asked if the paramedics had given her a sedative.

She shook her head; so did the Ramapo officer.

Good, Morrow thought. A sedated witness could be a challenge.

"I know this is difficult," Morrow said, "but I need you to give me every detail of everything that happened while it's fresh. Can you do that?"

Lisa's breathing quickened. Her gaze lifted to the big windows and the center's parking lot as if the murders were replayed out there.

"It was horrible."

For nearly half an hour, Lisa took Morrow through it all, telling him all she could remember from the lobby, then inside. One of the gunmen sounded American, another sounded foreign, European, maybe. Their movements suggested those of men in their late twenties, early thirties, though Lisa couldn't say for sure.

They wore motorcycle helmets with dark shields that

hid their faces. They had full-body suits that motorcycle racers wear. They were wearing gloves. As for weapons, all Lisa saw were handguns.

"Do you recall seeing any distinguishing marks?"

Recognition rose in her mind then vanished.

Distinguishing marks?

Awareness rose again before dissipating. Lisa couldn't remember. She shook her head.

"Are you sure?" Morrow asked.

Lisa blinked hard.

But something was there. Why can't I remember?

Because it's my fault.

Morrow pressed for other details. How were Lisa and the agent positioned? Show us the angle, show us the distance. Show us where on this floor plan. Where were the suspects? What were they saying?

"I know this is awful," Morrow said, "but it might help if you reenacted where the killer positioned the gun before he pulled the trigger.

Before he pulled the trigger.

If she hadn't dropped the gun, the agent might still be alive. Her guilt mounting, Lisa recounted how the agent had identified himself, directed her to get his gun, how she'd dropped it, how the gunman rushed to them.

She then lowered her head flat on the desk, atop the photos of her children, and positioned her fingers like a gun. With her trembling forefinger as the barrel, she pressed it to the side of her head.

"He never pleaded for his life like I did. He tried to help us."

Lisa sobbed.

The Ramapo officer comforted her.

Morrow gave it a moment and looked to the window; that's when he thought he saw someone at the edge of the lot. *The press?* As a precaution, he nodded for an agent to close the blinds.

Morrow returned his attention to Lisa, who was calmer. He had finished interviewing her for now and closed his clipboard.

"Thank you, Lisa." Morrow gave her his card. "Call me at any time if you remember anything more at all. I don't want to put you through this too many more times, but we'll talk again soon. Matt Bosh is here and he's going to help you now."

A second man, who had quietly entered the office, took Morrow's cue.

"Lisa, Matt Bosh. I'm with the FBI's Office for Victim Assistance. We're here to help you. First thing we want to do is get you into town to be with Ethan and Taylor, to make sure you feel safe and comfortable."

Bosh had white hair and a kind face.

Lisa nodded her appreciation.

She found a measure of composure and searched her bag for more tissue, suddenly remembering the magazine and comic book she'd bought for Ethan and Taylor; how items had spilled from her bag during the heist.

How they were lost.

Like so many things in my life.

Overwhelmed by a terrible wave of sadness, she called out to Morrow before he left the room. He stopped and turned, hopeful she'd recalled an important detail.

"Did you know him? The agent?"

"No."

"Did you know anything about him?"

"He was married. His wife is pregnant with their first child."

"Can you tell me his name?"

"Gregory. Gregory Scott Dutton."

Lisa turned back to the desk, stared at the pictures of her own children and tenderly collected them. Consumed with guilt because she was alive, she broke into tears again.

Watching her, Morrow grappled with his rising fury.

He didn't know if it was for the cold-blooded executions of these four people, or for his own death sentence. It didn't matter, he reasoned, heading for the door.

He took up his communion with the dead as if it were a shield and whatever anger he had, he kept caged. Glancing at the ID photos of the three guards and the young agent, Morrow made his way back to the killing zone, accepting that he was at war.

7

Time to roll the dice.

Gannon was at the tape, too far away to identify the woman in the office who was demonstrating a shooting to investigators.

Morrow, the FBI case agent, had to be among the small group gathered around the desk. Gannon needed to talk to him, but didn't know how much longer he'd be alone here. In the office, he saw someone looking in his direction. Then the blinds closed.

Damn.

He had to do something. A long moment passed.

Gannon whistled through his teeth at a detective who was standing in the parking lot near the office, reading notes. The man approached.

"What's the problem?"

"I believe Special Agent Morrow is inside. It's important I speak with him, briefly." Gannon gave him his card.

"Nobody's giving any interviews."

"Our stories go to every newsroom in the country and around the world. We can get information out fast. If you want to catch the bad guys, it might help you to talk to us."

Considering Gannon's point, the detective reassessed Gannon's card, looked back at the office, told him to wait then walked to the building. Gannon saw him at the door, talking to two men also wearing the standard FBI uniform of conservative jackets, white shirts and ties. One of them looked at Gannon, then his watch.

Then the two new guys started toward him.

This was his shot.

"What is it?" The first fed asked.

"You're Agent Morrow?"

"Right, who are you?"

"Jack Gannon, WPA. I understand you're the case agent?"

"Yeah, what's so important?"

"Can you confirm for the WPA that one of the four homicide victims is an FBI agent? And that it's believed he was going for his weapon when he was killed?"

Morrow's icy expression revealed nothing.

Gannon expected his questions to sting because they betrayed a leak. But that was not his concern. Leaks, tips, informants and anonymous sources were oxygen for reporters, and for cops like Morrow. The agent was about six feet, maybe taller, with a medium build. His chiseled, impassive face gave off the vibe of a man not to be messed with as he eyed Gannon.

But Gannon was no rookie, having experienced ordeals like a horrific interrogation by secret police in Morocco and being taken hostage by drug gangs in the slums of Rio de Janeiro. He was raised in a blue-collar section of Buffalo, New York. His old man was a machine operator in a rope factory and had a handshake that could crush bones.

Gannon could stand his ground with anybody.

"Is any part of my information wrong, Agent Morrow?"

"No comment."

"Do you have any key witnesses?"

"No comment."

"But you're not denying WPA's information?"

"I don't have time for games with you."

The second agent stepped closer to Gannon. "There will be a press briefing at the flags. We advise you to go there now."

A tense moment passed between them before Morrow and the agent walked off.

So did Gannon, his determination hardening with each step.

Twenty minutes later he was at the flagpoles.

Things had changed here since he'd ventured off alone to prospect for information. More than one hundred members of the Greater New York City news media had claimed a patch of space under the flags.

Any of these people could have the jump on me, Gannon thought, tapping his notebook against his leg while observing the rituals of a news conference.

The camera operator called for batteries, cables and switches from news and satellite trucks. Information concerning birds, dishes, coordinates and feeds was exchanged over harried calls that were patched to directors, booths and networks. TV reporters primped and preened hair and teeth, checked earpieces and handheld mikes.

Gannon saw Carrie Carter, with WRCX Radio 5 News, talking with a reporter from the *New York Daily News.* Then he saw Dixon finish a phone call and adjust his camera.

"Jack. Sorry, I didn't catch up to you. The desk wanted me to stay here. You find anything?"

"Only possibilities. What about you?"

"They moved my stuff. Great pickup. The desk says we

beat AP and Reuters with some of the big ones already. FOX, CNN, *USA Today,* the *Washington Post, L.A. Times, Times of London, Le Monde* in Paris, *Bild* in Germany and the *Sydney Morning Herald* have posted them already."

A sheet of paper appeared in front of Gannon, held by a cop distributing a short summary of facts on the crime. Gannon took it, read it over. Nothing here he didn't know. His phone rang.

"It's Lisker. Update me."

"They're about to start a news conference."

"What do you have?"

Glancing around, he lowered his voice to protect his information. "I got an account of what happened from a source close to the investigation, but it's going to take more work to flesh it out."

"What about suspects?"

"Nothing so far. Nothing they're talking about."

"They have any leads? What're they saying?"

"Not much."

"Well, what else you got?"

"That's it for now."

"That's it? We're going to need more to stay out front on this. We've sent people up to report on the manhunt."

"I have to go."

Several sober-faced men in suits and uniforms emerged at the microphones. The one who identified himself as FBI Special Agent Tim Weller then made introductions of the police people flanking him from Rockland County, Ramapo P.D. and the New York State Police.

In the seconds Weller took to prepare, it struck Gannon, as it often did covering major crimes, how this part of the process was a macabre juxtaposition. Here they were about to joust over information on a multiple homicide, while not far off, the bodies of the victims still lay under tarps in pools of blood.

And somewhere out there notifications would soon be made; somewhere out there wives, mothers, fathers, sons, daughters, sisters, brothers would be told the worst thing a human being could ever hear. Gannon knew the devastation, knew how the ground under your feet vanishes, how your world changes forever.

A memory shot through him.

The state trooper standing at his apartment door in Buffalo, holding his hat in his hand. He has shining brown eyes. A mix of cologne and unease as he clears his throat and confirms. "Jack Gannon?" Rotating the hat in his hand, saying, "I'm so sorry to have to tell you that your mother and father have been in an accident. A very bad accident. I'm so sorry."

Gannon shifted his concentration to the podium where Weller looked into the cameras and unfolded a sheet of paper.

"Let's get started." He read directly from the handout, offering little more than a bare-bones summary of the case: Police were searching for four armed-and-dangerous suspects wanted in connection with four homicides during the robbery of an American Centurion armored car while the crew was replenishing ATMs at Freedom Freeway Service Center at Ramapo. Three of the victims were armored car guards, the fourth a resident of Connecticut. At this time, their names are being withheld until tomorrow after their next of kin have been notified.

"We'll take a few questions now," Weller said, igniting a deluge.

"Is this in any way connected to terrorists?"

"Nothing's been ruled out at this time."

"How much cash was stolen?"

"That's undetermined at this time."

"Was anyone taken hostage when they fled?"

"We don't believe so. Nothing indicates anyone taken against their will."

"Can you estimate how many shots were fired?"

"We don't have that information at this time."

"Did the guards fire back?"

"It's unclear at this point."

"We heard the suspects fled on motorcycles, is that true?"

"That's our understanding. We hope to have more information later."

"There's some indication the power failed prior to the heist. Is this an inside job? Is anyone else involved?"

"All part of the investigation."

"Were security cameras working?"

"That's under investigation."

"We heard that maybe people outside took some pictures or video with cell phones?"

"We're looking into that."

"Have your searches on the thruway and in town yielded any leads?"

"Not yet."

"Can you tell us about the fourth victim?"

"As we've said, we'll have more information tomorrow."

For nearly half an hour the reporters were unrelenting with their questions. Many were repeated, frustration mounting until Weller concluded matters. "The investigation is ongoing. More information will be released at a later date."

Gannon sighed internally.

It looked as if his angle about the fourth victim being an FBI agent who'd died going for his gun remained his exclusive. Using his BlackBerry, Gannon typed an immediate update to the news desk at WPA headquarters with a note stating that he'd write a fuller feature once he got back. After he'd pressed the send button, he felt a tap on his shoulder.

"So this is it?" Katrina Kisko glowered at him. "This is what you couldn't tell me?"

"I didn't want to *complicate* things."

"I just don't get it, Jack. I am not your freakin' enemy. Besides, when a story like this breaks, you seriously think the *New York Signal* isn't going to know about it?" She shook her head. "You're still pissed at me, that's what this is all about."

"Well, you kind of just flushed me away, but that's fine."

"I'm sorry. I suck at that sort of thing, okay?"

"Sure."

"Can't we be friends? Maybe work together on this? I'll help you, you help me?"

Gannon smiled.

"I don't think so. You're forgetting, you're my competition, Katrina."

The warmth drained from her face.

"Fine with me, if that's the way you want to play it. You want to go up against me, the *New York Signal* and our two million online followers? Well, bring it on."

Katrina walked away.

That's the way I want to play it, Gannon thought.

As he and Dixon headed back to his SUV, he stopped at the tape, his eyes adjusting to the distance, and watched the crime scene technicians working around the victims.

He gave it a moment, out of respect for the lives lost.

8

Killers At Large After Armored Car Heist...

The headlines on the I-87 truck stop murders blazed along the news zipper that flowed around the old New York Times Building.

Updates also streaked across the news ribbons on neighboring buildings, intensifying the jumbotronic neon glory that was Times Square. But the full story would be forged about a dozen blocks northwest in the headquarters of the World Press Alliance.

After a hard drive from Ramapo into Midtown, the brakes squeaked on Angelo Dixon's SUV when he stopped in front of the WPA Building. Gannon got out, hustled through the lobby, swiped his ID badge at the security turnstile and stepped into the elevator.

The afternoon was fading and time was hammering against him.

While the elevator floor numbers flashed, he concentrated on what he had, what he had to confirm and how he would structure his story.

The doors opened on the sixteenth floor.

Gannon passed through news reception with a familiar

rise of pride as he swept by the wall showcasing some of the most stunning images taken by WPA photographers over the last century. Many were Pulitzer and international prize winners.

The news operation took up much of the floor. Executive offices lined the north and south walls. The floor-to-ceiling glass walls on the east offered the Empire State Building, Madison Square Garden and Penn Station. Looking west, Gannon saw the Hudson and New Jersey.

It was a far cry from where he'd started at the *Buffalo Sentinel*.

The WPA's newsroom was oversupplied with large flat-screen monitors tuned to 24/7 news networks around the world. They were mounted to the ceiling and overlooked the vast grid of low-walled cubicles where reporters and editors answered phones, engaged in interviews, huddled in quick brainstorming sessions or typed at their keyboards.

Gannon glimpsed a report on one of the TV monitors concerning the heist then glanced at Lisker's office. He was nowhere in sight. *Good, don't need him breathing over my shoulder,* he thought, settling in at his desk.

Logging on to his computer, Gannon suddenly detected the telltale smell of Armani cologne. Lisker had emerged at Gannon's desk, sleeves of his blue Italian dress shirt rolled crisply over his tanned forearms. His handmade Gucci tie was loosened.

"What do you have that's exclusive, Gannon?"

"The fourth victim was an FBI agent. He was killed going for his gun."

"What?" Lisker's eyes narrowed. "Why wasn't this in your earlier copy?"

"I still have to make some calls to confirm it and other information."

"Why didn't you make them on your cell and file from the road?"

"Some are sensitive. It's better to do the work here."

"Damn it, Gannon!" A few heads turned. "This is a news-gathering agency and news has a short lifespan, or did you forget that?"

"I need another hour."

"I'll give you thirty minutes and a warning— We broke this story. If we lose it now to AP, Reuters, the *Times*—to *anybody*—there will be consequences. Got that?"

Gannon did not look from his computer monitor. Katrina's threat to kill him on this story flashed through his mind.

"Did you get that, Gannon? Getting beat is not an option!"

"I got it."

"Good. You're my lead reporter on this until I pull you off. Hal Ford will send you raw copy from the others we put on the story. Weave their work into yours and move your ass."

Lisker left with Gannon's stare drilling into the back of his head.

Lisker had never been on the street. He'd never covered a fire, or a homicide; never had to ask an inconsolable mother for a picture of her dead child. Word was that all he'd done for years was rewrite corporate press releases. Beyond the fact that Lisker was married to the daughter of a WPA board member, it was a mystery how he'd ascended to his post, because whatever he excelled at wasn't journalism.

Gannon was a die-hard old-school, street-fighting reporter. Sure, he could file from a BlackBerry; text you copy. And he was fast. But the way he saw it, accuracy trumped speed. He was a relentless digger, hell-bent on getting things right. Being first to get it wrong does not enhance your brand. Gannon knew that firsthand; saw how sloppiness had destroyed the credibility of the *Buffalo Sentinel*.

But all that was behind him now.

He had to get to work.

As minutes ticked by, he shut out the activity around him and concentrated on writing about three guards killed in the heist and an FBI agent's self-sacrificing attempt to stop it. First, he searched online to check what competitors had filed. Nothing new, so far. Then he reviewed the raw copy. His colleagues were exceptional; their work was clean, well-written. But it didn't advance the story.

Juliet Thompson got the same statement the armored car company, American Centurion, had given everyone: "Our thoughts go to the families of the victims. The safety of our employees is of paramount concern. We are co-operating with the investigation and ask that anyone with information on the case contact local law enforcement." The company hinted that a reward was forthcoming.

Ron Schwartz had some strong stuff from retired guards on previous heists and the dangers of the job. "You live every second knowing all eyes are on you and somebody somewhere is planning to knock you off."

Veronica Keaton had local color, plenty of shock, outrage and fear. "This sort of crime doesn't happen here."

But the WPA had nothing from the inside.

We have to go deeper, Gannon thought. *Four people were killed and four people got away with murder and a lot of cash. We need to take readers inside. We need to find who did this and why.*

Gannon picked up his phone and called the private number for Eugene Bennett, a former professor who'd taught at the John Jay School of Criminal Justice before becoming a security consultant for the armored courier industry. Gannon knew Bennett from earlier stories and was certain that he would know what had happened in Ramapo.

No answer.

Gannon left a message then called another number. It rang in the Buffalo suburb of Lackawanna, where Adell Clark, an ex-FBI agent, ran a one-woman private detective agency out of her home in Parkview. She was a single parent with an eight-year-old daughter.

Several years back, when Clark was with the bureau, she had been shot while the FBI was staking out robbery suspects in Lewiston Heights. Gannon wrote about her struggle to recover from the wound to her leg. Since that time, they'd become friends, helping each other when they could. Adell should've heard something on the dead agent via the FBI grapevine, he thought.

Again, no answer.

Gannon cupped his hands over his face, checked the time, then began writing. He was five paragraphs into his story when his line rang.

"Jack Gannon, WPA."

"Gene Bennett."

"Thanks for getting back to me. I could use your help on the Ramapo thing, but I'm short on time."

"The usual deal, you keep my name out, okay?"

"Absolutely, what do you know?"

"The victims are three guards and an FBI agent from New Jersey."

"I got that, do you have names for the guards or the agent?"

"No."

"What was the agent doing there? Was he part of an operation?"

"No. From what I'm told, he was there on his own time, buying gas. He tried to get at his weapon when one of the suspects executed him."

"Executed?"

"A woman was on the floor beside him when he tried to get his gun. But the suspects saw him. They checked his ID, discovered he was an FBI agent, then shot him point-blank in the head."

"They made an example of him?"

"They knowingly and purposely killed a federal agent. That's an AFO—assault on a federal officer—which makes this a federal case."

"And there's an eyewitness? A female eyewitness?"

"That's right. She's crucial."

"Who is she? Is she an agent? Where is she?"

"I don't know. The bureau's keeping that tight."

"And the suspects? What about them and the take?"

"As you know, there were four. They got away clean on motorcycles, high-performance sport bikes, with an estimated six million in cash."

"They got away with six million on motorcycles? That's a lot of cash."

"Most of it was vacuum-packed-compact and easy to transport in saddlebags."

"I read a piece you wrote a while back in the *FBI Law Enforcement Bulletin,* where you said that historically, some armored car heists have been used to support bigger crimes by organized groups with an ideology, or with the desire to finance larger operations. Is there any indication this is a terrorist act, or guys on some sort of cause or mission?"

"Well, no doubt it was highly organized. It's too early to rule anything in or out. But this was a ruthless, chillingly cold hit."

"That's my lead quote from an industry insider."

"Just keep my name out of it."

Gannon checked the time, thanked Bennett and ended the call.

After he finished writing the story, he sent it to the desk and browsed the web again, monitoring the competition. So far, nobody had what the WPA had—the inside angle about an FBI agent executed while going for his gun in a six-million-dollar heist that left four people dead.

"Nice work, Jack," Hal Ford said after proofing Gannon's story and putting it out to some five thousand news outlets across the country and around the world that subscribed to the WPA wire.

Gannon went to the washroom and splashed water on his face. He was the lead on the heist murders until Lisker pulled him off. That meant he'd have to set aside anything else he was working on. He stared at himself in the mirror, kneading the tension in his neck.

I'm missing something.

It was near dusk when he collected his things in his bag and headed home for the day. Sirens echoed through the city as he walked east, concern gnawing in the pit of his stomach.

I don't know what it is, but I'm missing something on this story.

9

New York City

The Wyoming Diner was a classic eatery wrapped in battered chrome and blue trim. It was two blocks east of Madison Square Garden.

Gannon stopped off there to wait out the rush at Penn Station. A gum-snapping waitress—"What'll it be, hon?"—took his order: a club sandwich and large white milk.

While waiting, he used his BlackBerry to check his competition, trolling for anything breaking on the heist. Not much, so far. Good. His food arrived. So did an email from Lisker, in his typical jabbing style:

Strong pick-up on our exclusive. We're leading. Need new angle tomorrow.

Gannon chewed on his situation but failed to hit on a new angle. It'd been a long day and he was wiped out. After eating, he paid the bill, then went to a used-book store near Penn to think. It always stirred his imagination and his intent to write a crime novel one day, but the idea dissipated when his BlackBerry vibrated with an alert.

Reuters had just moved a story confirming 6.3 million dollars was taken in the heist and that American Centurion would offer a substantial reward for information leading to the arrest of the killers.

Okay, all they did was match us on the money angle. We're still ahead.

But the pressure to stay ahead was mounting. He had to find a new angle. For now, he needed to get home, to shower, get some sleep and come at it fresh in the morning.

The crush at Penn Station had barely subsided when he threaded his way through the vast low-ceilinged warren under Madison Square Garden. He scored a seat on an uptown train. Most of the WPA's married staff lived in New Jersey or Long Island, where real estate was affordable. He lived in the mid-100s and some days it could be a long ride.

For Gannon, New York was an adrenaline-driven power-drive through heaven and hell. Amid its majesty, there were the crowds, the traffic, the eternal sirens; and an array of smells like roasted nuts, grilled bratwurst, perfume, body odor, flowers and horse piss where the carriages lined up at Central Park between Sixth and Fifth Avenues.

He loved the way girls checked their hair in the reflection of subway windows; the way New Yorkers talked, like the time on Seventh Avenue he heard one woman tell another, "I'd rather gouge out my eyes with a curling iron than see that walking slime again." Or, the time he stopped to check that a man facedown on the sidewalk on Thirty-second Street was alive.

He was. Still, Gannon alerted a cop.

Yeah, Manhattan was a world away from Buffalo.

As his train grated and swayed, subway platforms blew by him like the moments of his life. He'd grown up in a tough neighborhood of proud blue-collar families who lived in small, flag-on-the-porch homes built after the Second World War. People there were die-hards who believed the Bills would win the Super Bowl and the Sabres would win the Stanley Cup.

He had a sister, Cora, older by five years. Mom was a waitress. Dad worked in a factory that made rope and would come home with calloused hands. Gannon remembered how the winter winds would tumble off Lake Erie and rattle his windows as he fantasized about being a writer. Cora nurtured that dream, taking him to the library. "You have to read what I read in high school if you're going to be a writer." Cora got him Robert Louis Stevenson, Hemingway, Twain; urged their parents to buy him a secondhand computer and encouraged him to write.

Jack and Cora were close, but eventually she grew apart from them all. Then she started taking drugs. So many nights were filled with screaming, slamming doors, silence and tears. She was seventeen when she ran away with an older addict.

Heartbroken, Gannon's mom and dad hired private detectives, flew to cities when they had tips. They never found her. It was futile and it broke his heart. He ached for her to come home. Then his anguish turned to anger for what she'd done.

Years went by. Cora was out of their lives.

His parents never saw her again. They never stopped searching for her.

After Cora left, he'd worked in Buffalo factories to put himself through college because his parents had spent nearly all they had looking for her.

All the while, he yearned to become a reporter and escape Buffalo for New York City and a job with a big news outlet. After college, he worked at small weeklies before landing a job with the *Buffalo Sentinel*.

The *Sentinel* would be his way out, he figured.

Then, while dispatched to a mall shooting in Ohio, he'd met a reporter with the *Cleveland Plain Dealer*. Daphne Newsome. They started dating. She was a free spirit. Her first name was Lisa, but she used her middle name, Daphne. She wanted him to move to Cleveland and work at the *Plain Dealer*. She wanted to have kids and settle down.

He didn't.

That ended it.

He threw all he had into his reporting and broke a major story. A charter jet en route to Moscow from Chicago plunged into Lake Erie off Buffalo's shoreline, killing two hundred people. The world press speculated that the cause was terrorism. But Gannon tracked down the pilot's brother and convinced him to share the pilot's last letter, which revealed his plan to commit suicide by crashing his jet because his wife had left him for another woman.

The story was picked up around the world.

It led to Gannon's Pulitzer nomination. He didn't win, but what he got were job offers with big news outlets in New York City.

But as fast as his dream came true, it died.

A few days after the offers came, a construction worker, who'd spent the afternoon in a bar, slammed his pickup truck into Gannon's parents' car, killing them both. He'd never forget that New York state trooper, standing at his apartment door, hat in his hand, then watching two caskets descend into the ground. After his parents' deaths, he was in no shape to do anything and declined the job offers. Months later, things had changed in New York.

The offers had dried up.

Gannon remained at the *Sentinel* until he was fired in a scandal over his refusal to give up a source on a story that linked a decorated detective to two women. One had been murdered—the other was missing.

No one believed in the story but Gannon. Everyone had rejected him, except Melody Lyon, the legendary editor at the World Press Alliance. She'd been watching him since his Pulitzer nomination and sensed something about his news instincts.

She hired him to work at the WPA in New York.

In the end, Gannon was vindicated.

Since he'd joined the WPA, he'd faced many ups and downs. But there were bright spots, like the recent one with his estranged sister. The circumstances were frightening, but he'd reunited with Cora, who had a daughter named Tilly. They lived in Arizona.

He smiled each time he reminded himself that he was an uncle now.

On the downside, Dolf Lisker was dragging the World Press Alliance through troubling upheaval. Like everyone, Gannon agreed that the newswires had to adapt to the struggling newspaper industry by strengthening content, particularly online content. Hell, the wire was the fore-runner of the internet—so most people got the concept.

What they didn't get was Dolf Lisker.

Unlike Melody Lyon, Lisker was a corporate sycophant rather than a journalistic champion. His so-called "person-nel efficiency model" was rumored to be looming; and his daily edicts with mantras like "brand thrust" and "maxi-mizing news value"—whatever the hell they meant—all worked to create a climate of fear for most WPA staffers.

But not for Gannon.

Being a reporter was in his DNA and he'd survived far worse than the ranting of a nonjournalist like Dolf Lisker. Pure journalism, the kind Gannon had devoted his life to, would endure long after the Liskers of the world had turned to dust.

And what about Katrina Kisko?

He'd never met anyone like her, a Brooklyn girl and a dynamite crime reporter who'd broken several major stories for the *Signal*. She had the killer instinct needed to survive the city's fierce news wars.

Gannon loved the way her hair curtained over her eyes when she wrote, the way she clamped her pen in her teeth as she typed, faster than anyone he'd known. There was an energy about her; an intensity that pulled him to her like a moth to a flame.

He'd fallen in love with her.

Katrina was thirty and when she'd started hinting about her biological clock and the possibility of living together, Gannon was open to the idea. For the first time, he started to think about settling down, thinking about kids, thinking about the long run.

The more he thought about it, the more he realized that Katrina was the woman for him, until he reached the point where he was bursting to tell her.

He'd taken her to their favorite Italian restaurant in Lower Manhattan.

They'd both had chaotic days and he was sure his news would sweep her off her feet. After they'd ordered, he'd reached subtly into his jacket pocket and felt the tiny box.

"I've been giving a lot of thought about us, the future," he said. His thumb traced over the box in his pocket as the candlelight lit her eyes.

"So have I, Jack. I've been thinking about our moving in together."

"Yes." He squeezed the box.

Katrina's BlackBerry vibrated.

"Sorry, I have to get this." Reading the message, she

chuckled at a private joke she didn't share. Then she texted a swift response, took a sip of her wine and a deep breath.

"Jack," she started, "I don't think it's such a good idea."

"What's not a good idea?"

"Our living together."

"What?"

"It'll just complicate things with our work. It would be too complicated for me."

"Complicate how? What is this?"

"I think we need a break." Tears filled her eyes. "This is hard. I'm so sorry, Jack."

The blow nearly winded him. He released the box in his pocket, tossed several twenties on the table and walked out. He kept walking that night until he found himself on the Brooklyn Bridge, staring at Manhattan. He contemplated the river for the longest time before he caught a cab back to his empty apartment.

The subway's automated public address called: 157th Street.

Gannon's stop.

His neighborhood was at the southern edge of Washington Heights, in the Sugar Hill district of Hamilton Heights. He liked it here. People were fiercely proud of the community and watched out for each other. On his way home, he stopped at the corner grocery for maple ice cream.

He did his best thinking with ice cream.

His building was a seven-story walk-up on 151st Street where he rented a fifth-floor one-bedroom for thirteen hundred dollars a month. It was clean, quiet, with oak floors, crown molding, milk-white walls and a whole lot of nothing else.

Sure, he had a few things: a used black leather sofa, a coffee table, a TV, a plain table and his personal laptop. Next to it, the *New York Times, News, Post, Newsday,*

USA TODAY and the *Wall Street Journal* stood in neat towers, like a newsprint shrine to his faith in the truth.

He flopped onto his sofa and spooned ice cream from the carton. Catching night breezes, soft laughter and the echo of distant sirens that floated through the window he'd opened, he assessed his day and his life.

Seeing Katrina had made him think of the little box with the ring he'd bought for her at Tiffany's. It was still in his nightstand. He didn't have the stomach to go back for a refund. Maybe because he hoped against all reason that Katrina would change her mind. That was before he heard she'd started dating a DEA agent a week after dumping him.

He should've tossed the ring off the Brooklyn Bridge.

A sudden wave of loneliness rolled over him.

Why?

He'd been a loner all his life. Was he feeling this way because he'd seen Katrina? Maybe it was his sister, Cora. Despite all the pain she'd endured, she'd found joy with her daughter, Tilly. It had forced him to take stock of himself.

I'm thirty-five. Do I want to spend the rest of my life alone?

Maybe he hadn't met the right woman yet.

Taking a hot shower, he considered the women he'd known. There was Sarah Kirby, the human-rights worker he'd met in Rio de Janeiro. There was Emma Lane, who lived out west. Then Isabel Luna, the journalist he'd met in Mexico, although she was married. Gannon could never forget her, or the others.

All of them had blazed through his life like comets.

As he brushed his teeth, his focus shifted to his story.

Four men died today.

He thought of the families of the guards, the agent. Man, his heart went out to them. He knew what it was like to be on the receiving end of that kind of news, when the ground beneath you vanishes and you plummet into a chasm of darkness.

Who did this?

Gannon fell into his bed, exhausted, set his alarm, then reached for his BlackBerry to check his competition again. Nothing new.

He had to find a fresh angle on the story.

Worlds had collided at the Freedom Freeway Service Center in Ramapo. For three guards just doing their job and an FBI agent.

I'm missing something.

Sleep was gaining on Gannon as he reread his work.

The witness.

She was beside the agent when he was murdered.

Who was she?

How did she come to be there? What had she been doing in her life up to that point? He had to find her. If he could put readers in her place, take them through that moment, well, that would be one hell of a story.

10

New York City

Two FBI agents escorted Lisa Palmer through a side entrance of the Westover Suites Hotel on West Twenty-ninth Street.

The men said little during the drive from Ramapo to Midtown and used a service elevator to take her to a twenty-fifth-floor suite of two large adjoining rooms.

To stem the adrenaline still rippling through her, Lisa held her bag tight and scanned the layout. Each room had two doubles and a single bed. There was a hint of Chanel as three women emerged to greet her.

"Hello, Lisa, I'm Agent Vicky Chan." The first woman extended her hand. She was wearing jeans and a blazer over a T-shirt.

"This is Agent Eve Watson," Chan said. The second woman, also in jeans, wore a New York Yankees sweatshirt. She had a firm handshake.

Chan indicated the third woman, wearing bifocals and a conservative skirt suit. "This is Dr. Helen Sullivan."

Sullivan sandwiched Lisa's hand in both of hers with warm concern. "Please call me Helen. I'm a psychiatrist with the FBI's Office for Victim Assistance. I'm here to help."

Lisa glanced around again, concluding that the bags in the other room belonged to the women. This looked like a sleepover with strangers. All the curtains were drawn. Outside, a passing siren underscored how Lisa's world had been turned upside down.

Chan touched her shoulder.

"We want you to feel safe and comfortable while you help us with the investigation," Chan said. "No one knows you're here. This location has not been disclosed. With the exception of Helen, we're all armed. The guys—" Chan cued the men to leave "—will be in the rooms across the hall."

"Where are Ethan and Taylor?"

"NYPD detectives are bringing them now with your friend Rita Camino."

"My kids must be scared. I haven't spoken to them yet. I—I—I feel like—damn it—" Lisa's heart raced.

"They'll be here soon," Chan said.

"Lisa." Sullivan stepped closer. "After an event like this, it's normal to go through a range of emotions."

Lisa shot her palm at Sullivan.

"With all due respect, Helen, don't tell me about my feelings, please. I went through hell when I lost my husband."

"Yes, I know. Matt Bosh briefed me on the phone. But Lisa, you're enduring a lot of trauma."

A tense moment passed as Lisa eyed Sullivan then Chan.

"Did the FBI find the monsters who did this?"

"We're still searching."

"Because I shouldn't be here right now," Lisa said. "I shouldn't be here talking to you, waiting to see my kids.

That bastard put a gun to my head! He wanted to kill me, too. And if that had happened, I would never see my kids again!"

Lisa dropped her bag and covered her face with her hands.

"Where are they? Oh, dear Jesus!"

The women moved to console her.

"It's okay," Sullivan soothed her. "It's okay. Your fear, guilt and rage—*anything* you're feeling—are natural reactions to this terrible event, which has hijacked whatever control you've had of your life."

Lisa cried softly and Sullivan passed her tissues.

"You and your children have already been victimized by your husband's death. This kind of trauma reopens the wound. Healing will take its own time. Everyone reacts differently. We know that Ethan and Taylor are your chief concern," Sullivan continued. "Don't underestimate their ability to cope. Children are perceptive. You should tell them, give them an idea you experienced something troubling. They may not need to know every detail, but they need to understand what happened to you. They need to have enough information so that they can help you heal."

Lisa nodded, touching the tissue to her eyes until she found a measure of composure.

"I'm sorry," she said. "It all happened so fast. I just stopped at a truck stop. I was just trying to get home." She ran her hands through her hair. "I have to fix myself up before the kids get here."

Lisa went to the bathroom where she switched on the light and stood before the mirror, still trembling. Helen was right. What happened today had torn open her wound, pulling her back over time to that night when she was...

...keeping the meat loaf and mashed potatoes warm while worrying. Bobby's so late. Why hasn't he called?

It's not like him. He always calls. Why doesn't he answer his phone? Staring at the clock over the fridge, the fridge door is feathered with Ethan's and Taylor's art and the picture she loved so much of all of them at the cabin by the lake.

Bobby's smiling right at her, just smiling, and the kitchen phone is ringing...Bobby? No. A stranger's voice asks: Is this Lisa Palmer? This better not be a telemarketer. Then the voice adds: the spouse of Robert Anthony Palmer?

The air freezes.

The "spouse" of Robert Anthony Palmer?

The official tone, the masked emotion stops Lisa's world because she somehow knows, the voice explains...it's the hospital...Bobby's been rushed to the intensive care unit... come right away...

From that point on, everything moved in hazy slow motion as if she'd been cast into a black hole. The aftermath of Bobby's death was surreal. People said things, but she didn't hear because she was consumed with pain.

She and the kids underwent counseling.

Still, it was so hard.

The first Christmas, birthdays, their anniversary were agony. Then she would see people she hadn't seen in years, who didn't know Bobby was dead, and they'd say, "How's Bobby?" She'd tell them and watch their faces and it got so she'd just avoid people. Then there were the people who did know and they'd avoid her at the mall or someplace, as if her grief were contagious.

The life Lisa had was over.

But she had to keep going for the kids. Each morning for the last two years, she confronted mountains of destruction, hopelessness and loneliness, taking them on one step at a time; as months then years passed she'd come to believe that she'd put the worst of it behind her.

Until today.

The pop-crack *of the gunfire, those poor guards, the chaos, the money bags splitting near her, Lisa dropping to the floor, her purse spilling the things she'd bought for the kids, the robber grabbing the money, the agent looking at her, his gun, she dropped his gun, the killer was on them, she looked into the agent's eyes, a good kind face—I love you, Jennifer—the muzzle flash, the deafening explosion of blood splattering his brain matter on her. The killer comes for her, his gun boring into her head...bringing it all back...*

Bobby.

We've already been through too much. I don't think I can bear this.

A vague prickling crept along the back of her neck as she looked at her shirt, discovering flecks of blood—*the agent's blood.*

Lisa leaned back against the bathroom door and slid to the floor, burying her face in her hands. In the stillness she begged God for her life back, pleading until a soft knock sounded at the door.

It was Vicky Chan.

"Lisa, someone's here for you."

"One moment."

Lisa collected herself, reached into her bag, changed her shirt, washed her face, brushed her hair, then opened the door to the sun. Ethan and Taylor were standing before her. She dropped to her knees and took them into her arms.

"Oh, thank God! My angels!"

After hugging and kissing them, she drew back to stare at her children. At Taylor, her turned-up nose and freckles.

At Ethan, calm and too mature for ten, and looking more like Bobby every day.

"I'm so happy to see you!"

"I'm happy to see you, Mommy." Taylor locked her arms around Lisa's neck.

"Hi, Mom. You're not hurt or anything?" Ethan asked, taking inventory.

"No, I'm not hurt."

Again, Lisa hugged them to her while shooting a glance over their shoulders and mouthing a big *Thank you* to her friend Rita.

Rita Camino was a self-described "divorced-no-kids-fun-loving-Jets-fan." She was a natural blonde in her thirties from Forest Lawn, Queens. For the last ten years, she'd been a senior cashier at the supermarket where Lisa worked. Rita was a rock-solid friend to Lisa, practically an aunt to the kids.

"We told them that you were fine but that there was a complicated, important family matter going on," Rita said.

"Ethan and I thought you were in big trouble," Taylor said.

"No, sweetheart, I'm not in trouble."

"What happened?" Ethan asked.

Lisa first introduced the children to the other women, then, after a nod of encouragement from Dr. Sullivan, she explained.

"I stopped at a gas station and I saw some people do some bad things to other people."

"What kind of bad things?" Ethan asked.

"I saw people get hurt. I saw bad guys hurt other people."

"Like a fight?" Ethan asked.

"Yes, sort of like a very bad fight."

"How bad were they hurt?"

Lisa glanced at Dr. Sullivan, who nodded.

"Honey, some people were killed."

Lisa watched Taylor's eyes widen and stroked her hair.

"It's sad, I know, sweetie," Lisa said.

"But—" Ethan looked around the room, processing the information "—you didn't get hurt?"

The gun pressed to her head. They don't need to know every detail, but they need to understand what happened.

"No, I didn't get hurt, but because I was there I need to remember everything for the police. It's important that I do it so they can find and arrest the bad guys. So our police friends fixed it so we can stay here with Vicky, Eve and Helen until we're done. That's why everybody has overnight bags. It's like a sleepover."

"How long will it be?" Taylor asked.

"A few days, then we'll go home. Did you guys get a chance to eat?"

The children shook their heads.

"Some chips and soda on the drive in," Rita said.

"Okay, how about we order pizza from room service?"

"And ice cream!" Taylor said.

"And ice cream," Lisa agreed.

While they ate, Lisa caught up with them on their school, their friends, upcoming parties, wants—"it's always something"—and the cabin.

"So it's really sold now, Mom?" Ethan asked while fidgeting with his small folding pocketknife. Bobby had given it to him a month before his death and Ethan cherished it.

"I'm afraid so, sweetheart."

"But we still get to go up one last time like you promised, right?" Ethan lowered his voice for privacy, knowing the FBI people were in the adjoining room. "We have to do the special thing for Dad."

"Absolutely. We'll go up once we get this stuff all sorted out. A promise is a promise."

Ethan brightened, so did Taylor. Their smiles were balm to Lisa and they spent the rest of the evening watching an animated movie together. Snuggling with them was the best medicine. Lisa drew strength from them and resolved to get back on track, seize her life back. After the movie ended, she got them into bed, smothered them with kisses before closing the door behind her and joining the women in the other room where they were watching an all-news network.

"How are they doing?" Rita asked.

"Good. They're strong."

"And you?" Sullivan asked.

"Better."

"You should know," Rita said, "that a cute FBI agent drove your car to your house and locked it in your driveway. I have your keys."

"Thanks."

"I told Nick at the store that you had a family emergency and you'll need some time. You should call him in the morning."

"I will if I am allowed." Lisa looked to Chan.

"Well, you're not under arrest." Chan smiled. "But Agent Morrow will be here in the morning. You can discuss it with him. As you know, he's concerned about guarding the seal of the investigation."

"Another thing," Rita said. "I also told Mrs. MacKay, the kids' principal, that an emergency came up, so you'd better call the school tomorrow, too, Lisa."

The TV's images flashed with a Breaking News update on Armored Car Heist Homicides.

"Here we go." Watson had the remote control and increased the volume slightly as the newscaster read the information.

"And this just in on that I-87 armored car heist that left four people dead in Ramapo, north of New York. The World Press Alliance, citing unnamed sources, is reporting that one of the victims was an FBI agent who was shot 'execution style' while going for his weapon and that investigators have a key eyewitness. Again, the WPA is reporting..."

Chan and Watson exchanged looks of concern.

"Whoa! Morrow's going to freak out," Watson said.

"A leak was inevitable," Chan said, "with so many jurisdictions involved and the New York and national media all over it."

"So much for his 'seal' on the investigation," Lisa said. "How would the WPA know about this?"

"Good reporters with good sources," Watson said.

The report made Lisa uneasy and she withdrew into her thoughts. Watson changed the channel to one showing *Casablanca,* and the women watched Bogart and Bergman in silence until the anxiety in the room gradually subsided. When the movie ended, Lisa got ready for bed. Sullivan, mindful of Lisa's anxiety, went to her bag.

"You're under a tremendous amount of stress and may have trouble sleeping," Dr. Sullivan said. "One of these pills will work fast and help you get the rest you need."

"Thank you."

They moved one of the single beds so Rita could sleep in the bigger room with Chan, Watson and Sullivan because Lisa wanted Rita to be near her and the kids the first night. Lisa also requested to have a room alone with her children. After taking the pill, she kept the bathroom door open so her room was awash in soft, soothing light.

After checking on Taylor and Ethan, she got into bed.

Did this really happen?

Her body was still quivering.

She struggled not to think.

Sleep came for her quickly just as...*on the bed beside her, inches from her, the killer's eyes burned with hate before she was face-to-face with the FBI agent.*

Gregory.

Staring at her, he said, "I love you, Lisa," before his face became Bobby's face and his head exploded in a never-ending stream of blood. The pressure of a gun against her head increased.

She woke, gasping, sat upright and waited to catch her breath.

She got out of bed, kissed Ethan and Taylor, then went to the sofa chair next to the window. Pulling her knees under her chin, she looked out at Manhattan's skyline.

Thank you, God, for letting me live.

Brushing the tears from her cheeks, she prayed.

The killers are out there. Please help the FBI catch them. Please. We need to put the pieces of our lives back together.

11

Thousand Islands—U.S. border with Canada

At that moment, some 350 miles north of where Lisa Palmer prayed, a fire raged in Ivan Felk.

Today's operation succeeded, even against the surprise counterattack. The FBI agent had tried to be a hero, a mistake that he paid for with his life. He was a casualty of war, like the guards.

So be it. We're all casualties of war.

Felk continued spooning cold baked beans from a tin can and watching the night from the cover of a tangle of brush on a small island in the St. Lawrence River. He considered the man beside him. Nate Unger, a country boy from La Grange, Texas, battle-weary and pathologically loyal to their mission, like all of Felk's men.

Like the soldiers I lost four months ago.

It was a doomed covert mission in the disputed frontier between Afghanistan and Pakistan. It had failed because it was supposed to—his team had been sacrificed. Felk's unit of professional soldiers had been hired by a global security firm contracted by coalition governments to carry out an illegal op.

No one acknowledged it.

Felk and his people were scapegoat soldiers; plausible deniability.

Before it was dismantled, the global security company was portrayed quietly through government-initiated rumors as "a group of dangerous rogues in a dangerous zone." The government that had hired the firm through covert branches denied knowledge of any sanctioned action within the disputed frontier.

Such action would be illegal, a violation of U.N. convention.

It never made the news. Felk's unit didn't exist. Their mission never happened.

But Felk and the surviving members of his team knew the truth. Three of his men were killed. Six were captured and were being held hostage for a twelve-million-dollar ransom by insurgents in a labyrinthine region that was impenetrable. The deadline to pay was in one month, or the "spies" would be beheaded. Coalition governments refused to acknowledge the demand, or get involved in any way.

Felk refused to let his men die.

He gathered the surviving men of his team and set out on a desperate mission to secure the payment and bring his people home; an act of vengeance against the governments that had abandoned them.

This was their new war.

Everything was at stake.

They would lay waste to anything that got in their way.

"Here they come," Unger said, handing Felk the night-scope.

It amplified the existing ambient light, capturing two brilliant green figures in a canoe, working their way across the river to their temporary camp on the island.

Rytter and Northcutt.

On time, just as they'd practiced. Felk went back to consulting the charts and testing his GPS unit, reconfirming their coordinates. Then he started on a second can of beans, finishing by the time the two others came ashore.

"Any problems?" Unger asked.

"None," Northcutt said.

"You take care of everything with your vehicle?" Felk asked.

"It's done," Rytter said. "We're hungry."

"Eat. Suit up. Then we'll move out."

A fire would risk attention, so the men ate in darkness as water lapped against the island. There was no need to talk. Each man had experienced the horrors of war. Each man had killed other people, many other people. As a loon cried, each man withdrew into himself to process the death and destruction they'd left in their wake.

They were an elite group, possessing the highest IQs and most sophisticated training of any professional fighting group on earth.

Before becoming a private operator, Erik Rytter, a twenty-nine-year-old engineer's son from Munich, was with the KSK—Kommando Spezialkräfte, a specialized German unit.

Ian Northcutt's father was a physicist at Oxford. They'd become estranged when Ian left Oxford University at age twenty-seven, just shy of getting a Ph.D, to pursue a military career, ultimately becoming a member of the British Special Air Service, better known as the SAS.

Felk and Unger had been with the U.S. Army's Special Forces before the CIA recruited them for its SOG, Special Ops Group. All of them had seen action in Iraq, Afghanistan and other hot spots around the globe before leaving government armies to become hired operators for private contractors, who in turn were hired by governments to help fight their wars.

They were highly skilled and highly paid to do the dirtiest jobs.

Now, all were committed to the rescue of their friends in an action they called Operation Retribution.

They'd researched and drilled until every move was committed to memory, like an intricate pass pattern. The irony of the targets, American Centurion and the Freedom Freeway Service Center, was not lost on them.

They'd rolled fast from Ramapo to where they were situated now: in Upstate New York's Thousand Islands region, a group of islands and shoals scattered in the St. Lawrence River, dividing Canada and the United States.

After the heist, they'd split into pairs, traveling on back roads. They'd hidden the motorcycles in wooded areas, where they switched to vehicles stolen from long-term parking lots at Newark's Liberty International Airport. They'd checked dates on dash-displayed parking tickets. The vehicles were hidden in isolated areas about a mile from their current location and would not likely be reported stolen for a week.

Felk reviewed their situation, recalling his research. He tapped his watch. The men prepared for the next stage by putting on wet suits.

New York state's border with Canada stretches 428 miles. But between the twenty-six points of controlled entry, most of that border is "porous," as an official for the New York Field Division of the Drug Enforcement Administration reported to Congress. The fact there are few natural, or man-made, barriers in the area to deter criminals was a key reason Felk chose this route for initial escape.

Felk and his men had a network of military friends everywhere, like-minded people who were always faithful. Their intelligence-gathering mission gave them the date and time that several million in unmarked U.S. cash was scheduled for delivery along I-87 by American Centurion.

They had yet to count all the cash, but the amount looked substantial and put them in good shape for the next stage of the operation.

After zipping up their suits, they checked to ensure their small cargo packs were watertight before breaking camp, stepping into their canoes and heading into a chain of small islands in a northerly course.

The Thousand Islands, whose number is estimated at eighteen hundred large and small islands, are eroded Ice Age mountaintops. Part of a chain of metamorphic rock linking the Canadian Shield with the Adirondack Mountains. By Unger's calculations, they still had a few miles to cover using a route that snaked along a necklace of small islands, many of them privately owned. In the distance, he saw the red beacons atop the spires of the bridges connecting the United States and Canada.

They traveled silently and unseen in the night, hugging islands wherever possible, ready at the first hint of trouble to vanish into a cove or inlet, or behind a jutting rock formation or trees that arched into the water. They heeded the approaching rumble of every motor, scrutinizing every vessel with their nightscopes, knowing they could easily encounter pleasure boaters, or an enemy.

The area was patrolled by the Ontario Provincial Police, the Royal Canadian Mounted Police, Canadian and U.S. Coast Guards, the U.S. Border Patrol, New York State Police and New York State Park Police. Rounding an island dense with pine, Felk was satisfied that they'd come upon the invisible point in the river that was the border. But his

relief was short-lived when he heard three soft knocks of
Rytter's paddle against the second canoe.

The alert for trouble.

On cue, the low distant rumble of a large inboard
echoed around the island. Alarm rolled through Felk. The
island nearest to them offered nothing but a rising wall
of flat, wind-smoothed rock. The rumbling was getting
closer. Nowhere to hide. Not a cove, inlet or tree. Nothing.
The men paddled furiously to round the rock face, hoping
some form of cover would present itself. Casting a backward glance, Felk saw the beam of a searchlight rake the
surface.

Whatever was approaching was gaining.

Both canoes moved swiftly and silently, rounding the
island until a good-size private dock reached out like a
helping hand. With military precision the men guided their
canoes to the dock. A large speedboat and two small boats
were moored to it. Quickly, they tied their canoes to the
dock, grabbed their packs and slipped into the water.

Keeping their eyes above the waterline, they hid behind
the dock's pilings. Felk manipulated the nightscope as a
boat emerged. He cursed under his breath after glimpsing
the word POLICE on the side. The boat's powerful light
swept across the dock and all the boats tied to it.

The engine stopped. The boat glided to the dock without a sound but for the gentle lapping of its wake.

"See." A woman's voice came from the boat. "He did
it again."

"Know what I think, Alice," the man at the wheel of the
police boat said. "I think you're just looking for a reason
to visit this guy again. I think you got a thing for him."

"Bring me closer. He keeps forgetting to moor his boat
properly. It drifts out into the shipping lanes. It's not safe,
Don. I'll tie it down."

The dock moaned as Alice hopped onto it.

From the water, Felk and the others watched through the planks as she moved strobelike above them in the light's beam. Felk reached down to his calf until his hand found the handle for a ten-inch hunting knife. He would seize her ankle and bring her down into the water with him. He indicated for Unger to be ready and Unger gave a slight nod. Felk signaled for Rytter and Northcutt to pass under the police boat to take care of her partner.

They vanished in the black water.

Felk caught the patch for New York State Police as Alice crouched to secure the mooring line of the speedboat. He saw the butt of her pistol sticking from her holster.

"Okay, Don, done."

"Sure you don't want to go in, bat your eyes and tell him you done good, Alice?"

"Knock it off, wise guy. Hold on. What's with these canoes? I don't remember him having canoes."

"Maybe he's got company, Alice."

"What the heck?" She walked along the dock, then halted directly above Felk. "Is there something down there? Don, bring the light over here."

12

Thousand Islands / Somewhere in Ontario, Canada

Felk swallowed air and submerged.

Underwater, gliding along the bottom, he swam from the dock. Behind him he saw fingers of light spearing the dark water where he'd been. Using one of the moored boats for cover he surfaced without making a sound.

His hand tightened on his knife.

He could see the female trooper, crouched on the dock, working her flashlight, trying to determine what she'd seen.

"Alice, come on," her partner called from the boat.

"I saw something down there."

"Likely a fish."

Felk heard a muted radio dispatch.

"We have to go, Alice."

Suddenly the radio burst with a repeated police call for immediate assistance, near Alexandria Bay.

"Alice, we've got to move, now!"

The patrol boat's motor grumbled to life and she leaped aboard.

After waiting several minutes for its wake to subside, Felk and the others climbed back into their canoes. They drove hard toward their destination, eventually coming to a large marsh and a welcoming symphony of croaking and chirping. The smell of fish and mud enveloped them as they set to work plunging knives into the canoes, weighting them down with rocks, sinking them and covering the area with cattails.

Once they'd moved to dry land, they changed into jeans, flannel shirts, woolen socks and hiking boots. They buried their wet suits and the things they no longer needed. Rytter clipped a digital police scanner to his belt, tuned it to frequencies for the Ontario Provincial Police and slipped on a headset. Northcutt monitored news reports on radio stations. Unger confirmed their location and their next destination point with his GPS unit.

"That way." He pointed to a forest that bordered empty, rolling farmland. It looked like easygoing. "We've got a hike."

As the group climbed a slope, Felk turned and looked back across the expanse of the river and the islands that straddled two nations. They'd fled the United States and entered Canada safely with millions in stolen cash strapped to their backs. This phase of the operation was behind them. Time to advance to the next.

Moving fast, the men soon entered a dense forest. It was the gateway to a rest stop along the Thousand Islands Parkway, a scenic two-lane highway meandering along the north shore of the St. Lawrence River. Parked vehicles dotted the lot, an RV with Alberta plates, a Porsche from Quebec, a couple of sedans from Ontario.

There it is.

Felk spotted a white Grand Cherokee bearing an Ontario plate with the numeric sequence 787. Leading them to it, he went to the driver's door. The window lowered to a man in his late twenties, alone behind the wheel.

"Waiting long, Dillon?" Felk said.

"Not long at all."

"Good, let's roll."

"Outstanding work, sir." The driver gave Felk a half smile, pressed a button and the Jeep's rear liftgate opened. After setting their gear in the rear storage area, they got in. The Cherokee wheeled quietly from the rest stop and west along the parkway.

Felk was in the front passenger seat next to Dillon, who was in charge of support for the unit in Canada. This operation had been planned, drilled and reviewed with a range of contingencies. Felk took nothing for granted, but savored a moment of relief, exhaling as he looked at Dillon in the glow of the dash lights.

Lee Mitchell Dillon. Age: twenty-six. Born in Scarborough, a Toronto suburb. His father was a doctor and his Montreal-born mother was a nurse. Dillon was fluent in French, Spanish and English. He held a master's degree in science from McGill University. He had seen combat in Afghanistan as a member of the Canadian Forces Joint Task Force 2, the JTF2, before he quit to work as a private operator with Felk.

The team was solid, not a weakness among them. Felk regretted that Sparks had refused to sign on. He was the only holdout. *Could Sparks be trusted to keep the faith? Should we guarantee that he does?* The troubling questions returned to gnaw at Felk until he shoved them aside to focus on the mission.

"News reports of the hit are being carried up here. It's a big story," Dillon said.

"We know," Unger said. "How much farther?"

"About forty-five minutes, give or take."

Traffic was nonexistent when they turned north on Highway 32, which cut across forests, farm fields and jagged rock exposures. When Highway 32 ended, they turned south on Highway 15, traveled another fifteen minutes beyond Seeley's Bay toward the Dog Lake area. Dillon slowed to a near stop at an outcropping of house-size rock. The formation nearly concealed the mouth of a dirt road that twisted into a thick forest, disappearing in the darkness.

Private Property Keep Out, a hand-painted scrawl warned from a sign nailed to one of the trees. They bordered the entrance like sentries. Overhanging branches engulfed the road, as if to underscore the notice.

Lit only by the Cherokee's high beams, Dillon proceeded along the narrow dirt ribbon, hugging small cliff edges.

"Some of the men behind Lincoln's assassination fled to this region," Dillon said as branches slapped at the doors and roof and gravel popcorned against the undercarriage.

The Cherokee arrived at a soft sandy path, curtained with tall shrubs. Then, through the bush, the headlights found a clearing and a cottage.

"It belongs to my buddy's uncle." Dillon killed the motor. "I told him I had some friends who wanted to fish. I've got full use for three weeks."

It offered seclusion on three acres.

Felk was pleased.

After they hauled in their gear, Dillon showed them around. The cottage was built with cedar logs. The lake shimmered beyond large windows that framed a stone fireplace.

The main floor had an open living-dining area with a large flat-screen TV hooked to a satellite dish. The kitchen had a freezer, stove and a fridge Dillon had fully stocked. The sink had a pump to draw clean well water. There was a small hot-water reservoir. Upstairs, there was a private master bedroom and two large spacious bedroom areas with two extra-wide bunks in the loft area. There was no indoor plumbing. No toilet. No tub or shower. There was an outhouse at the rear. The lake was where people bathed, Dillon said before offering the men cold Canadian beer.

"Luxurious compared to some assignments," Unger said.

"The Sheraton in Addis Ababa was comfy," Northcutt added.

"Beats the hell out of Afghanistan," Rytter said.

"Neighbors are rare in these parts," Dillon said.

"We'll cool off here for as long as we need before rolling on to the next stage." Felk indicated the sports bags. "We need a tally on the take."

The men opened all the bags containing the cash and other items from the heist. Dillon produced a money counter. As the men loaded cash in the machine, Felk took his gear upstairs to the master bedroom and stepped outside onto the upper balcony. He looked at the lake, tranquil under the starlight.

His attention shot back to the tribal regions of the disputed zone and he ran his hand over his stubbled face, knowing what was coming. The images were seared into his brain…

…the desecrated corpses of his men…corpses hanging from a bridge…dragged naked through a public square… pissed on, then dismembered…given to the dogs to finish off…the diseased three-legged mutt with a hand and forearm clenched in its jaws…

Three of Felk's men were killed.

Five escaped with him.

The insurgents set their price for the lives of the six they'd captured: two million per man. Total: twelve million in U.S. cash. Whether the insurgents would actually make the cash-for-lives exchange was not a factor for Felk. He would secure the ransom and bring his men home.

He would not fail.

Felk returned to the bedroom and switched on his laptop, a state-of-the-art model fully encrypted with a satellite link. He checked for new emails from the intermediary.

There was one.

It had a video. *A new video.*

Was this it?

Felk braced to look at it, preparing himself for the worst he could imagine. The insurgents had threatened to make execution videos of the beheadings.

If this was it, he was ready.

The image blurred then focused on a newspaper showing the date, indicating the recording was less than twenty-four hours old. From his limited grasp of Urdu, Felk recognized the newspaper. It was the *Daily Dunya Quetta.* Sometimes the militants used other newspapers from the region to verify the date of the video. This one was twenty-four hours old.

The newspaper vanished.

Now the camera was showing six unshaven men—his men—sitting on the floor in manacles and flanked by four men wearing hoods and holding large swords.

One of the hooded men stepped in front of the camera.

"Heed this message from the New Guardians of the National Revolutionary Movement," he said in heavily accented English. "Our court has tried these infidel spies and has found them guilty of crimes against humanity. The penalty is to pay the fine, or execution."

The footage cut to a hooded man stepping to one of the seated prisoners and forcing him to bow his head as a sword rose over it. The captors shouted at the bound man.

Fear filled the eyes of the other hostages. They were haggard, exhibiting signs of beatings, sleep deprivation.

Felk's stomach churned.

The man chosen for execution began moving, his back heaving up and down. He was sobbing. They've broken him, Felk realized, just as a horrible guttural keening distorted the video's sound.

"Ivan! Don't let me die!"

The man's cry pierced Felk.

The prisoner was his younger brother, Clayton.

"Ivan, please! Don't let me die!"

The first hooded man blocked the image, his head filling the frame again.

"You have twenty-six days to pay fine."

The video ended.

Felk's nostrils flared as he struggled to steady his breathing. It took a long moment before he could slow his heartbeat.

Unger knocked at the door.

"Ivan, we've got something coming up on a newscast from New York."

Felk joined the others in the living room. The cash was stacked neatly on the coffee table.

"How much?" Felk asked.

"Six point three," Northcutt said.

Felk acknowledged the amount just as VNYC cut to a news anchor at a desk. A Breaking News flag stretched across the screen's bottom.

"And this just in on that I-87 armored car heist that left four people dead in Ramapo, north of New York City. The World Press Alliance, citing unnamed sources, is reporting that one of the victims was an FBI agent who was shot 'execution style' while going for his weapon and that

investigators have a key eyewitness to his murder. Again,
the WPA is reporting…"

"An eyewitness? Jesus Christ, what could they have
seen?" Dillon asked.

"Nothing," Unger said. "No one saw anything. We took
every precaution. It's bull. What do you think, Ivan?"

Staring intensely at the TV news report, the image of
his brother still burning into his heart, Felk grappled with
self-reproach.

Why didn't I kill that bitch next to the cop?

Why did he hesitate? Was it because he was distracted?
Was it because she wasn't a cop? Was it because she
pleaded?

All he could do now was torment himself for his mistake.

I should've put a bullet in her head.

13

Morrow watched time tick down in the glowing green numbers of the clock on his nightstand in his home.

Three hours of sleep.

He deactivated his alarm before it was set to go off and in the darkness, he felt his wife's warmth against him, heard her soft breathing. Part of him yearned to stay here and hold her. Instead, he stared at the ceiling while self-reproach coiled around him for not telling Elizabeth what he was facing.

I can't. Not yet. Not after losing her mother and not with this case.

But you vowed to love, honor, respect her in sickness and in health.

I also have a sworn duty to see that justice is done for these four men.

I need to clear the case before I can tell her.

What if I don't clear it?

The notion of failure evaporated as scenes of the four notifications he'd made late yesterday swept over him again.

In Brooklyn, the first guard's wife had refused to let Morrow and the others into her home in Flatbush. A curtain had fluttered, someone had seen them coming to her door. Morrow shot glances at her priest, the FBI grief counselor and the armored car company exec, who kept adjusting his glasses. Through the door the wife said she'd heard news of a heist on the radio. "I know Phil was working up in Ramapo." She knew it but had refused to accept it: "It's a goddamn lie! It's not true!" She screamed through the door until Morrow noticed it was not locked, opened it and caught her in his arms just as she let go.

The second guard also lived in Brooklyn, in Bensonhurst, where he had recently separated from his wife. She was a bank teller in Gravesend. They took her into her manager's office to break the news. She went numb. Froze, except Morrow observed how she kept twisting her wedding rings.

The third guard was to be married in a few weeks. His fiancée shook her head, repeating "No! No! No!" then collapsed against the doorway of her apartment in the Bronx. They called an ambulance and two neighbors.

The last notification was some sixty miles north on 1-95 in Connecticut. The agent in charge of the FBI's New Haven Division met Morrow and two other agents at the Bridgeport resident office on Lafayette Boulevard. From there they went in separate cars to a tree-lined street where Special Agent Gregory Scott Dutton had lived in a split-level with his wife, Jennifer.

Others had joined them. Jennifer's father, who was a retired Hartford detective. They also called her priest. Jennifer's face contorted as if it had broken, when they'd confirmed her worst fear. "I kept calling Greg's phone, and calling and calling." One hand covered her face. The other covered her stomach as if to shield her baby from the nightmare that had befallen them.

In the shower, Morrow welcomed the hot needles of spray.

He would clear these four deaths.

Then he would clear his own with Elizabeth and Hailey.

By 4:45 a.m. he was dressed and ready to leave, when he peeked inside his daughter's bedroom. Hailey was a fourteen-year-old vegetarian, intent on becoming an environmental lawyer. Her walls had posters of rock bands he'd never heard of. She had a new poster he liked that said, Give Earth A Hug Today. She was pretty as hell, with her mother's eyes.

He could lose himself in their eyes.

Morrow was not afraid of dying. What he dreaded was the idea of never seeing them again. Yet, since Art Stein called, Morrow realized that a small part of him hoped that maybe, just maybe, the diagnosis was wrong.

It is an indestructible pillar of human nature to hope until the end.

He saw it in the victims straining from broken windows in the towers, waving shirts, jackets, flags of desperation, signaling hope to be rescued from the inevitable.

Then some of them jumped.

Morrow felt hands on his waist from behind.

Elizabeth, wrapped in her robe, turned him to her and kissed his cheek. She was warm and smelled so good to him.

"This is a terrible case, Frank," she said. "You were tossing and turning."

"I know."

"Let me fix you something before you go in."

"I'll take a bagel and some fruit to eat on the way. How's she doing?"

"She's got a new boyfriend. Jerrod."

"Do we like him?"

"Too soon to tell."

"Have they…?"

"She tells me she believes in abstinence."

"Do you believe her?"

"We have to trust her."

"Want me to polygraph her?"

"Seriously, is there something we need to talk about?"

"What do you mean?"

She pulled him away from Hailey's door.

"You've been acting like you've got something on your mind, and the weight thing."

"Just work, Beth. I've got a lot on my plate."

For an intense moment she read his face for any evidence of deception before shifting to another subject.

"I am so sorry about those guards, the agent. Did you know him?"

"No, he worked in Bridgeport. His wife is pregnant with their first."

Elizabeth shook her head. "I think that's about the worst news a wife could ever hear."

Morrow hated himself for not being able to tell her about his condition.

Not now. Just not now.

14

Morrow got behind the wheel of his bureau car, an old Taurus, but before he started the engine, his phone hummed.

He'd received a flurry of reports, including an updated version of the WPA story he'd seen last night. It quoted "unnamed sources," stating that an FBI agent was among the victims, that he was shot while going for his weapon and investigators had an eyewitness to his "execution."

Morrow cursed under his breath.

Unnamed sources.

This kind of crap was dangerous. Leaks kept the suspects informed. Morrow's phone vibrated again with a new message that seized his full attention.

It was from the director of the FBI.

"Agent Morrow. I want you to keep me personally updated on the progress of the Ramapo investigation."

Morrow took in a deep breath then let it out slowly.

It was 4:58 a.m. when he started the car and rolled from his modest colonial home in Pelham, working his way westbound on the Cross County Parkway. He made good time to the merge with the Saw Mill River Parkway until it continued south as the Henry Hudson Parkway in upper Manhattan. Then it was on to the West Side Highway and downtown.

Traffic was good at this hour.

He found a calming, classical music station and as New Jersey and New York streamed by him in the incipient light, he thought of what he was facing.

Lead agent for one of the FBI's biggest cases.

Death at age forty-two.

Morrow was not bitter, angry or fearful. He was grateful for what he'd had, for Elizabeth, for Hailey, for his parents. It had been a good life, growing up in Laurel, Maryland. His father was a Maryland state trooper. His mother was a dental hygienist. They were God-fearing, devoted parents.

After getting a degree in criminology at the University of Maryland, Morrow became a police officer with Metro D.C. While on the beat, he obtained a master's degree in law from Georgetown University where he'd met Elizabeth in the library. She was a research assistant for the U.S. Attorney General. Two years after he'd joined the FBI, they were married.

Morrow had had a good run with the bureau. He was recognized twice for exceptional service on organized crime and kidnapping cases he'd led in Chicago before transferring to New York, where Hailey was born. In New York he'd been assigned to the Joint Bank Robbery Task Force, working with FBI agents and NYPD detectives investigating major crimes like kidnappings, extortion, threats, bank and armored-car robberies.

In the wake of September 11, Morrow joined a special group of FBI agents that traveled to Afghanistan to question captured Taliban and al-Qaeda suspects.

He had devoted himself to keeping America safe. But even though Bin Laden was dead, there would always be a new threat, he thought, wheeling through Lower Manhattan, a few blocks from Ground Zero, before coming to the sentry posts and the barricades that sealed the streets surrounding Federal Plaza.

This quasi militarization was all in keeping with the so-called new normal, for the protection of the institutes and symbols of freedom that are sacrosanct. They define the nation. The security is insurance, he thought as the guard waved him through the check stop. That's when Morrow made a mental note to check his policy and federal death benefits for Elizabeth, to ensure that she and Hailey would be financially secure, that she would not have to worry about the house, about Hailey's college fund.

He'd take care of it.

As Morrow's car entered the parking garage he glanced up at his building, gleaming in the twilight like a bastion of justice. After parking, he swiped his security ID then stepped into the elevator.

As it climbed he checked his watch: 5:47 a.m.

The case briefing was at 7:00 a.m.

We'll see where we're at then, Morrow thought, stopping off at the cafeteria for a large strong, black coffee before continuing up to the twenty-eighth floor. He went down the main reception hall, passed the framed photos of executive agents, as he did every day. This time his thoughts lingered as he glanced at the display nearby, the one honoring agents killed in the line of duty as the result of a direct adversarial force. The Service Martyrs.

Now we have one more.

Entering his office, Morrow saw that most members of his squad were at their desks, working the phones and studying data on their computer monitors. He set to work, reviewing everything they had so far, and made notes to prepare for the briefing. Twenty minutes later, agents and detectives from a spectrum of agencies crowded into the same boardroom where Glenda Stark, the assistant special agent in charge, had first alerted them to the case less than twenty-four hours earlier.

The air was a mingling of coffee, cologne, mint and righteous determination. Copies of a stapled six-page summary of the incident, encompassing statements, diagrams and preliminary results and analysis of a scene search, were circulated.

After a quick roll call of those in the room and the people whose voices echoed through the speakers of the teleconference line, Stark got to the point.

"Four people are dead. It is our solemn duty to see that those responsible for their deaths are brought to justice. We will bring to bear the full weight of every law enforcement arm involved in this case to ensure that we prevail, and we *will* prevail."

As Stark let a moment pass, Morrow glanced around the table at the scattering of notepads, cell phones, coffee cups and morning papers. Every newspaper—the *New York Times, Newsday,* the *New York Daily News* and the *New York Post*—carried stories of the heist murders on the front page. He caught the glitter of traffic on the Brooklyn Bridge and the FDR Expressway. Radio stations would be reporting the story to commuters.

"Now," Stark said, "before I turn it over to Special Agent Frank Morrow, I want to emphasize that any unauthorized release of information on this case will not be tolerated. Leaks will be deemed an obstruction of justice. Is that clear?" Her eyes scanned the faces in the room. "A reminder, we've called a news conference for 11:00 a.m. Okay, Frank, over to you."

Morrow ran through key aspects of the investigation so far, then gave a brief background on the victims and the timeline of events as he flipped through the pages of the summary.

"You'll see here that during the heist, the restaurant's cook, who was out back, ran into the lot to a rig operated by a driver from Tennessee and urged him to call 911. The trucker got off a cell-phone photo of our suspects fleeing, but the quality is extremely poor. A retired parole officer at the gas pumps took a photo from another angle when he heard gunfire, but it's out of focus. And two Yale students got clear footage, but from a great distance. We're looking at it all, trying to enhance the images, but they're not very helpful."

Morrow hit on other key elements, most of which posed a challenge. The FBI's Evidence Response Team was still processing the scene.

ERT's work there so far confirmed that the service center's security cameras had been disabled and that no cartridge casings had been recovered; it appeared the suspects had collected them.

"All the kill shots were head shots. Preliminary information gleaned from the scene by ERT and the Rockland County medical examiner indicates the rounds used were 9 mm. One of the witnesses, a gun-store owner, suggested the suspects used Beretta M9s. So far we have no latents, no DNA. We expect to get an update from Ramapo this morning."

"These guys are smart, very smart," someone said.

Morrow nodded and continued. The Critical Incident Response Group, CIRG, had dispatched a team from the Behavioral Analysis Unit out of Quantico to conduct an on-site examination.

"Van, want to jump in here?" Morrow said.

The voice of Van Brogan, a BAU supervisory agent, crackled loud through the speaker.

"As you all know, our aim is to characterize the fugitive suspects to aid our pursuit and ultimately to provide interview strategies once we make an arrest."

"Glenda Stark here, Van. What can you tell us at this stage?"

"Obviously this attack was very organized, almost commando, militaristic in its execution. This kind of discipline is indicative of a number of possibilities—a group on a mission, possibly domestic terrorists, entwining an ideological motive with a financial one. The detached manner of the homicides, particularly once it was established by the suspect that the fourth victim was a federal agent, suggests ideological motivation typical of a crusade, or mission."

The briefing evolved into a short brainstorming session.

"Says here the loss was 6.3 million dollars— Was it an inside job? Did the suspects have help?" a New York detective asked.

"We're going through the background of every employee and ex-employee at American Centurion and the service center."

"Including the guards?"

"Everybody."

"I'd check with military records and polygraph, everybody," an FBI agent advised. "Get warrants for all phone records."

"What about confidential informants?" a Manhattan agent asked.

"Yes, we're asking everyone to press their C.I.'s. We understand American Centurion will put up a reward, and the bureau is also looking into a reward for information," Morrow said.

"Was Agent Dutton shot going for his weapon?" a New York detective asked.

"That's consistent with our information," Morrow said.

"What was he doing there?" the detective asked.

"According to his wife, he was restoring a 1930 Ford and went to Newburgh for a part. We found a headlight set in his trunk and receipt in his wallet."

As the briefing wound down, teams were assigned aspects of the investigation: canvassing, background checks on employees and reinterviewing witnesses. As they ended things, one agent asked Morrow a final question.

"What about the news report that says we have a key witness to Agent Dutton's homicide?"

"Everyone who was there is a key witness to the crime," Morrow said.

Not long after the briefing, after everyone had departed for their assignments, Morrow had a moment alone at his desk. He used it to stare at Lisa Palmer's driver's license photo. She was closer to Dutton's killer than anyone else at that scene.

You had to have seen something.

After the upcoming news conference he would go back to her. She was his thread to the killers. There was one more thing he would try to help her remember.

Morrow's cell phone rang.

"Frank, this is Gortman with ERT at Ramapo."

The supervisor agent sounded jacked on caffeine, breathless amid the excessive background noise at his end.

"What's up, Jim?"

"We've got something here—hold on. Can you hold on a bit?" Gortman turned to talk to someone before coming back to Morrow. "Okay, we're getting it ready to go for you to use at the news conference."

"Wait, Jim, what is it?"

"I thought Lanning told you, anyway, we've got something you'll want everyone to see. We got it from this place across the roadway…"

15

Four motorcycles rocket from the Freedom Freeway Service Center, disappearing down the roadway leading to on-ramps for the New York Thruway and a web of secondary highways and back roads.

The grainy images, lasting some ten seconds, were captured by an old security camera at a fabric warehouse called the Colossal Cloth Collection. The building stood about one hundred and fifty yards from the service center. Its rusted exterior mountings for the camera had loosened, leaving it susceptible to wind gusts. The distance and aging equipment resulted in jittery footage.

But for the FBI, this was a key piece of evidence.

"We believe these are our subjects," Special Agent Barry Miller told the reporters gathered for the press conference at Federal Plaza. The FBI showed the images on large monitors at the front of the room. Networks were broadcasting live. "We'll have copies for you and enhanced still frames of each vehicle. We'll run it three more times before we continue."

Jack Gannon was among the reporters, photographers and TV crews crammed into the room. Every news outlet in Greater New York had someone there. Angelo Dixon was at the back, lining up shots. Amid the unyielding glare of camera lights, Gannon studied the security video. Taking notes, he never lost sight of the human toll.

It was right in front of him.

The ghostly images of the killers in flight, juxtaposed with those of the four people they had murdered. The faces of the dead men stared from the enlarged photographs set up next to the monitors. The FBI was about to confirm their identities. Now, for the first time, the world would meet the victims.

There was the crew chief, Phil Mendoza: aged fifty-two, of Flatbush, Brooklyn, married thirty-two years, with three children and six grandchildren. Mendoza, a former U.S. marine, had nine years with American Centurion and was considered the old man of the team.

Next was Gary Horvath, aged forty-one, from Benson-hurst, Brooklyn. Horvath was recently separated after his nineteen-year-old son was killed when a rig hauling scrap metal rolled over his Honda on the Jersey Turnpike. Horvath was a former self-employed limo driver who'd put in seven years with the armored car company.

Then there was Ross Trask, twenty-four years old; the crew's rookie, who started with American Centurion two years ago. Trask was from the Bronx and was about to join the New York Fire Department. He was engaged to his high school sweetheart. She operated a hairstyling salon. Their wedding date was a month away.

The FBI agent was Gregory Scott Dutton, who'd joined the bureau in 2007. Right from the academy at Quantico, Dutton was assigned to the Bridgeport residency office in Connecticut. He'd worked on the joint-terrorism task force's investigation on the Bridgeport link to the attempted Times Square bombing. Dutton's widow was seven months pregnant with their first child.

The instant their names were released, reporters alerted their desks to dispatch people to track down their families, ignoring Agent Miller's pleas to respect their privacy.

The story was too big.

There were too many factors: four homicides, one of them an FBI agent going for his weapon, the 6.3 million dollars and the nature of the attack. The killing of the FBI agent was compelling. Since the bureau's creation in 1908, fewer than fifty agents had been killed as a result of direct adversarial force.

Gannon's call to the WPA went to Lisker.

"We've been watching the conference live," Lisker said. "We've sent people to The Bronx and Brooklyn to profile the guards. What do you have to maintain our lead on the story?"

Gannon cupped his hand over his phone.

"Nothing, so far. I'm working with my sources."

"After the press conference, I want you to help on the profiles of the guards. You and Dixon head to Flatbush. Profile Mendoza. I'll get Hal Ford to get you the family's address."

"What about the FBI agent?"

"Our Bridgeport stringer got his home number. No one's answering. The stringer's on her way to the house now, but we think the agent's widow is avoiding the press."

Gannon was uneasy with Lisker's micromanaging of the story. It would lead to problems. Gannon turned back to the news conference and surveyed the agents watching from the sidelines. The undercurrent of emotion seething beneath their grim faces was palpable.

For the FBI, this wound went deep.

Gannon found Special Agent Frank Morrow observing

from a corner and for one burning moment their eyes met, before Morrow suppressed a sneer and looked away.

Then Gannon saw Katrina Kisko, sitting midway at the side. She'd glared at him long enough for him to feel her wrath before she resumed focusing on the conference.

"With the support of American Centurion," Agent Miller said, "the FBI is offering a two-hundred-thousand-dollar reward for information leading to the arrest and conviction of the suspects. We're appealing to the public, to anyone with any information about this crime, to contact us."

The amount sent ripples of murmuring across the room.

"We'll take a few questions now," Agent Miller said.

The reporters asked about leads, evidence, Agent Dutton's action, FBI policy on drawing a weapon, safety and training of armored guards, statistics about heists, the high-performance sport bikes used for the getaway, the commando-style attack, the suspects, motive, number of agents on the case, the emotion, FBI vendetta, the risk of being an armored-car guard, the amount of money stolen, witnesses, links to other heists, the possibility of the crime being an inside job, the potential link to domestic or international terrorist groups.

For nearly forty-five minutes, reporters went up and down a range of aspects relating to the heist before Miller concluded.

"We'll call another briefing when more information is available. Thank you."

As the conference broke up, Gannon told Dixon he would meet him where he'd parked his SUV, then pursued Agent Morrow, who'd left the room alone. At the moment, Morrow was his only shot at a stronger angle. The agent was thirty paces ahead, about to round a corner, when Gannon called out.

"Excuse me, Agent Morrow?"

He turned, recognized Gannon and stopped. Gannon double-checked to ensure they were alone.

"Jack Gannon, WPA. We met at the scene."

"I know who you are."

"May I ask you a few confidential questions?" Gannon said.

The sternness of Morrow's face dared Gannon to continue.

"Look, I can understand that you and the agents on the case might be having a hard time and—"

"How's that? Now you know what we're going through? Did your 'sources' tell you how we're feeling?"

"No, I was just being respect—"

"You don't know dick, Gannon."

"Were the facts in my story wrong, Agent Morrow?"

Morrow didn't answer the question. Instead, he asked one.

"Who are your sources?"

"You're kidding, right? I'm not telling you who my sources are."

"I didn't think so. But let me enlighten you, all-star, if I fuck up, people get away with murder, maybe even die. If you fuck up, what happens?"

"Possibly the same thing."

"Is that right?" Morrow almost laughed.

"I'll tell you one thing—you can bet your pension your shooters are reading every word I write, wherever they are."

"Now you get why we don't want to talk to you."

"I see." Gannon tilted his head to the briefing room. "But you sure do need us to spread the word on your bike photos and reward. You have no problem using us like a fifty-dollar hooker. But when we dig, when we do a little journalistic investigating, well, that changes everything. Which brings me full circle— Was my information wrong?"

Morrow's jaw muscle pulsed.

"Just as I thought," Gannon said. "Well, think about this. WPA stories go everywhere, and I mean, everywhere. The killers likely read my stuff. I am a conduit to what they digest, Agent Morrow. Think that over."

Gannon's phone rang, Morrow walked away and he answered it. It was Dixon, anxious to get rolling to Brooklyn.

"On my way."

Gannon left.

As he exited Federal Plaza, he hurried to where Dixon had parked; a spot off Broadway on Chambers. Gannon was near the northwest edge of City Hall Park when across the street he spotted Katrina Kisko on a bench. She was talking to a guy in a suit and taking notes. Gannon recognized the man as a New York City police detective he'd met a couple of times.

He looked as if he was telling Katrina something significant.

16

New York City

The Blessed Virgin Mary ascended to heaven on a cloud of roses supported by angels in the framed print on the living room wall of Ana Mendoza's Brooklyn home in Flatbush.

"Mi Felipe!"

Ana hugged her wedding photo tightly, while clutching a rosary. Its beads ticked against the frame's glass as she rocked on her sofa, her face a portrait of agony. A grieving daughter on either side stroked her arms. Their tears fell on the younger Ana and Phil, who smiled at Gannon from a happier time.

"Why did they take my Felipe? Why?"

Ana's raw, choking sobs tore at Gannon. This was the part of his job that he hated, meeting bereavement face-to-face.

The Mendozas had agreed to allow him and Angelo Dixon into their home for the WPA's profile, to offer a tribute. A proud family, they struggled with their words in honoring their beloved husband, father and grandfather.

Throughout his years, Gannon had faced many situations whenever he made "death calls." People had cursed him, threatened him or slammed doors on him. He never took it personally. Rejecting him was their right. What amazed him was how most people had invited him into their homes, while they praised the dead, showed him pictures, stared blankly or cried on his shoulder.

No matter how any times Gannon had done it, he always believed he was trespassing on a private moment of mourning; that he'd only gained entry largely because the bereaved were stunned by their loss and vulnerable. He was always respectful of their suffering. Experience had taught him when to offer words of compassion and when to sit in silent understanding. At times like this, Gannon steeled himself to be at his very best because he believed this was one of his greatest duties.

The families of the dead deserved nothing less.

And so he was more than patient with Ana Mendoza as she fought her anguish to talk about her murdered husband.

"I had a bad feeling yesterday morning," Ana said. "I didn't want him to go in, but I never told him. I don't know why. Somehow, he must've known, because before he left he kissed me and said he loved me."

The house filled with sobbing from Ana's daughters and daughter-in-law. Her grandchildren, those old enough to grieve, cried too, while the little ones played.

"Why did they do this?" Esther Paulson, one of Ana's daughters, asked Gannon. "I'll never see my dad again. Our children are without their grandfather. Do these killers have a conscience?"

Esther's sister, Valerie Roha, hardened her tear-stained face. "We want the hammer of justice to come down hard on them," Valerie said. "It won't bring my father back, but he didn't deserve to die this way. None of them did. My father was a good man."

Gannon's gaze went to the mantel and framed photos of Phil Mendoza as a U.S. marine, local baseball coach, amid those of his children and grandchildren. Dixon's camera clicked as he shot Ana with her daughters in the seconds before she fell into a session of inconsolable weeping. The women helped her to her bedroom while her son, Juan, finished a phone call in the kitchen.

"…yes, I told the FBI this morning that Dad thought they were being watched… Right. I'll be there in about half an hour… Okay. Thanks."

After ending his call, Juan Mendoza, a New York City Corrections Officer at Rikers Island, took his mother's place on the sofa. His face was drawn. He hadn't slept.

"Got everything you need?" Juan asked. "Because I have to go."

Gannon seized this chance to build on the fragment of Juan's telephone conversation that he'd overheard.

"Juan, I'm sorry, but I need to ask you about this. As you know, there've been rumors that investigators think this could be an inside job—"

"Are you saying that my father or his crew—"

"No! No. Forgive me. No, nothing like that. Let me clarify. There's speculation that someone inside the company tipped the suspects about the route and the amount of cash your father's crew was carrying. Have you heard anything on that? Did your dad raise any concerns on that, given all his years on the job with the company?"

Juan clasped and unclasped his hands while looking long and hard at Gannon, thinking carefully about the question. Then Juan's red-rimmed eyes shifted to the wedding photo his mother had left on the coffee table and his focus seemed to drift before he spoke.

"A week or so before the attack, my dad and I went to a Yankees game. He rarely talked about his job, when out of the blue he tells me that he thought someone was casing his crew for a hit, that he'd sworn he'd seen the same guy appearing at various drops and that he was thinking of doing something about it."

"Did you tell the FBI this? Did your dad tell someone, give you details?"

"Whoa! What are you doing? You're writing this down?"

Gannon looked up from his notebook.

"I want to use it in the story."

"No. No way."

"Why not?" Gannon shot Dixon a glance, then looked at Juan. "You know we're journalists and this information is critical. I could keep your name out of the story. Have you told any other reporter about this?"

"No. I haven't. No, don't write that. I shouldn't have said anything—look, I'm not thinking straight."

"But Juan—"

"No. Don't use that. I take that back. Sorry, but I'm kind of messed up right now, okay? You saw my mom. Forget what I said. I misspoke myself." Juan cleared his throat. "Please do not write that. I have to meet my brothers-in-law to pick out my dad's casket, okay? Do you understand?"

Gannon swallowed his disappointment and, out of respect, agreed not to use the information from Juan Mendoza.

"So what're you going to do, Jack?" Dixon asked later when they were in his SUV, heading for the Brooklyn Bridge. "That sounded like a dynamite lead. One of the dead crew providing a tip on the killers?"

It was dynamite, but the circumstances put Gannon on a

moral and ethical tightrope. As they crossed the Brooklyn Bridge over the East River, he searched Lower Manhattan's skyline for a solution.

17

New York City

Lisa Palmer flinched, pierced by the image of muzzle fire.

The memory vanished as she let out a breath.

Shivering, she hugged herself and continued looking out the window at the city. At times she felt like a prisoner here.

I want my life back.

Her hotel was not far from the Empire State Building. Maybe they could take the kids there, or go to Central Park? It'd been a long time since they'd seen the sights.

Bobby used to take them on Sundays.

Turning from the window, she picked up her tea, sipped from the cup, gazed at Ethan. His thumbs blurring, he was engrossed in the beeping and pinging of a computer game on his portable player. Taylor was rewatching the animated movie they'd seen on TV last night. She liked to do that. She was smiling, listening on a headset.

Rita was on the sofa chair reading a James Patterson thriller.

The irony was not lost on Lisa.

The room was tranquil except for the storm of confusion

raging in Lisa's mind. After checking the time, she rapped softly on the connecting door to the agents' room. She entered and Vicky Chan let her use her laptop again to catch up on the latest news coverage on the heist. Lisa couldn't shake her unease with the WPA's stories highlighting an eyewitness to the FBI agent's "execution-style" murder.

How could this reporter, Jack Gannon, know so much?

Lisa, Chan and Eve Watson watched the live news coverage of the FBI's press conference. It was excruciating seeing the faces of the murdered men. Lisa gasped when she stared into Agent Gregory Scott Dutton's eyes again.

She thought of his wife.

Widowed while pregnant.

Lisa whispered a prayer. Her heart went out to her and to the families of the guards. The report then broadcast the security camera pictures.

The killers. Look at them, speeding away. Escaping. They're out there.

To get away cleanly after such a monstrous act was an outrage. She hated them for the worlds they'd destroyed; hated them for shattering the fractured life she was painfully rebuilding before she stopped for gas at the Freedom Freeway Service Center.

God, she wanted it back, wanted it all back…Bobby… everything…

Sitting there at Chan's laptop, Lisa saw flashes of herself that first time Bobby came through her cash at the supermarket, devastatingly handsome, his cart loaded with TV dinners, canned beans, chili, cold cuts, chips and beer.

"You got a lot of single-guy food there," she teased him.

He smiled back.

He was shy, but after that he came through her cash almost every week. Each time he'd make some conversation, starting by reading her name tag.

"You got a boyfriend or anything, Lisa?"

"Depends. You got a girlfriend or anything, whatever-your-name-is?"

"No, and my name is Bobby."

That was it.

Not long after that, he asked her out. They had pizza, went to an Al Pacino movie. Then they walked, talked. They started dating.

Bobby's family name, Palmadessalini, was shortened to Palmer at Ellis Island. He'd had an older sister who drowned at Coney Island when he was three; he barely remembered her.

His mother died of cancer ten years ago and his old man died of heart failure last year. Bobby was a mechanic. He had a mortal fear of snakes. He liked the Yankees, the Jets, Springsteen, fixing things, helping people.

Lisa was an only child, her father left home when she was eight, leaving her mother, a part-time waitress, to raise her alone. Life was a struggle. She fought with her mother because she drank too much and dated too many men. Lisa got her cashier's job when she was still in high school. She'd dreamed of going to college, of being an interior decorator and maybe moving to Florida or California.

It never happened.

Her mother got sick and Lisa had to work full-time at the supermarket to help pay the medical bills.

Then her mother died.

"And, well, that's pretty much my life so far," she'd told him.

They'd dated over a year when Bobby asked her to marry him.

It was a small wedding, just a few friends. They went to Atlantic City for their honeymoon, worked hard, saved and bought the house when Lisa got pregnant with Ethan. The cabin Bobby had inherited through his family was their treasure and their asset. After they had Taylor, Bobby was talking about opening his own shop, Lisa was thinking about college courses, they took trips to the cabin, took the kids to Disneyland.

It was all beautiful until the night Bobby never came home.

Sitting here, staring at Chan's laptop screen, Lisa realized she could never have that life again; that she needed to move on. She needed to put everything—Bobby's death, the shooting—behind her. She sat in contemplation until Chan repeated her question.

"Lisa, did the news reports help you remember any details?"

"I'm sorry, no. Can you tell me how long before we go home? We have things we need to take care of."

"Agent Morrow can discuss that with you," Chan said, checking her messages on her BlackBerry. "He'll be here soon with Dr. Sullivan to see you."

Lisa informed the agents that she needed to make calls concerning her kids' absence from school and her job. After Chan cautioned her about discussing the case, she directed Lisa to the desk to use Agent Watson's cell phone. Its number could not be identified by recipients.

First, Lisa called the principal's office at Ethan and Taylor's school. She was on hold for two full minutes before Chandra MacKay came on the line.

"Mrs. MacKay, this is Lisa Palmer. I wanted to let you know that there's been a family emergency and my son, Ethan, and my daughter, Taylor, are going to miss school for a few days."

"I'm so sorry. Is it a death or illness in the family?"

"A bit of a family crisis… I wish I could tell you more."

"Well, I hope things work out. If they're going to be absent for a few days, our policy requires a note, a doctor's note if they're away for medical reasons. I'll inform their homeroom teachers."

Lisa thought Dr. Sullivan might be able to help provide a medical note or something. Next, she called the Good Buy Supermart that bordered Rego Park and Forest Hills in Queens. Above the chaos of ringing registers, she heard someone answer.

"Hello, Good Buy."

Lisa always thought of the Beatles song whenever she called the store.

"Nick Telso, please."

"Hold, please."

Lisa pictured Nick—excessive hair gel, the tight shirt and gum chewing. He had managed the store for five years, promoted from running the produce section. Lisa was one of his best cashiers.

"Good Buy Supermart, Nick Telso."

"Nick, it's Lisa. I won't be in today. I need to use a couple of banked days." Lisa heard Nick flipping pages of the schedule near the phone in his office.

"You're scheduled for two. This is short notice, Lisa. I could dock you."

"I'm sorry. It's a family crisis. I'll need a few days."

"How many are we talking, Lisa? One? Two? I got to change the shift schedule and there'll be a lot of squawking."

"Counting today, possibly four?"

"Four? What the hell happened, did someone d—"

She knew he was going to ask if someone died, but caught himself when he remembered who he was talking to.

"It's something with my kids, Nick. I'll tell you more later."

"All right, all right, I'll put you down for a two o'clock on the tenth. Call me if anything changes."

"Thanks, Nick."

Hanging up, Lisa stared at her reflection in the mirror before the desk and followed the worry lines drawn in her face before she returned to her room.

Ethan was on one of the beds. Legs crossed, his eyes darted from his game player to his mother then back again.

In that instant, Lisa read it all. He was carrying a world of worry on his shoulders, far too much for a ten-year-old boy. His father's sudden death had accelerated his maturity and sharpened his intuition. He'd grown protective of her and Taylor. Studying his face, Lisa thought he was in a silent battle with resentment, anger and fear.

She would talk to him later.

Taylor seemed to be fine, smiling, watching the movie, sipping juice.

"So, how are things looking?" Rita asked.

Ethan, his nose in his game, listened intently for his mother's answer.

"I called the school, the store and let everyone know that we're going to be away for a while. So we've got some breathing room," Lisa said. "Thank you again for dropping everything to help us."

"No problem, kiddo," Rita said. "I have to get back home tonight, got a shift in the morning, but then I'll come back here to help with the kids. Want me to pick up anything?"

"I'll let you know." Lisa tugged Taylor's headset off. "Some more people are coming to talk to me. They'll be here any minute. I was thinking that you guys could go with Rita, Vicky and Eve to Times Square. I'll give you some money. You could ride the Ferris wheel at Toys "R" Us then go to Central Park, or the Empire State Building."

Taylor loved the idea. While she and Rita went into the bathroom to get ready, Lisa talked with Ethan, who pretended to be more interested in his game.

"What's on your mind, hon?"

"How much longer before we can go home?"

"I don't know, a couple of days, maybe."

"*A couple of days?* I thought it was just going to be one night."

"I don't like this either, but I have to help the FBI. I'll ask them about it when the senior agent gets here. He seems to be the boss. So, how are you doing?"

"Are we moving to California?"

"What?"

"I heard you talking on the phone last week."

"I'm not sure about everything yet."

"I don't want to move. All my friends are here."

"I know. We need to talk about it."

"But Mom...?"

"We'll talk about it, Ethan, okay?"

He looked at his game, letting a few moments pass.

"But we're going back up to the cabin to do what we have to do for Dad, right? You promised."

"Yes, we still have it for a few more weeks. I promise we'll go back for one last visit."

"Did you really see people get killed?"

"Yes."

"And you're okay, really?"

Lisa searched his face and by the way he was scrutinizing hers, she could only imagine how she must look to him. He'd already lost his father and to see his mother facing a new psychological tsunami had to be terrifying for him.

It broke her heart.

"Mom? Are you really okay?"

Lisa recalled Dr. Sullivan's advice.

Tell them. Give them an idea you experienced something troubling.

"It was horrible, Ethan, but I'm doing the best I can to get through it."

He took her hand. "It'll get better when we can go home, Mom."

She nodded through her tears. Lisa sat that way with her son until Taylor and Rita were ready. That's when they heard Morrow and Sullivan arrive through the FBI agents' room.

Agent Frank Morrow arrived with Dr. Helen Sullivan, who had left that morning for meetings at the FBI's New York Division. Morrow approved Agents Chan and Watson going with Rita and the children. He sent one of the male agents with them and had the other remain across the hall.

"Are you comfortable here?" Morrow asked when he and Sullivan were alone with Lisa.

"Yes, but we want to know when we can go home. The kids have school, I have my job and bills to pay."

"We understand that. But we'd like you to stay. We need you to keep helping us at this stage."

"I thought you brought me here to be safe in case the assholes were trying to find me."

Morrow nodded.

"That's part of it. We wanted to isolate you from the scene, the chaos. Give you a chance to recover. We've done that with some of the other witnesses as well."

"And what about the killers finding me? They took our cell phones."

"We talked about this. They burned the phones. We've retrieved them and are keeping them as evidence. We're trying to check calls to determine if anyone was working with them. From what we determined, the suspects had no time to gain any personal information to use for intimidation."

"So they don't know who I am or anything about me?"

"That's our feeling and our Behavioral Analysis Unit, the guys who profile criminals, tell us it's unlikely our subjects would pursue witnesses. Remember, they took pains to ensure no one could identify them."

A mild wave of relief rolled over her.

"So I can go now?"

"We'd like you to consider one thing that may be crucial."

"What's that?"

"From all our interviews, we've determined that you are our key witness. You were closer to the homicide of a federal officer than anyone else there. You had to have seen a detail, a scar, a tattoo, jewelry, something unique about the gun, shoes or clothing."

"But I told you everything. Everything."

Morrow threw a glance to Helen Sullivan. It was her cue.

"Lisa, when someone witnesses a horrific crime, they often have trouble recalling the details of what they've seen. The trauma obliterates it. But studies show that the unconscious mind has recorded all the information, including the most disturbing parts."

"You may not recall seeing the details we need," Morrow added, "but they're there."

"So what are you asking me to do?"

"We'd like you to submit to a special interview," Sullivan said. "In the file it's known as a cognitive interview."

"Is it hypnosis?"

"No, not exactly. It's an interview technique to help you remember details. If you cooperate, I'll conduct a few sessions."

Lisa stared off, considering the request. A distant siren resurrected the sensation of a gun drilling into her skull.

"Will you do it, Lisa?" Morrow asked. "It might be our only hope to arrest the people who did this."

She swallowed and nodded.

"All right."

"Good," Morrow said. "We can get started right away."

18

New York City

It was midafternoon when Gannon returned to WPA headquarters from the Mendoza home in Flatbush.

He'd missed lunch and stopped for a sandwich at the deli on the building's main floor. No egg salad left. Ham-and-cheese would do. He grabbed chips and a ginger ale, then swiped his ID badge through the security turnstile.

As the elevator carried him to the newsroom, his dilemma ate at him.

Juan Mendoza had revealed a major aspect of the case: before the heist, his father, the lead guard, had feared his crew was being secretly targeted for a hit.

The story practically wrote itself.

But if Gannon reported it, even using Juan's information anonymously, it meant not keeping his word with a grieving source—an ethical and moral violation. If Gannon didn't report it, he risked getting beat on the story, a costly professional defeat.

There was only one way around it: independent confirmation.

He had to nail this angle from his sources.

And he'd better do it fast, because it was a safe bet that

the family had spoken to other news outlets. *Who was Juan on the phone with at the house?* There was no telling what he may have let slip to other reporters.

The elevator doors opened and Gannon hurried through the newsroom to his desk. Immediately he put in calls to Eugene Bennett at John Jay, his cell and home phones. Next, he tried reaching Adell Clark. Then he left messages for Brad West, with the New York State Police.

Somebody's got to come through for me.

He opened his notebook, tore into his food and reread his notes. Between bites, he made asterisks alongside key points he would use. After eating, he crumpled the wrappers and paused to scan his desk.

Unease pinged at him.

I'm forgetting something. What the hell is it?

"I didn't see you come in." Hal Ford stood before him. "How soon before you file?"

"What do you mean? I just got here. And I already filed from my BlackBerry right after the news conference while Dixon drove us to Brooklyn."

"We moved that story long ago," Ford said. "Lisker wants to move a feature on the victims' families ASAP. Didn't you get my email?"

"I got the one that said we had the afternoon to write the profiles, because they were going later this evening."

"I sent you another one." Ford glanced across the newsroom toward Dolf Lisker's glass-walled office. Lisker was at his terminal reading his monitor. "He changed his mind," Ford said. "Everybody's filed. He wants you to pull it all together ASAP into one large, updated piece that has everything—the profiles of the three guards and the agent and hard news on top." Ford turned and said over his shoulder. "I'll send you everyone's raw copy. Get on it and get it to me, pronto."

Gannon looked at his screen and shook his head.

He needed to hear from his sources. He made a quick round of calls, to no avail. He sent them emails and tried texting.

Come on. Somebody's got to be around. Come on.

All of his efforts to reach his sources were futile.

He started working as fast as he could, assembling the large feature, pulling in the profiles and comments from the families and friends of the FBI agent, the guards, inserting paragraphs on the security video images of the suspects, the reward, updating the investigation.

The story wasn't quite there. He had to break news and the piece he needed was from Juan Mendoza. None of his sources had returned his calls. He was wrestling with whether to use Juan's information when his line rang.

"You done yet?" Ford asked. "Lisker wants to move the feature."

"Five more minutes."

"Hurry up."

Gannon gave it a moment to consider Juan. He'd probably talked to other reporters. All right. He made a decision.

More like a rationalization. Whatever. Screw it.

He would use Juan's information.

He started writing a new lead, topping the story with what Juan had told him, but attributing it to "a source." This would be another solid exclusive for the WPA.

It would also be wrong. Wrong. Wrong. Wrong.

Deep in his gut Gannon knew it. He'd given his word to Juan. He could not burn a guy on the day he was buying a casket for his murdered father.

"Jack," Ford called again. "I need that story now!"

"Hang on!"

Gannon lined up his cursor, pressed the delete button

and watched the exclusive element of the feature vanish. He gave the story a fast read, correcting typos and garble, then sent it to Ford.

"You've got it, Hal."

Gannon got up, went to the far end of the newsroom, looked out at the Hudson, New Jersey and took stock. He just didn't burn people. That was not how he maintained his credibility with his sources.

But he had to advance the story. He had to keep the WPA ahead.

What am I missing? Am I forgetting something?

He considered possibilities. He could press Adell Clark and Brad West on any intel on how the investigation was going. He could even try pushing Frank Morrow, the case agent, one more time. Or, he could head back to Ramapo. Work the staff of the service center. But the WPA's stringer was already doing that.

What about Gene Bennett?

Bennett was his inside source on New York City's armored-car industry. If it was an inside job, he could go to Gene for help pursuing staff at the armored-car company American Centurion.

Gannon headed back to his desk, stopping off at the kitchen for fresh coffee, remembering what Bennett had told him: there was an eyewitness, a woman who was on the floor beside the agent when he was "executed."

If I could find her, put readers in her shoes, give them a sense of who she is, what was going on in her life the instant she walked into a tragedy, it would be a hell of a story. It would take readers inside the heist.

As he settled back into his desk, his newsroom phone rang.

"Gannon, WPA."

"Did you see what the *New York Signal* just posted?"

Gannon's attention jerked to Dolf Lisker's glass-walled office to find him glaring from his desk across the newsroom.

"No, I'll call it up now."

"We've just lost our lead. What you just filed is substandard. The *Signal* hammered us. I told you that getting beat is unacceptable. I'll be sending a memo to all editorial staff. Meantime, get your ass on the street and get us back in front!"

The *Signal's* story landed on Gannon's monitor like a blow to his midsection. Seeing Katrina Kisko's byline was the uppercut.

Deadly Armored Car Heist an Inside Job:
Sources Tell *Signal*
by Katrina Kisko
The *New York Signal*
The killers behind the commando-style robbery of an armored car that left three guards and an FBI agent dead at an I-87 truck stop likely had inside information.

Sources among FBI agents and NYPD detectives investigating the heist say…

Damn it. There it was: the credit to "NYPD detectives" told Gannon that Katrina got her info from that NYPD guy he'd seen her with at City Hall Park after the press conference. It was such an obvious angle, too.

He'd missed it. Katrina didn't. She'd taken him to school.

Gannon swallowed the humiliation, then shoved files and notes into his bag and left. As the elevator descended, temptation rose. Gannon could annihilate her story by using Juan Mendoza's explosive revelation.

It would be sweet to hit back.

On the street, Gannon hailed a cab.

"Anywhere near Central Park."

It would be so easy to use Mendoza's information. Lisker would love it. But the glory would be short-lived. Gannon had to adhere to his own code. His word was his word. He did not give up sources and he did not burn them.

That's how he lived with himself.

Compared to what the Mendoza family and the other families of the dead men were suffering, Gannon's wound of being journalistically whopped was nothing.

But it stung.

He'd been beaten by the woman who'd dropped him. It was over with Katrina, so forget about her, he told himself after paying the driver and walking toward the park to decompress as sirens wailed behind him.

Before entering, he bought an ice-cream cone from a vendor, vanilla. He often came to Central Park to reassess matters, and was relieved to find an empty bench in the shade by the time he finished his cone.

He sat down, took a deep breath and let it out slowly. He cupped his face in his hands and rubbed his eyes before they traveled over the park, then to his bag on the bench beside him.

That's when it hit him.

The thing he'd forgotten. It all came to him with clarity. He had a collection of about two dozen printouts, notes and fragments of information, ideas and tips that he collected in a folder labeled To Be Checked Before Ruling Out.

He'd thrown the file into his bag.

Gannon followed a fundamental rule to check every piece of information against any live story he was working on for any possible connection, something he learned long ago from an old battle-weary crime reporter in Buffalo.

"You never know what you're sittin' on, kid."

With all the distraction and pressure arising from the Ramapo heist, Gannon had forgotten to check it against his file.

His mind started racing, for there was one item that screamed to be checked: the anonymous call about an impending threat to national security that came in about a week before the Ramapo robbery.

Yes, at first Gannon had dismissed it as useless babble from a nut-job. A lot of people from the crazy train called the WPA. *"I know who killed Kennedy. The pope's an alien, I have proof. I own the Brooklyn Bridge."* But Gannon's gut convinced him that his caller could have something. He sounded so apprehensive, so frightened on the phone and kept his promise to call Gannon back at suggested times.

Gannon reviewed all the notes he'd taken from the calls, checking the quotes and things he'd flagged.

"This is big! I swear to God what I'm telling you is true!"

"I'll bring the confirmation you'll need."

"It involves an operation, a mission, an attack on America."

He checked everything against what he knew of the heist.

It was a commando-style attack akin to a military mission or operation. It encompassed the execution of an FBI agent, a representative of the federal government. Is that in line with "an attack on America?"

Eventually, the caller had agreed to meet Gannon and bring him documented confirmation but was a no-show.

That was that. Gannon had never heard from him again.

That was three days before the heist—then nothing.
Radio silence from the tipster.
Could the calls be linked to the heist?
Was it a long shot? Or was it a lead?
"You never know what you're sittin' on, kid."
Gannon read over his notes.
What if there's something here?
Could he afford to spend time looking for this guy?
Could he afford not to?
As Gannon continued scrutinizing the note, his heart beat faster.
He had to find this guy.

19

"Are you comfortable, Lisa?"

She was sitting in a finely upholstered wingback chair with her legs resting on a matching ottoman. Dr. Sullivan sat across from her in the hotel's luxury suite. Morrow had arranged use of the top-floor room.

The curtains were drawn, the lights dimmed.

It was quiet, calm.

"Yes, I'm comfortable."

Along with Sullivan and Morrow, FBI Agent Craig Roberts was with them, making a video recording of the session of Lisa's cognitive interview. While he adjusted the tripod and camera, Sullivan ensured Lisa was ready by confirming that—other than the mild sedative she'd given Lisa last night—she was not under any medication. Lisa was rested and had eaten half a muffin and fruit that morning.

"Are we set, Craig?" Morrow was anxious to proceed.

"Good to go."

The red recording light blinked.

The yellow legal pad on Sullivan's lap was filled with

handwritten notes. After making a formal evidentiary introduction on the video, she began.

"Lisa, I spent much of last night and this morning reading reports and witness statements. I've reviewed yours several times and I'd like you to think back. Go back to about one hour before you stopped at the service center. Tell us what you were doing, thinking. Then take me into the center with you. I want you to recall everything you see, hear, smell, taste, feel, right up until police arrived."

Lisa nodded. She took a deep breath, wiped the corner of her eye and spoke in a steady tone of her everyday ache from Bobby's death; of the kids; of selling the cabin; of the idea of moving to California.

"I came off the thruway at Ramapo because I wanted to get a snack for myself and gifts for the kids, a magazine for Taylor and a comic book for Ethan."

Lisa remembered waiting in line to pay, seeing the armored truck arrive, the guards entering the main lobby, the motorcycles, the riders coming in behind the guards. But she couldn't remember details; not their clothing; they wore racing suits, helmets with dark visors. She couldn't remember shoes, or jewelry, or anything, because her attempt was overwhelmed by...*the popping sounds of the guards being shot...and blood everywhere.*

"I'm telling myself this can't be real and they're ordering us to put our cell phones on the floor and get down on our stomachs with our hands behind our heads."

The shooters do the same with the center's staff and other customers.

Some of the bundled cash had tumbled near Lisa and all the items that had spilled from her bag to the floor. One of the gunmen brushed against her, grunting as he collected the cash, tossing it into a bag.

She was terrified and prayed to God for help.

"Then the man next to me—" Lisa's voice broke "—tells me he's a cop and asks me to help him reach his gun."

Lisa recounted how she tried to help but dropped the gun; how the gunman rushed to them; how he put the gun to the agent's head; how the agent looked into her eyes before the explosion splashed his brains and skull fragments on her face; then feeling the gun drilling into her head; expecting to die.

Lisa remembered how everything smelled like lemon floor cleaner; how she was numb, feeling nothing except the dead man's warm brain tissue.

"It burned on my skin, searing me, branding me, because it was my fault he was dead because I dropped the gun and now I was going to die!"

Lisa saw her reflection in the face shield of the killer's helmet; then how, for a burning moment, she saw through its semitransparency, saw the killer's eyes, ablaze through the blood flecks.

Speaking haltingly in spasms, Lisa explained how she lay on the floor waiting for death; how her heart hurt, hammering so hard against her ribs; how when she was waiting to die she saw Bobby, the kids; that time stood still until the police came.

Lisa closed her eyes. Tears rolled down her cheeks as she gasped for air.

"I'm sorry, I can't remember any more."

Sullivan saw Morrow watching from his chair in the corner. He leaned forward with his elbows on his knees and cupped hands to his face in frustration. Sullivan resumed concentrating on Lisa.

This was a process.

It took time.

"It's okay, Lisa. You're doing fine." Sullivan passed her

a tissue, then poured a glass of water for her and waited as she collected herself.

"Are you ready to continue?"

Lisa blinked back her tears and nodded.

"For this next stage I need you to try to remember every single detail, no matter how trivial. Don't hold back. No matter how unimportant it seems, I need you to tell me, okay?"

"Okay."

"Good. I want you to try to recall everything in reverse, going back from when the police arrived until when you walked into the center. Okay? Please, try recalling it all in reverse and noting every little detail that comes to mind."

"Everything?"

"Yes, like how the shooter held the gun, what angle, the grip he used. Did he wear gloves, how was his arm and hand extended. Did you see his neck, his skin, his wrist, a watch, a scar, moles, hairs? Did he have an accent, the tone of his voice, everything."

Lisa nodded, repositioned herself, and for the next twenty minutes narrated events starting at the end and then going backward. Sullivan made notes and was encouraged at the outset, but eventually this technique, like the previous one, failed to yield anything new.

Lisa apologized.

"It's okay," Sullivan said. "This is hard. Not many people can do this the first time. Are you up to trying one more method?"

Lisa nodded.

"This will be the most difficult. You can decline and we'll end the session, but I'm asking you to put yourself in the position of the shooter and then the agent."

Lisa gave Sullivan an are-you-serious look.

"This sometimes works," Sullivan said. "Try thinking what they would see from their perspective. If it's too traumatic, I can end the session."

Lisa contemplated what Sullivan had asked, then imagined herself back at the center, but as the killer, extending his right arm and the gun, pressing it against the agent's head with such malevolence.

I love you, Jennifer.

Squeezing the trigger, the deafening bang, the instant explosion, like Kennedy's head in the Zapruder film, firing brain tissue across her face, marking her for death with the agent's skull fragments.

Now he presses the gun into her skull.

"I am the killer. I see Lisa's fear. I taste it. I savor it as she begs for her life. This is it. This is my chance. I should pull the trigger; just kill her while she's lying there begging to live, the agent's blood on her face, oozing under her. But I hesitate. Why? The other gunman is yelling that we have to go. It's over."

Lisa shook her head and stared at the hotel room carpet as if she saw herself on the truck stop floor, as if watching the entire scene unwinding right in front of her.

"It's over."

She did not feel Morrow's gaze on her.

He was on the edge of his chair, poised to somehow reach into her memory and haul in everything, the way a trawler's crew pulls in a drift net. He could no longer hold back.

"Lisa, wait." Morrow still believed critical details were locked in her head.

"Frank." Sullivan's tone cautioned him, but he shrugged her off.

"Lisa, you were right there, practically touching the killer," Morrow said.

Lisa nodded, eyes fixed on the carpet.

"You must've seen something about the shooter. What did you see?"

For a time Lisa did not speak. She just looked at the carpet.

"Lisa?" Sullivan's tone was softer. "What do you remember?"

Lisa said nothing.

Frustrated, Morrow stood, hands on his hips.

"What do you see?" he asked.

Lisa started shaking her head again until her face gave way to anguish. She caught her breath as a great choking sob burst from her throat and she crumpled into tears.

"I see the dead agent's face staring at me and it melts into Bobby's face staring at me and both of them are telling me it's my fault. I dropped the gun. It's my fault…he was going to kill me. Why didn't he just kill me?"

Sullivan went to her, put her arms around her.

"It's all right," she told Lisa softly. "We're going to end the session. It's all right." Sullivan took her hand in both of hers. "It's not your fault. What happened was not your fault. What you're feeling is natural and you did very well today. None of this is your fault."

Sullivan gave her tissues and water. Soon Lisa's crying subsided and she went to the bathroom to recover her composure. Morrow went to the window where he cracked the curtain, looked out at New York and contemplated all that he was facing. Then he turned to Sullivan, who was making notes.

"She's our only hope," Morrow said. "I *need* her to remember something, anything."

"I know. But it's like she hits a wall. Like something's blocking her from retrieving the information we need."

"What is it?"

"It's the trauma. Her ordeal has obliterated her recollection of details."

"Even the smallest thing?"

"Frank, you have to allow for what she's been through—having brain matter splashed on her, having been that close to the murder, having a gun to her head, preparing to die. She's grappling with guilt over the agent's death while still mourning her husband. We're asking a hell of a lot of this woman."

"I've got four homicides and four killers at large and right now she's my best link to finding them. There has to be something more we can do."

Sullivan bit her bottom lip and looked at the bathroom door.

"There's another method I could try."

"Let's do it then."

"You have to understand, she's psychologically exposed. This one is dangerous. It could push her over the edge."

"We have to do it. This is not the time to pull our punches."

20

Dog Lake, Ontario, Canada

Ivan Felk unfurled a map of San Francisco on the cottage's dining table.

"Huddle up, time for review."

Using a pencil, he made a small X on Market Street and began detailing the next mission for Rytter, Unger, Northcutt and Dillon.

"This is the Federal Reserve Bank of San Francisco. It's on Market but occupies much of the block bordered by Main Street, Mission and Spear, with security cameras at every point."

Felk spread an array of photographs of the building.

"The rear receiving dock has seven loading bays monitored by cameras and a manned loading-control booth… here. The dock opens to a parking lot protected by a steel bar fence that is security gated. There."

Felk tapped his pencil to an enlarged color photo.

"The delivery entrance is off Main Street, here. There is a guard station with a reinforced hydraulic crash gate that can stop twenty-five thousand pounds at 35 mph. The exit is also equipped with a crash gate that opens onto Spear Street. Any questions so far?"

Felk glanced at his squad and took a moment to consider them.

They were the survivors of Red Cobra Team 9; men who were largely hated in their own countries; asked to do the secret, dirty work of the very governments who'd hired them, betrayed them, disowned them and left them to die.

These men were a rare tribe, baptized in blood, bonded by their loyalty to each other. Felk glanced at them with pride as they drank from their coffee mugs. They were the best of the best; fighting machines with their shaved heads and goatees, each with hardened biceps sleeved with swirling tattoos. As with Ramapo, each man was betting his life on the next mission. They'd committed every point of the San Francisco job to memory.

Felk continued.

"According to our intel—and this came at a very high price—on the sixteenth, the bank will process an order of ten million dollars to be shipped to federally insured banks in Hawaii. A three-man crew from Ironclad Armored Courier will transport the cash to its cargo terminal at Oakland International Airport."

Felk positioned his laptop on the table and consulted it.

"In addition to GPS, Ironclad's truck has an engine kill switch, which can be activated remotely via satellite by Ironclad's dispatcher. The dispatcher can override the driver and stop any truck in their fleet at any time, to counter hijackings, thefts, robberies."

Felk had photos of Ironclad's depot in Millbrae.

"As some of you know, we have an ex-contractor friend, Dante. After his tour of Iraq, he worked with classified nuclear national security systems at the Livermore lab before the economy took his job. It left him bitter and in debt. We hired him.

"Dante has demonstrated to us that from his laptop, he can bypass Ironclad's online security, seize control of the truck and shut it down at any point. He killed the engine on an Ironclad truck making deliveries in San Bruno. The company thought it was a stall-throttle issue."

"We could've used him at Ramapo," Unger said.

"He wasn't available for that stage." Felk tapped the map. "Let's review assignments. We have a cache of equipment in a storage locker in Daly City, with new bikes. We had help purchasing them. On the sixteenth, Unger and I will surveil the Ironclad truck. We'll follow it when it exits the reserve, over the Bay Bridge and into Alameda County. The rest of you will join us when the truck leaves the eight-eighty for the airport.

"At that point Dante will remotely detonate two small IEDs we'll set up in safe areas at a school and a mall near the airport. That will create enough fear and chaos to occupy emergency services. Within minutes after the IEDs go, the truck will be on a clear strip of Air Cargo Road. Dante kills the truck's engine. It stops and we move in fast.

"In California we'll obtain a new frequency device through Dante that jams all cell phones and radio messages in a half-mile radius. The crew and any wireless user witnessing our operation will be rendered incommunicado.

"Rytter and Unger will first affix C4 to the truck's driver and passenger doors. Dillon and I cover up front. Rytter and Unger then affix C4 to the rear doors. Northcutt covers. We detonate, toss flash bangs into the truck, immobilize the crew, offload and haul ass on the bikes to the vehicle switch point in San Leandro. Then we drive to our meeting point in Sacramento where we courier the cash to our contact in Kuwait City, just like we'll do with this cash tomorrow. Dillon will ship it to Kuwait from couriers in Kingston, Ottawa, Toronto and Montreal."

Felk glanced at the Ramapo cash, neatly arranged beside other bags of items in a far corner. The cash was wrapped with bands stamped Imitation Studio Prop Supplies—Movie Prop Notes Not Legal Tender.

"We had considered shipping the money by air transport in steel coffins—a repatriation of human remains—but that method is subject to greater Customs scrutiny, including X-ray screening, so we decided to be obvious.

"Shipping by movie prop money courier is a huge risk, but this is the fastest way to move our cash, under the circumstances. We're shotgunning the delivery in several small packages through different courier companies to reduce chances of the entire load getting tripped up in Customs somewhere. Our Kuwait City contact will arrange to ship the cash to Karachi. After San Francisco, we all meet in Karachi, pick up the cash and equipment. We then go to Quetta, contact the go-between and use the money to lead us to our guys and lay waste to the fuckers who took them."

Felk paused to take a hit of coffee from his mug.

"Tomorrow we'll disperse and all move out. We must meet by the twelfth at the hotel in San Francisco to give us plenty of time for a few dry runs. You all have cash and credit cards. Travel any way you like to get there. I think it should be less risky entering the United States—they're not expecting us to be entering the States. Besides, they've got no description of us. They have nothing. No one knows what to look for."

"But the news reports say they have an eyewitness," Northcutt said.

"I think that's bullshit. We were careful. We took steps. We left nothing to ID us, no DNA, no casings, nothing."

"What about the reward?" Dillon said. "What if someone gives us up?"

"No one will give us up. Everybody helping us is in some way tied to the people we're going to rescue. They're all part of this."

Felk went to his laptop and activated the latest video of his members being tormented by the insurgents holding them. He turned the screen to Rytter, Unger, Dillon and Northcutt and looked them in the eye.

"This could be any one of you. We will not leave our men behind. We are at war. If the guards in California resist, kill them all."

The meeting ended with each man retreating into his thoughts.

As they prepared for travel, they contended with the horrors that haunted them. They were ghosts of what they once were. It was an unspoken truth they'd recognized about themselves in the shadows of their darkened eyes. They were chained to their comrades taken hostage and the sword of Damocles hung over all of them.

We are the dead, the dying and the damned, Felk thought. *We have nothing to lose.*

Watching Dillon pack the Ramapo cash for shipping, Felk took interest in one of the small bags Dillon had repositioned. It contained various items Rytter had scooped up with the cash that had spilled onto the service center's floor. Rytter had kept them because he figured they might hold potential use for the squad.

Felk examined the FBI agent's badge and his ID.

Special Agent Gregory Scott Dutton stared at Felk from his laminated ID photo. All-American pumped with righteousness from Bridgeport, Connecticut. Felk looked through Dutton's wallet. It held about a hundred in cash, credit cards, bank card, loyalty cards; a receipt for a headlight set from a Newburgh, New York, dealer. A woman's face beamed at Felk from a snapshot.

That would be the wife.

Felk looked back at Dutton's bureau ID. The agent's eyes were burning bright, duty-bound; fated to make a stupid move. Yet some of the news reports portrayed him as a hero who'd sacrificed his life. Probably get some sort of hero's full-color honor-guard funeral at Arlington. Felk sneered.

What did his men get for their sacrifice?

They were dragged through a backwater street like animals, their bodies desecrated.

And what about his men held captive and tortured?

What awaited them if Felk's squad failed to deliver the ransom?

Decapitation.

There'd be no honoring of their work; the risks they took, the price they paid, the blood they'd given, the toll exacted. No memorials. They were throwaway heroes, every one of them.

Including his younger brother.

Clayton.

"Don't leave me!"

Staring out the window to the lake, Felk suddenly saw himself at ten in Ohio during winter.

Just him and Clay, getting set to play hockey on the frozen pond near the house. The Felk brothers are the first of the boys to arrive for the game. No one else is in sight and Clay's practice pass bounces over Ivan's stick and the puck glides far over the ice.

So very far.

Ivan skates after it over smooth-as-glass ice, so clear he can see the muddied bottom with undulating grass, even fish, it's like he's flying until the air cracks and the

*ice collapses under him and instantly he's in the water,
so cold it punches his breath from him as he plunges to
the bottom where he drives his skates into the mud and
pushes up, breaking the surface, body stabbed numb, ears
ringing with hysteria.*

"Clay! Help me, Clay!"

*In his thrashing panic Ivan sees his little brother skat-
ing...AWAY! OH, GOD, HE'S SKATING AWAY! NO!*

"Clay, don't leave me! C-C-Cla—Clay—HELP ME!"

*At eight years old, Clay's heart is nearly bursting, skat-
ing so hard to old man Corbin's dock, and the post that
has that white old-fashioned lifesaver with the rope. Snow
covers the ice and now Clay's running on his skates, snot
tears tightening on his face as he yanks and jerks and pulls
the rope and trips and runs then skates while crying choking sobs, hearing Ivan's screams, praying he's still thrashing in the water. Clay skates, but it's so far and the rope's
uncoiling behind him, but Clay skates and skates and like
Dad showed them drops to his belly on the ice near Ivan
and slides the lifesaver to Ivan who gets it over his arms
yelling, "Pull, Clay!" Clay slides to the end of the rope,
digs in his blades, feeling the weight of his big brother's
life at the end and Ivan feels the strength of Clay's will
dragging him from the icy jaws of death, wrapping his
jacket around him and practically carrying him to old
man Corbin's door where there's a hot stove going inside
pounding on that stinking cracked door hearing his old
mutt yapping the old man's eyes JESUS! Ivan's covered in
ice his lips are blue heat spills from the house and Clay's
begging help my brother please! Oh please help him...*

Felk turned from the window to his computer and replayed the last video from the insurgents, his rage building as he watches the sword rise over his brother's head as
Clay's cries echo with his own from the pond.

"Don't let me die! Ivan, please! Don't let me die!"

Hang on, I'm coming, Clay.

Felk swallowed and turned back to the bag of items collected by Rytter from the service center. *What's this?* There was something else that got swept up with the cash Rytter had recovered.

It was a plastic photo-ID employee card for Good Buy Supermart.

Felk looked at the woman on the card.

Her face was familiar: She was the woman next to the cop.

Was she the eyewitness? Was she the threat, the one thing that could stop them? No. No way. She didn't see anything.

Right?

She didn't see anything. There's no goddamn way a supermarket clerk can stop this operation. Who is she?

He studied the ID

Lisa Palmer.

Felk stared at Lisa's face for a very long time.

21

Tense from a troubled sleep, Jack Gannon woke early.

In the predawn light he saw his files blanketing him, fished out his splayed notebook and paged through his late-night thoughts on his tipster.

Mr. Anonymous could be linked to the heist.

In the wake of the murders, the caller's cryptic information now rang too many alarm bells. Gannon had to steal time to chase this lead down, but couldn't tell anyone what he was doing.

If it dead-ended, then no one would know.

If it turned out to be something, he'd alert Lisker.

Following a hunch never sat well with editors and, unlike some reporters, Gannon never oversold a story.

He started a pot of coffee then climbed into the shower.

After a breakfast of microwaved bacon on a cold bagel with lettuce, tomato and mayo, and orange juice, he fired up his laptop and got to work. He downed his coffee while checking the major news websites to see if his competition had advanced the story.

Nobody had hard news, mostly rehash. All was good until he read the lead item from the *New York Daily News*.

$6.3M Armored Car Heist Killers Fled Upstate

The ice-cold killers who vanished with $6.3M after gunning down three guards and an FBI agent may be in Upstate New York near the Canadian border, sources told the *Daily News.*

Gannon cursed. The *Daily News* reported that locals near Alexandria Bay, New York, told police they'd spotted sport bikes that fit the general description of those in nationally broadcast security video. The exclusive gave the tabloid the jump. Expecting Lisker to call soon and scream at him, Gannon turned to his work.

He would devote as much time as he could get away with to pursuing his instincts on the caller. Then he'd turn to another angle: New York State police trooper Brad West, his friend who'd helped him at the scene.

Later he would press Brad to get his wife, the Ramapo cop, to help him find out more on the eyewitness. There had to be a way to get to the woman who saw the FBI agent's murder up close.

For now, Gannon laid out every note he had on his tipster.

Judging from his voice, Gannon placed the guy in his late twenties. He was plain-speaking, maybe a blue-collar background, sounded concerned, troubled. He kept calling Gannon *sir.*

Military?

There wasn't a whole lot of solid information. Gannon was mindful of the caller's tone and his genuine fear, as again he scrutinized the key aspects of the content of his calls.

"This is big! I swear to God what I'm telling you is true!"

"It involves an operation, a mission, an attack on America."

Then Gannon told him there was nothing he could do with vague, groundless information, that he needed something solid to support it, like documents or some sort of evidence. Gannon thought that would scare him off, as it did with most calls of this nature, but his tipster surprised him by agreeing to meet.

"I'll bring the confirmation you need."

They'd agreed to meet at a diner near Times Square. Gannon waited there, but was stood up and never heard from the guy again.

That's how it ended.

Gannon checked the timeline.

That was three days before the heist.

Damn, he needed to find this guy, to determine if his tip was valid.

What if it was somehow connected to the murders? What happened?

Gannon went online, panning the social chatter on Facebook, Twitter and other social networks for anything related to the heist that might be a lead. Nothing useful surfaced.

He went back to his notes, recalling how his tipster had called him five times over ten days. Caller ID showed that all the calls came from pay phones in New York City. At the time, Gannon figured there was no use following up the numbers, but now he realized the pay-phone numbers were his only connection to the caller.

Gannon had noted the dates and times of the calls. Two came from two different phones in Manhattan, but three of the calls came from the same number. The guy could've been calling near where he lived or worked.

The number started with 914–969.

That was a prefix primarily used in Yonkers.

With everyone using cell phones, pay phones were disappearing; the WPA had done features on the trend. Gannon used online directories and quickly located the pay phone his tipster had used three times. It was in the 300 block of Warburton Avenue in Yonkers.

Within minutes, Gannon was in his old Pontiac Vibe, northbound on the Henry Hudson Parkway. Whenever he could, Gannon avoided driving in New York. The traffic and parking were nightmares. But this morning he needed flexibility and took his car.

Traffic was good and the city was coming to life by the time he arrived in Yonkers. The moment he found a parking space on Warburton, his cell phone rang. It was Lisker.

"Where are you, Gannon?"

"Yonkers. I'll be in a bit later."

"What are you doing there?"

"I'm chasing something."

"What? Be more specific."

"I'm chasing an angle about the heist being an inside job."

"What? The *New York Signal* had that yesterday. Did you see this morning's *Daily News?*"

"Yes."

"We got beat again. Will your lead top the *Daily News?*"

"I won't know until I check it out."

"Be quick. CBS News just said a massive ground search for the suspects will be launched today near Alexandria Bay. We're sending people from our Syracuse bureau. I want you on standby."

"Okay."

"We're losing this story, Gannon. We need to break

this thing wide open! They tell me you're good, but I'm not seeing it."

"I'm pushing my sources."

"Push harder."

Lisker ended the call.

Gannon exhaled.

I'm on the ropes here. He took a hit of coffee from his commuter mug and sent texts to Brad West, Adell Clark and Eugene Bennett.

He got out of his car and walked the block and a half to the pay phone.

There it was.

A pedestal style with a metal enclosure scarred and laced with graffiti.

Gannon confirmed the number and took stock of this section of the avenue: a mix of small businesses, a deli, a check-cashing store, a florist, a beer wholesaler, auto shop, electronics store, hair salon and farther down, an assortment of tired-looking postwar homes and small apartment buildings.

Gannon had done his homework. He knew buildings on the east side of the two-way street backed on to the Old Croton Aqueduct Trailway. It was a long narrow park. Due east of it was Pine Street, where David Berkowitz, the killer known as the Son of Sam, lived before he was arrested.

Welcome to the crime beat.

Gannon popped a stick of gum into his mouth to help him think. There was one very slim chance he'd get anywhere with this lead.

Security cameras.

Covering crime, he knew that most businesses invested in a good security system to reduce the risk of theft, vandalism, liability and to lower insurance rates. These days most systems were digital, making it easier to store video records indefinitely.

Standing at the pay phone, he turned three hundred and sixty degrees, eyeing all the stores, checking off those with a line-of-sight for cameras. He had the time of the last call he'd received from this phone. He had to determine which stores had cameras; if they were angled to capture enough of the street and the phone clearly; and if he could persuade them to check their archives for him.

Easy.

Yeah, right, he told himself.

In a city where everyone was suspicious of everyone, he knew it would be as easy as asking for someone's wallet.

What did he have to lose?

The phone stood directly in front of the Big Smile Deli Mart.

Gannon would start there.

22

The deli mart was a two-story weather-beaten redbrick building with a retracted roll-up steel door.

The store was open for business. Customers were coming and going.

Outside, it had two exterior stands. Fresh, terraced selections of tomatoes, peppers, onions, mushrooms, lettuce were on one side of the door. Apples, pears, oranges, bananas, lemons and grapefruit filled the other stand.

There was a neon beer sign flickering in one window.

Inside, the store's hardwood floors creaked. The air smelled of damp cardboard and nearly soured milk. Its four aisles were narrowed between shelves jammed with groceries. The cold case had beer, soft drinks, milk, eggs, yogurt, ice cream and butter. The deli counter had a display case with an array of meats, salads and pastries.

A slender Middle Eastern man in his early seventies stood behind the counter. A security camera was mounted on the wall above him, angled over the register and the door with an unobstructed view to the street and the pay phone.

This held promise, Gannon thought.

The old man's droopy dark eyes took quick note of Gannon's interest in his camera while he rang in the purchases of the three customers at the counter.

Gannon wanted to approach the clerk when he was alone and walked down an aisle to buy some time. There was a man wearing a Yankees cap at the newsstand flipping through *GQ* and an old woman browsing the deli display case. A younger Middle Eastern man and older woman were working behind the deli counter. Both wore white aprons.

When the counter traffic cleared, Gannon approached the old man.

"Excuse me." He placed his business card on the surface over the lottery-ticket case, opened his wallet to his press badge. "I'm a reporter with the World Press Alliance and I was hoping you could help me."

The man glanced at Gannon's ID, then his card, without touching it. His impassive face bore a pencil mustache. Gannon continued.

"I'm trying to locate a man who called me from the pay phone out front and I thought maybe if we could view your security camera's recordings it might help."

The old man shrugged and shook his head.

"It's important," Gannon said. "I'd be willing to compensate you."

The man shook his head. His eyes shifted to the younger man who'd come from the deli to the counter, likely the old man's son.

"Who are you?" the younger man asked Gannon.

Gannon identified himself and started repeating his request before he was cut off by the old man, who issued a stream of what Gannon guessed was Arabic to the younger man.

As the two men talked, the old woman, wiping her

hands on her apron, joined them in a heated three-way conversation. Gannon knew his request had hit on some deep-seated emotions. The younger man turned to him.

"We can't help you."

"It's all right, I understand."

"No, you don't. After 9/11, our store was robbed. My father was beaten. Two years ago, we were robbed again and the scum dogs told him they had a right to his money because he supported al-Qaeda. They were ignorant racists. My parents are Americans. They've lived here for forty years. I was born here. We pay taxes, we vote and we mind our own business. He would like to help you, but he's afraid there would be repercussions. Okay? So unless you're going to buy something, I'm sorry, but we must ask you to leave."

Gannon thanked them.

After he left, he headed for the check-cashing office across the street.

Eyeing the security camera over the counter, Gannon was satisfied that it was aimed at the door and the pay phone.

"May I help you?" asked an Asian woman in her twenties, wearing a blazer and a smile that weakened a bit as Gannon explained. When he finished, she said, "I'll ask my boss," and picked up a cell phone.

Gannon knew it was futile here.

He turned to the window and she relayed his request. While waiting for the predictable answer, his attention went across the street to the floral shop beside the deli mart. A shapely woman was tending to the flowers in the street display.

"I'm sorry," the Asian woman said, and Gannon turned. "But my boss says you have to make your request to corporate security downtown." She jotted down the number on a corner torn from the back page of the *New York Post* she was reading and passed it to him.

The business next door was an electronics shop.

Gannon saw the shop's security camera trained at the proper angle. He looked to the counter and the balding manager with an assortment of pens jutting from his pocket protector. An older woman was trying to understand his directions on how to program her cell phone.

"Be right with you, sir," the manager said.

Gannon nodded, went to the side of the store and stood before the array of big-screen TVs, watching a replay of last night's Yankees game.

At that moment, a second man entered the store. Gannon recognized him as the guy reading magazines in the deli mart, the Yankees cap.

"They sucked last night," the ball cap guy said, joining him at the TVs.

He was about fifty, six feet with a potbelly straining a mustard-stained Mets T-shirt. The cuffs of his jeans were frayed and the guy needed a shave, a haircut and, judging from his greasy strands, maybe a shower.

"Yeah, that's too bad." Gannon moved to the display of laptops.

"I might be able to help you," the ball cap guy said.

"Sorry?" Gannon turned back.

"I overheard you in the deli asking about security tape and I might be able to help you."

Gannon doubted it.

"How can you help me?"

"I'm with a Community Watch program." He nodded upward. "I live on the second floor above this store and I keep electronic surveillance of the street. I work closely with the NYPD."

"Is that right?"

"Yup, and if we can reach an agreeable consulting fee, I could check my recordings for the dates you're interested in."

"And what fee would be agreeable?"

"Seeing how you work for a big news agency, let's say one thousand."

"Too high." Gannon smiled. "I don't even know if you have what I'm looking for, and if the quality is acceptable. I'll give you fifty to check and another fifty if you have what I need."

"Make it two hundred in total."

"One-fifty, and only if you have what I need, in good quality. Agreed?"

The ball cap had to scratch his whiskers to decide.

"One-fifty, fine."

"Let me get your name and ID first. Got a driver's license?"

"Driver's license? What do you need that for?"

"My personal security against getting ripped off."

"Well, I'm not too sure about that."

"That's what I figured. Have a nice day." Gannon started to turn.

"Hold on." The ball cap guy reached for his wallet and handed Gannon his license. His name was Jerry Falco. He was fifty-three. Gannon took down all his information before Falco snatched his license back.

"Satisfied?" Falco asked.

Gannon presented him with a business card and his WPA ID.

Falco eyeballed him for several seconds then invited Gannon to follow him. They went outside to the door between the electronics shop and check-cashing office. Falco pressed buttons on the security keypad, opened the door for Gannon. The building reeked of cats. Gannon tried not to breathe deeply as Falco led him up a narrow wooden staircase.

There were two apartments with scuffed doors across from each other. The walls were webbed with cracked plaster. Neither door had a number or nameplate. Falco's keys jingled as he inserted them into the lock and turned. Before opening the door, he hesitated.

"I need you to wait out here a bit while I go in and tidy up, all right?"

"Sure," Gannon said, thinking, *I'll just hold my breath and try not to inhale a fur ball.*

Falco opened the door, entered then shut it. In that instant, Gannon thought he saw a camera on a tripod aimed at the street below.

Weird.

But Gannon also glimpsed a display of photographs taped to a wall; a collection of shots of the flower shop and the shapely woman he'd just seen tending to her flowers.

Was this guy some kind of voyeur or peeping perv?

As Gannon contemplated the question, his BlackBerry vibrated.

The number was blocked. Gannon answered, keeping his voice low.

"Jack, this is Brad. I got your message."

"What's up with Ramapo?"

"Buddy, I wish I could help you, but they've tightened things up."

"Can you give me a hypothetical?"

"Afraid not. I had to make this call from a safe phone. I wish I could help, believe me. I have to go."

"Wait, wait. If you were me, where would you go right now and what would you do?"

A long silent moment passed.

"Hypothetically?"

"Yes."

"I'd haul myself back to the service center as fast as I could right now."

"What's going on, hypothetically?"

"I would just do it. Get there and watch and learn. I have to go."

Gannon stood outside Falco's door. Should he go to Ramapo now or wait? He wrestled with the decision amid the sounds of furniture being rearranged in Falco's apartment. If he didn't go to the center and missed something, Lisker would nail his balls to the newsroom wall.

"Mr. Falco!" Gannon knocked hard on the door. "Mr. Falco, I have to go!"

Falco's door opened about six inches.

"I'm sorry, Mr. Falco, I have to go, but I'll be back."

"I don't understand. I only need a few more minutes, then you can come in and I'll help you find what you're looking for."

Gannon held up a crisp twenty, folded around his business card.

"This is for you. I will be back. I really need to do this, but I have to go. Believe me, I want to see your stuff and we have a deal, but I have to go."

Falco inspected the twenty as Gannon rushed down the stairs, to the street and trotted to his car.

23

Morrow stopped the car at the main entrance of the Freedom Freeway Service Center.

Dr. Sullivan, in the front passenger seat, turned to Lisa in the back.

"How are you holding up? Are you sure you can you do this?"

Lisa was looking directly ahead, her hands clasped together in her lap as she struggled with the panic rattling through her.

A part of me died here, Lisa thought.

She'd agreed to return to the center this morning after two more difficult and fruitless interviews the previous night. Sullivan had said that research showed that on-the-scene sessions increased the accuracy of memories and the chances of unlocking suppressed details.

But there were risks.

As the engine ticked down and Morrow consulted his phone, Sullivan searched Lisa's face and touched her hand.

"Remember, we discussed the downside, Lisa."

Lisa nodded. Reliving the event also increased the potential to intensify the emotional fallout and further traumatize the witness.

"After I do this, my kids and I are going home, okay? That was the deal. I will do everything I can to help you catch these monsters, but my kids and I need our lives back. We've got a lot to sort out, you know?"

"I understand," Sullivan said.

Morrow finished on his phone.

"Let's go, we're ready."

With the exception of a few emergency and service vehicles, the parking lot was deserted. A teenage boy wearing a Freedom Freeway T-shirt and ball cap was trying to corral the discarded ribbons of yellow crime scene tape slithering across the lot. The service center's big sign out front said SORRY TEMPORARILY CLOSED; so did the one printed in block letters on the sheet of paper taped inside the glass door.

The flutter and clang of the flagpoles underscored the quiet.

Morrow held up his palm, indicating that he, Lisa and Sullivan would wait outside the entrance as Agent Craig Roberts, holding a walkie-talkie, exited to greet them.

"Almost ready now," he told Morrow. "Heads-up, manager behind me."

"Got it," Morrow said.

The FBI's Evidence Response Team had been poised to clear and release the scene last night when Morrow alerted them to hang on to it. The delay frustrated Mac Foyt, the center's manager, who had followed Roberts outside to plead to Morrow.

"Agent Morrow, we were told we could open this morning."

"I'm sorry, Mr. Foyt. We're going to need a little more time."

A breeze kicked up the pages on Foyt's clipboard and lifted his tie as he undid the collar button on his white shirt and tried to make a case.

"We're respectful of what happened, don't get me wrong," Foyt said. "We're cooperating, but I'm getting calls from companies that are planning routes, fuel schedules. I've got my staff on hold, a hell of a lot of business on the line."

"We ask for your patience a little while longer, Mr. Foyt," Morrow said.

Roberts clipped a small microphone to Lisa's collar. It was wired to a pack she'd helped him fasten to the side of her waist.

"Good. This will pick up everything you say," Roberts said as the walkie-talkie he'd set on the ground crackled. Roberts grabbed it, spoke into it, then to Morrow and the others.

"Ready," he said, then turned to the manager. "Mr. Foyt, you'll have to excuse us, but we need you and your staff to clear the area now."

"It's just me and Aaron." Foyt grimaced and whistled to the teenager in the lot. As they walked together to a Cadillac Seville parked some distance away, Sullivan acknowledged Morrow's nod and turned to Lisa.

"We're going to begin. All set?"

As if cued, the air split with motorcycle engines starting up and Lisa caught her breath. Four of them idled about fifty yards down the roadway beside a white unmarked panel van.

"Now? We're doing it now? I thought we'd walk in and talk first."

"No, we have to replicate the event cold, like this. It's the most effective way." Sullivan put her hand on Lisa's shoulder. "We've used statements to re-create everything as accurately as possible. The people in the vehicles and inside are all law enforcement—FBI, state, local."

Roberts held the door open for Lisa.

It was moving too fast. Lisa took a breath, then entered with Sullivan beside her, encouraging her to narrate every memory, sensation and detail.

Upon stepping into the lobby, Lisa's skin tingled and the small hairs at the back of her neck prickled. The scene was otherworldly. Nearly two dozen casually dressed men and women were at the ATMs, or looking at the big map, or in the store, or the lobby. She recognized Detective Percy Quinn and Anita Rowan with the Ramapo P.D.

Oh, God, just like before, yet different.

There was an eerie, deceiving quiet; a funereal air. There was activity, yet it was as if the service center were a mausoleum, empty of life.

As if she were watching ghosts.

Sullivan was beside her, gently urging her to report details.

"Don't hold back, Lisa," she whispered.

Lisa swallowed.

"I remember I needed to pee then get some magazines and a snack … The air-conditioning felt good, people were at the ATMs…people were in the store… I went to the store, picked up snacks and magazines. I got in line to pay and remember it was taking a long time…"

As she went through the chronology of events, recalling how the lights went off then on again, how she paid for her items, how she started back across the lobby, she glimpsed Roberts talk into his walkie-talkie and soon two men entered with a cart and bags.

The guards.

Lisa froze.

Through the window she saw the white van doubling

as American Centurion's armored car. Then she heard the motorcycles, saw men in racing suits and helmets with dark visors enter, extend their arms, shape their hands, their forefingers, as if holding a gun.

Pop! Pop!

Lisa flinched as the ghost killers shouted the firing sounds. Her heart beat faster as she detailed events, moment by moment.

Even the scene outside was replayed.

Inside, the killers barked commands. Lisa went numb. Her legs crumpled and she was on the floor—*in the very same spot*—it was absent of blood, absent of death, but reeked of industrial bleach.

Oh, God, no!

A man was on the floor beside her, facing her, about the same age as the agent, and he started saying, "I'm a cop...my gun's on my hip under my shirt...slide closer, lift it out...tuck it under me...I can get off shots..."

Lisa's thought process spun into a whirlwind of what was remembered, what was re-created and what was real.

Everything went blue.

She can't breathe as her trembling hand reaches for his weapon...she can't feel it because she knows what's coming...she drops it and the gunman rushes to them with such fury, seizing the weapon, the man's wallet, extending his arm, his hand, his gun finger...

Lisa recounts every detail, when she is overcome.

"NO. GOD, NO! DON'T KILL HIM!"

But the gunman shouted.

BANG!

Lisa spasmed as her memory replayed the hot splatter of blood—the explosion.

The killer moved to her.

No, wait.

In that instant, as the killer's finger pushed violently against Lisa's skull, it happened. In the terrifying moment between one death and her life, it happened. Her heart skipped.

Time stopped.

With the unbearable pressure mounting on her skull, the horrifying images rewound to the shooter placing his gun against Agent Gregory Scott Dutton's head. His last words—"Jennifer, I love you"—roared in Lisa's ears and memory rewound a bit more to that sickening instant when the killer extended his arm and the cuff of his racing suit slipped back and in a searing telltale flash Lisa sees...

SHE SEES IT!

Lisa grabbed the shooter's arm, clamped it in a viselike grip.

"A tattoo!" she shouts from the floor. "He's got a tattoo!"

Morrow's eyes widen. Jerked into action, he pulled out his notepad.

"Help her up! Quick!" Morrow said. "Lisa, please, can you sketch it now!"

Lisa was sobbing convulsively as Sullivan helped her to a sitting position, passed her the pad and sat on the floor with her.

"It was like a snake caught in ropes," Lisa managed to say through her tears, struggling to steady her hand as she drew. "The snake's head was up like it was going to bite, its mouth open, showing fangs, and the ropes and things were kind of braided."

After several moments, Lisa passed her sketch to Morrow.

"Please, don't ask me to do any more today. Please."

"No, Lisa. We're done for today. You did very well. Everyone did very well," Morrow said, then huddled around her drawing with other investigators.

Sullivan comforted Lisa, praising her amid her quiet sniffles. They sat that way for a long time. Someone brought Lisa a Coke while Morrow and the others absorbed the break, quietly sending emails and making calls. Morrow approached Lisa, apologetic. There was one more thing. He asked Lisa to allow an NYPD sketch artist to work with her at fine-tuning the tattoo image when she returned to the hotel.

"It won't take long. It's important," Morrow said.

Lisa agreed.

Off to the side, Agent Roberts was on the phone to Agents Vicky Chan and Eve Watson. He was arranging to drive Lisa back to the hotel in Manhattan so she could work in the room with the sketch artist before collecting Ethan and Taylor and going home to Queens.

Then Agent Roberts, another agent and Dr. Sullivan prepared to leave the service center with Lisa. They were outside the entrance when Morrow caught up to them.

"Lisa." He took her hands. "Thank you. I know this was painful."

"Catch them, Frank."

"We will. I've taken care of whatever you may need at your house while we continue investigating. From surveillance to having someone stay with you, if you want."

"Well, our lives have already been turned upside down."

"Whatever you're comfortable with. Think it over and let us know."

"Okay." She tried to smile before noticing someone approaching.

"Excuse me, Agent Morrow?"

Everyone's attention shifted.

"Jack Gannon, World Press Alliance. Sorry for interrupting, but I was wondering if you could update your progress on the investigation?"

Morrow was quick to respond.

"The investigation continues. We have no further comment at this time. We'll update the press when we have something."

"And here?" Gannon looked at Lisa and assessed that she was not a cop. In fact, she looked familiar. *Was this the woman he'd seen with Morrow before?* "What can you tell me about the nature of your investigation here? I'm sorry, miss, you are...?"

"I—I—" Lisa shot a look to Morrow. "I'm not sure I can—"

Morrow's jaw tightened.

"She has no comment at this time." Morrow positioned himself between Gannon and Lisa. "Now, if you'll excuse us, please."

"Is that right, miss? Does Agent Morrow speak for you?"

"Beat it, Gannon," Morrow said.

"Let me pass you my card."

Before Gannon could pull a business card from his wallet, Roberts, Morrow and the other agent got Lisa into an FBI sedan.

As it wheeled away, Lisa's eyes met Gannon's.

She kept looking at him until the car disappeared toward the thruway back to Manhattan, her children and her life.

24

A cobra, entwined in thorns, hood flared, fangs exposed.

Experts said it represented a feared killer ready to strike from the depths of its agony. The black-and-gray drawing filled the large monitor in the boardroom at the FBI's Manhattan office.

"This is a solid break for us," Morrow told the investigators who'd gathered for an emergency case-status meeting late in the day.

Lisa Palmer's sketch had been enhanced to a sharp pencil image of the deadly snake. Its body twisted with bramble, circling the wrist of the suspect who'd murdered FBI Special Agent Gregory Scott Dutton and at least one of the three guards.

"To date, we still have no latents, no casings, no plate, no DNA. This descriptor is the strongest lead we've got so far. It came from our key eyewitness this morning."

Morrow said it had emerged after interviews with a psychiatrist and was reliable. The witness had been positioned next to the shooter's wrist. Earlier in the day, after recalling the tattoo, the witness worked with an NYPD police sketch artist to ensure accuracy of the detail. The image had just been submitted to the Integrated Auto-mated Fingerprint Identification System, which also held information on tattoos, scars, photos and other physical characteristics on some sixty-six million people.

"We've also submitted it to every possible U.S. agency—military, prison security and gang task forces at national, state, local police levels—alerting them to look for any individuals bearing a similar tattoo. We've advised they exercise extreme caution and alert us."

Glenda Stark added: "We've also alerted Interpol, U.S. Customs, airports, train and bus terminals. But we're not releasing the information to the press at this time."

Al Dimarco, a New York detective with the Joint Bank Robbery Task Force, stared at her from his status sheet over his bifocals.

"Why not?" Dimarco was puzzled.

"We're pressing intelligence sources first," Morrow said.

"Meanwhile, you go with this needle-in-a-haystack search for your cobra killer?" Dimarco said. "Cripes, blast the tattoo to the press, it goes viral and the whole freakin' world is looking for our guy within hours, Frank."

For a second, Morrow envisioned a *New York Post* headline: FBI Search for "Cobra Killer." Morrow respected Dimarco, a legend with the NYPD, but had always con-sidered him to be too cozy with the New York press, liked to see his work on the front pages.

"Yes, Al, we could give it to the press, but we believe our subjects don't know we have it. If we told the press, we'd be giving our edge to the suspects, who could take every effort to cover it. These guys are good. Let's work quietly with intel first. The tattoo could be the key to us grabbing the whole crew and its network. If we blast it through the media, we alert the subjects that we're coming."

Dimarco shrugged. Morrow flipped through his file before stressing his point.

"You all got the handouts and the e-version, but I'll state the obvious—we want everyone who is canvassing and recanvassing to show the tattoo, especially to employees at the service center and American Centurion."

"Hold up, I've got another question," Dimarco said. "If these guys are so smart, why did they leave a living witness?"

"They left a lot of living witnesses," Morrow said.

"I'm talking about our tattoo witness here," Dimarco said. "She was less than two feet from the shooter. He had a gun to her head, then pulled away. They'd already knocked down four. Why didn't they put her down?"

"I would say they were sensitive to response time. They were working by a clock. They could've seen people in the parking lot making calls," said Percy Quinn. "Witnesses reported seeing one shooter urging the gunman to leave the scene. We figure they feared they were taking too long and that locals were responding."

"That's plausible," Morrow said. "Unless you've got another theory on that, Al?"

"No, but it's very fortuitous that she was not killed."

"We have no reason to suspect she was involved, if that's what you're getting at, Al?"

"No, it just struck me as odd."

"She begged for her life," Morrow said.

Glenda Stark requested Morrow move the meeting along.

"All right, updates," Morrow said. "Going around the table—what do we know from confidential informants, what are we hearing from the street?"

"Even with the reward, we're not getting much," Tony Carza, a New York detective, said. "It's an indication that these guys are not known locally."

"The call line, tips?" Morrow asked.

"Got about sixty that we're following," Agent Hughes said. "Half of them related to possible sightings of the sport bikes from the public appeal using the security video, but nothing concrete."

"Financial?" Morrow asked. "Anything from banks, casinos, on large amounts of cash, wire-transfer services?"

Agent David Whitfield, an expert in white-collar crime, reported that nothing unusual had surfaced that could be tied to the heist.

Morrow took a moment to think.

"All right, we know that these guys knew to be there at that time," he said. "They knew to hit that truck at the top of its route when it was heavy. What about the Freedom Freeway? Percy, who has access to delivery and pick-up times?"

"Mac Foyt and his secretary, Betsy Leeds. They handle the receipts. American Centurion services the ATMs on the same trip roughly every five days, although they float the times and dates."

"And how is that communicated to the center?"

"Verbally. American calls Betsy or Foyt. We looked at both, but they have been cleared. Leeds is a choir leader at her church."

"And the staff?"

"We're working our way through background. Len Purdy, the dishwasher at the restaurant, did time at Rikers ten years ago. He stole Corvettes and Ferraris and lived it up in Atlantic City. His buddies at the Bottoms Up, a local dive bar, claim he wondered about knocking off an armored car, but Purdy says it was bar talk. The only risk he takes is with lottery tickets."

"That it?"

"We also looked at Amy Danson, a clerk at the center's grocery store. Her husband is doing a hard stretch at Northern State in Newark. She visits him every weekend."

"What's he in for?"

Special Agent Stan Garlin with the Newark office said Tyson-Lee Danson had held up four liquor stores.

"Two in Trenton, one in Bayonne and one in Hoboken. He used a sawed-off shotgun. He's a crackhead with a low IQ. We don't think he is in the same league as our Cobra guys," Garlin said.

"That's it for the center so far," Quinn said.

"Al, what's the status with the task force and Armored Centurion? Do we know if our subjects had help there, or got access to routes and logs?"

Dimarco adjusted his bifocals, wet his index finger on his tongue and turned to his notebook.

"The company is cooperative as we continue to interview staff. As you know, every hire is prescreened, polygraphed, fingerprinted, criminal checks are made. So the list is fairly clean. We've got a lot of young security guards, retired cops, ex-military, the usual mix."

"And support staff?"

"We're working through all staff. We're also looking at all former employees, anyone with a beef, anyone facing financial stress, the usual."

"What about the routes? Did they print them out?"

"All documents were printed, given to the crews. When routes were completed, the data was entered into the company's computer and the paper was shredded," Dimarco said. "We're building a pool of staff we'd like to reinterview. Some have already submitted to a polygraph. This afternoon we'll have warrants for all phone records, computer records of all staff."

"I'll join you on the reinterviews, Al," Morrow said.

"We've set them up for tomorrow."

"Okay," Morrow said. "That just about wraps it up, but before we break, I want to underscore that we have a lot of people helping on this case, but unauthorized release of information to the press will be regarded as obstruction. You all know that." Morrow's eyes went around the table and lingered on Dimarco just long enough for his point to be made.

As people began collecting their notes and phones, Glenda Stark interrupted them with an announcement.

"One last thing. The funeral for Special Agent Dutton will be held in Bridgeport, Connecticut. The director will be attending. The day and time is still being sorted. Everyone in law enforcement is welcome."

It was late by the time Morrow got home.

He dropped his jacket on a chair and made his way to the kitchen. The lights were dimmed, but the counter and table were spotless. Not a dish or leftover in sight. Exhausted, he loosened his tie, glanced at the mail, then went to the living room. On his way, he met Beth, descending the stairs.

"How did it go today?" she asked.

"We got a break."

"Good, I'm glad. We got pizza. There's plenty left in the fridge."

By his wife's tone and the shine in her eyes, he knew all was not well as they went to the kitchen to talk.

"What is it?" he asked.

"Pepperoni."

"No, what's bothering you?"

"Jerrod told Hailey he likes someone else. She's taking it hard. She's in her room and won't come out."

"I'll go talk to her."

"No, she's being consoled. Text support from her friends."

Morrow accepted that there were places a father couldn't go.

"Is she going to be okay?"

"She's upset now, but she'll be fine. It turns out they weren't *that* involved. Better this happened now, rather than later. Are you going to eat some pizza?"

"No, I'm not hungry. How was your day?"

"Crappy."

"Want to talk about it?"

"Did you eat downtown?"

"No, I was working. I'm just not hungry, Beth. What is it?"

On the brink of saying something, Beth searched his face. Reconsidered, blinked several times and waved it all off. Morrow figured—*hell, hoped*—it was all to do with Hailey or Beth's job.

"I'm going to have a shower, then look at some reports," he said.

Later, in the living room Morrow reviewed where they were on the case. He flipped through all the agencies that would be acting on the alert for the tattoo. It was a good lead. Dimarco was right, it was tempting to circulate the info through the press, but they needed time.

He scanned some of the agencies. Air force, Office of Special Investigations, army CID, U.S. Marshals, Homeland Security, the Defense Intelligence Agency, Marine Corps Intelligence and the Naval Criminal Investigative Service. On and on it went. Somebody would have to come through. Dimarco and the task force were going full bore on the armored car company. Piece by piece they were getting closer, Morrow could feel it. If they could get another break...

He would clear this case.

He had to.

"Frank?"

Beth stood before him.

"Tell me what's going on," she said.

"What do you mean?"

"I was doing laundry and I found this in one of your shirts."

It was a business card for Dr. Arthur Stein, oncology specialist.

"I want the truth, Frank." Her chin crumpled. "I deserve to know." She nodded upstairs. "We deserve to know."

Morrow looked at his wife. His mind raced back to the moment he'd first set eyes on her; then to the moment they were married; then to the moment when Hailey was born.

"Tell me, Frank."

Something caught in his throat. His Adam's apple rose and fell before he found his voice.

"I've got cancer. It's terminal. I'm sorry."

"Cancer? What? No. No."

"I've got just over a year."

Beth shook her head.

"No." She kept shaking her head. "No, there must be a mistake."

"There's no mistake."

"There has to be, Frank! We'll find another doctor. We'll—"

He took Beth in his arms, holding her as she cried softly so Hailey wouldn't hear.

Suddenly overwhelmed by the pain of leaving them, he closed his eyes hard.

25

Gannon sat alone in a booth of the Moonshade Café and gazed into his second mug of coffee until the sting of self-rebuke subsided.

It was coming up on an hour since his disastrous confrontation down the road at the service center with Agent Morrow's group.

It was not Gannon's best moment.

He'd been borderline rude in scrambling to read the situation. He hadn't expected to come upon Morrow leaving the scene with a woman who appeared troubled.

Something had happened in there with her. She had to be Morrow's witness. I was so close, but I dropped the ball. What happened with that woman in the center?

Gannon searched the cream clouds of his coffee for the answer as he tried to determine his next step.

Time was slipping by.

Maybe he could salvage something out of the incident, shape it into a story? He needed help. Using his BlackBerry, he sent a message to Brad West, his state police source who'd tipped him to coming to the center today.

Am in your hood, got time to meet?

Gannon knew he was pushing things, but he had few options. Eugene Bennett hadn't responded to his latest request, and he hadn't heard back from Adell Clark. At the moment, Brad was his best shot.

After sending his message, he checked for any breaking stories on the heist. Nothing new had surfaced. The search upstate was the lead story of the day. Part of him wished he was up there. It was easier to report and if they made an arrest it would bust things wide open.

Lisker had also dispatched staff from the WPA's Rochester bureau to support the team from Syracuse. They'd already filed words and images from the scene. The hunt had built-in drama, made for good pictures—helicopters, dogs and cops on ATVs combing the region—but so far it had failed to yield anything.

At least we're covered there, Gannon thought, determined to follow his instincts and keep digging, just as Brad West responded to his message.

Where R U now, Jack?

Ramapo, Moonshade Café.

Meet us in 20 min at Jade Sun Chinese place S. of Southfields on 17, just N. of 17A on the right.

OK.

Us? Who is 'us'? Gannon wondered.

Ten miles later, he arrived at the Jade Sun. Parked among the pickups and commercial vehicles. He noticed an unmarked police car.

Who belongs to the unmarked?

Gannon looked it over before he entered the diner. It smelled of deep-fried food. Cutlery clinked along with the hiss of running water and Johnny Cash singing "Ring of Fire." Half the tables and booths were in use. Trooper Brad West was in uniform, occupying one side of a booth opposite a woman in a West Point sweatshirt and jeans.

"There he is." Brad smiled at Gannon, offering his hand and a seat beside him as the woman turned.

"This is my wife, Detective Anita Rowan with Ramapo P.D. Anita, this is Jack Gannon, a reporter with the WPA."

"Hello, nice to meet you." Gannon shook Anita's hand.

"I was telling her," Brad said, "how if it wasn't for you, the charity in Buffalo would have tanked. When I went to Jack, he wrote a fantastic story on the front page of the *Buffalo Sentinel*. That got us the benefit concert, and the donations rolled in like water over Niagara Falls. I told him he had a friend for life here. How ya doing, buddy?"

"Good, thanks, Brad. I appreciate this."

"No problem, sit down. Ya hungry? The egg rolls are deadly here." Brad glanced at the waiter. "My treat."

"No, thanks."

"Ya sure?"

"Just a ginger ale, maybe."

"Can I get a ginger ale?" Brad repeated to the server, turning to Gannon.

"You're all he ever talks about," Anita said to Gannon, twisting a straw through her fingers. He sensed unease behind her smile. He was walking a tightrope. Brad West had a big heart. He trusted Gannon with his job and now he was going to extend that trust to include his wife, who, from the way she was working that straw, was apprehensive.

"How can we help you, buddy?" Brad said.

"Wait," Anita asked. "You're not going to use names or anything?"

"Don't worry," Brad said. "I told you, Jack's a good man."

"I protect sources, I don't use names."

Anita studied her straw.

"I saw you back at the center," she said, "through the glass, outside with Agent Morrow."

"You were there, inside?" Gannon said.

"Yes."

"Can you tell me what you were doing?"

"Helping with the investigation."

Their food arrived, a heaping plate for Brad, who dug in, and a salad for Anita. It was followed by ginger ale for Gannon, who sipped some, deciding it was time to play his cards.

"Maybe you could help me confirm a few things?" Gannon asked Anita.

"Maybe."

"The woman with Morrow, who looked a bit distraught, that was a witness, right?"

"Right," Anita said.

There's my confirmation, Gannon thought.

"And the FBI brought her back to the scene today?" he continued.

"Uh-huh." Anita took a forkful of salad.

"Walked her through the scene, I imagine."

Anita nodded.

"She must be the key witness?" Gannon asked.

"I can't say."

"Is she from the city, or local?"

Anita hesitated as she picked through her salad. Tension mounted with every passing second of silence. Gannon threw a look to Brad, who nodded at Anita to continue.

"I'm sorry," she said. "Brad, I'm just not comfortable doing this. I mean, I just came from the center. I don't feel right about this. You two go way back, but this is not something I do. I'm sorry."

"Honey, I trust him completely."

"It's okay," Gannon said. "I understand."

"Anita, you can trust him," Brad said.

"What I don't get—" she stabbed her salad with her fork "—is why do you need to know? That's part of a police investigation."

"He needs to know because he's reporting on the heist," Brad said.

"I asked *him,* Brad."

"Journalists investigate, too," Gannon said. "I've got a tip, a long-shot tip I'm working on that may be connected to the case."

"What is it?"

"It's a bit vague right now, but it's possible someone with advance knowledge on the case contacted the WPA."

Anita put her fork down and turned to Gannon.

"If that's true, you should tell the FBI."

"I'm not a police informant. I'm a journalist and I investigate independently."

"Except when you need our help, like now."

"Anita," Brad said.

"It's okay," Gannon said. "I understand, and I apologize for making you uncomfortable. As for my tip, I'm not certain of its reliability and I'm still looking into it. Please keep that confidential. Look, I should be going."

"Hold up," Brad said. Then he turned to Anita. "Jack is the best journalist I know. When a charter jet crashed in Lake Erie near Buffalo, everyone said it was terrorism. Truth was, the Russian pilot committed suicide. Jack got the story and was nominated for the Pulitzer. Then there was the Styebeck case. Remember? The murders tied to a suburban-Buffalo detective? They fired him for protecting sources on that story, right, Jack?"

"Yes."

"Turns out, Jack was dead on the money on Styebeck," Brad said. "Anita, I help him not because he helped save my charity, but because he gets to the truth and never ever gives up his sources. He's honorable."

Anita stared at her husband. As she ate her salad, she weighed her words carefully before she turned to Gannon.

"What are you going to say in your story, based on what I told you?"

"I'll say investigators returned a key witness to the scene of four murders and walked her through the tragedy in an effort to find the fugitive killers, something like that."

"And to whom will you attribute the information?"

"Sources."

"That's it?"

"Yes, for that part, then we'll have some background and updates, like with the search upstate."

"We're hearing there's nothing to that," Brad said. "Something about the veracity of the information, or some confusion."

"We have people up there reporting. And we'll add other aspects to the story."

"Are you good with that, Anita?" Brad asked.

"Tell me what happened in Buffalo on the cop case," she asked Gannon.

"No one believed my reporting, including some senior police officials who pressured the paper until I was fired."

"And?"

"I was not wrong."

Anita nodded thoughtfully.

"You can use what I told you, Jack."

"Thank you."

"No names, got that?"

"I got it."

Back at his desk in the WPA's headquarters, Gannon typed quickly, assembling the wire service's main story on the search for the killers in the interstate armored car heist.

"I like your stuff, lead with it. It's exclusive news," Lisker had acknowledged. "Everybody and his dog will have the story on the 'futile search' upstate."

It took less than forty-five minutes for him to write the full piece. He sent it to Hal Ford on the desk, Ford gave it a quick edit before putting it out to all WPA subscribers.

Gannon went to the window and massaged the back of his neck.

He was beat.

The sun had set and the horizon had dissolved into a swath of pinks and blues. He looked at the Empire State Building rising from Manhattan's twinkling lights and reflected on Anita and Brad, who seemed to be suited to married life.

What was that like?

Gannon glanced at the empty desks of people who'd already gone home to their families in New Jersey, Westchester or Long Island. He glanced at the framed photos of their kids, wives and husbands, beaming through the chaos of stylebooks, notes, newspapers and assorted messes.

In the end, family is what mattered.

Gannon had his sister and niece in Arizona, but beyond them he had no one.

Nobody waiting for him.

Nothing to rush home to but an empty apartment.

Empty.

That's how he felt.

He thought of Katrina for a second.

Then he turned to the skyline and somewhere in the night he saw a face he'd seen earlier that day.

The witness.

What had she endured? What was her story? Who was

she? Where was she from? What was her situation? Married? Single? Involved?

In the moment their eyes met at the service center something had connected between them.

A longing?

A deep sense of loneliness?

Give your head a shake.

He was too tired to think straight; crazy to believe that he'd somehow made a spiritual, cosmic bond with the witness.

All right.

But he needed to find her, that much made sense.

Four funerals were coming and he was determined to take the reader into the heart of this story—the whole story.

"Jack!" a news assistant called out. "Call for you."

He took it on his landline at his desk.

"Gannon."

"Mr. Gannon, this is Jerry Falco, in Yonkers."

"Mr. Falco, yes, sorry."

"I may have what you need. Are you still interested?"

Gannon checked the time.

"Yes. I'm very interested."

26

VIA passenger train number 45 edged the windswept shore of Lake Ontario, swaying gently through the picture-postcard towns and farm fields east of Toronto.

Ivan Felk had an economy-class window seat. Few people were aboard. The aisle seat next to his was empty. So were the seats near him. Yet in the soothing rhythm of the train's *click-clacking,* Felk seethed.

The previous night, he'd sent a message to the untraceable account of the insurgents holding his men. In it, Felk had claimed responsibility for the deadly heist outside New York City and sent news reports, all to confirm his team's actions to secure the ransom by the deadline.

The insurgents responded with a new video.

Felk viewed the images on his laptop: the camera panned over the aftermath of his team's failed military mission in the region's frontier city; then to the desecration of the dead; then to the torment of the hostages. The footage then cut to a man before a plain black backdrop, his face concealed in a black scarf with only his eyes showing.

Felk locked onto them.

The insurgent gave readings from the glorious text, his voice traveling through Felk's earphones. Then he switched to English.

"Heed this message from the New Guardians of the National Revolutionary Movement. We acknowledge your work to collect the fine. We must see your continued atonement for crimes committed by the invading infidels. We must see evidence in America of further work to collect the remainder of the fine. Full payment must be received by the last day of this month, or the infidel spies will be executed."

The man concluded with another tribute from the holy text; then the footage showed the blade of the executioner's sword resting on the neck of a hostage: Felk's brother.

Clay, oh, Jesus, hang on. I'm coming.

Felk snapped his laptop shut, yanked out his earphones.

I'm going to waste these mothers.

He ran his fingertips over his chin.

Calm down. Focus. Focus. Focus.

His mind scanned the operation.

Dillon's assignment was to ship the movie-prop cash to Kuwait, then join the others in California. They knew the method was a gamble, but it was a risk they had to take.

The team had split up.

Each man was now traveling independently to San Francisco. How they got there was their choice. Supported by their network of friends, they each had counterfeit passports, ID and credit cards and several thousand dollars in cash. They would meet at the hotel in San Francisco by the twelfth, ample time to conduct surveillance, drills, set up the IEDs far in advance of when they needed to launch the mission.

Each soldier knew his job.

Each one was sworn to duty.

Life and death.
We will not fail.

Felk looked through his window to the south.

Somewhere beyond the great, endless lake and its seamless meeting with the sky, he saw himself back in Ohio in the wood-frame house where he and Clay grew up.

It was a little nothing-ass speck of a town at the fringes of Youngstown, in the graveyard of factories, steel mills and the American dream.

Their old man was a Vietnam vet, a U.S. marine who did two tours. He'd survived Khe Sanh and came home with a mangled leg to work at an AljorCor Aluminium plant before it closed. Then he worked the Old River Metal foundry before he was laid off.

He always drank, but by then he drank more.

Sometimes he hit Ivan and Clay, but they forgave him. He was their dad and they knew he had problems. For years they heard him screaming in his sleep at night— heard their mother comforting him.

She used to come home, her hands raw, from her job in the VanRoonSten meatpacking house. After it ceased production, she got a job on the line at the Steel Gryphon power-tool manufacturing operation. But Steel Gryphon was sold and the work went to Mexico. After that, his parents bounced downward to jobs that paid less and less.

One night, when he'd been hitting the sauce pretty good, the old man opened up to Ivan and Clay.

"Your mother will kill me for telling you this, but you're old enough to hear the goddamn truth," he said between pulls on his beer. "I won't tell you the things I seen in the war. You can't understand unless you were there. But the only time I felt alive was when I was in the shit. I swear to God. And nowadays, I wake up feeling dead, you know?" He pointed his fingers, holding his burning Lucky Strike, at his sons. "Take my advice, boys, enlist. We're all gonna die. Just depends how—day by day, earning eight-fifty an hour, or serving your country on a field of goddamn glory."

Things never got better for his family.

As his parents' savings melted, their desperation rose. They struggled not to show that they were losing their dignity a piece at a time.

Ivan remembered his mother gathering up her jewelry— her engagement ring, a necklace, earrings the old man got her one anniversary, her mother's wedding ring. She put them in a plastic lunch bag. "It's just things I don't need anymore," she told him, but the look on her face said otherwise when she took them to the jeweler. She came home looking older, but with seven hundred dollars that she used to pay for groceries and a heating bill.

After that she found part-time work cleaning the restrooms at the Eastwood Mall.

Ivan and Clay worked, too; pumping gas after school, shoveling snow, landscaping, giving what they could to the household. But it was never enough because their parents were unemployed for long stretches.

Then came the day his mother never returned home from work. The bus driver found her at the end of his route, thought she'd fallen asleep.

Brain aneurysm, the doctor said.

That was the day God abandoned Ivan and Clay Felk.

After they buried her, the old man turned to stone.

He hung on for about a year, sitting alone in the dark, nothing but the swish of the bottle keeping him company until the night of the firecracker explosion. They found him in his living room chair, with the framed wedding picture in his lap under his brains. He'd put his pistol in his mouth and joined her.

Ivan was twenty. Clay was nineteen.

This was the story of Felk's working-class family in the broken heart of the Rust Belt. His estranged uncle drove his battered Dodge from Akron to help get a lawyer to take care of selling the house and everything.

"I shoulda tried to visit more. I'm sorry, boys. You can come stay with me and Aunt Evie for a bit to get things figured out. Got a room over the garage."

The man was a stranger to them. They weren't listening.

One week after he left, Ivan signed up with the U.S. Army.

He tried to persuade Clay to enlist with him.

"No, I'm going to California," Clay said.

"To do what?"

"Make surfboards. Live by the ocean. Put Ohio behind me."

"You don't know jack about surfboards. Enlist. Let's give that to Mom and Dad as our way to honor them. We'll keep on fighting. For them."

Clay caved to his older brother and signed up for the U.S. Marines, ultimately becoming a Scout Sniper. Clay saw action in Iraq and Afghanistan. He was good at his job.

Ivan did well in the army and, like his brother, was a superb soldier. It wasn't long before he was recruited by the CIA for its Special Ops Group.

The covert missions with SOG gave him access to classified procedures, technology, off-the-manual operations, intelligence experts, mercenaries, ghost teams, networks and murky entities thriving throughout the region.

That's where he befriended Rytter, from Germany, and Northcutt, from England. The three elite soldiers gave consideration to the lucrative life of private contractors. In the post–September 11 world, it was a growth industry.

When their time was right, they quit their government jobs and established Red Cobra Team 9, a private professional security company. Felk persuaded Clay to join. The team enlisted trusted friends. Red Cobra Team 9 had lucrative subcontracted orders via larger companies contracted to complete secret missions for the CIA and other intelligence groups. They did the dirtiest of jobs. They were "plausible deniability."

Scapegoats.

During a clear night on a covert rescue operation in the mountains of the disputed region between Afghanistan and Pakistan, Ivan and Clay watched the constellations wheel by from their camp.

"We're a long way from Youngstown, bro," Clay said.

"Better than bagging groceries or pumping gas," Ivan said.

"Dad would be proud. These are fields of glory."

The brothers spent the rest of that night reminiscing. It was a good night for them, the last time they had a chance to really talk. Several months later, they went out on the team's last mission.

The horror of it blurred across Felk's memory with a shrieking grind of steel on steel and his body jolted.

The CN Tower and Toronto's skyline rose before him as the train eased into Union Station, where Felk got into a cab.

"Take me to the airport, please."

"Which one? Island or Pearson?"

"Toronto International Airport."

"That's Pearson," the driver said.

27

Toronto, Ontario, Canada

Lester B. Pearson International Airport, named after Canada's fourteenth prime minister, was one of the busiest hubs in the world.

Felk's cab ride from Union Station downtown to northwest Toronto took some forty-five minutes. As the airport came into view, he consulted the ticket he'd purchased online.

"Terminal One," he told the driver when they neared the exit ramps for departures.

The driver nodded. "Where you headed?"

"New York," he lied.

Inside the terminal, Felk went to the self-service kiosk to check in. He submitted his counterfeit passport, followed the prompts on the touch screen. He was not checking in any bags. He had one carry-on. The night before, he'd gone online and submitted his advance passenger information to expedite the process. Now it took little more than a minute for the kiosk to dispense an electronic boarding pass for his flight to San Francisco.

He moved on to the U.S. Customs and Border Protection Preclearance section of the airport. He showed his boarding pass to the attendant, who directed him to fill out a blue U.S. Customs card.

Felk completed the form, then moved through the area, joining other travelers in the line that snaked before a row of busy inspection booths, where he'd be processed for entry into the United States.

He surveyed the people near him: a wrinkled slack-jawed man clutching a U.S. passport who kept asking the elderly woman with him to repeat her mundane comments. "I said, it's eighty degrees in Miami!" There was a young woman behind them wearing a Johnny Depp T-shirt, nodding her head, earphones leaking music as the thumb of one hand worked the phone she was holding. Her other hand gripped the handle of a pink suitcase that had a tiny stuffed bear chained to one of its zippers.

As he neared the row of booths, Felk heard the mechanical *clunk-chunk* of officers using the admittance stamps on passports. Then he heard something that pulled everyone's attention to booth number nine.

"Did I wave you forward, sir!" a female CBP officer barked.

A short, heavyset man stopped dead in his tracks.

"Get back behind the red line!"

His face crimson, the man stepped back.

Disbelief at her rudeness rippled through the line. Felk was fourth from the front and did not want to draw number nine. Her hair was pulled back into a tight bun, accentuating her stern face. She could have been in her thirties; and by the way she seized her water bottle, she could have been in battle. As she guzzled, she kept one eye on the line as if they were advancing enemies, even pink-suitcase girl with the teddy bear.

Felk took stock of the other officers nearby. Number seven was a white-haired grandpa who seem bored but calm, and number eight was a twenty-something guy, all spit and polish and worthy of the corps. Then there was number nine.

What was her freakin' problem? Felk wondered.

The CPB officer at number nine was Magda Vryke, and her problem was manifold.

Today was supposed to be Magda's day off but fat-ass Daisy called in sick, which was total bull. Then, as Magda was leaving for work, feeling pissed off and bloated, her life partner, Lynne, told her she wanted to back out of their condo purchase. *What the hell?* And when Magda arrived at Pearson, she found a dump of new alerts on her computer monitor: three new "PAs," her name for Parental Abductions; one from France, one from Austria and one from Italy. And there was an advisory for a German chemical engineer with suspected links to terrorist factions who may be en route to the United States.

All were Red Notices with Interpol, which meant the subjects were to be detained on sight and arrested by local authorities.

And—we're not done yet—some several hundred miles south in Washington, D.C, the Office of Enforcement at U.S. Customs and Border Protection headquarters had processed an urgent alert from the FBI through Homeland Security to all CBP Preclearance facilities.

It advised to "detain any subject bearing a tattoo similar to the image shown." Magda Vryke had glanced at the cobra-in-barbed-wire-bracelet picture; read the background history. She was familiar with the high-profile armored car heist murders in New York City. But the alert puzzled her and she gave her head a little shake. If anything, those guys would be fleeing the States, not entering.

Whatever, Magda thought as she screwed the cap back on her water bottle and smacked her booth light.

"Next! Come on, step up!"

Ivan Felk arrived and placed his documents on her counter.

"Where are you going today, sir?" Magda Vryke folded his Canadian passport, cracking its spine before inserting it into her passport reader.

"San Francisco."

She eyeballed him, then the passport photo on her monitor, to make sure they matched. Felk was wearing jeans and a long-sleeved turtleneck sweater that complemented his muscular build. He was clean shaven, as he was in the photo.

"Purpose of your trip?"

"Visit friends, see the sights, vacation."

Magda punched a few commands on her keyboard.

"Where were you born, Mr. Chapman?"

"Belleville, Ontario."

"Don't they have a big base out there?"

"That air base in Trenton is close by, just west."

"Drove by there once. Impressive." Magda stamped his passport. "Have a nice trip."

"Thank you."

He'd just been admitted entry into the United States. Felk collected his papers, gripped the handle of his bag. *Almost there.* He exhaled as he moved on to the next stage of the process, preboard security screening.

It was on the next level up.

The lines were jammed. People were moving slowly through the scanning stations. Felk saw security cameras everywhere. Occasionally he recognized fellow travelers from preclearance. This area was operated by the Canadian

Air Transport Security Authority. As Felk moved through the line, a CATSA officer directed him to a screening station.

He joined the hundreds of passengers in the global choreography of loading luggage on the conveyor belts, extracting laptops, removing belts, shoes, jackets, emptying pockets and depositing everything into trays. At the direction of the screening officer, Felk stepped through the scanner.

It sounded.

Damn it.

"Step forward and extend your arms, sir."

He took a quick deep breath and complied as the officer passed a wand over his body, stopping near his right wrist.

"Pull back the sleeve of your shirt, please, so I can have a look."

Felk hesitated, trying to remember, trying to calculate the risk.

"Are you refusing, sir? I need you to pull back your sleeve."

"Oh, no, sorry. No."

Felk rolled back his sleeve immediately, angry at himself for forgetting his watch.

"There you go," the officer said. "Sir, go back through, put the watch on a tray to be scanned and come back."

Felk did everything successfully and went to the end of the conveyor to collect his luggage and laptop where another officer was waiting.

"Is this your computer, sir?"

"Yes."

"Could you put it aside here, and turn it on for me?"

"Yes."

Felk had taken steps to remove everything incriminating on all the drives when he was on the train. He'd stored the videos online in email accounts. Nothing was on the laptop drives.

He'd also erased his history.

The officer used tongs and a patch of cloth to chemically swab the computer. Then he put the sample in a microwave-oven-size machine to determine if Felk had been handling explosive compounds.

Then it hit him.

The guns! Christ, the guns!

He'd forgotten about the guns and ammo Dillon had shown him at the cottage. He'd washed his hands, but was it enough not to set off any alarms?

Damn it.

Casually putting on his belt, Felk tried to read the face of the screening officer studying the swab results on the screen.

This could be it.

He swallowed hard. He could flee, but they had his photo. He couldn't believe that it could be over. Just like that. His body tensed. He thought of Clay, the other men, and begged fate for a break.

No, please, no.

"You're good, sir," the officer said.

Felk nodded with a smile, his tension melting as he collected his things and headed to his gate, just like any other passenger at any other airport at any other time. No one could have imagined what he and his men had done, or what they were going to do.

Ninety minutes later, the thrust of his Air Canada Airbus A319 pushed him back into aisle seat number 23C. As the jetliner climbed and leveled, he savored a measure of relief.

That he'd gotten through without any problem told him

that the team was clear. They'd gotten away from Ramapo cleanly. The FBI had nothing on them. Felk was on track to the next step of the operation at five hundred and fifty miles an hour. He lowered his seat and closed his eyes.

As he fell asleep he was haunted by the face of the eye-witness.

The supermarket clerk.

Don't worry about her. We were careful. She saw nothing that could hurt them.

Nothing.

28

Lisa Palmer's two-story frame house was at the edge of Rego Park.

Mature maple trees lined the sidewalks of her block, shading the small, neatly clipped front yards of the post-war homes. Most were fenced and displayed small signs alerting potential intruders to their security systems. A few front doors were fortified with ornate steel.

It was a pretty neighborhood of fourth- and fifth-generation Irish, Italian, Russian and Jewish immigrants that had evolved to include new Albanian, Korean, Colombian and Iranian Americans.

How long since I left to close the deal on the cabin at Lake George?

Four days? Five days?

It didn't matter, Lisa thought.

After everything that had happened, seeing her home again was balm.

Lisa and the kids took it all in from the back of Vicky Chan's FBI car after it had rolled off Queens Boulevard, on to Sixty-third, then down their street.

They'd left their Manhattan hotel earlier that afternoon.

"What lovely gardens." Dr. Sullivan was in the front passenger seat.

"People take care of things here. It's a good neighborhood," Lisa said.

"My GPS is wonky," Chan said, confirming the address. "It's 87-87?"

"Yes, not much farther."

"Can Mallory come over for a sleepover?" Taylor asked.

"Not for a few days, hon."

"Can I go over to Jason's?" Ethan asked.

"No, sweetheart. I'd like you to stay home until we get back to normal."

"When will that be, Mom?"

"As soon as I can make it happen."

Rita Camino and Agent Eve Watson were already waiting at Lisa's house and came out to help with the bags.

"Go check out the kitchen," Rita said after hugging the kids.

Ethan and Taylor rushed off, then shouted back, "Cake!"

The words Welcome Home! were inscribed in blue on the white icing.

"Chocolate, your favorite," Rita said. "I got Burt in the bakery to make it. I told him it was for my aunt Louise's release from the hospital."

"Thank you." Lisa hugged Rita. "You're the best."

"Just want to help out by sweetening things." Rita smiled.

After chatting over cake and coffee, Lisa gave Dr. Sullivan and Agent Chan a tour of her home, starting upstairs with the three small neat bedrooms—hers, Taylor's and Ethan's—and a full bathroom. Then down to the finished basement. It had a guest room and smaller bathroom, which they'd once planned on turning into an apartment for additional income.

Chan left her bag on the bed. The plan was for her to bunk in the guest room, to stay with Lisa and the children for as long as Lisa wanted. In a private moment, Lisa tapped Chan's sidearm under her T-shirt.

"Vicky, please keep that concealed as much as possible, for the children and me. I've seen enough of guns."

"I was thinking the very same thing." Chan touched Lisa's shoulder before she and Watson went outside to check Lisa's doors, windows and her security system.

Dr. Sullivan went upstairs to talk with Ethan and Taylor, who were showing off their rooms. Rita, the eternal saint, insisted on cleaning up in the kitchen while Lisa grabbed her bag and went to her office alcove off the living room to make some calls.

First, she checked her messages.

There was an automated announcement from the school on an upcoming parent–teacher night; a dental-appointment confirmation for Taylor; a message from Lisa's friend Sophia: "Where are you? I've texted you a gazillion times. Did you sell the cabin? Are you coming to live in California? Call me, text me, anything."

Then there was a message from the bank. "Donna Madsen, Mrs. Palmer. When it's convenient, could you come in? We need you to sign…" That call was followed by a prerecorded telemarketing message—"Congratulations, you're the lucky winner"—then another message from Sophia. "Getting ready to fly to London and still haven't heard from you. I'm getting a little worried, so can you get back to me, please?"

Lisa wanted to text Sophia, but as she reached for her bag she realized that her cell phone had been taken in the crime. It triggered a sudden memory of the killer's gun against the agent's head then hers.

Focus on the here and now.

She would email Sophia later and let her know she'd "lost her phone," but that everything was fine.

Right, fine in that I am alive.

Stop it. Concentrate on being a mom, on getting a grip.

Good advice, she thought, shuffling through her mail, most of it bills. She needed to get back to work. She'd planned to give it one more day before getting back into things but seeing the bills, she reconsidered the need to wait. Lisa called the school, informing the office that Ethan and Taylor would return to class tomorrow. Then she called the supermarket. She'd return to work tomorrow. Nick, her boss, was pleased.

Then she went through her bag and searched in vain for her work ID.

Where did I put it?

It was foggy as she went back over everything from her last shift. She had gone home from work and got ready for her overnight trip to the lake. She recalled holding her ID in her hand at some point. She always put it in her bag.

But it wasn't there.

Maybe she left it on her dresser, or night table?

Entering her bedroom upstairs, she heard Dr. Sullivan's muffled voice from down the hall. She was gently explaining to Ethan and Taylor how even though the bad guys "are likely very far away," it was important to keep "all this stuff with the police secret so the bad guys didn't know, so the police could catch them."

This is the toll exacted on my family.

Lisa was hit with a sudden wave of sadness. She didn't know if it was the room, a flash of Bobby, or something else. But having to swear her children to FBI secrecy because she'd witnessed a bloodbath, two years after their father had died, was a lot to ask.

This whole freakin' mess was a lot to ask.

Lisa's eyes stung.

She went to her dresser and traced her fingers tenderly over an elegant marble box, the cremation urn that held some of Bobby's ashes. She roiled with emotion. It triggered the raw sensation of loss. Something had been stolen from her—the fragile peace of mind that she and the children had painfully rebuilt?

Hang on. Just hang on.

As a jetliner from La Guardia screamed its ascension across the distant sky, Lisa touched the corners of her eyes.

No, I refuse to let those monsters win. These bastards had no right to do what they did. I am taking back control of my life. I'll spend every second of it praying for the FBI to catch those fuckers.

Looking at the urn, her heart aching, she assured herself that she would go back to the cabin, make their final tribute and start living the rest of their lives.

She'd do it for the kids, for Bobby.

And for me.

"Lisa?"

She turned to Dr. Sullivan.

"How are you doing?"

Lisa touched a tissue to her eyes. "You won't believe me, but I feel stronger."

"I believe you."

"Just by being here, I feel like I am getting some control again"

"Lisa, of course you have to resume your life. Just know that it's okay to accept any feelings, bad dreams, fears, anxieties. It's all part of the trauma. Take your time, deal with them and move on. It's part of the healing. To some extent you've already done that with Bobby and you're still doing it."

"It's so hard."

"Having us all around may give you a false sense of external security, might delay your healing. However, while you may be a little emotionally vulnerable, I sense that you're very strong, incredibly strong, actually."

A few moments of silence passed before Dr. Sullivan said, "I think Eve and I should go soon. You need to get back to your sense of normal. You have my number, so you or the kids can call me at any time for any reason."

Dr. Sullivan hugged Lisa.

"Thank you."

Downstairs, Eve Watson told Lisa her house was secure then passed her a business card with numbers penned on the back.

"The NYPD will have unmarked units swing by regularly, 24/7. Here are the precinct duty-desk numbers."

Lisa nodded. Then, as Chan joined them, she lowered her voice.

"I plan to send the kids to school and get back to work tomorrow. I'm thinking after tonight, we should be okay on our own. What do you think?"

"Whatever you are comfortable with, Lisa," Chan said. "We can stay with you as long as you like, but there's been no evidence of a threat. Remember, our Behavioral Analysis Unit doubted that the suspects would have cause to attempt to pursue any witnesses. They don't know who you are or where you live. They're probably long gone from the Greater New York City Area."

"Did anything come out of the tattoo yet?" Lisa asked.

Chan and Watson exchanged glances.

"We can't say," Watson said.

"Are you serious? After all I've gone through to help?"

"I'm sorry. It's for operational reasons," Watson said.

"Morrow's orders," Chan said.

Stung, Lisa realized she could learn more on the case

from the press. The insult of shutting her out only fortified her decision about sending the kids to school and going back to work.

Watson was looking at her BlackBerry. "I just got this via the Hartford office. Agent Dutton's funeral will be in two days in Bridgeport."

"I want to attend," Lisa said. "Will I be permitted?"

Chan and Watson threw her question to Dr. Sullivan.

"I'm the last person he saw," Lisa said. "I need to be there."

"I'll give Morrow the heads-up," Chan said. "We can take you."

After Watson and Dr. Sullivan left, Rita said her good-byes, too. Later, Ethan and Taylor played a computer game in the living room. Chan went to the guest room and worked quietly on her laptop while making calls on her cell phone. Lisa went to her own home computer, sent an email to Sophia, then started laundry.

In her small utility room, Lisa held fast to the thera-peutic virtue of an ordinary task while she grappled with the aftermath of the last few days, and years, of her life.

As she loaded the washer, she reflected on Bobby's death and widowhood, which was something that only happened to old ladies.

Or so she'd always thought.

I'm only thirty-one.

Nothing made sense to her. The life she'd known with Bobby was behind her. Selling the cabin was a turning point, a rose on the casket of a dream. She was preparing to move on when this—this horror happened.

I was a heartbeat away from death.

But she survived.

And she would endure. She had no choice. She'd pull herself out of this pit.

I'm strong.

With the machine loaded, she leaned against it and hugged herself.

Taking comfort in the washer's calming drone she slid her hands up and down her arms, thinking that it had been so long since she and Bobby had been—well—two years.

Two years.

Amid her emotional inferno, she acknowledged an aching, buried deep in her anguished loneliness, and she found herself thinking of a man she'd met hours earlier.

That reporter who'd approached her in Ramapo at the service center.

Jack Gannon.

Lisa had read his stories. He seemed to know as much about this case as the FBI; enough to piss off Morrow, so he must be good.

Gannon had been a bit pushy, but he didn't come across as a jerk, which was her impression of press people, at least from movies and TV shows. Sure, that's dumb, but this Gannon guy was different.

In the moment they'd met she'd sensed something she liked about him. He had a good face, a kind face, and the way he stood up to Morrow—*"Is that right, miss? Does Agent Morrow speak for you?"*—he'd exuded an air of confidence and trustworthiness.

She remembered how he'd kept his eyes on her as they drove away.

She knew because she'd kept her eyes on him.

29

Jack Gannon hit the buzzer a third time at the outside entrance to Jerry Falco's apartment above Save-All Electronics.

No response.

Frustrated, he turned, thinking that maybe Falco was at the Big Smile Deli Mart across the street. Then he heard movement inside the entrance landing. A man bent by age, wearing a fedora, sweater and baggy pants, pushed through the door.

Gannon held it open for him.

"Excuse me, sir. I'm looking for Jerry Falco."

The man stopped.

"Who?"

Gannon spotted the hearing aid under wisps of silver-white hair.

"Falco. Jerry Falco. I'm supposed to meet him here at noon."

"Falco? That kook?" The man started down the street. "Upstairs."

Kook?

Great. This is what I'm dealing with. A pervy kook who

can't answer his own door, Gannon thought, taking the creaking stairs and nearly choking on the smell of cats. Gospel music leaked from somewhere into the gloomy hall as he banged on Falco's door.

Gannon couldn't meet with him last night because he got tied up in the newsroom. Falco had agreed to meet today at twelve noon sharp, to discuss reviewing his "video surveillance of the street for the time and date in question."

What are the chances this weirdo can help me?

As a reporter, Gannon had met enough oddballs to know that you could never assume who was a waste of time, and who was going to come through for you unless you invested some shoe leather.

Trouble was, he didn't know how much longer he could continue searching for his tipster. If he didn't find something soon, he'd have to give it up. Lisker was breathing down his neck for another exclusive. He wanted him to help Chad Feldman, the business reporter, investigate American Centurion. Feldman had heard that the FBI–NYPD Joint Task Force was going harder on the armored-car company than anyone had imagined.

We get the sense something could break there, Lisker said ten minutes ago in an email to Gannon. Call me.

Gannon considered telling Lisker about his tip.

But what would I tell him?

He didn't trust Lisker to understand the gut feeling he had about it and would bet a month's salary that Lisker would force him to report on it prematurely, which would only guarantee his source would never surface again. It could also point the way for the competition, who could take the story away from you. No, he could not tell anyone at the WPA, not until he found his source and confirmed his veracity.

Gannon would call Lisker later.

But he was running out of time.

He hammered on Falco's door again.

"Jerry, it's Jack Gannon from the WPA!"

Locks clicked and the door across the hall cracked as far as the security chain allowed. A woman with white hair curled tight and pinned down everywhere glared at him. She cradled a cat in her arms while another one threaded between her ankles.

"Who the hell are you?"

"I'm a friend of Jerry's."

"He's not home, get out."

"Do you know where I could find him?"

"It's Wednesday—if you're his friend you'd know."

"I'm his new friend…I just met him yesterday. Is that a calico?"

"On Wednesday mornings Falco meets his parole officer, then he goes to the Dented Tin Can."

"The what?" Gannon was lost. "His parole officer?"

"Didn't he tell you he's done time in the big house?"

"For what?"

"Some friend you are."

"We just met. What's the Dented Tin Can?"

"It's the hellhole bar two blocks north."

"But it's noon."

"That's where he is."

The Dented Tin Can was in a crumbling brick building. It had neon signs behind its barred windows and it sat between two trash-filled alleys. Inside, the light was dim. Gannon waited for his eyes to adjust as a ballad yearned from the jukebox for a lost love.

He thought of Katrina before he was distracted.

Worse than Falco's building, this place reeked of stale

beer, cigarettes and melancholy. The bar was scarred, the bar stools patched with duct tape. Affixed to one of them was a middle-aged woman who looked as if she'd put on her makeup during an earthquake. She pointed her cigarette and two inches of ash at the bartender, telling him that childhood trauma caused her problems. "Freakin' stepfather. Did I tell you what he did?"

Jerry Falco was alone in a booth hunched over a copy of the *New York Post* and four—Gannon counted—four empty beer bottles. *It's barely afternoon. Was he wearing the same clothes he wore yesterday?*

"Mr. Falco? Jack Gannon, WPA. We have a meeting?"

Falco lifted his head from his paper.

"Who are you?"

"Jack Gannon, the reporter. We met yesterday." Gannon slid into the booth. "You were going to help me review some security video?"

Falco took a pull from his beer, stuck out his bottom lip, shook his head.

"I don't know you."

Gannon recoiled. What was this? He couldn't be *that* drunk.

"I gave you twenty bucks. We made a deal. You were going to help me. You called me last night, you said to meet you at noon."

"Fuck off and leave me alone, asshole!"

Was this guy on meds? Gannon was at a loss, when he felt a big hand on his shoulder.

"Let's you and me talk, pal." The bartender nodded to the bar, taking Gannon out of earshot. Gannon gave him a brief summary, then the bartender said, "You don't really know Jerry, then?"

"No, what's his story?"

"A long time ago he was a network-TV news editor. He

drove home drunk after a party and killed a little girl. He
did time, got beat up in the joint. He's not all there, see.
He's been in and out of jail ever since. He gets by on a
small inheritance."

"He was supposed to help me with his video work. I
need to see it."

"Buy him a meal."

"What?"

"After he sees his parole officer, he comes here and
cries in his beer. Food usually brings him back, closer to
normal."

About an hour later, Falco's recollection returned after
he ate the clubhouse sandwich Gannon bought him. "Let's
go," Falco said, still enveloped by despair when, without an
apology or explanation, he led Gannon to his apartment.

It was cleaner than Gannon had expected. He was acquainted with the photographs of captured video stills on
the walls of the woman at the flower shop across the street.
Gannon now noticed inspirational passages of Scripture
scrawled on paper taped near the photos, passages about
forgiveness, redemption.

Very weird.

Before the windows there were three tripods with cameras aimed at the street. Falco sat at a desk that looked
like a TV-editing suite, with small monitors, consoles and
electrical equipment.

"I keep a vigil on the neighborhood and send police
anything suspicious I see." *Like the woman at the flower
shop,* Gannon thought. "You were interested in a call made
from the pay phone?" Falco asked.

"Yes." Gannon gave him the time and date.

Falco entered commands on a keyboard and a sharp
color-video image with a date graphic appeared on a moni-

tor. It showed the street, the pay phone. Then the activity began moving backward at high speed.

"This will take a moment," Falco said. "I got this equipment from a friend at Channel 88. It's older." Falco turned to Gannon. Seeing him fixated on the photos of the woman, Falco said, "It's not what you think."

"Sorry?"

"I'm not a peeper or a voyeur or anything."

"No, it's okay."

"About fifteen years ago, a little girl died because of me."

"I'm sorry about that."

"It was my fault and I'll carry that mistake to my grave. Had she lived, she'd be the same age as Florence, the woman across the street in the pictures. It gives me comfort to see how she would be doing in her life, had she lived."

Gannon just nodded.

"Here we go." Falco stopped the rewind on the time and date of the last call Gannon had received on that phone from his tipster.

"Jesus."

The monitor showed a clear image of a man using the pay phone. Falco's keyboard clicked and the image got larger. The man was white, medium build, brush cut, olive-green T-shirt, jeans.

"That's your guy, right?"

It had to be him. Gannon double-checked the date and time.

Incredible.

"Yes. Can you make a color print from this still now, then send me a clear electronic version? You have my email address on my card?"

"Sure, for three hundred dollars."

"No, I wasn't going that high."

Falco raised his index finger over the delete key and held it there.

"Okay, okay, three hundred."

Gannon hurried down the street to the ATM machine, his heart racing as his tipster's words echoed.

This is big! I swear to God what I'm telling you is true!

30

American Centurion's depot was on Rockaway Boulevard among the acres of storage operations, customs brokers and freight-forwarding agencies clustered around Kennedy.

It was situated in a warehouse equipped with cameras, loading bays secured with razor wire, motion sensors and a round-the-clock K-9 security team.

At 6:30 a.m., Agent Morrow and Detective Al Dimarco met with other investigators there to continue their work.

Moe Malloy, company founder and CEO, was on the loading floor flipping through pages of his clipboard amid the grind of diesel engines. Malloy was resuming operations today. But detectives and agents were stopping the trucks before they moved out, requesting guards expose their wrists for inspection, then showing a photo or something to the crews.

"What's going on?" Malloy asked Morrow and Dimarco in the gruff, cement-mixer voice he was known for.

Morrow opened a folder and showed Malloy the cobra tattoo.

"Does this look familiar to you?"

Stress lines cut deep into Malloy's craggy face, the manifestation of the strain of three murdered employees, a six-million-dollar loss, a maelstrom of insurance claims and the stench of police suspicion that someone inside his company was responsible. He hadn't slept since the attack.

"No. It's not familiar to me. Should it be?"

"It could be a factor," Dimarco said. "Have another look. It's a tattoo."

"Everybody and their mother has a tattoo." Malloy re-examined it and shook his head. It was not familiar to him or to his crews on duty that morning.

The three men went to Malloy's second-floor office. He shut the door, offered Morrow and Dimarco fresh coffee while they glimpsed 747s lifting off, near enough to rattle windows.

The rattling propelled Morrow back to Beth, shaking in his arms after he'd told her about his condition. How she held on to him through the night; how Hailey sobbed when they broke the news to her the next day.

"We just have to carry on," he told them, thinking of the September 11 jumpers who'd had no time to say goodbye.

Malloy's question brought Morrow's attention back to the case.

"Are you any closer to nailing the fuckers who hit us?"

"That tattoo's a good start," Morrow said.

"What about upstate? Did you find the getaway bikes?"

"Not yet, it's only a matter of time."

"You guys keep saying that, but I don't know if you're ever going to find these cocksuckers."

"We're working on it," Morrow said.

"You're working on it?" Malloy scratched under his chin, his jaw muscles pulsating. "You're working on it. You want a dose of honesty?"

"Sure," Dimarco said.

"It makes me want to puke when I see that shit in the press that you think this is an inside job."

"These guys knew exactly what they were doing, Moe," Dimarco said.

"We think they had help," Morrow said.

"Bullshit. Not in my yard. I built this company from nothing. I was a tow-truck driver from Uniondale when I towed a beat-up armored truck. The bankrupt company couldn't pay. I kept the truck and started my own business with it. That was twenty-two freakin' years ago. Now I got a fleet of twenty-five rigs, one hundred people on the payroll. Not one loss. Not one problem. American Centurion is financially sound. We're audited every six months. We're inspected. We're fully insured. We're solid. Our operational policy is one of the best. Our contracts are competitive, our staff screening and training is intense. I *am* the company. This is my life's work. We're cooperating with you, volunteering all our records, phone, computer, every damn thing you ask for. For you to imply that this was an inside job is insulting to me and to Gary, Ross and Phil, the outstanding men I lost."

"I appreciate how difficult this is," Morrow said, "but the subjects knew where to go, when to go, and that the truck was heavy. Do you think that was a lucky guess, Moe?"

Malloy turned to his window, ran a hand across his face and watched another jet lift off. Morrow and Dimarco allowed him a moment.

"Some of the guys are pissed off at me. They say I'm starting up too soon, that it's disrespectful to Phil and his crew. I know it is. But goddamnit, we got contracts and deadlines. I got three funerals coming up. We'll have to shut down again for each of them. Everybody here is torn up. This is killing us," Malloy said. "So what do you need today, just showing that tattoo picture around?"

Dimarco opened his folder, handed Malloy a sheet of paper.

"We need to reinterview these people."

"But you already polygraphed them, like you did with everybody."

"Yes, and we'd like to talk to these people again."

Malloy let out a long, slow breath.

"Lester's here. I'll call Donna."

Lester Ridley's huge tattooed biceps flexed when he folded his arms. He eyed Morrow and Dimarco, sitting across a small table from him in an otherwise-empty office.

Morrow scanned his file again. Lester was thirty-two, had five years with the company as a driver. Before that he had seven years with the army. Lester had two little boys. His wife, Roxanne, ran a day care out of their home to help with the bills.

"You grew up in Levittown. Your mother raised you alone after your father walked out," Morrow said.

"So what?"

"When you were seventeen you got into a jam. You and two older guys knocked off a liquor store. You pleaded out and gave up your friends. The D.A. ensured you had no record. This was a little something your prescreen missed. Nobody here knows but us," Morrow said.

Lester pressed his thumb and forefinger over his mustache and blinked.

"You and Roxanne are sinking in debt. You missed a mortgage payment and the bank's leaning on you, isn't that right, Lester?" Dimarco said.

"That's none of your business," Lester said.

"The results of your polygraph were inconclusive. We need you to tell us all you know about the hit," Morrow said.

"I told you everything."

Morrow glanced at his watch.

"This is what's going to happen," Morrow said. "Very soon Roxanne will likely call you. She'll be upset because FBI agents will be in your home, in every room, executing search warrants. They'll seize your computer, go through your house. We will obtain your phone records, credit card and bank records. We'll know who you called, who called you, who you emailed. Tell me, what are we going to find, Lester?"

Lester's chest rose and fell as his breathing quickened.

"Nothing."

"Hold up your hands, show us your wrists."

Dimarco checked them for tattoos. Nothing of note. Then he slid the sheet bearing the cobra tattoo toward Lester.

"You're familiar with tattoos, who do you know that has one like this?"

Lester glanced at it.

"I never saw one like that. I already told your guys out there."

"Lester, this doesn't look good for you," Dimarco said. "Make it easy for yourself, for Roxanne and the boys. Protect yourself, like you did when you were seventeen. You probably didn't mean for anybody to get hurt in Ramapo. Tell us what happened."

Lester shook his head, tears came to his eyes and he looked off.

"Phil, Ross, Gary, they were my friends. I got money problems, but Roxanne's brother's going to give us a loan. Help us out. Yeah, I got into some trouble when I was a kid, but the two douche bags set me up. Why are you wasting time on me when you should be looking for the scum who did this? You two are assholes, you know that?"

"Lester." Dimarco leaned into his space. "We got four murders, six million in cash gone. People tend to lie when we ask questions. When our examiner asked you if you had any financial stress, you said no. When we checked, we found that you owe close to two hundred and fifty thousand dollars. This is how you help your friends, Lester, with lies?"

"I got nothing to do with this, I swear."

"Let's see what we find out with the warrants later," Dimarco said.

Lester's cell phone rang.

"Roxanne, I know, I know...take it easy..."

Less than fifteen minutes later, Donna Breen arrived with her husband.

Morrow and Dimarco asked him to wait outside as they interviewed her. Donna was nearly eight months pregnant. She apologized as she positioned herself into a cushioned chair that Morrow rolled in from the office nearby.

"I'm sorry. I can't stop crying."

Donna was Moe Malloy's young cousin, a churchgoing newlywed. She had worked at American Centurion for three years as an office assistant who handled personnel files. She did not undergo a polygraph because of her condition, and her preliminary interview the day before was curtailed because of nausea.

Morrow consulted the interviewing agent's note: "Subject is cooperative, credible and may possess useful information on other employees. Reinterview recommended."

Dimarco showed her the cobra image.

"No, I've never seen that one before, but there are a

lot of guys here with tattoos, you should have them show you."

"We're checking," Morrow said. "Donna, you indicated you had insights on ex-employees. Tell us what you can, starting with Felix Johnson."

"Felix? Oh, he was a piece of work, sexist and offensive. The guards are screened and trained, but that doesn't mean they have what it takes."

"Right, did Felix have a grudge?"

"I doubt it. He was just lazy. He missed a lot of work and when he showed up he didn't want to work. Moe let him go."

"And Bonita Irwin?"

"Bonita was sloppy. She got written up for not keeping her log up-to-date, forgetting her weapon, forgetting to lock the truck after her route. Moe had to let her go. But I wouldn't say Felix or Bonita had a grudge."

Dimarco and Morrow asked a few more questions before wrapping up. As Donna rose from the chair to leave, a thought occurred to her.

"You should show the tattoo to Gina when she gets back."

"Gina?" Morrow asked.

"Gina Saldino."

Dimarco flipped through his notes and found a question mark by her name. No one had interviewed Gina Saldino, an office worker.

"She's on vacation," Donna said. "She left about a week ago."

"What can you tell us about her?"

"Very quiet, shy. I think she broke up with her boyfriend. He could've been in Pakistan or someplace like that. She only mentioned it once when I saw her crying at her desk. She never talked about it again. She was sad and private, almost mousy, but good at her job. She never made any mistakes."

"What was her job?"

"She helped Moe and Butch Tucker finalize the routes, the schedules, the size of deliveries. I mean, Moe and Butch controlled the info, Gina put it on a spreadsheet and gave it to the crews, and input the data later."

Morrow threw a silent question to Dimarco.

How did we miss this?

31

Thirty miles north of JFK, Gannon stared at Falco's "surveillance" photo of the man using the pay phone.

This is my caller.

Gannon's pulse quickened as once more he checked the time and date of the picture with the time and date of the last call from his tipster.

Oh, yeah, it's him. No doubt about it.

But Gannon's elation began evaporating soon after he'd thrust the three hundred bucks into Jerry Falco's hand and asked him if he'd recognized the man in the photo.

"I've never seen that guy before, nope."

Gannon left Falco's building and went across the street to the Big Smile Deli Mart where he showed the eight-by-eleven color shot to the manager and his family. Still wary of Gannon, they gave it a cursory glance.

"No, we don't know him," the old man said.

"He never comes here, this one," the woman added.

Gannon had to believe them; he had no choice. But before leaving the store, he bought an issue of *Sports Illustrated* magazine and tucked the photo inside to protect it. He then showed the picture to people at neighboring

businesses: the florist, the check-cashing office, the electronics store, then to the bartender at the Dented Tin Can.

Nothing.

He soon realized that he was facing a needle-in-a-
haystack search and all he had was a picture of the needle.
But it did not diminish what he felt in his gut. *There's
something to this. Don't give up.* He was determined to
take his search beyond the immediate area, when his phone
rang.

It was Lisker.

"Did you arrive at American Centurion yet?"

"No."

"Where are you?"

"I'm in Yonkers."

"Yonkers? You're still poking around there? What's
going on?"

A long moment passed.

"Gannon?"

*You're going to have to play a card here. You've in-
vested a lot of time chasing this hunch. You're getting
somewhere, but there's no guarantee it will pay off. You
can't give up on it and you can't give it up to Lisker. Not
yet. Lisker's not a journalist. He doesn't understand a gut
feeling when a frightened source calls. Don't blow this.*

"I'm pursuing a difficult angle, one I think is tied to
the heist."

"What? You know I like all leads outlined to me first?"

"Well, I don't work that way. I'm a reporter, not a bu-
reaucrat. I follow my instincts, not a template. Do you
want memos, or exclusives?"

Lisker said nothing and Gannon filled the silence.

"Let me follow this my way and see where it goes."

A long stretch of tension crackled between them before

Lisker said, "You've got until four this afternoon. Then I want your ass in my office."

Gannon headed down Warburton Avenue, walking a tightrope between Lisker's wrath and a story that may not exist.

What if I'm dead wrong and wasting time?

He had to stop thinking about it, tend to his business and keep digging. It's what he did best. So he kept pushing it, block after block, visiting pizza shops, pawnshops, barbershops, a porn shop, a jeweler's, a liquor store, a pet store. He asked bus drivers stopped at red lights, a cab-driver waiting on fares, two NYPD cops who'd pulled over for coffee from a pastry shop.

As time ticked by, Gannon slipped further and further down the rope of futility. He must've walked twenty blocks by the time he entered Big Picture Used Movies and Rentals. Next to it was a tanning salon and a Greek take-out place. Leaning on the counter, waiting for the clerk to finish a phone call, Gannon was thinking of packing it in soon, getting a cab back to his car and bracing for a showdown with Lisker.

"Can I help you find something?" The clerk was tall with oily hair, a bad case of acne. He could stand to eat a sandwich or two.

"I need your help." Gannon opened the magazine to the photo, which was getting creased from so many showings. "I need to locate this man. Does he live around here?"

The clerk held the sheet three inches from his nose. Gannon anticipated the usual head shake, but this guy—Oren, according to his name tag—blinked a few times.

"Yes, I think so."

Gannon's heart skipped a beat.

"You're sure?"

"This looks like a police surveillance photo," Oren said.

"Are you a cop? Do you have identification? What does this concern?"

Oren seemed sharp enough to trust. Gannon reached for his wallet, showed him his World Press Alliance ID and dropped his voice.

"I'm a reporter with the wire service. I won't tell you where I got the picture, but I can tell you that it is extremely important that I locate this man. We were supposed to meet a few days ago, but he vanished and he never gave me his name. Naturally, I'm concerned. He may be tied to something bad. If you help me locate him confidentially, I will share all the information I can."

Oren weighed Gannon's request, excused himself, then went to a female clerk organizing DVDs in the horror-supernatural section, showing her Gannon's photo. They both shot looks at him before she came to the counter. Her name was Greta. She stood about five-three, had pierced eyebrows and a black Cleopatra-helmet of hair.

"Is this matter connected to our store in any way?" Greta asked.

"Not at all, I'm just trying to locate him."

"And what does it concern?"

"He's vanished. He was supposed to meet me, but never gave me his name or address. He had information on something very important. It's not a police matter."

"How come you don't have his address?"

"Because he indicated he was hiding. I'm a reporter and he called me for help anonymously. Now I need your help."

"How did you get this picture?" Greta asked, handing it back.

"Look, no one needs to know how I found him. I've come this far to you, and you don't know who has helped me along the way. I will keep it that way. I protect sources."

She moved to the keyboard and started typing, staring at her monitor.

"You'll keep the store's name out of any stories?" Greta asked.

"Yes. I need to find him."

While looking at her monitor, Greta tapped her fingers on the counter. Gannon noticed she had little flowers painted on her red-glossed nails. She tapped for several moments before coming to a decision.

"His name is Harlee Shaw," she said.

"Harlee Shaw, okay."

"He likes classic war and Westerns." She consulted her monitor. "He's got *The Searchers* and *The Dirty Dozen* out and both are overdue."

"I see." Gannon knew she was on the brink of sharing what he needed. "And you've got his address there?"

"Uh-huh." She blinked thoughtfully.

Greta reached for a notepad, clicked her ballpoint pen and jotted down an address, tore the sheet and gave it to Gannon.

"It's about four blocks," she said.

"Thank you." Gannon tucked the information in his pocket.

"Be careful," she said.

"Why?"

"He's very strange."

Oren nodded in wholehearted agreement.

"That's why we're helping you," Greta said. "We think he needs help."

"What do you mean?"

"Once I heard him in the store arguing with disturbing intensity."

"Who was he arguing with?"

"No one."

Gannon's heart sank as he started walking to the address.

In minutes he'd gone from the high of finding his source, to the low of finding out that he was a whack job. Taking stock of all the energy he'd invested exhausted him, but he would see this through. Like a losing team, Gannon would play out the clock, he thought as he came to Shaw's building. It was an eighteen-story apartment complex built in the 1970s with blond brick in the vintage of industrial eastern European blandness. To Gannon it bordered on Section 8 housing.

In the secure glass-walled lobby he went to the tenant directory and pressed the intercom button for number 1021, Shaw's apartment, according to the video-store information.

No response.

As expected.

He tried two more times without success. When two white-haired women arrived from the elevator to exit, Gannon inquired about Harlee Shaw.

"Never heard of him," one of them snapped.

The women eyed Gannon from head to toe and were careful to ensure the security door locked behind them before they left. Gannon didn't care. He'd come too far to give up. He returned to the directory, pressed number 402—the button for the super. Within ten seconds the intercom speaker came to life.

"Yes?" A woman's hurried voice.

"I'm Jack Gannon—"

"Are you here for a rental?" The woman cut him off.

"No. I'm concerned about a tenant." Gannon glanced up at the camera recording him.

"Which one?"

"Harlee Shaw, in 1021. I have business with him and

I'm concerned for his safety. I haven't heard from him. He doesn't answer his phone. It's been a few days. I really need to check on his welfare."

Gannon counted the seconds passing and got to five.

"Who are you?"

"Jack Gannon. I'm a reporter with the World Press Alliance." Gannon held up his photo ID to the camera.

"Step inside, please, and wait. I'll be right there."

The lock on the interior glass door buzzed and Gannon stepped into the lobby. A few minutes later, to the jangle of keys, a fast-walking woman of about fifty, wearing a T-shirt and jeans, arrived.

She looked Gannon over after they'd stepped into the elevator.

"A reporter, huh?"

"What do you know about Harlee?" Gannon asked.

"He lives alone and keeps to himself. Bet you hear that a lot." As the car rose, she picked her way along her key ring. "I'm sure you know there are a ton of laws and policies about entering an apartment without permission."

"I know."

"But I have discretion if I think it's an emergency," she said. "Mr. Shaw's late with his rent. He's never late and I ain't seen him. He hasn't answered my calls on the phone and at his door, or picked up his mail. And now you're here with a concern. I'm likely wrong, but I consider that an emergency and reason to check on his welfare. My name's Shelly."

"Jack Gannon."

"Yeah, I saw that on your ID."

The elevator doors opened on the tenth floor. Shelly led the way to unit 1021 and knocked hard on the door.

"Mr. Shaw! Mr. Shaw, are you okay?" Shelly called.

Again, she rapped loudly then pressed her ear to the

door. She turned to Gannon, shook her head, then inserted her key. As the door cracked, Gannon detected an odor. Then saw the security chain.

This is not good, he thought.

Shelly surprised Gannon when she produced a tele-scopic metal hook. She extended it, and with one expert move, used it to unfasten the chain, as though she'd done this before.

"Mr. Shaw!"

Noise from near and distant units, TVs and voices, filled the hallway, but inside everything was silent. The odor grew more intense as Shelly pushed the door open.

As they went down the apartment's hallway, Gannon glimpsed the small kitchen, saw the table cluttered with take-out-food wrappers. A mountain of filthy dishes rose from the sink. Bugs feasted on the garbage strewn on the floor. It was hard to breathe.

"Mr. Shaw!"

As they entered the edge of the small living room, Shelly seized Gannon's arm and released a guttural wail.

"Jeezus!"

Within a split second Gannon's skin tingled, his mind struggled to comprehend what he tried to process as an elaborate joke.

It had to be a joke.

Something was waiting for them on a sofa chair. He saw a pair of boots, pants above them. Feet and legs in the boots, a T-shirt, a bare arm with an empty hand curled like a claw; another arm with the hand clamped on the end of a long-barreled gun pointed to where a head would be. A broom handle was inserted into the trigger guard of the gun. The head had been divided by a powerful explosion, the way a cannonball would plow through a pumpkin, propelling glops of cranial tissue in a volcanic eruption to the wall, the ceiling, the sofa arms, the table beside it.

Gannon fought to breathe normally, to think.

Shelly recoiled to the nearest wall, biting her fingers between spurts of, "Oh, Jesus! Oh, Christ!"

Gannon turned to her.

"Listen to me, Shelly. Do not touch anything. Go now to the nearest phone, not the phone here, and alert police. It looks like a suicide."

She started nodding.

"Do it now, Shelly! I'll wait here."

Gannon did not want the 911 call on his cell phone. He wanted the super to make the call. The instant she left, Gannon battled the roaring blood rushing in his ears. His heart was racing as he worked to gain control.

He only had a short time.

The apartment would be sealed once the NYPD arrived.

He reached into his pocket for his digital camera and began taking pictures of everything, including the blood-spattered note on the table. It looked as if it was written in ballpoint.

I never meant for this to happen.
I am so sorry, Harlee.

Gannon took pictures of the note.

Then he flipped the camera to video mode. This was his only chance to look for answers about Harlee Shaw, his anonymous caller. Without touching a thing, Gannon recorded all that he could.

When he heard the sirens, he left the apartment and stepped into the hall. Shelly was sitting on the floor, back against the wall, knees pulled to her chest, hugging herself and cursing softly between pulls on her cigarette.

32

Lisa opened her closet.

Hanger hooks scraped on the rod as she rifled deep into her never-wear stuff and pulled out the dress, still protected in a Spring Breeze Cleaners plastic bag.

A chill shot through her.

She'd only worn it once.

I can't do this. Yes, you can. You need to do this.

Lisa looked at the dress, swallowed and began rolling off the plastic.

Rita got it for her at Kim's Dresses in Forest Hills because Lisa couldn't function at that time. It was a simple cotton wrap, knee length, three-quarter sleeves with a modest neckline.

Black.

Lisa put it on and stood before her full-length mirror, which Bobby had fastened to the inside of the closet door for her. The mirror used to stand in the corner.

How many times did I bug him to screw it to the closet door? Then one day—surprise. Done. He was like that, turning little things into gifts.

The dress fit. In fact, it was a bit loose. She'd lost a few pounds, but it worked. She slid her feet into low-heeled black shoes. Her hands shook a little, giving her trouble with the clasp when she put on her pearl necklace, a birthday present from Bobby.

She got it, adjusted it. When she looked into the mirror the full impact hit her and her knees weakened. She gripped the closet door to steady herself. Of course, this is what she'd worn to Bobby's funeral.

The official uniform of the grieving widow.

She let the tears come.

Will it ever stop hurting? Help me through this, Bobby, because I have to do what I have to do.

Ethan surfaced in the mirror, watching from her bedroom door.

"What's going on, Mom?"

She continued facing the mirror, blinking back her tears. "I'm getting my things ready."

"For what?"

"Vicky and Eve will pick me up in the morning to go to the funeral for one of the people who got hurt."

"Do you have to go?"

"Yes, to show my respect. It's just for the day. Rita will be here. Sweetie, we talked about this yesterday. Are you okay? How's school going?"

"Good."

"Don't you have some homework to do while I'm gone?"

"Just geography, we have to draw a map."

"Better get started today. Now, you haven't told anybody about us helping the police and stuff."

"No."

"Good."

"Mom, we're still going up to the cabin like you promised, right? We have to."

"Yes, Ethan. Nothing's changed, okay?"

"Okay."

"So what's bothering you, then?"

"I don't want to move to California, Mom. It'd be like leaving Dad forever."

The hurt in his voice was too much for her and she went to him, dropped to her knees and took him into her arms.

"We can never ever do that." She put his hand over his heart, covering it with hers. "He will always, always be with us, wherever we go. Your father is part of us, part of you, Taylor and me. Wherever we are, he is with us and will always, always be with us. Do you understand that, honey?"

"I think so."

"Good." She smiled, brushing at her tears, kissing him softly, seeing so much of Bobby in his face. "That's good."

The next morning, Agents Vicky Chan and Eve Watson arrived just before seven. It was surreal for Lisa, saying goodbye to Taylor, Ethan and Rita just as she did a week ago.

Because this time she did it as a federal witness to four murders and this time she did it in mourning clothes.

She took a deep breath.

Chan and Watson wore blue conservative blazers and skirts.

Aside from threads of small talk, the car was quiet as Chan pulled on to I-95. The drone of the freeway traffic fit with the funereal mood and residual tension. After all that she'd given the FBI, Lisa was feeling shut out from the case. She had wanted to ask the agents if the FBI was any closer to making an arrest, but killed the thought. Earlier, they'd made it crystal clear to her that if something had happened they would not tell her. They'd got what they needed from her—at least that's how she interpreted it.

Any new information Lisa got came from the press, particularly Jack Gannon—that good-looking wire-service reporter. Her face reddened. She shouldn't be thinking about him like that. Anyway, this Gannon guy knew things, she thought as they rolled through suburb after suburb.

Lisa was happy they had finished with the hotel, glad to be home with the kids without the FBI living with them, smothering them. She had declined Dr. Sullivan's offer to accompany her to the funeral. "Events like this can be traumatic. They can rip open wounds, resurrect pain," Dr. Sullivan cautioned.

Like I didn't know.

Lisa was determined to face this on her own terms.

She had resumed piecing her life together. She'd already put in a few shifts at the supermarket. Funny, when they made her a new photo ID to replace her old one, it felt as if she had started over. Here was the new Lisa, her first official "after-Bobby" photo.

None of the girls at the supermarket pressed her too hard for missing a few days. Most of them knew she'd gone upstate to sell the cabin. And when she added the cryptic "unexpected family issues," nobody inquired. Some may have speculated that it probably had something to do with the kids or the cabin. For the most part, everyone tended to leave Lisa alone, and her boss was happy to have her back. The FBI agent's funeral fell on her day off, so it worked out. With the exception of Rita, no one knew she was the FBI's key witness to the armored car heist.

Being back at her checkout was both therapeutic and depressing. Lisa had glanced at the older cashiers, the near-retirement lifers, then at the new girls, and for the first time she saw the timeline of her life at the Good

Buy Supermart. This was all there would be for her. She thought of what she'd endured; realized how life was so fragile, so short. Then she thought of her old dream and her chance to start a new chapter of her life in California.

It's scary, but we're going to do it. It'll be best for all of us. Life's too short to live it with regrets.

About an hour after they'd left Queens, they approached Bridgeport, Connecticut. Chan guided them to Saint Patrick's Church using the GPS unit on the car's dash. Traffic was backed up already, uniforms from Bridgeport P.D. were directing.

"It's not just the director who's coming from HQ," Watson said as they inched along North Avenue, "it's the U.S. Attorney General and a ton of dignitaries. I heard they were expecting two thousand people from law enforcement."

"Full ceremonial honors," Chan said, nodding to the corner of the parking lot and the satellite trucks and news crews from New York, Boston, Hartford, Philadelphia, New Haven and many others, including some of the national press from Washington, D.C.

After parking, they'd come up to Morrow and Dr. Sullivan talking with others gathered near the large overflow canopies. They'd been erected on the lawn next to the church over rows and rows of folding chairs, big-screen monitors and speakers linked to microphones set up in the church.

"How are you holding up?" Dr. Sullivan asked Lisa.

"Okay, I guess. I'm taking it moment by moment."

"That's all anyone can do." Morrow squeezed her shoulder.

"How is Jennifer Dutton doing?" Lisa asked.

"Not so well, as you might imagine. But she wanted to be here for Greg. Her father is at her side and her doctor is here," Morrow said before he was approached by a grave-faced man.

"Excuse me, Agent Morrow, but the director is ready for your briefing now. He wants to make a press statement afterward."

After Morrow left, Lisa, Chan and Watson entered the church. Seating was prearranged; theirs was midway, left side, at the main aisle. The church smelled of candle wax and fresh linen. Whispers and nervous throat clearing echoed. A choir sang hymns. Lisa looked at her funeral card and the program, which was outlined in calligraphy.

Agent Gregory Scott Dutton smiled at her from the cover.

"I'm a cop...my gun's on my right hip, under my shirt."

She touched her fingertips to his face.

I'm so sorry.

The service commenced with the procession of altar boys and the priest, the casket rolled behind them, trailing the fragrance of the flowers that draped it. The casket was followed by Jennifer Dutton, seven months pregnant, sobbing while her father, the former detective, held her close to him as they walked. They passed only a few feet away...Lisa could feel Jennifer's gasps, saw the talons of agony cutting into her face with such force something in Lisa's heart gave way. Lisa gripped the wooden pew in front of her as a wave of anguish overwhelmed her, sending her tumbling back...back to that horrible moment... when her telephone rang in her kitchen...

...the spouse of Robert Anthony Palmer?

...it's the hospital...Bobby's been rushed to the intensive care unit...come right away... Rita hurried over to watch the kids...Lisa raced to the hospital...nearly blowing red lights...battling tears...I'm coming...everything moving in a slow-motion dream...no...she was dreaming...

she was dreaming...the hospital's antiseptic air...the P.A. calling doctors...the reception...I'm Lisa Palmer...yes...my husband, Bobby...this way...in that room...Jesus God... her knees buckling...he's on the bed...the machines... Bobby...! Is that Bobby?...his head is a turban of bandage...she's numb...someone's telling her...a doctor someone...Bobby had stopped to help a woman with her car stalled on the freeway when a big rig swayed...the surgeon is saying...significant head trauma...saying the pressure on his brain...can't relieve the pressure...not much time left...so sorry...but I made meat loaf...Bobby loves meat loaf...she was going to surprise him with apple pie... they'd fought over a bill...a freakin' useless bill...now... Bobby...cuts on his face...she's got his hand trapped in both of hers...her tears flow over her wedding ring...over his wedding band...that face when he first asked her... "So what are you doing Saturday?"...for the rest of your life...she's squeezing his hand...she can't let go...don't you leave me, Bobby...! the alarms are beeping...screaming... nurses are telling her it's time to let go...she can't let go... the alarms...she's screaming...you have to leave...Mrs. Palmer, you have to leave...I'm so sorry...we did everything we could...he's gone...we're so sorry...one last look and an undefined energy burned through her with a brilliant light...

...light...

The light.

Lisa twisted her wedding rings and gazed up at the light streaking through the beautiful stained-glass window. Wishing all of this was a bad dream as she tuned in to the eulogy given by the director of the FBI.

"...Greg did not hesitate to take action in order to save

others, even if it meant sacrificing his life. He gave us the ultimate gift for which we suffer an unbearable loss…"

Several pews from where Lisa grappled with her anguish, Agent Frank Morrow wrestled with his anxiety for Beth and Hailey, who were facing a life without him.

They were still in shock, still reeling from learning of his terminal condition. He wished to hell he could alleviate their suffering and help them through this. God, all they needed was a break. One break to clear this case, then he could deal with his own life and the time he had left.

Was he just praying?

Hell, now, that's something he hadn't done in a while.

At that moment in Queens, as Ethan Palmer worked on his homework, he thought of his mother in that black dress.

It was the dress she wore at Dad's funeral. Wearing it today had made her sad again. He didn't like seeing his mother sad.

Or his sister.

He glanced from his homework at the kitchen table to the living room where Taylor and Rita were playing a video game with the sound off. Ethan liked living here. He'd lived here all his life and he didn't want to move to California and leave everything behind.

It would be sort of disrespectful to his father.

Ethan picked up his small pearl-handled penknife. His dad had given it to him on his birthday and he treasured it. Such a cool little knife. He never went anywhere without it.

If they moved away, he'd miss his best friend, Jason. He'd be the new kid at school and that would suck. And worst of all, maybe his mom would find a new boyfriend who would become his new dad. He didn't want a new dad because he loved his dad and missed him so much it hurt.

But his mom was already making big changes, like selling their cabin.

Dad loved the cabin. Ethan loved it. Taylor and Mom loved it, too. They had the best times there, swimming, fishing, roasting hot dogs on sticks over a campfire and looking up at the stars.

Mom cried when she tried to tell him why she had to sell it; that with Dad gone, things were harder now. Things had changed. Ethan begged her not to sell it. But what could he do? He was just a ten-year-old kid.

What would Dad tell him?

Buck up and be a man, son. Look after your mom and your sister.

Ethan put his knife down and went back to putting the final touches on the map he was drawing for school. Mrs. Chambers said it had to give directions and distance from Queens to a favorite place. Ethan did a map to the cabin at Lake George. He had all the information from a copy of an old map Dad sketched once for Arnie, his friend. Now, it was like Dad was helping him with his homework.

Pleased with the results, Ethan pinned his map on their message corkboard by the back door for Mom to check. Then he wrote on the calendar square for next Saturday, "going to the cabin."

He sure missed his dad, all right.

Ethan grabbed his knife, left the kitchen, went upstairs to his mom's bedroom to do what he always did when he felt this way.

He went to her dresser, stood before the special marble box and caressed it with his fingers. He knew it was a cremation urn that contained some of his father's ashes. Ethan slid his arms to either side of the box, drew his face near, turned his head and pressed his cheek to the top, feeling its surface against his skin.

"I miss you, Dad."

In Bridgeport, Connecticut, Agent Dutton's body was committed to the earth. At the graveside ceremony, the FBI director presented Jennifer Dutton with the FBI's Memorial Star, a medal given to the relative of an agent whose death was caused by "adversarial action." Then Jennifer Dutton's father held her as her husband's casket was lowered into the ground.

After the burial, hundreds of mourners gathered for the reception at the community hall near the church. Jennifer sat in a chair while she, her father and family members formed the funeral receiving line.

This was it.

This is where Lisa needed to do what she had to do.

She took her place in line along with Chan and Watson. It moved slowly. As she neared the family, Lisa noticed the funeral director's staff delicately attempting to keep the line flowing with respectful requests to "please keep your condolences brief, please, thank you."

But Lisa needed to do more than console Jennifer.

As she got closer she heard people say, "I am so sorry for your loss," "Greg was such an amazing person," "Our sympathy to you," "We're going to miss him."

Lisa found herself standing before Jennifer Dutton, looking into her face, pale, broken, bright red veins webbing her tear-stained eyes. *I know your pain. I know you are not here, that you're falling through an abyss right now, but I need to break through. I need you to hear me.*

Lisa took Jennifer's hand. It was warm, weak.

Lisa held it tight.

"Jennifer, my name is Lisa Palmer. You have my deepest condolences."

Jennifer nodded, but nothing registered.

"I was with your husband when he died."

Chan turned and Watson shot a look at Lisa, who with measured words continued attempting to penetrate Jennifer's grief.

"I was there when it happened."

"Excuse me—" Chan's voice was soft "—this isn't the appropriate time."

Jennifer blinked as if awakened, her attention focusing.

"There's something I must tell you," Lisa said, bending, nearly on her knees so that she was face-to-face with Jennifer, never letting go of her hand. "I have to tell you what he said before he died."

Jennifer's free hand flew to her mouth, her face crumpling with fear and an aching to know at the same time.

"We're so sorry…" Chan grasped Lisa's shoulder firmly.

"Yes," Jennifer said to Lisa. "Tell me."

"He said, 'Jennifer, I love you.' Those were his last words. I know, I was on the floor next to him. He tried to do the right thing. To save people. I held his hand as long as I could."

A harsh, throaty cry rose from deep within Jennifer, forcing her to lift her head back to release it. All attention went to her and to Lisa. Her father put his arms around her as concerned mourners strained to see, prompting Jennifer's doctor to approach her.

Chan and Watson tried to move Lisa away, but Jennifer wouldn't release her hand.

"No!" Jennifer groaned to the others. "Let her be, let her be."

Lisa remained rooted until Jennifer was able to speak again.

"You know, I felt him that day, felt him call out to me," Jennifer managed to say, her voice a rasped whisper. She pulled Lisa to her and the two women, bonded in grief, held on to each other.

"Thank you for this. Thank you for telling me," Jennifer said.

Much of the return drive to New York was passed in silence as Lisa suffered the unspoken wrath of Agents Chan and Watson for her perceived violation of FBI etiquette or protocol.

Lisa did not care.

Widow to widow, she knew what had to be done.

Lisa had to give Jennifer Dutton what was rightfully hers.

33

*W*here's *Rytter?*

Ivan Felk swallowed whiskey, gritted his teeth and looked out from the hotel's rooftop bar at the lights necklaced across the Bay Bridge.

It was late.

Unger, Northcutt and Dillon had checked in, but not Rytter. *Where the hell was he?* As Felk searched his phone yet again for messages, he'd received a new one from their support man in Kuwait City.

All props arrived safely. We're awaiting next stage of the production.

That was good, significantly good. But Felk's relief was short-lived.

The operation's next stage would originate across the street in less than a week, at the Federal Reserve Bank of San Francisco. He needed every squad member here, now.

Rytter was missing.

Today was rendezvous day. It was critical they prepare. They had to check their gear and then drill. Felk put his phone away, gulped the last of his drink, tossed some bills on the bar. He turned to leave, when the flat screen above the bar stopped him cold.

A national news network was reporting from Bridgeport, Connecticut, on the funeral for FBI agent Gregory Scott Dutton *"...who, along with three guards, was murdered in a commando-style six-million-dollar armored-car heist in Greater New York City. Our correspondent Frances Felder is at the ceremony where dignitaries from Washington, D.C., paid tribute to the fallen agent. Frances... Yes, John, it was an emotional service with Agent Dutton's pregnant widow receiving the FBI's Memorial Star on what the director of the FBI called a painful day in the bureau's history—"*

Painful? Those fuckers don't know what pain is, Felk thought.

My men were betrayed and sacrificed defending you and assholes like you. And you praise this guy for his stupidity—for trying to stop the rescue operation of our brave people. You praise him? He's not a hero, he's a lesson, and you'd better learn it—anyone who gets in our way is an enemy combatant.

The news report ended, but Felk's anger roiled as the glass-pod elevator descended seventeen stories inside the hotel's colossal atrium. The others were waiting in the main-floor bar. Unger had flown directly to San Francisco. Northcutt flew to Los Angeles then drove up. Dillon flew to Seattle and drove down. Rytter had flown to Chicago and was driving across the States from there.

"Anybody heard from Erik?" Felk asked the others.

No one had anything to report.

"Shit. We can't wait. Let's move out. Dillon's got a van."

They went southbound on the 280, a multilane freeway of red-and-white lights that wove through a galaxy of terrace-hilled suburbs to Daly City. The self-storage outlet was near the Metro Mall and the Home Depot.

"You take care of things, Dillon?" Felk asked.

"Yes, the van's rented on one of the counterfeit cards."

Felk wanted this inspection done late at night. Fewer eyes around. As with most stages, they'd been supported through their network of trusted friends. Details were sent to Felk through an encrypted email and a key had been left at the hotel for him, under his alias. Using the information, he guided Unger as they navigated around the facility to unit 90, their unit.

They backed the van to it.

They had 24/7 outside access.

Felk pressed the unit's password on the keypad then inserted the key into the steel lock. Metal rumbled as they raised the steel door. It was ten feet by twenty, plenty of room for their needs. It held motorcycles and large storage crates. They set to work inspecting their equipment, weapons, ammunition, clothing, wiring, hardware and other items. One isolated tub contained several white blocks of C4 packed in white Mylar-film wrapping.

"Looks good," Unger said.

The *snap-click-clack* of the men making a closer examination of the M9 Beretta pistols and the M4 carbines pulled Felk back to Red Cobra Team 9's assignment—the last mission.

Under layer upon layer of secrecy, they were subcontracted through a private security firm that was hired through the CIA to hunt and neutralize terrorists in the western frontier—a no-man's-land straddling the border between Afghanistan and Pakistan that had been lost to al-Qaeda.

The territory was a whirlwind of militia cells, insurgents and tribal forces responsible for hostilities against all western troops. It took years before coalition leadership negotiated conditional peace with clan leaders, sweetened with humanitarian aid, but balanced on the condition that western troops would never enter the designated zones of the territory.

The peace actually took hold until western intelligence suggested insurgents were using those zones to plot devastating attacks against local governments who'd allied with western governments. Red Cobra Team 9 was hired for a covert mission to remove targeted leaders in the forbidden zones.

The night drop was done with radio silence.

Felk's squad fell to earth never knowing that the intelligence on which they had staked their lives was false, that it was part of a calculated strategy to draw out militia cells for a larger "eradicating" action by coalition groups. But it could never be known that it was the western alliance that had violated the agreement. All Felk knew at the time of his team's unsanctioned mission was that he needed every man on his squad to do the job.

Just as he needed every man now to finish it.

"Ivan?"

We did not come this far to fail—not with my brother's life on the line.

"Ivan?" Northcutt had asked him a question. "We just got a message from Rytter. He's in Nebraska."

"Nebraska? Why is he so late?"

"We don't know. He isn't answering."

34

Trooper Duane Hanson with the Nebraska State Patrol finished his coffee and took stock of the vast windblown plain while rolling westbound on Interstate 80.

He was just beyond the exit for Brule, midway through his shift, thinking about lunch at Thorsen's Diner in Big Springs and maybe hitting the books again. He had five years with uniformed patrol and was working on getting selected for the Investigative Services Division.

Making the Cold Case Unit was his dream.

He'd studied, applied and written the exam. His interview was in three days. The brass at Troop D headquarters in North Platte was encouraging. Captain Wagner liked him, and Lieutenant Tolba let slip that Hanson had scored the highest he'd ever seen on an ISD exam.

It likely helped that Hanson was a voracious reader and had a near-photographic ability for retaining details, especially when it came to a "Be On the Lookouts." While most guys scanned the local, state and national BOLOs, Hanson devoured them every day.

It would be sweet to make it into ISD, he thought, plus, there'd be the little pay boost. He flipped down his visor to a pretty woman smiling at him from a small color snapshot.

Darlene.

He'd met her in high school. They'd been married six years now. She was doing well selling real estate. They'd started talking about buying that property down by the river, starting a family.

Something came up on the right lane.

A Chevy pickup passed him, coming close to breaking the limit. *No, that won't do.* Hanson pushed his old Crown Victoria Police Interceptor until he overtook the pickup, got in front of it and slowed things down to the proper speed limit.

Sometimes they just need me in their face, to remind them to abide by the law of the land. Hanson glanced in his rearview mirror. Looked like a young ranch hand, who gave a tiny embarrassed wave.

Hanson smiled to himself.

Reminds me of me, he thought as something blurred by both of them.

"What the hell? Now, *that's* a serious violation."

Hanson hit his lights and siren. The Ford's big eight roared as he reached for his radio and alerted his dispatcher.

"Seventy-eight-ten westbound on eighty at Brule in pursuit."

"Ten-four, seventy-eight-ten, description?"

"Looks like a white Chrysler, maybe a three hundred. Man, he must have a Hemi in that thing. He's up to one-twenty-five, maybe one-thirty. Light traffic. Road is good."

Hanson's chase did not last. The driver pulled to the shoulder. Hanson eased up behind the vehicle. It was a Chrysler 300, looked like a rental. Hanson called in the tag, an Illinois plate. Then he gave the location, grabbed his book and got out of his car.

As he approached the driver, his training kicked in.

Be alert. Expect the unexpected.

One occupant. Hanson inventoried him: white, male, in his thirties, clean-cut, military-style brush cut. Blond. Tattooed and well-built; jeans, plain white T-shirt.

"Good afternoon, sir. What's your rush?"

"I'm sorry. I lost concentration on my speed. I apologize."

The accent was European, German, maybe.

"Back home on the autobahn there is no limit."

"Well, this is Nebraska, sir, and our limits are clearly posted. If you exceed them, you break the law. Where you headed?"

"I'm on holiday."

"Right, that doesn't answer my question."

"I was going to meet a friend on the West Coast."

"Okay, well, I'm going to have to see your license and registration."

"Of course, Officer. This car is a rental."

Maybe it was the guy's accent, his body language or something in the air—Hanson couldn't pinpoint the reason, but he was getting a weird vibe. The driver got the registration from the glove compartment, pulled his license from his wallet and handed both to Hanson.

In that instant, he noticed a tattoo on the driver's wrist, not quite covered by his watch.

Hanson clipped the information to his book.

The driver was Dieter Windhorst of Hamburg, Germany.

"That's a pretty sophisticated watch you got there. Are you a serviceman?"

"I was in the military."

"It's a small world—my dad was with the corps, he's got a watch like yours. Would you mind if I had a closer look?"

As the driver considered Hanson's request, the corners of his blue eyes crinkled and he moved his arm so Hanson could look at the watch.

"It's quartz," the driver said. "Dual time, has temperature, altimeter."

"Very cool, may I see it?"

The driver hesitated at the casual forwardness of the American cop, unlike police in Europe. It bordered on amusing. Clearly thinking cooperating might help the situation, he shrugged.

"By all means." The driver removed the watch and gave it to him.

"It is also waterproof. Quite good."

Hanson held it close, but was actually noting the driver's wrist tattoo, a cobra in a strike position entwined in wire.

Unease pinged in the pit of Hanson's stomach.

"Yup, Dad's wasn't that good. Very cool." Hanson returned the watch. "Thanks. Hang tight, partner, it'll take a while to process your information and to write you up for the infraction."

"I understand. My apologies." The driver replaced his watch.

In his car, Hanson radioed for an NCIC check on the car and Dieter Windhorst of Hamburg, Germany.

"Ten-four."

"And please make an urgent check with Homeland and the FBI. I think we've got something here. Can you send backup to my twenty? No lights or siren. I need them now."

"Roger that."

Hanson's pulse quickened as he flipped through the BOLOs on his clipboard. He stopped at an FBI alert displaying a clear illustration of a tattoo depicting a cobra, fangs bared and braided in barbed wire.

Damn, he glanced toward the car, *that's it.*

The alert warned that any subject bearing the tattoo could have links to four homicides arising out of the armored car heist in New York City. The subject should be detained for questioning by the FBI. Approach with extreme caution as the subject is considered armed and dangerous.

"Seventy-eight ten subject vehicle a rental out of Chicago, O'Hare. Copy?"

"Ten-four."

"Lessee is Dieter Windhorst, German national. I'm shooting the particulars to you now." Hanson checked his small mobile computer. No outstanding warrants or wants.

"What about Homeland, FBI and Interpol?"

"Stand by."

"What's the ETA on my backup?"

"Not good, seven-sixty and seven-eighty-one are tied up with an overturned cattle truck near North Platte."

Hanson dragged the back of his hand across his mouth.

He'd seen news reports of the armored car robbery in New York.

Four homicides, three guards and an FBI agent.

"Seventy-six to dispatch. What's the situation with county, any chance of any backup within five?"

"Not looking good. Seventy-six, NCIC has a supplemental from Interpol and Homeland. Passport for Dieter Windhorst of Hamburg, Germany, is flagged as lost slash stolen from Schiphol Airport, Amsterdam. Do you copy?"

Damn, that's him. I got a world of trouble sitting in front of me.

Each passing second increased the chances of the driver

realizing that Hanson knew he was a wanted man. He could run.

"Seventy-six. Copy. The subject is consistent with the FBI BOLO, NCIC number W581898201. I'm going to bring him in."

Hanson flipped down his visor, glanced at his wife's face and activated his PA system.

"Sir, would you please remove your keys from the ignition and drop them outside your window! Extend your hands outside the window, exit the car and lie flat on your stomach with your hands behind your back!"

The driver did not respond.

Hanson cursed under his breath.

If he runs, I'm screwed. I have to do this now.

Hanson stood six-two, weighed two hundred pounds and was a former defensive tackle at college. He'd made all-state. As a state trooper he faced many difficult situations and drew on his football days whenever he had to get physical. He was quick, smart and strong.

But this guy gave off an icy vibe.

Hanson would prefer backup right now.

"Sir, please follow my instructions."

Another moment passed and Hanson met the driver's stare in the rental's rearview mirror for nearly a minute before the driver's body shifted.

He removed the keys. They chinked to the ground.

That's good, Hanson thought. *But this ain't over.*

The driver then extended his hands and opened the driver's door from the outside. Keeping his eyes on Hanson, he raised his hands, palms open. He came to the rear right of his car and got on his knees, then lowered himself onto his stomach, lying flat on the ground.

He placed his hands behind his back.

And waited.

"Don't move, sir!"

His pulse galloping, Hanson got out of his car, drew his gun from his holster and trained it on the driver. As Hanson approached him, he pulled metal handcuffs from his utility belt and tossed them on the ground next to the driver, keeping his gun steady.

"Close one cuff on your left wrist, let me hear it lock. Leave the other cuff open and place your hands behind your back. Do it now, please."

Very slowly the driver complied. He was a big guy. Hanson estimated that they were a match in weight and height.

"Thank you. Now spread your legs."

Hanson holstered his gun, moved quickly to place his knee on the driver's back, to slip the open cuff on his free wrist. But the suspect made a lightning twist of his body, drove Hanson into the ground, smashing a fist to his head, striking like a snake for his gun. Vision blurred, senses floating, Hanson clawed to regain control. His football years and police training fueled by adrenaline rocketing through him, he got his hands on his gun.

Too late.

The driver's steel grip was already on the Glock.

Oh, Jesus, he's got my gun, got his finger on the trigger.

Hanson crushed his hands around the driver's, who was angling the gun at Hanson. Reaching deep for every iota of strength, Hanson growled to fend off the barrel that was slowing turning toward him.

This guy's strong. Fight. Fight. Fight.

Hanson shifted his weight and summoned strength he didn't have.

A prayer and Darlene's face blazed across his mind as he gave all he had to the battle just as the gun fired.

35

New York City

Jack Gannon arrived in the WPA newsroom needing an afternoon coffee, but there was no time. Lisker had seen him and called his desk phone.

"In my office, *now!*"

Two days had passed since Gannon and the super had discovered Harlee Shaw's corpse.

Through the glass walls of Lisker's office, Gannon recognized the two men waiting with Lisker as the detectives who'd first questioned him at the scene, Mullen and Walsh.

This is not good.

He'd never expected them to show up at the WPA unannounced. As he cut across the newsroom Gannon's throat went dry. He hadn't given Lisker the full picture on his tipster's death. All that he'd told him was that his tip may have dead-ended.

Now, with two detectives from Yonkers waiting for him in his boss's office, he realized that he'd made a mistake.

Gannon's mistrust of Lisker stemmed from his time at the *Buffalo Sentinel,* where his managing editor had burned him. The editor betrayed Gannon's confidence to the person Gannon was investigating. The incident had left

Gannon with a pathological aversion to telling any editor about any major lead he was working on until he had the story locked up.

Since learning Harlee Shaw's identity, Gannon had spent every free moment secretly digging into his life for any connection to the Ramapo heist. He had the suicide note committed to memory:

> I never meant for this to happen.
> I am so sorry, Harlee.

Did Shaw mean his suicide or the murders in Ramapo? Was Gannon unraveling the conspiracy behind four homicides and a 6.3-million-dollar heist? Or was he mired in the sad case of a disturbed man?

Harlee Shaw grew up in Hoboken, New Jersey, was a former member of the U.S. Army, saw action in Iraq then came home to a job in private security. Shelly, the super, told Gannon that Shaw was a lonesome type, very sad. Shelly figured it was a result of his time in Iraq. But Gannon was unable to link Shaw to the heist.

So far.

He needed to keep digging.

He also needed to keep pressing his sources to help him get an interview with the woman who'd witnessed the FBI agent's murder. There was a compelling story to be told. But he shoved all that aside and entered Lisker's office, braced for his wrath.

"Park it, Gannon." Lisker, leaning on his desk, arms folded, indicated the small meeting table where Mullen and Walsh were seated, wearing rumpled suits and stone-cold faces. "Apparently you're acquainted with these gentlemen from the Third Precinct of the Yonkers P.D. They dropped by so you could further enlighten them on your involvement in the tragic case of Mr. Shaw."

"My 'involvement'? Am I going to need a lawyer here?"

"No, unless you did something criminal." Walsh opened his notebook. "We just have a few follow-up questions. We've gone over your statement and we'd like you to elaborate on your dealings with the deceased and how you came to be at his residence on the day of his death."

As Lisker's gaze burned into him, Gannon cleared his throat.

"Well, as I told you, he called me anonymously a few times, claiming to have a tip on a big story. He would not give me his name. We get calls like these, most are from nut-jobs."

"So why did you seek him out?"

"I don't know what it was but I had a gut feeling about him. He said he had a big story about national security, but as for the details, he was vague, cryptic and scared. He called about five times and finally he agreed to meet me but never showed."

"If he didn't give up his name, how did you know where to find him?"

"I tracked his number to a pay phone in Yonkers, asked around and that's how I located him."

"So it was important that you find him?"

"I had a gut feeling, so I put in some time."

"I'm curious..." Walsh looked at his notes. "Shelly Konradisky, the super, told us that you stayed alone in Shaw's apartment right up until the time help came after her 911 call. What did you do in there?"

"I just took stock of the room."

"Really? You touch anything? Take anything?"

"No."

"Response time was sixteen minutes. Seems like a long time to keep a corpse company."

"Journalistic curiosity."

"Bull-fucking-shit, Gannon," Mullen said. "Why were you interested in finding Harlee Shaw? What were you looking for in his apartment?"

Gannon's Adam's apple rose and fell. After assessing his situation, he decided to show his hand.

"All right. Whenever he called, he would call me *sir*. I pegged him for military, or ex-military. To me he sounded genuinely frightened about something. And when he agreed to meet, he said he would bring documents to prove his claim of a pending security threat. Now, all of this could have been part of a psychological problem. I've encountered my share of disturbed callers. I don't know about this case. He was a no-show at our meeting. Three days later, the hit at Ramapo happened, a commando-style armed robbery."

"So?"

"After that, I never heard from him again and I got thinking, what if his tip was related to the heist?"

"That's a big-ass what-if, Gannon," Mullen said.

"You never followed a hunch?"

"What was it you said? You get nut-job calls," Mullen said.

"Did Shaw ever give you anything to support his claims?" Walsh asked.

"No, but I found out he was ex-military and worked in private security."

"Private security?" Mullen snorted. "He was a mall cop, with a drinking problem. He talked to himself and was undergoing counseling. Did you know all that?"

"No." Gannon swallowed hard. "Did he have a criminal record?"

"No record."

"If he's a psych case, then why are you guys so interested in my interest in him?"

"Because a suicide is a crime scene until we release it. You mucked around in our crime scene and we want to know why," Mullen said.

"So it was definitely a suicide?"

"According to the Westchester County medical examiner's preliminary report," Walsh said.

"Did his counselor tell you what drove him to it?"

"He was despondent over losing some of his buddies in Iraq."

"I found out he did a tour with the U.S. Army."

"Two," Walsh said. "After that he went back as a contractor, came home all messed up and decided to eat his gun."

"I think we're done here," Mullen said.

"Are you going to pass this case to FBI agent Morrow?"

"Who?" Mullen asked.

"The case agent on the Ramapo homicides."

"What for?"

"To look into a possible link between Shaw and the heist."

Mullen threw a glance to Walsh that had the beginnings of eye rolling before Walsh said, "We'll take that under advisement, Jack. Thank you."

Walsh concluded the interview by closing his notebook.

After the detectives left, Lisker closed his office door and held up his thumb, keeping it a quarter inch from his forefinger.

"I am this close to firing you."

"Why?"

"Insubordination, violation of newsroom policy, near-criminal behavior."

"I was following a lead."

"That's why two detectives were here? You embarrassed the WPA."

"I was doing my job. Most editors practiced in journalism support their reporters."

"Shut up and listen. From this point on—"

A knock interrupted Lisker, and Beland Stone, the WPA executive editor—everyone's boss—stuck his head in the office.

"Dolf, those revenue reports are in. I need to see you and Wallace in my office in two minutes."

"Of course." Lisker waited for the door to close then continued. "You're off the heist story."

"What?"

"Here." He turned to his desk and passed Gannon a news release for a national dog show at Madison Square Garden. "While you are still employed here, you'll be our new color writer. Start by covering this."

"You're joking."

"Go with the photographer and get us a color story with art."

"You're serious?"

"Get out."

Gannon returned to his desk with anger rippling through him.

Okay, I screwed up, big-time, but no way will I give up on this story.

He took several deep breaths and began scrolling through the newswire, struggling to think. He stared blankly at the screen waiting for his heart rate to level off as he clicked through story after story.

I've put in too much time, called in too many favors.

I know there is something there. I'll go rogue if that's what it takes. I'll bust this story. There is something there.

Gannon closed his window for the newswire, went to a hidden file on his computer's hard drive and opened it. Images of Harlee Shaw's decomposing body blossomed in vivid color on his monitor. Gannon studied them, unsure what he was looking for.

"What the hell is that?" Angelo startled him from behind.

Gannon's first inclination was to hide the photos. But he had an idea. Checking the area to ensure he and Dixon were alone, Gannon explained the photos. Fresh eyes may find something.

"A typical suicide…" Dixon shrugged. "Now, when I was in Iraq, I saw some real damage, man. Come on, we have to go to the dog show. Photos of those mutts usually get good pick-up."

"Wait, keep looking. Is there anything that strikes you as different?"

"Cripes, Jack." Dixon took his mouse, clicked through, zooming in professionally on certain details. "It's a suicide. The guy no longer wanted to breathe, it's in his note."

"But what else?"

"He no longer wanted that tattoo, either?"

"What?"

Dixon enlarged the area of Shaw's wrist and pointed to the discoloration.

"See, he was fading a tattoo. Whatever he had there, he no longer wanted it. Looks like a snake or something. Come on, let's go."

"Hang on."

Gannon drew his face close to his monitor, puzzling at the tattoo, not sure what to make of it. Was this something?"

Gannon's cell phone rang.

"Gannon, WPA."

"Jack, its Adell."

The sound of his best source, Adell Clark, the ex-FBI agent from Buffalo, took his thoughts back to his hometown.

"Adell, it's been so long."

"I'm sorry I've been out of reach, I'm in Chicago on a case and it's been time-consuming."

"I understand. How's your little girl?"

"Oh, she's a handful."

"Pretty soon the boys will be knocking on your door." He smiled.

"Jack, I got your messages and I've been following your stories on the case. Listen, I just picked something up from a friend with the Chicago FBI that may help you."

"In Chicago?"

"No. It's a big break and it's in Ogallala, Nebraska."

36

North Platte, Nebraska

The man known as Dieter Windhorst drifted toward death.

He'd lost his struggle for State Trooper Duane Hanson's gun when a bullet smashed through his jaw, shredded his optic nerve, then tore into the frontal lobe of his brain.

He'd been rushed from Ogallala, an hour east, to Great Plains, a regional trauma center in North Platte. After three hours of surgery, he lay shackled at the ankle to a hospital bed, his condition deteriorating. In the chair next to him, an FBI agent snapped through *Field & Stream* magazine, keeping a vigil punctuated by the squeak of soft-soled shoes on polished floors as the nurses checked on him at twenty-minute intervals.

It'd been some twenty-four hours since Trooper Hanson had stopped him.

The doctors said the patient was unlikely to survive much longer.

Across town, in a third-floor room of North Platte's federal building, a bland three-story red stone structure that evoked a 1960s high school, a growing team of investigators was at work dissecting the mystery surrounding the suspect.

Agent Frank Morrow had arrived with several New York agents the previous night, joining FBI agents from North Platte, Omaha and Denver who were crammed into a meeting room along with local and state investigators. The ad hoc local task force used secure laptops and cell phones to work online and through teleconference calls to federal agents in Chicago, Washington, D.C., Quantico, Manhattan, the NYPD and the bureau's legal attaché at the U.S. embassy in Berlin.

The Ogallala stop was a critical break.

Morrow agreed, the subject's cobra tattoo was consistent with Lisa Palmer's description of the one wrapped around the wrist of Agent Dutton's killer.

Who is our subject? Will he lead us to the others?

They had to confirm his identity.

North Platte P.D. got a clear set of the driver's fingerprints, which were now being processed through databases in the United States, Canada and Europe, while an Evidence Response Team from the FBI's Denver office processed his car and the scene.

"We need to ID this man and put him at the scene in Ramapo, or in the area at the time of the hit," Morrow said.

So far they had received nothing on the prints.

But with each piece of evidence, the scope of the investigation broadened. Chicago confirmed the car was rented at O'Hare. Then Homeland confirmed an air ticket for Dieter Windhorst on an Air Canada flight direct to Chicago from Toronto. Toronto Police Service, the Ontario Provincial Police and the Royal Canadian Mounted Police were investigating the subject's activities in Canada under the alias Dieter Windhorst.

In Nebraska, in the lining of the subject's jacket, the

ERT had found a credit card in the name of Hans Ballack of Munich. Credit card security confirmed Ballack's identity had been stolen. The card was shut down after one recent fraudulent use at a motel in Teaneck, New Jersey.

"This charge puts our guy, whoever he is, twenty minutes and twenty miles from the heist the day before it happened. He checked out the morning of the crime," Morrow said before requesting emergency warrants to search the New Jersey motel room the subject had rented and check the IDs and rooms used by every guest. "The heist crew may have launched from this motel."

At that point identification of the subject's fingerprints had been confirmed via Interpol, Europol and the BKA, Germany's equivalent of the FBI.

Suspect identified as Erik Rytter, age twenty-nine. Last known address, Munich. No criminal record, no arrests, convictions or warrants. Not even a traffic infraction.

According to the BKA, Rytter was a former member of the Bundeswehr, Germany's national defence force. He completed two tours of Afghanistan with the Kommando Spezialkräfte. He'd been a sniper and an explosives expert. Upon returning home to Germany, he pursued a Ph.D in chemical engineering at university but left to become a professional soldier, taking a job with a private international security firm with contracts in Iraq. From there, Rytter's trail got murky as he continually subcontracted himself to shadowy companies.

The BKA was sending agents to interview Rytter's relatives and friends.

Rytter's military expertise and his potential network underscored Morrow's concern about the people behind the heist. This was no ragtag crew. Morrow updated the Joint Terrorism Task Force, Homeland and several other national security agencies for help probing Rytter's background as more questions arose.

Was Rytter ever legitimately in the United States under his real name? If so, what was his status? Who were his associates, what were his activities, his travel patterns? Did he have any affiliation with anyone at American Centurion? Did he know Gina Saldino, who gave the crews their delivery spreadsheets?

And where was Saldino?

They'd failed to locate her so far. That Saldino, who had access to all information on routes and deliveries, would take a vacation without any contact information a week before the heist was an aspect of the case that troubled Morrow.

Was she involved?

Morrow returned to his files to review statements and reports, when his cell phone rang.

"Morrow."

"It's Darby at the hospital. He's regained consciousness, but it doesn't look good."

Kyle Rice, with North Platte P.D., got Morrow into his unmarked Ford and they roared to the hospital in minutes. Morrow badged his way to Rytter's room just as Darby exited, shaking his head. Behind him nurses were drawing a sheet over the body before the door closed.

"He never said a word, Frank," Darby said before Morrow was paged to the phone at reception.

"Morrow, FBI."

"Captain Wagner, with State Patrol."

"Yes, Captain."

"We're getting calls from local press following up on the bare-bones news release we issued yesterday on the shooting. Now, we don't want to jeopardize your case, but what more can we tell them at this point?"

"We'd prefer you say nothing further about the suspect. Only that his identity is under investigation."

"Can we tell them the FBI is involved and this is linked to your armored car heist?"

Hell, no. The last thing Morrow wanted was the three other suspects to learn what had happened. He wanted to use the advantage the FBI had at the moment to capitalize on leads that could bring them closer to the others.

"No. Keep it low-key for now, please."

"Low-key?"

"Yes, it's crucial for some of the leads we're pursuing."

"You know, Agent Morrow, sooner or later this thing is going to blow open. It was our trooper who put his life on the line to bring in your suspect."

"Yes, it was outstanding work."

"Damn straight, and we'd like to inform the public about it."

"I appreciate that, Captain, but we need time before we can release more details."

"I hear you, Agent Morrow. We'll keep things low-key for now, out of respect for the FBI man and the guards you lost back east in the heist."

"I understand and I appreciate your help, Captain."

Morrow hung up, ran a hand over his face.

"Excuse me, Agent Morrow?"

He turned and his stomach tensed.

"Jack Gannon, WPA, New York. Can I get a moment with you?"

37

North Platte / Ogallala, Nebraska

Morrow's face flashed with disbelief.

He did not need this. Not now.

"Can you just give me a few minutes?" Gannon asked.

Morrow stared at him.

Early on he'd accepted that this case was high profile, involving many jurisdictions; that leaks were inevitable. But Gannon's presence meant he had been tipped again and the continued betrayal was an insult Morrow couldn't stomach.

His eyes burned with a dangerous fury.

He walked away.

"Sir," Gannon persisted, "is this your shooter from Ramapo? Is this one of the killers?" He started down the hall after him. "Agent Morrow, you know I'll do a story with or without your help."

Before Morrow turned a corner, he mumbled something to a uniformed officer who sent Gannon back to the reception area.

Frustrated, Gannon sat in a cushioned chair.

Morrow's presence confirmed a significant development. Gannon could use that, but where did he go from

there? After considering matters, he pulled out his Black-
Berry and scrolled through his notes, only to be hit with a
text pressuring him to deliver something. New York feared
the AP would beat the WPA to the arrest story and wanted
him to file immediately.

Damn it, I just arrived here. Story still developing, he
responded, to buy time as he reflected on his ordeal and
his next step.

To get to North Platte he'd taken an early-morning flight
direct to Denver, then a one-hour hop in a Beechcraft twin-
prop. Then he'd rented a car. But it was not the trip that
kept adrenaline pumping through him, it was the terms.
First, he'd broken his own rule after he'd been tipped. He
rushed to Lisker, begged him to forget the dog show and
put him back on the heist story by promising an exclusive.

"One of the suspects has just been arrested near Ogallala, Nebraska. No one knows yet. It's all ours. Send me
there now."

Lisker weighed matters.

Then, thinking of costs, because that was always
Lisker's first concern, he tried WPA's Omaha and Denver
bureaus, but staff members were out of town on other assignments. They had a student stringer out of North Platte.
But that was too risky.

"I'll send you—on one condition," Lisker told Gannon.
"No doubt you've heard the WPA is facing staff reduc-
tions. I don't care how good your reputation is, your insubordination and this episode with the police makes you
a prime candidate for termination."

"I was just doing my job."

"If you want to keep it, you'll give me an exclusive on
an arrest in the heist murders. If you don't— Well, think
of Nebraska as the potential graveyard for your career."

Right, well, fuck you, Gannon thought, sitting there in

the hospital waiting room, the pressure on him mounting. He would not fail. He would not let a guy like Lisker bury him. There was a story here and he'd pull it together.

One way or another, he'd deliver.

North Platte was a small town but it was pure freakin' luck that he'd encountered Morrow. The fact the FBI's case agent was here confirmed the significance of the traffic-stop shooting. Gannon had to piece something together fast. He went to the Nebraska State Patrol's website. The news release on the stop was still not updated. It was the same one he'd printed off before he left. Beyond the time and date, it said nothing about the magnitude of the incident.

A trooper with the Nebraska State Patrol Troop D Headquarters—North Platte, stopped a 2011 Chrysler for speeding westbound on Interstate 80, near Brule.

Upon checking the driver's credentials, the trooper determined that the white male driver fit the description for a wanted subject and proceeded to arrest him.

During the arrest the subject grabbed for the trooper's sidearm. In the struggle the gun discharged. The subject suffered a serious gunshot wound and was taken to hospital in North Platte in critical condition.

No other details available at this time.

Gannon exhaled.

His next step was to find the unnamed trooper who took down the suspect. He'd put in a call to the State Patrol but they refused to provide more information. His only option at the moment was a suggestion texted by the stringer,

Trevor Reece, a part-time freelancer for the *Underground Movement,* an online student arts-and-entertainment newspaper.

Troopers hang @ 6 Bees Roadhouse W of NP off I-80. Big sign can't miss it.

Gannon left the hospital and drove there.

Encouraged at seeing three marked State Patrol cars among the vehicles in the lot, he parked his rented Chevy, sat on a stool at the counter and took a quick inventory.

It was a popular place, nearly every table and booth in use. Conversations, the strains of a Garth Brooks ballad and the smell of coffee filled the air. He noticed three uniformed cops sitting together in a corner booth with a man in jeans and a gray sweatshirt.

After ordering a cheeseburger platter, Gannon studied the mirror which reflected the booth occupied by the troopers. It allowed him to stare without being obvious. Within a few seconds he'd detected fresh cuts on the face of the man wearing jeans and a sweatshirt. As the man talked, Gannon studied the way he gestured and the faces of his trooper friends. They were engaged, as if he was telling an enthralling tale.

I don't believe this. It has to be him.

Feeling time slipping by, Gannon went to the table.

"Forgive me for intruding." Four sets of eyes turned to him as he nodded outside to the patrol cars in the parking lot. "I figure you're with the State Patrol and I sure could use your help."

"What's the problem?" one of the uniformed men asked.

Gannon produced his ID.

"Jack Gannon, I'm a reporter with the World Press Alliance in New York."

"Afraid we can't help you with that," said one of the troopers, cuing soft laughter at the table.

Adapting to the mood, Gannon played along, smiling as he fumbled in his pocket for his faxed copy of the State Patrol's news release, unfolded it and held it up.

"I've got to file a story about the trooper who made this stop that resulted in the suspect's getting shot in the struggle."

"What about it?" one of the troopers asked.

Gannon saw eyes shift to the man with the fresh scrapes on his face, and knew.

"I'd like to interview the trooper for the WPA. Our stories go across the country and around the world. I understand he's a hero and what he did was connected to a major case in New York City. I just flew in and I'm on deadline for the wire service."

"You call him a hero?" One of the troopers smiled into his coffee and winked at the man in plainclothes.

"Sure, why not?"

"We call him Duane who shoulda waited for backup."

As soft chuckling rippled around the table, Gannon waited, then asked, "Could you guys help me find him so I could interview him?"

Someone kicked the man in plainclothes under the table.

"Hey, Duane, seein' how you didn't make the Cornhuskers, this is your only chance to be famous. The man came all the way from New York City."

The man in plainclothes lowered his head and shook it, giving off an aura of gentle shyness, until a cell phone was held before him by one of his friends.

"Check with the lieutenant for the green light. Maybe you'll get on Leno."

"Or *COPS?*" Another trooper laughed.

Duane took the phone and turned to Gannon.

"Give me a minute. I'll let you know, okay?"

"Sure, I'll be at the counter eating my lunch. I appreciate this. But I really am on a tight deadline."

Buoyed by the break, Gannon dug into his meal. Between bites, he received a call from Hal Ford.

"How's it going? Any chance you're about to file?"

"I should have something to you in ninety minutes."

"Ninety minutes? That's a lifetime."

"Sooner if I can."

"Lisker is sharpening his fangs, so it better be a big scoop."

"I'm working on it."

By the time Gannon finished eating, all the troopers had gathered at the cash to pay. After they left, the one Gannon was waiting on approached him and introduced himself.

"Duane Hanson." He shook Gannon's hand. "I've got about fifteen minutes before I have to go. Hope that works for you."

"I'll make it work, thanks."

Hanson nodded to an empty booth in a far corner.

At the table, Gannon sensed the younger man was masking something unsettling. Only hours ago he'd struggled with one of the Ramapo killers who'd tried to end his life. As Hanson began recounting what happened on Interstate 80 near Ogallala, Nebraska, his tone darkened and he chose his words very carefully.

"My lieutenant said I can't tell you everything because it's all part of the FBI's investigation, especially now that he's dead."

"Dead?"

"Died in the hospital a little while ago." Hanson glanced out the window, the light accentuating his abrasions as he pondered the interstate stretching west to the horizon. "It's a hell of a thing. It could've been me. A hell of a thing."

38

The employee lunchroom at the Good Buy Supermart was near the produce section and always smelled of lettuce, apples and earth.

It had a battered time clock for punching time cards, a kitchenette, six chrome-trimmed table-and-chair sets, a message board for schedules, union meetings and used items for sale. Judy was offering a baby stroller; Wanda, recently single, was selling a man's watch that was "never worn." Smoking in the lunchroom had been banned for years, but fresh-air zealots complained of a lingering stench.

Today, the usual cashiers yammered in the usual bitch-gossip sessions between the afternoon-evening shifts. None gave a second thought to the TV above the row of lockers. It was always on, usually tuned in to a talk show. But today, the Breaking News banner that crawled along the bottom of the screen seized Lisa Palmer's attention.

...A suspect in the armored car heist that left three guards and an FBI agent dead in New York has died in Nebraska after struggling for the gun of the state trooper

who'd stopped his car for speeding, the World Press Alliance is reporting…

Lisa caught her breath, covered her mouth with her hand and battled the noise to listen to the report, which offered few details.

"You all right, hon?" Pam Horowitz, the most senior cashier, asked.

Other than Rita, no one at work knew of Lisa's role in the investigation.

"I'm fine. Something caught in my throat. Got any gum, Pam?"

Five minutes later, alone in the parking lot, chewing on bubblegum behind the wheel of her Ford Focus, Lisa let go.

Oh my God! Was this true? Did they really get one of them?

She fumbled through her bag for her new cell phone, called Frank Morrow's number. It rang through to the FBI's New York Division.

"Agent Morrow is out of the office," an assistant said. "May I take a message?"

"This is Lisa Palmer. I really need to speak to him, or Vicky Chan, or Eve Watson. It's about the Ramapo case."

"I'm afraid no one is available at the moment."

"It's important I talk to somebody. I'm Lisa Palmer. I've been working with them on the investigation."

"Yes, I'm aware of who you are," the assistant said. "But they are all unreachable at the moment, so if you'll just leave your number, Lisa—"

"They have it," Lisa said. "They have everything. I just need to talk to someone about what happened in Nebraska. I have questions."

"Yes, I understand."

"Can I speak to their boss? Or their boss's boss?"

"I'm sorry, Lisa, that won't be possible."

Lisa's breathing quickened with her rising frustration until she gave up, left a message and gathered her thoughts. She turned on her car radio, set it to scan, hoping to land on a news report that would tell her more about what had happened in Nebraska.

She left the parking lot bound for the school to pick up Ethan and Taylor. She drove through Queens, needing to believe that the Nebraska incident was good news. If they got one of the bastards, it meant they were making progress, getting closer to the others.

Which one was it?

Lisa stopped at a traffic light and a memory blurred in front of her.

The smell of lemon floor cleaner...her reflection in the black shield of the killer's helmet...his anger boring into her through the blood splatters...his gun drilling into her skull...

Was it him? The one who murdered the agent? The one who wanted to kill her? Which one was it? How did they get him? Was it because of her telling them about his tattoo?

A horn sounded behind her. The light had turned green. But the questions wouldn't stop, so Lisa pulled over, took out her phone and sent texts and emails to Morrow, Chan and Watson.

Please get back to me. I need to know what's happening.

When she got the kids, she held off telling them. First, Lisa wanted to learn more directly from the FBI, but no one was responding. She hid her unease by singing along with rock songs on the radio. The last one was Queen, "Somebody To Love."

It was not until they'd pulled into their driveway and Lisa killed the Ford's engine that her phone rang. At last, she thought, unlocking her back door and deactivating her home security system with one hand, keeping the phone to her head with the other.

But it was not the FBI calling.

"My God," Rita said. "Did you hear the news?"

"About Nebraska?"

"Yeah."

"Yeah, I saw it at work in the lunchroom."

"It's fantastic, Lisa. Did the FBI tell you what happened?"

"Not yet. I got messages in, but they're not getting back to me and it's starting to piss me off."

"Well, it's still all good news. I mean, they got him way out west, a billion miles from here. And the creep is freakin' dead."

"Yes, that's good."

Lisa made the kids spaghetti for supper but used every free moment to go online and to monitor news reports on TV for more on the case. It was futile. She was unable to find anything beyond the first report.

Rita was right.

Lisa had to accept that what happened was "all good." The fact they got one, and got him so far away, and that he was dead made her feel safer, lightened the weight of her worry.

She smiled to herself when she glimpsed Ethan's map on their corkboard near the fridge. He'd done a good job. It reminded her that they had important things to take

care of. She had to get ready for their trip—the last one—
up to the cabin.

She had to get ready for the rest of her life.

By early evening, after they'd finished supper, after
Lisa had washed the dishes and put them away, she still
hadn't heard a response from the FBI. It ate at her—feeling
shut out—and she resented it. She couldn't understand
and would never accept why Morrow and the others were
ignoring her, especially after all she'd been through; after
all she'd done to help them with the case.

Maybe something else was at work; something more
going on?

If that was the case, she deserved to know.

Why won't someone help me?

At that moment, it dawned on her that all the news reports had attributed the story to the World Press Alliance,
the wire service where that reporter, Jack Gannon, worked.
Lisa's keyboard clattered as she searched his name and his
story emerged online.

Life-and-Death Struggle with Murder Suspect on a
Nebraska Highway
Jack Gannon
World Press Alliance
NORTH PLATTE, Neb.—Minutes after Trooper
Duane Hanson pulled over a speeding car from Il-
linois cutting west along a windblown stretch of In-
terstate 80, he was locked into a battle for his life.

It ended in the death of a fugitive suspect wanted
for the cold-blooded murders of three armored car
guards and an FBI agent in the recent 6.3-million-
dollar heist out of Greater New York City…

Lisa read Gannon's entire story.

It was compelling and it proved to her that he knew a

great deal about the case, certainly more than she did. It brought her back to her questions and concerns over why the FBI had not responded to her calls. She contended with a growing fear that something was going on, something that the FBI agents were unwilling to share with her.

"Mom!" Ethan called downstairs from his room. "Is it bath night tonight?"

"Yes, do you need towels? I'll be right up!"

Lisa continued searching Gannon online, finding photos from his days at the *Buffalo Sentinel,* his Pulitzer nomination and stories he'd done across the country and around the world for the WPA. He came across as a guy who was confident, rough around the edges, but who had a good heart. He was easy on the eyes, too.

Lisa saw that he worked out of the WPA's world headquarters in Manhattan; saw the phone number and his email.

She bit her bottom lip.

Should she contact him for help?

39

Ivan Felk was in his hotel room, reviewing street maps on his laptop, when his screen chimed with a news alert.

The *New York Times* posted a breaking newswire item online three minutes ago.

Ramapo Heist Suspect Dies In Nebraska

What the hell?

Felk read the story fast.

The car was a rental from Chicago, heading west on the interstate. The driver was shot after he struggled for the trooper's gun and died later in hospital. The *Times* attributed the story to the World Press Alliance. Felk read it a second time.

But how did they link this to the heist?

Rytter was not named, and there were few other details. Still, the facts, and what Felk knew, were enough to convince him it was Rytter who had died.

A moment passed as he absorbed it.

Erik was dead.

Damn it.

This jeopardizes the mission.

What happened?

They were all professionals, the best of the best. They all knew going into this that there was no guarantee they'd come out alive. But they were not prone to mistakes. Rytter was careful, meticulous at eliminating risks.

How the hell did this happen?

Felk went to his window, looked down at the Federal Reserve Bank across the street and assessed the situation. Rytter was a strong soldier, a good man. They needed him. Every member of the team had a specific job that was crucial to the next stage of the operation. Rytter was his lead explosives expert, his best C4 man.

What do I do now?

Felk forced himself to stay calm, to think. They had to adapt just as they did in battle. When you lost a man, you adjusted and you advanced the mission.

Rytter was dead. But how did they link him to the heist?

Someone was knocking on the door.

In the peephole, Felk saw a fish-eyed version of Dillon and let him in.

"You see what happened in Nebraska?" Dillon asked.

"I saw. Where are the others right now?"

"I don't know. What're we going to do, Ivan?"

"We keep going."

"But we need Rytter."

"We carry it and we keep going. Unger's good with explosives."

"What about Sparks?"

"What about him?"

"He's a good explosives man. We've got time to bring him in."

Felk considered it, but the Sparks option came with challenges.

"He's been having a hard time," Felk said. "That's why

we didn't want him operational. He's unstable. Besides, he's already given us support, gone as far as he can go."

"But we need help. You could have him here in a matter of hours. We could get him up to speed. Sparks could do this with his eyes closed."

It was true.

When Sparks could function, he was outstanding. Having lost Rytter, they were now facing an extraordinary situation. Felk went to his laptop, opened a hidden file that contained phone numbers, then picked up his untraceable cell phone and made a call.

He got a recording:

The number you have reached is no longer in service.

"His number doesn't work. Hang on."

Felk called again to be sure he hadn't misdialed, and got the same message.

"Maybe he changed it?" Dillon said. "Call his building."

Felk went back to his laptop for the name and address of the building then went online for the super's number and called it. He expected a recorded message, but after three rings, the line was answered.

"Oceanic Towers, Shelly Konradisky."

"Hello, I'm trying to reach the tenant in 1021, Harlee Shaw. His number may have changed—"

"I'm very sorry, are you a friend?"

"Uh, yes. Would you have his new number?"

She cleared her throat. "You must not know what happened."

"No, what do you mean?"

"I am so sorry to be the one to tell you but...um... Harlee died."

"He died?" Felk shot a look to Dillon, whose eyes widened.

"Yes, I'm so sorry."

"What happened?"

"I'm afraid he took his own life."

"How?"

"With his gun."

"Jesus." A long moment passed before Felk said, "I knew he was having trouble from his time in the war."

"Yes, it's just terrible what our boys go through over there."

"When was this?"

"The day before yesterday."

"Who found him?"

"I did. Well, me and a reporter."

"Reporter?"

"Yes, he wanted to talk to Harlee."

"What reporter? Why?"

"I'm not too sure, some kind of story about war vets, maybe?"

"What's the reporter's name?"

"I have his card right here. Jack Gannon. Do you have a pen? I'll give you his contact information. He's from the World Press Alliance."

Felk took it down.

"Did Gannon say anything about why he wanted to talk to Harlee?"

"No, I'm sorry. I didn't get your name?"

"Wayne McCormick."

"And how did you know Harlee?"

"We went through basic together. Thanks for helping me."

"I am so sorry about your friend, Wayne. It must've been terrible what he went though overseas."

"It was."

Felk hung up and turned to Dillon.

"I got your end of that," Dillon said. "What's the reporter part?"

Felk shook his head in deeply troubled thought.

"Find Northcutt and Unger and meet me in the park at that spot in front of the port building in thirty minutes. We have to assess."

Dillon left. Felk returned to the window and dragged the back of his hand across his mouth.

No other option existed but to advance the operation.

They were at battle, taking losses, but they would adjust. They had time to evaluate resources and adapt the mission. The clock was ticking down on them. He replayed the older video from militants of the Revolutionary Movement showing his men unshaven, gaunt, cadaverous, eyes enlarged to dark pools of fear. He braced as a hooded captor raised a sword above his brother's head.

Ivan, please! Don't let me die!"

We're coming, Clay. Nothing's going to stop us.

Staring down at the Federal Reserve, Felk counted the days before the bank would process the ten-million-dollar order to be transported by armored car to Oakland International Airport.

They had time to prepare.

Still, he was assailed by the unknowns, questions that loomed large, eclipsing everything, gnawing at him.

How did they link Rytter to the Ramapo hit? They had to know something. *Are they getting closer to us? What if Rytter talked before he died? What about Sparks and the reporter? A* reporter? *Goddamnit. Take it easy. Harlee didn't know about California. But he knew about the operation. But he wouldn't have told the reporter anything. Sure, he was a bit unstable, but he wouldn't betray the operation to this reporter—Gannon, Jack Gannon.*

Why was that name familiar?

Felk went to his laptop and looked at news reports he'd saved.

Christ.

Gannon wrote the Nebraska story. But there was another reason his name rang a bell with Felk. He went to the first news reports on the Ramapo heist.

There it was.

Jack Gannon with the World Press Alliance. He was the first to report that the FBI had an eyewitness.

Eyewitness.

It all came back to her.

That bitch from Queens.

40

Erik Rytter extended his arms through the driver's window. He dropped his keys to the ground, got out of his car, raised his hands, palms out, walked to the rear right of his car and got on his knees.

"Don't move, sir!"

The air tightened in the twenty-eighth-floor boardroom of the FBI's Manhattan office where investigators were watching twenty-six minutes of digital recording made by Nebraska state trooper Duane Hanson's in-car camera. Morrow had lost count of how many times he'd viewed it in North Platte and during his return flight to New York. Now he was using it to kick off today's case-status meeting and brainstorming session. The window shades had been drawn to dim the light.

The deadly takedown played out on the room's large monitor. Rytter disappeared from view. Hanson approached him, gun drawn, issuing commands, disappearing from the frame, leaving the audio to replay the life-and-death struggle, the firecracker pop of the gunshot, Hanson scrambling to his car, his frantic call for an ambulance.

The recording ended with murmurs and paper shuffling around the table as the shades were opened.

"This break is critical," said Glenda Stark. "We must capitalize on it. We've got a lot of ground to cover. We'll update and assign. Over to you, Frank."

"First," Morrow said. "I want to stress that the tattoo is our key fact, the evidence that led to Rytter. It may lead us to the others and result in their prosecution. It's all linked to our eyewitness. The tattoo is absolutely holdback from the public. Our objective is to find the other suspects, not spook them. Is that understood?"

Morrow's eyes inventoried the faces at the table before he continued with the warrants executed at the Heavenly Rest Motor Inn in Teaneck, New Jersey. An FBI Evidence Response Team was still processing the room rented under the name Karl Ballack.

"Nothing has surfaced yet, but the clerk recognized Rytter as a guest. We're running the room's phone and all pay phones in the vicinity and checking cameras in restaurants and gas stations nearby."

Morrow said agents were showing Rytter's photograph to staff at the Freedom Freeway Service Center in Ramapo.

"We're still working on that front," Morrow said. "We are also asking the NYPD, the counties, New York and New Jersey to circulate his photo with motorcycle shops and tattoo artists."

As for other areas, Morrow said that Canadian authorities had confirmed capturing Rytter on security cameras at Toronto's Pearson International Airport. Prior to that, the Royal Canadian Mounted Police had nothing more on his movements in Canada. Nothing had emerged yet showing entry into Canada from the United States. Morrow said it was believed Rytter entered Canada from the States using false identification, or entered at an unsecured point in the border. Meanwhile, he said, U.S. federal aviation security cameras picked him up at Chicago's O'Hare.

"We're interviewing a dentist from Milwaukee. She sat next to him on the Toronto-to-Chicago flight."

Morrow used the remote for the monitor to show a time-line in development. "This is where we pick him up." Dates and times starting with Rytter in Teaneck, New Jersey, then in Ramapo, New York at the heist, then to Toronto, the flight to Chicago, the car rental and his death in Ne-braska.

Details of Rytter's entry into the United States in the time prior to the heist were uncertain. Rytter's genuine German passport did not show any entry into the States, according to American and German security.

"Again, he may have entered this country with coun-terfeit ID."

"What do we know about his background and asso-ciates?" an agent from the Department of Homeland Se-curity asked.

For the benefit of those who had just joined the case, Morrow summarized. He said that the BKA was inves-tigating Rytter's activities in Germany. "They are inter-viewing his relatives and friends and so far they tell us that Rytter was private and secretive. He was a former member of the Bundeswehr, Germany's national defence force. What they've learned is that after he completed two tours of Afghanistan with the Kommando Spezialkräfte, the elite KSK, he became a private contractor with a number of murky security firms with contracts and subcontracts in Iraq and Afghanistan. He never talked about what he did. It's believed to have been his last known area of em-ployment."

"Are we able to get to any of the contractors he worked for?" asked an NYPD detective with the joint task force.

"Not yet," Morrow said. "We've got the CIA, Defense and State Departments Intelligence looking into that aspect. It's a world of ghosts because many of the contracts are linked to national security."

Morrow wrapped up the meeting and nodded to Dimarco. The NYPD detective had spent much of his time peering over his bifocals at his own status sheets. As the room cleared, the two men talked quietly.

"Anything on Gina Saldino, Al?"

"No. Her friends have no idea where she went for vacation. She did withdraw three thousand in cash before her holiday, but since then we've got no action on bank accounts or credit cards."

"Phone records?"

"Nothing."

"I don't like this," Morrow said. "She's an unknown factor."

"We'll keep on it. Are you ready to go?"

"I have to take care of something. Why don't you grab a coffee downstairs. I'll meet you there."

The Nebraska shooting was front-page news in New York where the media had inundated the FBI with calls and emails demanding more information on the dead suspect. The New York FBI office had prepared a short press release. Morrow needed to review it before it went out to ensure it did not hamper the investigation.

The draft gave the time, date and location of the traffic stop in Nebraska and a summary of the incident, without revealing key details. It confirmed that the suspect was Erik Rytter, a German national from Munich. It stated that Rytter was a former member of the Bundeswehr, Germany's national defence force. Morrow revised the wording so that it said: *It is believed Rytter participated in the armored-car heist at Ramapo. The investigation continues.* Morrow did not want any other details released.

Less than forty minutes later, Dimarco guided the NYPD's unmarked Chevy along the Van Wyck Expressway. While Dimarco took a cell-phone call, Morrow considered Jack Gannon. That guy was good, always ahead of everyone on the story. Morrow admitted a begrudging admiration of Gannon. He was a relentless digger, so well sourced he was dangerous. Morrow would have liked to have been allied with him. They could have helped each other.

In another life, maybe, Morrow thought as his phone vibrated with a message: A text from his daughter, Hailey.

I love u daddy, when r u coming home?

It stopped him cold.

He blinked at it, then rubbed his face, struggling to remember the last time he was with his family. Not long after unloading the news of his condition on Beth and Hailey, he'd rushed off to Nebraska then rushed back to New York and back to the case. Hell, he was unable to recall when he'd last held his wife and daughter. He was such an SOB for not considering their feelings.

Christ.

But he couldn't just sit at home, accept his death sentence and curl up. He needed to rage against it, rage against the pain and exhaustion he sometimes felt. He needed to see this case through. The fight was keeping him alive.

He answered Hailey:

Be home as soon as I can tonight.

They were now about two miles along the Van Wyck, when Dimarco ended his call and turned to Morrow.

"You okay, Frank?"

"Just a little jet-lagged from the flight."

"That was Moe Malloy at American Centurion. He's got his people on-site, ready and waiting."

"Good."

So far, the FBI had cleared Lester Ridley, a driver for the armored car company and an ex-serviceman. The search warrants had not revealed anything. In fact, his story that his family would help him with his personal debt had been verified.

But in the wake of the development with Erik Rytter, Morrow and Dimarco needed to reinterview Ridley and three other drivers with ex-military backgrounds, to determine if Rytter had any affiliation with American Centurion, or with any of its personnel through any military network or association.

Malloy had cleared a room for the two investigators who would talk to the guards one by one. Morrow flipped through the files. Ridley was up first, his attitude hardened by being in the crosshairs.

"Our apologies for putting your family through the wringer," Morrow said.

"You assholes don't care."

"Hey!" Dimarco said. "You lied to us and gave us reason to look at you. You could've been charged with obstruction in relation to four homicides. Want to swallow that and cooperate? Now, do you know this guy?"

Dimarco slid Ridley photos of Erik Rytter: a recent one on a slab in Nebraska, in profile, without showing the damage from the bullet; a close-up of Rytter's wrist with the cobra tattoo; and two others provided by German authorities.

Ridley shook his head.

"I never saw that guy or heard of him."

"The tattoo?"

"Nope. Just like I told you before."

Ridley had been with the U.S. Army Corps of Engineers, in Baghdad's Green Zone.

"We were trying to rebuild their country in the middle of a war and people were trying to kill us. I got in and got out. There was so much crap going on. I did my duty and came home. And that tattoo… Hell, everybody had tattoos." Ridley held out his arms, sleeved in them.

It was going to be a long day.

Dimarco got fresh coffee for Morrow and for himself. Next up was crew chief Cal Turner, aged thirty-six, who'd been with the 82nd Airborne.

"Is he the shooter?" Turner stared at the photos.

"That's what we want to determine."

Turner took a long look.

"I was in Afghanistan chasing the Taliban." He shook his head. "I knew a few German soldiers but not your guy there. He doesn't ring a bell. But out there, you never knew who the enemy was half the time."

"Tell us about contractors," Dimarco said.

"I never paid much attention to that," Turner said. "Sure, there was a lot of money to be made, but to me it's a death wish. Why would you sign on to that? Just for a few more bucks. I'll tell you something, the guys that did it had different DNA. They were wild, crazy, some of the best soldiers in the world. But if you got home intact, you've won. So why would you go back?"

Morrow got up and paced a bit while kneading the back of his neck until the door opened.

Lori Schneider, a driver, was next. The thirty-five-year-old mother of three boys had served with the U.S. Army's 507th Maintenance Company.

"I was a mechanic," she said. "I helped support Patriot antimissile batteries in Baghdad."

Schneider said that she didn't know Rytter or his tattoo, had never seen or heard of him until now.

"You really think he did it? He's one of them?" She gazed at his picture, her chin crumpling. "I was close to our guys, to Ross, Phil and Gary. Being dead is too good for this fucker, way too good."

"What about contractors?" Morrow asked. "Lori, what's your knowledge of them from your tour?"

"I just did my job." She shrugged. "I heard the stories, how they were always getting into trouble and were exempt from prosecution. Cowboys with guns. I just did my job and looked out for my team."

The day had passed in large chunks and Dimarco wanted more coffee. Dennis Hagler, a driver for American Centurion, was the last ex-soldier they needed to talk to. Hagler had been a sergeant with the First Battalion, 87th Infantry.

"Our squad had a lot of casualties—IEDs mostly— but when we tangled with insurgents near the Tajikistan border with Afghanistan, we wasted them. I saw a lot of guys blown to pieces, but I never questioned the mission. I understood why we put it all on the line to do what we had to do. I'm glad they got Bin Laden, wish I was there to pull the trigger."

"Does Rytter look familiar to you?" Dimarco asked Hagler. "Had you ever seen him around the depot or on any routes?"

Hagler scratched his chin then shook his head.

"No."

"Does his tattoo look familiar?"

Hagler shook his head.

"We understand Rytter worked in Afghanistan and Iraq as a contractor. What are your thoughts on this and what's happened?" Dimarco asked.

"Over there you heard rumors of some illegal stuff—Special Ops, Black Ops, creepy CIA ghost friends, that's about it. Just a lot of beer talk," Hagler said. "With Rytter, you think that the people who did this were ex-military looking for a big payday?"

"What do you think?" Morrow asked.

"Maybe. That's one theory."

"Got another?"

"Well, maybe they hit us for the cash to fund something?"

Morrow and Dimarco exchanged looks.

"Like what?"

"I don't know. It couldn't be for the Taliban or al-Qaeda, that's what the sheikhs are for. It would have to be something personal, maybe? I don't know, some cause or crusade." Hagler shook his head. "I could be wrong, it might be some ex-mercenaries looking for a big payday. Who knows."

It was midevening by the time Morrow pulled his car into the driveway of his home in Westchester County. His body felt as if his weight had doubled.

In the kitchen he made a chicken sandwich, which he ate with a glass of milk. Then he had a sliver of his wife's homemade apple pie. Beth was in the living room on the phone to her sister. She nodded that Hailey was upstairs. Morrow went to check on her, but heard the shower going. He went to his study and started reviewing files.

Rytter had given them a major break.

They needed to advance it.

He got an email from Art Stein about another appointment, then went back to his files, scouring them for anything he'd missed until his vision blurred, his eyes closed and he drifted off.

He was dreaming about an ocean beach, when he felt a butterfly caress on his cheek and woke to see his daughter.

"Hi, sweetheart."

"Dad." She knelt before him, her face a portrait of sadness. "Dad, how can I graduate, how can I go to college, get married, have kids, without you there?"

Morrow pulled her to him and she sobbed in his arms.

As he held her he realized he was still gripping the file for Donna Breen, Moe Malloy's cousin, who'd informed them about Gina Saldino. A light flickered in a corner of his mind, something that Breen had told him about Saldino.

That she had a boyfriend who had been in Pakistan or someplace like that.

Could he be ex-military?

Could he be Erik Rytter?

41

Gannon's 737 from Denver landed with a thud at La Guardia.

He took a cab directly to World Press Alliance headquarters.

As the car cut across Midtown Manhattan traffic, he consulted the checklist he'd started on the flight. His first priority was to learn all he could about Erik Rytter of Munich, the man FBI had identified as the dead suspect in Nebraska. Where did Rytter fit in with the heist, with American Centurion, with any part of the case? He'd search databases, records and archives. And although it might be prickly with some of them, he'd go back to all his sources for help.

Gene Bennett at the John Jay School of Criminal Justice was reluctant to talk to him, but Bennett had a line into the industry that reached inside American Centurion. He'd keep trying with him. Gannon would also sound out Brad West, with the New York State Police, and his wife, Anita, at Ramapo P.D.

It was 2:55 p.m., when he arrived at the WPA building.

In the elevator, he remembered Adell Clark.

He needed to thank her for tipping him off on Nebraska. Adell always came through. He'd go back to her, too, he thought as he hurried through the sixteenth-floor reception area. He had just made it to his desk and set down his bags when a news assistant trotted up to him.

"Hey, Jack, you're supposed to join the editors in the story meeting now. They're all in the conference room."

The midafternoon story conference was in progress. Nearly a dozen senior editors were at the polished table in the glass-walled room with its panoramic view of Madison Square Garden and the Empire State Building. When Gannon entered and took a seat, attention shifted to him as if he'd been the subject of conversation.

"Welcome back," Lisker said. "I was just telling Beland and everyone how we followed our hunch on that tip we had on the suspect out west."

"Our hunch?" The tip "we had." What? Did I fall down the rabbit hole? Lisker threatened to fire me and here he is taking credit—hell, stealing it—to cover his non-journalist ass. Look at him, attempting a smile as if smiling were the most unnatural thing for him.

A nod was all Gannon could manage.

"You knocked it out of the ballpark for us, Jack," Beland Stone, the WPA's executive editor, said. "A clean kill against our competitors. Your item from Nebraska was one of the finest examples of breaking-news feature writing I've seen in recent memory."

"Thanks."

"We got great pick-up," Stone said. "And it got stronger in Europe after we updated with the German aspects. We need to keep in front."

"We want you to continue being our lead reporter on the story," Lisker added, still through his stupid grin.

"This is an important story," Stone said. "We'll keep

hitting it from all angles. Where are the other suspects? Where's the money? What did they want it for? Are they tied to other heists? What links this Erik Rytter, an ex-German soldier, has to the heist? How did they know to grab him?"

Gannon nodded respectfully to what was obvious.

"We're putting everything we can on this story," said Carter O'Neill, who ran the WPA's domestic bureaus.

"All our bureaus in Germany are on it," said George Wilson, who was in charge of WPA's foreign bureaus. He leaned to a speaker. "Franz, can you update us?"

From Berlin, the voice of Franz Dalder, chief of the WPA's German bureaus, echoed through the speaker.

"Yes, as I was telling you, our sources with the German national police inform us that they are helping the FBI with information on Rytter. He was a former soldier and then worked as a contractor in Afghanistan and Iraq. We are trying to confirm if he worked for a private security firm subcontracted for Black Ops for the CIA."

"This adds a new dimension to the crime," O'Neill said. "Was the heist an operation to raise funds for a bigger attack? Remember, the 9/11 guys spent a lot of time in Germany."

"We will investigate all theories and work with Jack Gannon," Dalder said.

Margot Cooke, the WPA's features editor, leaned forward, tapping a pencil into the palm of her hand.

"Jack, we discussed this, you've reported that there's a key eyewitness. We should try to give readers an anatomy of the heist, take readers inside, put them in that truck stop, provide a portrait of how everyday life can change in a heartbeat."

Gannon nodded.

Having just stepped off an early-morning four-hour

flight across the continent, he had a lot to take in. When the meeting ended, he returned to his desk, grappling with a mix of fatigue, adrenaline and stress. He turned on his computer, took a breath and began sorting out what he needed to do.

Sources. Right. Sources.

He started by putting out calls, sending texts and emails to all his sources. Then he sifted through his messages, notes and files. Was he forgetting anything? Was he over-looking any aspect of the story? He could go home, but why bother?

Nothing was waiting for him there but the furniture. Besides, he'd never get a seat on the train. It was practically rush hour.

His line rang. The number was blocked.

"Jack Gannon, WPA."

"Hey there, so you're back from the great plain."

Recognizing the woman's voice, Gannon rolled his eyes and tightened his grip on the phone as if stepping into battle.

"Hello, Katrina."

"Congratulations on kicking everyone's ass on the story."

"What do you want?"

"Wow, you're cold."

"I'm sorry, how nice to hear your voice."

"Now, now, Jack. Come on, be nice."

"Why are you calling?"

"Well, I wanted to take you out to dinner."

"The last time we went to dinner, things didn't go so well."

"Come on, Jack, can't we be adults about things?"

"Why do you want to take me out to dinner?"

"Aren't we still friends?"

"What?"

"I thought we could talk."

"About what?"

"Look, I heard a couple of detectives paid you a visit, something about a crime scene in Yonkers, and I thought we could compare notes. You know, team up. I'll show you mine if you show me yours kinda thing?"

One bitter second ticked by, then another and another before Gannon cursed under his breath, shook his head and stared across the newsroom at nothing.

"I don't believe you," he said. "You're a real piece of work."

"What do you mean?"

"You want to pump me as if I was one of your sources. You're shameless, you know that. You'd probably sell your firstborn for a story."

"Hey!"

"Goodbye, Katrina."

Gannon thrust his face in his hands.

Katrina was getting close.

Those Yonkers cops who were pissed at him, what were their names? He searched his notes: Walsh and Mullen. Maybe they were her sources? Katrina could've called them, trolling for stories, and they tipped her to his work on Harlee Shaw?

One thing was certain: Katrina's call was a double-barreled blast of reality. She was sniffing around on Harlee Shaw's suicide, his mystery tip. She was breathing down his neck.

Jesus.

He rummaged through his files. He hadn't even fleshed out who Harlee Shaw was. Not so far. He'd failed to track down any friends or family members. Here it was; the file on what he had, mostly through military records. Shaw was former U.S. Army, 75th Ranger Regiment, who saw action in Iraq. The military-records guy Gannon had talked to was chatty and hinted that after Shaw left the army, he may have been a contractor in Afghanistan. Gannon couldn't confirm it.

Rytter was a contractor. What if Shaw was connected to Rytter? What if he knew about the heist and had been trying to tell Gannon about it? What if Katrina beat him on connecting the dots, confirmed everything and stole the story from him?

Stop this. You're driving yourself nuts. Do something.

All right, he'd call Shelly Konradisky, the super, and ask if she'd heard from relatives about holding a funeral, or clearing the apartment.

Gannon reached for his newsroom landline when it rang.

Another blocked number. Katrina? Or, maybe one of his sources?

He took in a long, exhausted breath.

"Jack Gannon, WPA."

A moment of silence, then Gannon said, "Hello, anybody there?"

"Sorry, are you the reporter who's writing stories on what happened at the truck stop in Ramapo, the murders and the robbery?"

He didn't recognize the caller's voice: female, New Yorker, maybe his age. He had a digital recorder wired to his phone; he switched it on and the tiny red recording light glowed.

"Yes."

"And you wrote this latest one, about the suspect they got in Nebraska, who is now dead?"

"Yes. Is that why you called?"

"No. I don't make these sorts of calls."

These sorts of calls?

The woman's tone, her underlying nervousness, she had his attention.

"Why don't you start by telling me your name and how I can help you?"

"I need to be anonymous."

"Why?"

"I'm sorry, but I don't want to give you my name. Not now. But I have to know that you protect sources."

"I do."

"Are you required to give anyone the name of your sources?"

"Usually a senior editor, but they're bound to protecting a source for our news organization, just like me. So why are you calling?"

"I need…" She paused to clear her throat then came back, her voice stronger. "I need to know a few things."

A red flag went up.

Careful, Gannon warned himself, he didn't know who was on the line, but sometimes criminals got calls into reporters to see what they knew, or what their police sources had told them, about the investigation into a crime. On this call, he wasn't sure.

"What do you need to know and why do you need to know it?"

"It's about the suspect they got in Nebraska."

"What about him?"

"Is he the killer?"

The killer? Gannon thought it was a strange question. Weren't all four suspects killers?

"What do you mean?"

"Is he the one who shot the FBI agent?"

Gannon held his breath at the way she'd asked—

no, hurled—the question, propelling it with such raw intensity, barely containing her emotions.

"Can you tell me if he's the one who killed Agent Dutton?"

Gannon's gut screamed that this woman was viscerally tied to the case. She was either the agent's widow, or someone else linked to the agent's death.

"I don't know for sure."

"But you have sources, good sources who know what's happening. You seem to know as much about this as the FBI. What do you think?"

Gannon assessed everything, then he asked a question.

"Do you know FBI agent Frank Morrow?"

A long moment passed.

"Yes."

There it is. This woman is involved somehow.

"Have you and I met?" he asked.

He heard the caller swallow hard before she answered.

"Indirectly."

"Are you the woman who witnessed the FBI agent's murder?"

Another agonized stretch of silence passed.

"Swear to me and to God that you protect sources," she said.

"I do."

She waited.

"I was next to him when it happened."

His pulse accelerated. *Don't lose her.*

"It must've been horrible for you."

"It was."

"Would you consider meeting with me, just meeting, so we could talk further, maybe help each other?"

Another long moment passed with Gannon watching time tick down on the newsroom clock.

"I'll consider it."

Gannon heard movement on the caller's end of the line. "Wait! Wait!"

The line went dead, leaving him to fear that he'd lost his chance with the witness. He tried working, but his mood darkened. It was not going well. None of his sources had responded and he wasn't getting anywhere.

After two hours, exhaustion was weighing on Gannon and he began gathering his things for the commute to his empty apartment in Washington Heights. He was thinking of grabbing a club sandwich at the Wyoming Diner before heading over to Penn Station, when his line rang.

"I called you a little while ago about Nebraska and protecting sources?"

"Yes, I remember. Will you meet with me?"

"If you agree to a few conditions, I'll meet you tomorrow afternoon."

"I'm listening."

"No interview, no recording, no cameras. We just talk."

"Agreed."

"You give me your word?"

"I give you my word."

"I'll call you tomorrow with the time and location."

42

San Francisco, California

At 2:45 a.m., Ivan Felk woke in his hotel bed.

He did not know why he had awakened until his secure satellite cell phone rang again.

The caller's number was blocked.

He answered, heard four seconds of static, then an automated message: "The N.G.N.R.M. has sent you an important communication."

Felk sat up.

Wide awake, he went to his laptop, logged on to his encrypted email account to find a new video attachment. He connected his headphones and turned up the volume. As it loaded, he braced for the worst.

The new footage was confusing. It focused first on another laptop screen, blurring as it sharpened to the online edition of the *New York Times*. The camera shook while zooming in on the date, confirming the recording had been made within the last twenty-four hours.

It then scanned headlines before locking on one that Felk already knew: Ramapo Heist Suspect Dies In Nebraska

The camera held the headline for several moments then

the laptop lowered to the head and shoulders of a hooded figure who spoke in clear, accented English.

"This new communiqué from the New Guardians of the National Revolutionary Movement amends the fate of the invading criminals who are guilty of crimes against humanity."

The camera panned to Felk's men all kneeling on a barren concrete floor. They were skeletal as a result of being underfed. Their full beards accentuated their hollow eyes. Several large men in hoods worked at positioning the hostages' hands behind their backs with flex-cuffs.

The hooded spokesman resumed.

"The news report shows us your recent failure and deteriorating ability to gather the funds necessary to pay the fine to spare the infidels from their execution."

The camera pulled in on a cinder block set between the legs of the first kneeling hostage. Two men set his hands on top of it.

"To inspire you to deliver the fine in full by the deadline, the court has authorized us to begin prosecution by removing—"

"Oh, Jesus," Felk said aloud in his quiet room as the captors spread the man's fingers so that one index finger was exposed on the cinder block.

"—a finger from each man now."

A large blade glinted, pressed down on the finger, swiftly crunched, as if cutting celery, severing it cleanly from the hand. Spurting blood cascaded over the cinder block as the man's screaming pierced Felk's ears.

"God, no. Damn it, no!"

The injured man's hand was wrapped in a towel, the finger held to the camera, then tossed out of frame. Off-camera dogs yelped and Felk shut his eyes to the horror. For the next thirty minutes, he endured the screaming as one by one each of his men lost a finger, including his brother, Clayton.

Felk shook with rage as tears rolled down his face.

"I swear we are coming to get you and we will waste the motherfuckers. I swear to God."

After it had ended, Felk sat on the side of his bed with his head in his hands until dawn broke over San Francisco. The entire time his thinking had been crystalline while hate-fueled adrenaline pulsated through him as if he were in a firefight.

He analyzed their situation.

The mutilations resulted from Rytter's arrest and death. Rytter's arrest must've arisen from information police possessed. What did they know? The press had reported early in the case that the FBI had a key eyewitness to the federal agent's shooting.

If it was true, that witness had to be the woman beside him.

She'd looked right at Felk, pleaded for her life.

Why did I hesitate? Why? Why? Why? Fuck, I don't know why.

It was a mistake to let her live.

What did she see?

Goddamnit.

By 5:00 a.m., Felk had summoned the others to a briefing in his room for 6:00 a.m. He showed them the grisly video, explaining its link to Rytter's arrest, which had to be linked to the witness.

"What did the FBI get from her?" Felk said. "What could they know?"

"How can we be sure it's her and not someone in our network who may have gone to the FBI for the reward?" Northcutt asked.

"Because anyone who knows anything of our mission

is involved," Felk said. "Everyone helping us has a connection to our men who are being held hostage. There's
no way in hell they would give us up."

"So what could this woman have seen?" Unger shook
his head. "We were so goddamn careful. We took shell
casings. We left nothing—no DNA, no debris. We took
out their security cameras."

"We were covered in racing suits," Northcutt said. "We
wore helmets with dark glass, gloves. Nobody could see
anything."

"How close was this woman to you?" Dillon asked Felk.

"Less than three feet, maybe two," Felk said. "She was
on her stomach, on the floor, right beside the agent."

"Why don't we reenact it and see if that helps?" Dillon
said.

"Okay, get the gear. Bring up my suit, gloves, helmet
to the room. We'll do this ASAP."

Within twenty minutes Dillon had returned with a large
sports bag. Felk stripped down to his T-shirt and boxers,
then got into the one-piece leather racing suit. He pulled
on his boots, strapped on his motorcycle helmet and tugged
on his gloves.

"Unger, you're the agent, get on the floor on your gut,
here," Felk directed him. "Northcutt, you're the witness,
get next to him here and turn your head like this.

"All right, I was standing like this and I put my gun
on his head like this." Felk slowly shaped the fingers of
his right hand into a gun and lowered it to Unger's head.
"Northcutt, your head is turned facing Unger's, so you're
watching the gun on him. What do you see?"

As Felk extended his gun hand, the cuff of his racing
suit slipped back.

"Freeze," Northcutt said, raising his hand to touch the

Red Cobra Team 9 tattoo wrapped around Felk's wrist. "I see your tattoo."

Felk raised his wrist to study it in disbelief.

"Fuck!" Felk said. The others looked at their own wrists as if they were passports to doom. Felk tore off his helmet, unzipped his suit, cursing under his breath. He shoved his gear in the bag, dressed, went to his laptop and started working.

"What are we going to do?" Dillon asked.

"Stay true to our mission," Felk said. "We've taken losses, but we're not going to abandon our people. We're handcuffed to the schedule of that armored car shipment to Oakland International. We've got to hang on for four days."

"But we're vulnerable, Ivan." Unger took uneasy inventory of the others.

"Don't you think I know that?" Felk said.

His anger rising, Felk rummaged through his other bag until he found Lisa Palmer's photo-ID employee card for Good Buy Supermart.

He held it up to the others.

"This bitch will not bring us down!"

43

Lisa.

That was the only personal information Gannon's caller had given him when she phoned him this morning.

She'd set their meeting for 4:30 p.m. at a McDonald's in the Rego Park area of Queens. Gannon's dashboard clock read 4:15 p.m. As he guided his Pontiac Vibe along Queens Boulevard, he estimated he was eight blocks away; glad to take Queens traffic over Manhattan's nightmare.

Nightmare.

He thought briefly of Katrina.

How did it go so wrong?

The fact she'd dumped him underscored the emptiness of his life. To hell with her, he thought as the golden arches came into view.

Concentrate on work.

He was onto something big here.

After parking and heading for the door, he checked out the news boxes on the street displaying the *Post,* the *Times* and *Daily News.* Each paper had a heist item on the front page. The story was still huge and Gannon could not afford to blow it. Sure, he'd gotten a few lucky breaks, but he'd invested a lot of sweat, too.

He'd worked it, no doubt about it.

As he stood in line for a small coffee, he hoped that "Lisa" wouldn't stand him up. He understood that she was nervous and that this was an audition of sorts for him. He'd done a few of these dances with sources in the past and usually they went well. Usually, he got the story.

But experience taught him to never, ever take anything for granted.

He found an empty booth and flipped through a copy of the *New York Daily News* that someone had left. Then he checked his BlackBerry for updates. There were snippets here and there but nothing major. Lisa, his witness, was the story right now.

In their last call he'd started describing himself before she'd stopped him. "I know what you look like and you know what I look like. We met at Ramapo when I was with Morrow."

Gannon kept a vigil on the after-school, after-work customers streaming into the restaurant. He studied the women who resembled Lisa before he spotted her entering the side door. She scanned the dining area and upon seeing him, she approached his table.

"Hi, I'm Lisa." She had a nice smile, pretty eyes.

"Jack Gannon." He stood, shook her hand.

"I'm sorry to have to meet here but we've got a lot on the go these days," Lisa said. "I'm so thirsty. I just need to get a drink, can I get you anything?"

"No, let me get it for you."

"You don't have to."

"Please, I need a fresh coffee. Have a seat. What would you like?"

"Okay, a small Diet Coke, thanks."

When Gannon returned with the drinks, it became clear to him by the warm casual way Lisa carried herself, without pretense, that this was her McDonald's, and he was a guest on her turf.

"Thanks for coming out to Queens," she said.

"Thanks for agreeing to talk to me."

"This is off the record, not for print, or whatever you guys say."

"Yes," he said. "So can you tell me a bit about yourself?"

Lisa glanced out the window then at her hands.

"My husband was killed two years ago. He was a mechanic. He stopped to help a stranger fix their car on the Grand Central Parkway when he was hit by a truck."

This added a new dimension.

"I'm so sorry."

Lisa's eyes shone. "It's been hard, but we take things day by day."

"I understand," Gannon said. "My parents died together in a car accident several years ago in Buffalo, where I grew up."

"That's sad," Lisa said.

"I take it you live in Queens?"

"Yes."

"Where do you work?"

"I'm a supermarket cashier."

Gannon smiled.

"My mother was a waitress much of her life."

As they talked he found a lot to like about Lisa, she was blue collar, working-class, just like him. They quickly grew comfortable with each other as Lisa told him how she'd grown up poor in Queens, forgoing college to work, getting married, having two kids and then facing her husband's sudden death. To Gannon, she was getting on with her life as a single parent with a kind of heroic dignity. After some twenty minutes, Gannon figured it was time to get down to business.

"So you witnessed the agent's murder?"

"Hold on. It's just like we agreed, you can't take notes and you can't report anything until I agree to an interview later. That's our deal."

"All right, that's our deal."

"Give me your word."

"I give you my word."

"The FBI would go nuts if they knew I was talking to you. But I'm a witness, not a criminal. I'm free to find out what I need to know."

"So what do you want from me?"

"Tell me about this case. You seem to have good sources. You seem to know everything."

"Not as much as the FBI. Wouldn't they keep you informed?"

"They're guarded. After I helped them on this case, after they got what they needed, they seemed to have forgotten about me."

"But they have victim witness programs."

"They've got a process for keeping witnesses and victims informed after an arrest has been made. They'll keep you updated on the status of a prosecution. But it's different with a live investigation."

Gannon nodded.

"They want it sealed so they can make arrests," he said.

"Is this guy they got in Nebraska, this Rytter, is he the one who killed the FBI agent?"

"Why is that important?"

"I was on the floor next to the agent when it happened. Some of his blood splattered on me."

"What?"

"Then the killer put his gun to my head. I begged for my life, he hesitated and one of the others pulled him away."

Images swirled before Gannon. He was on the brink of a powerful story.

"And you helped ID the killer for the FBI?"

"I'm their key witness."

"How? What did you see that identified him?"

Lisa shook her head.

"I don't think I should say."

She glanced at her watch, then toward the play area, as if she was here with someone else. Gannon sensed his time was running out.

"Didn't they put you in any kind of witness protection?" he asked.

"They offered, but their thinking was that since the killers did not know my identity, they wouldn't look for me, or any of the victims. The killers took all our cell phones and burned them. The FBI said they would flee the area, and what happened in Nebraska convinces me that they were right about that."

"So what happened immediately after the murders?"

"The FBI took me to a hotel and got a psychiatrist to help me with the trauma and to remember details of the agent's death."

"Did the psychiatrist hypnotize you or something?"

"Something like that. Then we had an FBI agent live with us in our home for a while, but we really didn't like it. Before all this we were preparing to move across the country, to get on with our lives after my husband's death. I had debts. I had to sell our cabin, our only asset. It's been complicated and stressful."

"I see."

"So it would give me peace of mind to know that the

bastard who killed the agent and almost killed me is dead. Can you help me with that?"

Gannon looked at Lisa.

"I'll work on it. But I need you to promise me exclusivity. I want to tell your story."

"You give me your word that you will keep me informed on everything. Then, once we know the FBI has this thing under control, I'll give you your interview. I'll tell you everything."

"Deal. How can I keep in touch with you?"

"I'll give you my new cell-phone number, but it might not work all the time."

"What do you mean?"

"Before this happened, I had just sold our cabin upstate. We're going up for one last visit to close it. The cell-phone service is not reliable up there and we don't have a land-line."

Lisa's attention shifted beyond Gannon to another part of the restaurant. She nodded to someone. Gannon turned to see a woman and two children coming to their table.

"Can we go now, Mom?" Ethan asked.

Smiling at Gannon, Lisa said, "This is my posse, Ethan and Taylor. And this is my friend Rita."

Gannon shook hands with everyone.

"I have a niece and I'm guessing she's about your age, Ethan."

"Cool. What school does she go to?" he asked.

"I'm not sure, she lives in Arizona."

"It doesn't snow there," Ethan said.

"Not too much."

"Does Santa still go if there's no snow?" Taylor asked.

"I'm pretty sure he does," Gannon said, noticing Ethan's pearl-handled penknife clipped to a small chain on his belt loop.

"I like your knife."

"My dad gave it to me as a present before he died."

"Oh, I see."

"My brother lives in Buffalo." Rita changed the subject for the kids. "I work with Lisa. Sorry, I looked you up on the internet, Jack. You used to write for the *Buffalo Sentinel*."

"That's right," Gannon said and smiled at Taylor. "We get a lot of snow in Buffalo."

"Do you have any kids, Jack?" Rita asked.

"No, no kids. I'm not married. Got a sister in Arizona and a niece."

"Time to go, Mom?" Taylor asked.

"Time to go," Lisa stood.

"Wait." Gannon fished out a business card with all of his contact information and gave it to Lisa. "This is how you can reach me, or get word to me. There's a toll-free number on there."

"Could I have one? I collect cards," Ethan asked.

"You collect sports cards." Rita laughed.

"Sure, buddy." Gannon stood and gave him one. "It might be worth something someday."

Gannon sat down.

Watching Lisa leave with her children and her friend, he shook his head at what had just transpired, recalling when he first saw her at the Ramapo truck stop office, with her head on the desk, reenacting the shooting.

Now, seeing her walk across the McDonald's parking lot, he was in awe of this young widow from Queens, who had just promised him an unbelievable story.

44

"I never saw her! I swear I never saw her!"

In the wake of the tragedy, the distraught driver of the B68 city bus had told police that he was northbound on Coney Island Avenue at Avenue Y when the woman appeared before him in the crosswalk.

"She was just there! She looked dazed. I couldn't stop!"

The impact had hurled the woman some forty feet in the air to the hood of a cab. Blood gushed from her and she barely had a pulse when paramedics arrived and took her to Coney Island Hospital.

En route, she opened her eyes and asked for a priest.

The woman's name was Gina Saldino.

Emergency staff first stabilized her then assessed her chances of surviving beyond twenty-four hours at less than ten percent. Gina was able to talk for short drug-hazed periods to Father Edwin Davis, the on-call priest who'd responded to her request. Once Davis understood what Gina was telling him, he'd summoned the two NYPD officers who were in the cafeteria completing paperwork on the incident. Gina Saldino was employed at American Centurion, the armored-car company.

"She says she has information about the heist," the priest said.

The development set in motion a series of urgent cell-phone calls, emails and texts pinballing across the NYPD and the FBI's New York Division.

Ninety minutes later, FBI special agent Frank Morrow and NYPD detective Al Dimarco arrived at Gina's bedside, along with an agent who set up a video recorder. Her face was a net of abrasions, contusions. Her lip was split, her left eye was patched. Along with Davis, a doctor and nurse were present to monitor Gina's vital signs as she struggled to unburden her conscience.

"My boyfriend is Tim Shepherd…ex-army…a private contractor for missions in Afghanistan…ghost work… Tim taken hostage with other soldiers for ransom…no government help…no one knows…secret mission was illegal…his friends showed me the video…horrible… going to decapitate him…they needed ransom money to save them…I gave them routes and schedules…to save them…his friends were going to take the money…American Centurion's insured…no one would get hurt…no one would die…I'm so sorry…"

Her monitors beeped. The doctor grew concerned as she floated on clouds of grogginess. This was Morrow's only chance and he pressed the doctor to let her continue.

"I took vacation," Gina said. "Hid in an old friend's apartment…Sheepshead Bay…tried to reach Raife…is Tim okay…? Raife didn't answer emails…what happened…? Raife…no answer…I'm sorry for the guards…I knew them, Phil, Ross and Gary…the FBI agent, his poor wife, ohm God…my fault…can't sleep…can't think…I walk and walk…my fault…"

"Who is Raife? Who did you give routes to, Gina?" Morrow asked. "Give us names."

"Rups. Raife." She coughed. "Upshaw."

"Who?"

"Raife Upshaw, his name is Raife Upshaw. Post office box in San Francisco."

Alarms on the equipment monitoring Gina's vital signs sounded as her condition worsened. The doctor and nurse took control, but things were looking bad. The alarms kept going.

The doctor shook his head.

Morrow and Dimarco left the room and immediately put out calls for information on Raife Upshaw.

Morrow alerted his squad to start the process for warrants on any postal box registered to Raife Upshaw in San Francisco, and for the immediate arrest of an individual known as Raife Upshaw for his role in the homicides of three guards and the assault on a federal officer.

This was a major break.

As Dimarco drove them over the Brooklyn Bridge back to 26 Federal Plaza in Lower Manhattan, Morrow continued working the phone. His team had already alerted the San Francisco FBI, the San Francisco Police Department and the California Attorney General's Office.

Morrow alerted his supervisor and reached out to the CIA, State and the Pentagon for help on an ex-U.S. soldier named Levon Upshaw working with private security teams contracted for operations in Afghanistan.

By the time Dimarco and Morrow reached the twenty-eighth floor, the FBI had a file on their target: Levon Raife Upshaw, aged forty-one, of the San Francisco suburb of San Mateo, California.

Upshaw had no criminal convictions, no arrests and no warrants. He had one five-year-old traffic offense for speeding, fifteen miles over the posted maximum.

Much of his work history was classified.

Upshaw studied engineering at Caltech but dropped out to join the Army Corps of Engineers, then became a member of Delta Force, eventually recruited into Task Force 88, joining one of the "hunter-killer" teams in the search for Bin Laden.

Then he left the army to take jobs with private security companies contracted to do high-priced work for governments around the globe.

"Put this guy on the same team as Erik Rytter and you get a sense that the crew behind our heist is our worst nightmare," Dimarco said.

Upshaw's California driver's-license picture stared back at Morrow from his computer monitor. All the warrants they needed were nearly done.

"We're gaining on them, Al," Morrow said before taking a call from his supervisor.

"Frank, this is Crawford. We need you on the next plane to San Francisco."

45

San Francisco Bay Area, California

The Upshaw home was in San Mateo's North Shoreview neighborhood between the Bayshore Freeway and San Francisco Bay.

The small three-bedroom bungalow sat far back from the street on a deep, narrow lot. Through his binoculars, the San Francisco FBI SWAT commander saw movement in the house.

It was suppertime.

The San Mateo Police and San Mateo County Sheriff's Office had set up the outer perimeter. They had choked off traffic into the area and quietly cleared residents of all surrounding homes from the potential line of fire. The faint drone of highway traffic on the 101 echoed off the sound wall, and an ominous hush fell over the area.

The FBI's SWAT team had taken positions around the house.

Given that the subject was wanted in connection with four homicides, including the death of an FBI agent, and given that the subject was ex-military, a firearms expert in possession of weapons, the team poised for a no-knock forced rapid entry.

The commander made final checks with the team leaders at the front and rear of the house.

All was good.

The commander said, "Go!"

Flash-bang grenades smashed through windows and heavily armed SWAT members in body armor charged through the front and back doors, shouting orders to: "GET ON THE FLOOR, NOW!" to the teenage girl, woman and man who were eating pizza.

"What the hell is this?" the man protested while on his stomach, as his hands were cuffed behind him.

After his sobbing wife and daughter were removed from the house, unharmed, he confirmed he was Raife Upshaw.

The SWAT team sat him at the kitchen table.

The smoke cleared, the chaos gave way to calm. Several agents in FBI windbreakers entered the house and began searching it while other agents entered the kitchen. Frank Morrow sat down across from Upshaw, placed warrants on the table and read him his rights.

"You'll see in the warrant, Raife, we have you for being an accessory to the murders in New York. You might as well have pulled the trigger."

An agent standing behind Upshaw, who'd inspected the former soldier's tattoos, shook his head at Morrow, indicating no cobra tattoo on his wrists.

Unknown to Morrow, to the FBI, to just about anyone, Upshaw had endured many trials over his years as a soldier hunting terrorists. Once, he'd been captured and tortured by the Taliban. He was held for nine days before he escaped by killing three of his captors with his bare hands, nearly tearing the head clean off one of them.

The FBI, with their team jackets, cologne and spearmint breath, were an annoyance because Upshaw had no option to kill them. He exercised his right to remain silent with cold-blooded intensity.

This was an affront to Morrow and all that he stood for.

Since he'd looked upon the corpses of Phil Mendoza, Gary Horvath, Ross Trask and Agent Greg Dutton on the floor of Freedom Freeway Service Center, Morrow was consumed with one ambition: to find their killers.

Lisa Palmer's eyewitness account gave Morrow a break, Rytter's arrest in Nebraska got him closer and Gina Saldino's deathbed confession got him here, at the burning edge of the truth.

As far as Morrow was concerned, his life and his death were linked to the men who died in Ramapo and the men behind the killings.

His supreme duty was to see justice done and put it all to rest.

Now that he was this close, he would not relent.

Morrow found a framed family photograph and set it on the table before Upshaw.

"Think of them, Raife. If you cooperate and tell us how we can find the others, we'll take it into consideration."

Upshaw said nothing.

Morrow leaned into his space.

"Do you want to sleep in a cell tonight?"

Upshaw said nothing.

"This is not about loyalty. Somebody already gave you up, Raife. That's what brought this party to your home," Morrow said. "Eventually, you'll be identified to the world as 'one of the plotters against America' in the armored-car heist. You'll be helpless in a cell while reporters and patriots hound your wife and your daughter. Your husband's a traitor. Your daddy's a terrorist."

Morrow let out a long sigh.

"And the fact you put your life on the line for this

nation, risked it all in some backwater shit hole chasing the enemies of America, will be flushed away, Raife."

Not far off they heard a computer printer. An agent brought Morrow several articles from New York newspapers about the heist in Ramapo and Rytter's arrest. Morrow scanned the articles and placed them before Upshaw.

"Interesting you would have these on your computer, Raife." Morrow scratched his chin. "I'm sure we'll find all kinds of enlightening evidence once our cyberpeople take it apart, along with every aspect of your life."

Upshaw said nothing.

He never asked for a lawyer, he barely reacted. For nearly two hours Morrow carried on what amounted to a monologue.

Then Upshaw said, "I want immunity."

"We'll need your information to determine if that is even possible."

"I want immunity."

"Give us the information and we'll raise immunity with the U.S. Attorney's Office."

"I had no part in the heist."

"And you can prove this?"

"I will prove I was in California when it happened."

"Did you plot it?"

"No."

"Don't lie to us, Raife."

"I had no part in it."

"Gina Saldino says otherwise."

"Gina who? Never heard of her."

"She sent you schedules and routes for American Centurion."

Upshaw shook his head.

"You have a post office box in San Francisco."

"That's not against the law."

"She mailed you information about routes and schedules. Who did you give the routes to, Raife?"

"That never happened."

"Who are the players?"

"I don't know."

"Don't take me in circles, Raife."

"I don't know."

"That isn't much of a case for immunity, Raife. We are
going to go through your phone records, computer records,
bank records, everything in your life that touches you.
Your balls are in a vise and I'm going to tighten it. You're
going to hear them pop, Raife."

"All I did was secure a self-storage locker. I don't know
why or for whom. A friend of a friend asked me to do a
favor—that's it."

"Where? Where is this locker?"

"In Daly City, JBD Mini-Storage, unit ninety."

For the next thirty minutes Morrow tried to extract
more information from Upshaw.

It was futile.

The FBI took Upshaw into custody and released his
wife and daughter.

"We'll see how your information plays out, Raife."

Investigators then moved swiftly to obtain and execute
warrants on JBD Mini-Storage, unit ninety, where they
seized a cache of motorcycles, M9 Beretta pistols, M4
carbines, clothing, wiring, hardware. When they found
the C4, they called the bomb squad.

The storage facility's security camera provided images
of four men and a California license plate of a van backed
to the unit. The plate showed the van was rented at San
Francisco International Airport by a Devon Farrell of
Toronto. The Ontario driver's license copied at the rental
agency for Devon Farrell was counterfeit. Further checks

showed a Devon Farrell was a guest at the Hyatt Regency San Francisco on the Embarcadero waterfront.

"That's across the street from the Federal Reserve Bank," Morrow said as his squad headed to the hotel. "What are the odds they were setting up to hit one of the trucks there?"

Unlike with Upshaw, the FBI needed to make a swift low-key takedown without SWAT. Showing warrants and badges got the attention and cooperation of the hotel's management who let Morrow and several agents wait in Farrell's room. Two SFPD detectives were strategically positioned down the hall. They'd waited about two hours when Morrow got a heads-up over his radio seconds before the locked clicked.

In a heartbeat, two agents seized Farrell, got him to the floor, handcuffed him then positioned him on the king-size bed.

Morrow held up his FBI ID and proceeded to read Farrell his rights.

"You're under arrest. You have the right to remain silent…"

Farrell didn't speak as his fingerprints were rolled on the window of a portable scanner and processed.

"Tell us about that tattoo around your wrist." Morrow held up a copy of the sketch from Lisa Palmer's description. "Looks just like this one."

Farrell said nothing while agents searched his room. It didn't take long before the prints confirmed Farrell was Lee Mitchell Dillon; age, twenty-six, of Toronto, Ontario, Canada.

The Royal Canadian Mounted Police provided more background on Dillon. "What a surprise," Morrow said, reading the information on his phone. "You've seen action in Afghanistan with the Canadian Forces Joint Task

Force 2. I bet you know Erik Rytter. Things didn't end well for him."

Dillon said nothing.

"Where are your other friends, Lee?" Morrow asked. "Are they in this hotel?"

Morrow's attention moved from Dillon to the hotel phone-message pad an agent held up between the fingers of his latex-gloved right hand. Morrow stepped closer, reading notations beside the names Unger, Ian and Ivan.

"Would these be the room numbers of your friends, Lee?"

Morrow raised his walkie-talkie.

The cable car for the California Street line stopped in front of the Hyatt.

As Ivan Felk walked around it toward the hotel's entrance, he grew concerned. Among the taxis, shuttles and parked cars in the circular driveway were four sedans that bore rear dash-mounted emergency lights—the hallmark of unmarked police cars.

What's going on?

The lights weren't activated, no one was in the cars, but muted police cross talk spilled from the open windows. Felk tried to decipher the coded chatter without being obvious, but the radios were too low.

Wary, he entered the hotel, reviewing the team's last steps for risk factors. They'd drilled in the morning, rechecked the armored-car route then met at the Plaza across from the Ferry Building to go over the mission again. Then they parted, intending to meet up at the hotel bar about now.

The guys should be in their rooms, or arriving, Felk thought as the escalator delivered him to the mammoth lobby. He looked for any connection to the units out front but saw nothing at the registration desk, nothing at the reception area and nothing by the bar.

Felk joined the throng of tourists waiting at the elevators. Judging by the accents of the conversations, they were likely a charter group from Europe. The chime sounded, doors opened and he squeezed into the next elevator car.

Most of the people joining him inside were silver- and white-haired travelers, excited at having just returned from Napa. Except for the man in front to his left, who was subdued. He was about Felk's age, the same height with a solid build and an earpiece in his right ear. Felk figured him for a tourist on an audio-guided walking tour, but after deeper assessment of the man's haircut, his jacket with an ever-so-small bulge consistent with a shoulder holster, Felk pegged him for what he was.

A cop.

The doors closed and the glass-capsule elevator car rose. Floor by floor the open-terraced balconies that ringed the massive soaring seventeen-story lobby sailed by. A tinny transmission leaked from the cop's earpiece, just loud enough for Felk to hear because of his proximity.

"...they got our guy in room 1640 and we've got to..."

Felk's eyes widened slightly.

That's Dillon's room near the top floor.

"On my way," the cop said softly into the walkie-talkie wired to his earpiece.

Felk swallowed. *What the hell—they got Dillon?*

Every instinct told him police were here to take them down.

They're moving on us right now.

As the elevator slowed for its first stop, Felk saw clear across the expanse to the lobby's distant far side at the moment— *Damn, that's Northcutt walking to his room.*

Felk calmly excused himself around the cop to get off

on the seventh floor with two giggling seniors. The cop stayed in the elevator. Felk went to the balcony and focused on Northcutt, who was one floor below and half a football field across from him.

He could not risk shouting a warning and it was too far to run.

Felk took out his encrypted cell phone and called Northcutt's phone. Northcutt was ten paces from his door when his phone rang. *Come on.* He saw Northcutt answer while fishing out his room key.

"Yes," Northcutt said as he inserted the plastic key into the lock.

"Do not go in!"

"What?" Northcutt pushed the door.

"It's me. Step away from your door—"

Too late.

Northcutt stepped into the room. As the door started closing behind him, Felk saw shadows move, then, through the phone, he heard Northcutt's shout drowned out by desperate scuffling.

Everything went quiet.

But Felk's connection to Northcutt's phone remained live. He heard breathing for one moment, two, three, four—*damn*—then Felk shut his phone off. And even though his was untraceable, he removed the battery to kill any chance of tracking his signal.

Shit! Fuck! Christ!

All the saliva evaporated from his mouth like he was in a firefight. They were under attack and they were losing.

Fuck!

Felk dragged the back of his hand across his mouth. *Don't go to your room! Get out, now!* He had his laptop in his satchel, passports, cash and credit cards, nothing in his room but clothes, toiletries, fucking fingerprints and fucking DNA.

Fuck!

He got back on the elevator and descended to the lobby, went to a public phone and called Unger.

"Hello?"

"Where are you?"

"About a block away from the hotel."

"Don't go to your room!"

"What's up?"

"DO NOT GO TO YOUR ROOM!"

"Okay, what's going on?"

"Enact the withdrawal plan now!"

Some ninety minutes later, Felk and Unger were at a sandwich shop table near gate five, in the post-security area of Oakland International Airport's terminal one.

Felk's concentration was welded to his laptop's screen and keyboard as he worked. Unger pretended to read the copy of *USA TODAY* that was concealing his face. In fact, he was scanning the area for threats.

Earlier, Unger had nearly lost his breakfast as they passed through security. He'd made a comment about lost luggage when the security officer asked about his all-but-empty new travel bag and new toiletries. Unger had kept the sleeves on his denim shirt buttoned to the cuff and struggled to remain calm, but his stomach had spasmed.

They'd made it through. They were lucky—*this time*.

Every move was a high-stakes risk now. Sooner or later the FBI would identify them. Sooner or later their pictures would be everywhere. They'd have to run forever. The mission was falling to pieces.

"You haven't answered me. What are we supposed to do now, Ivan?" Unger kept his voice low. "They got Rytter,

Dillon and Northcutt. It's only a matter of time before they get us. It's over, done. Finished."

Felk's nostrils flared as he worked. He was consumed with rage so intense it blinded him to all reason. Even the logic he understood was overtaken by the bile and vengeance coursing through him. It shot from the images that assailed him—images of Clay and the icy water, his mother's funeral, his father's suicide, the degradation of his men, the video of dismemberment, the threat to behead his brother.

Nothing could save them now.

It all came back to the witness.

It had to be because of her—no, *it* was *because of her.*

Their sacrifice, their blood, all their rescue work destroyed because of this fucking supermarket clerk.

Lisa Palmer's New York State driver's-license photo stared back at Felk. He'd contacted intelligence sources who'd provided him with her home address in Queens.

Felk turned the laptop for Unger to see.

"This is our target," Felk said. "She will suffer beyond comprehension for what she's brought down on us."

"What? Are you crazy?"

"She's an enemy combatant."

"What are you talking about, Ivan? I thought we were going to disappear."

"I need you for one last mission."

Unger's eyes filled with fear and the realization that Felk was losing his sanity, just as a boarding call for their United flight was announced.

Direct to La Guardia in Queens, New York.

Like Dillon, Ian Northcutt had been identified through his fingerprints.

Northcutt, like Dillon, had the cobra tattoo around his wrist.

And like Dillon, Northcutt had refused to speak to Morrow.

Upon searching Northcutt's room and trash, agents found notes about the Federal Reserve Bank. Morrow noticed in the case files that a snapshot obtained by German police of Erik Rytter showed him in combat fatigues with his arm around Northcutt, against a scenic mountain range.

Morrow's team and a second team with the San Francisco police waited in hotel rooms for the two other men.

All they had were aliases, no photos, no IDs. The San Francisco FBI's Evidence Response Team was standing by for the warrants needed to collect fingerprints and DNA from the toiletries. Other investigators tried tracking credit card and phone records for the rooms and the names used by the guests, which were aliases.

Hours passed without either of the two men showing.

During the whole time, Dillon and Northcutt never voiced a single word.

"These cobra guys are bound to their code," Morrow told NYPD detective Al Dimarco later over the phone. "It looks like they were going to hit the Federal Reserve Bank across the street. They had enough firepower to make it a military operation. At least we stopped that and we got three of them."

We're tightening the noose.

Morrow, standing at a window in the FBI's San Francisco office, ran a hand across his face as he took in the city's skyline.

But we still have two unknown killers at large.

46

Hours later, across the country from where Upshaw, Dillon and Northcutt had been arrested, a rented Chevy Tahoe SUV rolled through Lisa Palmer's sleeping neighborhood at 1:46 a.m.

"There it is. Eighty-seven, eighty-seven," Felk said. "Take it slow."

They crept by a two-story wood-framed house with a Ford Focus in the driveway. The front yard had a waist-high steel fence displaying a small sign for Vital Guardstop Security Systems.

"Take the next left—" Felk opened his laptop "—and go for five or six blocks before circling back."

Unger was uneasy as he drove.

According to the information they'd obtained, Lisa Palmer was thirty-one, widowed, two small children, worked as a supermarket cashier.

She was the FBI's key witness, Felk was certain. He was the only one who'd seen her face up close.

This was insane, Unger thought as he guided them through the edges of Rego Park.

So much was at stake. They hadn't even done a basic

recon of the place. They had no idea how well it was secured, or if there were patrols. It might be under surveillance. Hell, she could have cops in her house with her as
part of some kind of witness protection. Unger was deeply
committed to Felk, the team and the mission, but this was
nuts. The mission was over.

"Okay, take us back to the house," Felk said. "I need to
work on the security system."

"Why are we doing this?" Unger said.

"She's the enemy. I told you."

"I think we should forget it."

"She has to pay—this is retribution."

"Maybe you're beating yourself up for not removing
her at the start. Maybe you're taking this witness thing
too personally."

Felk stared at him.

"What did you say?"

"This does not help us."

"What the hell's wrong with you?" Felk dragged his
hands over his face. "This bitch should not be alive! We've
lost this whole fucking operation because of her—*our
people will die because of her!* And you think we should
just walk away?"

"We have to accept what's happened."

"I do. We're at war and she needs to suffer, like our
people have suffered. She has to pay for what she did."

"But this is a suicide mission."

"Our lives have been a suicide mission, Nate! Shut the
fuck up and pull up to her goddamn house now! That's an
order!"

Unger moved the SUV near the house.

While Felk changed into dark coveralls and boots with
covers, Unger eyeballed parked cars lining the street for
any telltale sign of a police car. Then Felk concentrated

on his laptop. He used techniques he'd learned from intelligence experts to disable Palmer's home security system. He searched for Palmer's home wireless network; they'd named it "Palmer4" and it displayed on his laptop. He used a CIA program he'd obtained from a friend that was able to decrypt their password and bypass her internet security walls. Palmer's home security system had a base station connected to Palmer's landline. The keypads, motion detectors and sensors on the doors and windows were all linked via wireless. The security company was remotely monitoring the system 24/7 through Palmer's landline, but Felk disabled the wireless sensors and detectors without triggering any alarms on the company's master console.

"Done."

Felk opened the equipment bag he'd picked up earlier from a military friend in Brooklyn. Felk slipped on a small wireless headset that was linked to a walkie-talkie. Unger slipped on a headset as well, then adjusted the digital emergency scanner that was monitoring police radio chatter in the area.

"Test one, two, three." Felk tested their communication system.

"All good. Loud and clear," Unger said.

Felk slid a bone-handled hunting knife with a ten-inch blade into his pocket, tugged on latex gloves.

"You listen for police and keep me posted. This won't take long." Felk got out and headed to the house. He took a few steps, then, like a cat, slipped into the darkened backyard.

He went to a rear basement window and carefully removed the exterior exhaust vent for the dryer. He reached inside and using a small mirror and penlight, unlatched the window with surgical smoothness.

"Okay, I'm in the basement," he whispered into his headset to Unger.

"All clear out here."

Felk slipped on a small headlamp and moved toward the stairs, constantly checking his surroundings with each step, pausing to listen for any movement in the house.

Quickly and soundlessly he searched the basement, then headed for the stairs to the main floor. He was careful to place his foot on the part of the wooden stair secured to the side, which reduced creaking.

In silence he ascended to the small hall landing area near the back door. His light found small sneakers, jackets, caps, school backpacks then a corkboard with a calendar, dates marked; some sort of drawing.

Moving on to the kitchen he detected traces of pepperoni and onion in the air. An empty pizza take-out box was set on a counter, near a rubber trash bin and recycle tub, all staged as if they were to go out in the morning.

On the counter next to car keys and a second key ring, he saw a hand-written to-do list and he studied it. They were leaving in the morning. Where? Thinking, he stepped back to the corkboard and the calendar. Tomorrow's date was marked "We go to the cabin." Felk realized the drawing next to it was a map from Queens to a lake in upstate New York.

Felk considered it before moving on.

Outside, Unger glimpsed curtains moving in the darkened second-story window of a house several doors down.

A man with a phone in his hand searching the street?

"Felk?" Unger whispered. "I think we're being watched by a neighbor. Step it up."

"Roger," Felk whispered.

He moved with care throughout the main floor. It was

neat and empty. Scrutinizing the small office area, his interest went to a file. Flipping through it, he recognized real estate papers, a Post-it note with contact numbers, names, an agent's business card and one for Jack Gannon, a national reporter with the World Press Alliance in Manhattan.

Felk cursed to himself.

He waited until his heart rate leveled then went to the stairway, relieved the stairs to the bedrooms were carpeted. Again, he took pains to place his foot at the side of each step to minimize creaking.

He killed his headlamp when he reached the top.

By his count there would be three people sleeping on this level.

Slowly he reached for his knife.

The nearest bedroom door was open. He controlled his breathing as he inched toward it. He could start with the woman, slip in, hand over her mouth, tell her who he was and why she was going to die just before he plunged the blade into her throat, up to the hilt, just as he did at the militia camp in the mountains.

Killed six of them in their sleep.

Never knew what hit them.

Felk stood at the darkened doorway and let his eyes adjust to inventory the bedroom. The figure in the bed was large enough to be an adult. Steady breathing.

It had to be her.

Felk tightened his grip on his knife, feeling his rage swirling. As he prepared to step toward the bed, a watery explosion sounded.

A toilet had just been flushed.

He'd missed the line of light under a door—a bathroom door.

With nowhere to hide, Felk retreated to the stairs, descended a few, his eyes at floor level. Bright light flooded the hall and a small girl in a pink T-shirt left the bathroom, shut off the light and padded right in front of Felk.

Outside, Unger's eyes locked on a marked NYPD unit cutting slowly across the intersection half a block from his SUV.

"Jesus!"

In the house, a woman's groggy voice called from the bedroom Felk had wanted to enter.

"Taylor, is that you, hon?"

The girl turned and went to the bedroom.

"Yes."

"You feeling okay?"

"I just had to pee and I think my tummy's a little sick from the pizza, too many pepperonis."

"Get in bed with me, sweetie, and get some rest for our drive in the morning."

Felk reassessed.

He'd give it fifteen minutes for them to fall asleep, then do them both, then the second kid.

Unger's pulse soared.

A second NYPD car rolled down the street, side searchlights raking over the houses.

"Abort, Felk! Police out front!" Unger whispered, slouching down in the rental.

He held his breath and didn't move as light shot through the SUV accompanied by faint police radio traffic as the patrol car passed.

The neighbor must've called.

Far down the street Unger saw uniformed officers,

flashlights sweeping, going house to house, checking front and back doors.

"Abort now! Abort now! Meet me at the rendezvous point."

Once it was clear, Unger reached under the instrument panel, disconnected his lights, started his rental and drove off without being seen. He drove about a quarter mile to a Mobil gas station.

Unger had quit smoking in high school, but went inside and bought a pack of Lucky Strike. Outside, he reconnected the lights. Then he lit a cigarette and drew on it while waiting for Felk. He hated the taste, got out, crushed it under his foot. Then he went back inside and got a Coke and some gum.

Felk was leaning against the car, waiting for him.

"Did you do it?"

"No, I've got a better plan. We're going to need a few things."

Felk showed Unger the picture of the map on the corkboard he'd taken with his cell phone before he left.

"We'll do it there tomorrow. The bitch and her pups will suffer a long, slow agonizing death."

47

Gannon arrived at the WPA newsroom about 1:15 p.m.

This was his day off, but he couldn't let go of the story. Not when he was about to deliver Lisa's eyewitness account.

It would be an emotional powder keg, he thought, stopping off at the editorial post office boxes. WPA reporters still got snail mail, mostly from businesses selling something, or groups seeking coverage, or kooks ranting. Today, Gannon found three pieces of junk mail and a small padded envelope waiting in his slot.

The return address, scrawled in block letters in blue felt-tip pen, hit him like a bullet:

Harlee Shaw. #1021 Oceanic Towers. Yonkers.

The envelope was plastered with stamps of U.S. Marines raising the flag at Iwo Jima. There was no zip code for the WPA—it had been added in ballpoint pen. He tore it open, nothing inside but a memory card about the size of a stick of chewing gum. He went to his desk, fired up his computer and inserted the card. He plugged in his earphones, cranked up the volume.

The card contained a single item: a video labeled Classified.

Gannon glanced around for privacy then clicked on it. The video opened with a man in his thirties sitting alone talking to the camera.

"If you're seeing this, then I'm dead. I came to you because I followed your stories with the World Press Alliance. You do good work, and after we talked on the phone I figured you for being someone I could trust.

"I never meant for things to happen the way they did. I'm so sorry. I'm very messed up. My name is Harlee Edward Shaw. Sometimes they call me Sparks. I grew up in Hoboken, New Jersey. I enlisted in the U.S. Army and was with the 75th Ranger Regiment. I saw action in Iraq and Afghanistan. After three tours, I left the army to work for private security companies contracted for covert ops.

"Nearly six months ago our last mission was a horrible failure. Our team was sacrificed for an illegal 'ghost' operation. This is our story."

The video cut to a jerky night-vision montage from a helmet-cam point of view, showing footage of members of a military unit jumping from a plane at night, parachuting into rugged terrain.

The video cut to soldiers on foot patrol at night, moving quickly at the edge of a settlement. Shaw's off-camera voice mixed with the breathless voices and sounds of the footage.

"We're now in a denied zone between Afghanistan and Pakistan. We're here to support local friendlies by removing several hostile leaders aligned with al-Qaeda."

Suddenly the camera shakes as the video flares with orange flashes and deafening earth-shattering explosions. Tracers rip through the night, inches from the camera, *twanging-whizzing-plunking* mixes with shouting, cursing and screaming.

"We've been ambushed!"

Shaw gets down, digs in with his buddies. They return fire, fighting back as explosion after explosion tears up the world around Shaw. A hot, muddied clump lands on his lap, the camera turns to—a human face—there is only the face—eyes open wide, mouth an O of surprise.

The mouth is moving, gasping!

Shaw screams

"Billy! Oh, God, Billy!"

Shaw's agony overtakes the fury of battle.

The video cuts to dawn and Shaw narrates.

"Billy's gone, Kleat's gone and Big John. They're all gone. The enemy outnumbered us. They overran us in the night. Six survivors of the squad retreated to a new position. Three of our men were killed; six of our team were captured. From our location we could see the enemy celebrating their victory by desecrating the corpses of our fallen men. It went on for days."

The video jumps to a long grainy shot of three bodies hanging from a bridge, then dragged naked through a public square while laughing children followed. Townspeople urinated on the corpses, then they were dismembered; village dogs carried off body parts, others were burned.

"We wanted to get our six men out. Through surveillance we determined their location and launched a night-rescue attempt. Again, we came under heavy fire, were repelled. Luckily we took no casualities and retreated. We had no support. Promised support never showed. We realized we were set up, sacrificed. So we began a long hike from the zone to the nearest coalition outpost. We wanted to regroup and rescue our men. Along the way we met an international aid group that agreed to serve as our go-between with the insurgents and the local clan leaders.

"Eventually, word came back to us that our men were being held by assholes calling themselves the New

Guardians of the National Revolutionary Movement. They said our guys had been tried and found guilty of crimes against humanity and had been sentenced to beheading unless we paid a twelve-million-dollar fine. Now, as I make this video, the deadline to pay is nearly upon us.

"When we turned to our contractors to reach out to coalition governments for help, we were warned that we had most likely 'committed unsanctioned acts of war,' and that we were contractually bound to silence, and disclosure of any information would lead to our prosecution. This thing never happened, they told us—which meant our men had been left to die.

"This was a betrayal. It was unacceptable to us. We took action. We quietly reached out to our friends for support and launched Operation Retribution. Our objective was to take strategic military steps against the powers who sacrificed us, to obtain the ransom and save our men."

The video cut back to Harlee Shaw in his Yonkers apartment and panned the newspaper reports on the four killings in the Ramapo heist.

"But I could not go through with it. It was meant to be bloodless, but I knew people would die. Too much was at stake. I backed out. I'm so sorry, for deserting my people, for everything that happened the way it did, for the guards, the agent. I don't know what's going to happen to our guys overseas or even if they're still alive. God help them and God help me. All I can see is Billy's face on my lap—he haunts me.

"Mr. Gannon, I leave it all with you now.

"Goodbye."

The video ended.

Gannon cupped his hands over his face. This was unbelievable. How would he approach the story now? He had to report this. But there were complications.

He took stock of the newsroom.

He'd have to go to the senior editors. They'd likely have to call the WPA's lawyers. All right, before he went to the brass, Gannon looked at the memory card, then back at his monitor. He immediately duplicated the video and emailed a copy to his private online account.

The instant he finished, his landline rang.

"Jack Gannon, WPA."

"Hi, it's Lisa, from the other day."

"Lisa. I thought you were out of town."

"We're north of Albany at a little place call Hudson Falls, on our way to our cabin," she said. "I'm ready to give you the interview tomorrow, so why don't you come up tonight. I've got your card. I'll text you directions before my phone goes out of service. It's about a four-hour drive. There's a good motel you can stay at. We can talk in the morning."

"Great, I'll leave this evening. But why the sudden change?"

"I thought it would be good for me now, you know."

"No."

"Well, since they got the other three guys in San Francisco."

"What?"

"I just heard it on the radio news. I figured you knew?"

Gannon looked around then went online. His news alert had been turned off. He typed a few commands and there it was—*damn*—the Associated Press had just moved a story quoting law enforcement sources in San Francisco stating that three people had been arrested in the Bay Area in connection with the murders of three guards and an FBI agent during a 6.3-million-dollar armored car heist in New York. The arrests followed the death of another suspect, Erik Rytter, a German national with a military background who was fatally wounded struggling for a state trooper's gun after a traffic stop in Nebraska.

"I just got it now."

"That makes four," Lisa said. "That means they got all of them. That was our deal, so I'll tell you my story in the morning."

Gannon spotted Lisker across the newsroom, storming his way.

"Yes, send me the directions," Gannon told Lisa. "I'll be there tonight. Wait! Is there any contact number or email for you? Didn't you say something about poor phone or internet service?"

"There's none in the area where our cabin is. We can meet at the motel café. I'll put the time and stuff in my directions."

"Gannon!" Lisker shouted. "Conference room! Now!"

Hal Ford, Carter O'Neill, George Wilson, Margot Cooke and Lisker had gathered at one end of the table, huddled around the teleconference speakerphone.

"How did we get skunked by the Associated Press?" O'Neill asked. "Gannon, did you have any inkling of this?"

"No, nothing."

"How the hell did we get such a butt-whooping?" O'Neill asked.

"They've got good sources in the Bay Area, Carter," the voice of Jasmine Lane, the WPA's San Francisco bureau chief, crackled over the speaker. "They're strong here, but we're chasing it."

"We break news, not learn it from competitors," O'Neill said.

"Jasmine, do you want us to send Gannon out to help?" Lisker said.

Gannon objected and was shaking his head.

"No, let us work on it," Lane said. "We'll match it and advance it."

"Jasmine, this is Jack. I've got calls into my sources. I'll send anything I pick up. I also have a couple of breaking elements that I need to discuss with everyone here."

"Thanks, Jack. Any help will be appreciated," Lane said.

Margot Cooke, the WPA's news features editor, said, "With four suspects arrested, it sounds to me that the FBI may have them all now."

"Looks that way," Ford said.

"So," Cooke continued, "if it's winding down, we're going to want to get into the anatomy of the heist. Jack, can you draft something for us?"

"Yes, but first, there's something you have to see."

Gannon quickly explained to the editors who Harlee Shaw was, his connection to him and Shaw's suicide. Lisker pursed his lips but said nothing as Gannon then inserted the memory card in the conference room laptop and played Shaw's video. As it ran, a few jaws dropped and a few heads shook. Afterward, the editors started into a debate on what to do.

Didn't the WPA have an obligation to tell the FBI it had received this video? Was it not a case of domestic terrorism? But was it the role of the WPA to be a police informant? Didn't journalists have a duty to be mindful of national security? Didn't the WPA have a moral right to find out who the hostages were and alert their families? What impact would this video have in the investigation? Would reporting it have an impact on the lives of the hostages? Did the FBI know? Was the video authentic? How could they confirm it? What if the FBI was planning a news conference to say it had cleared the case with these latest arrests? What if the FBI released details of the heist and stole the WPA's thunder?

Gannon then compounded matters when he revealed his developing exclusive with Lisa, the eyewitness.

"Here's what I think," he said. "We have a chance to put this all together," Gannon said. "Given the nature of Shaw's situation, my gut tells me that we're the only ones who have his video. I feel the same about the witness. I don't think anyone can catch us now."

"After what just happened with AP in San Francisco," Wilson said, "I wouldn't be so cocky, Gannon."

"Normally I would agree," Gannon said, "but I think we may be holding the biggest pieces of this story in our hands right now."

"What're you getting at?" Lisker said.

"In his video, Shaw says six guys survived. Shaw's dead, four have been stopped. That means there could still be one more at large that no one, except maybe the FBI, is aware of. Or—" Gannon held up a finger "—or maybe they picked up associates of the group, which makes all of our speculation meaningless. Bottom line, this might not be quite over yet."

"What do you propose we do?" O'Neill asked.

"We pull out all the stops to learn more about the San Francisco arrests," Gannon said. "We get our Washington bureau to pump national security sources on the video and the 'illegal mission' in Afghanistan."

"Then what?" Ford asked.

"You give me twenty-four hours to go upstate and get the witness exclusive. We write what we know, then tell the FBI that we're going with the story, tell them what it is, ask for comment and then we let it go as our exclusive?"

Gannon glanced at all the editors as they considered his proposal, then he looked at the wall with the time zone clocks.

"I like that approach," Cooke said.

"By seeking comment we're alerting the FBI to what we have, I think that's fair," O'Neill said.

Lisker grabbed his BlackBerry and started a message.

"I'm alerting Beland. Gannon, you've got twenty-four hours to pull this all together."

48

Lake George, New York

Maybe the worst is behind us.

After talking with Jack Gannon, Lisa echoed the same hope she'd had the last time she'd driven on this highway, when she'd signed the papers to sell the cabin.

It was over a week ago, but it felt like a thousand lifetimes as memories pulled her back...*to Ramapo and...the gunfire...the killing of the guards...the agent beside her...the killer is on them...the agent's eyes...I love you, Jennifer...the warm bloody spatter...the killer drilling his gun into her...she sees Bobby...he tells her to fight...it's not your time...fight for everything that matters...*

Bobby.

She missed him, ached for him as she glanced in her rearview mirror at Ethan and Taylor, sleeping.

Lisa blinked back her tears as she drove.

She was seething at the killers.

What gave them the right to destroy lives? Who were these animals? She hated them, thanked God they were caught. Three arrested in San Francisco and one dead in Nebraska; the tally was now four, the radio news report said.

Four. It was done.

Lisa had found a degree of comfort in the outcome. And if the FBI got them because of her help, she was glad. But she prayed she would never have to face those murdering bastards again.

Not in court, not anywhere.

Not ever.

She questioned whether she should've called Chan or Morrow to let them know that she was going out of town. "Keep us informed of your whereabouts in case we need to contact you," they'd told her at the outset. But they seemed to have forgotten about her, or were slow to confirm with a phone call what she'd already learned on the case from the press. She dismissed the thought of calling the FBI.

It was over.

She needed to look after her kids, move on with their lives.

As Lisa drove she embraced the beauty of this secluded section of the state. The magnificent Adirondacks rose in the west. Vermont, with its rolling Green Mountains, was a few miles east. She felt safe here, sheltered and ready to do all the things she needed to do. She looked forward to seeing Jack Gannon again, to telling him her story. She liked him.

He was a good guy.

Talking to him, letting the world know exactly what happened would be therapeutic for her, it would help her heal. She could close a chapter of her life and start living the next one by focusing on everything that matters.

...fight for everything that matters...

She glanced in her rearview mirror again.

Ethan and Taylor had awakened and were peacefully watching the scenery roll by.

Her angels.

On the seat between them was the handmade wooden box holding the marble cremation urn containing Bobby's ashes. Ethan and Taylor each rested a hand protectively on it in a scene that warmed Lisa's heart.

Yes, she thought, concentrating on the road ahead, *maybe the worst was now behind them.*

49

Following several hundred yards back of Lisa's car, in a rented SUV, Ivan Felk adjusted the tuning dial on the dash-mounted radio.

"Did you hear that?"

"Just the tail end before it cut out," Unger said from behind the wheel.

It was a few seconds after the hour and one static-filled station's newscast had led with something about "the armored car heist in Ramapo."

Felk found a clearer station in time to hear a fuller news report, which summarized the Associated Press story.

"...*three people have been arrested in San Francisco in connection with the murders of three guards and an FBI agent during a 6.3-million-dollar armored car heist in Greater New York City. The arrests follow the death of another suspect—Erik Rytter, a German national with a military background who was fatally wounded while struggling for a state trooper's gun after a traffic stop in Nebraska...*"

After swallowing the news, the muscles along Felk's jawline spasmed and he glared at the mountains.

"Three? Who else did they get?" Unger asked.

"Maybe Dante, or Upshaw, all because of her!" Felk glowered at Lisa's Ford far ahead in the distance then slammed both palms violently on the dash. For nearly half a mile, his anger faded into the tense hum of the SUV's radials on the asphalt. Unger tightened his grip on the wheel.

Thinking.

Police actually had three of their people. They should get out of the country, now. It was worse than Unger thought.

"Ivan, what if she's leading us into a trap? What if they're watching us? We could still pull out…the mission's over."

"It's not over. Not while I'm breathing."

Felk dragged the back of his hand across his mouth.

His squad was decimated, his other men, his brother, were all facing death. Clay's pleas on the video, and Felk's own from the frozen pond in Ohio pierced him—*"Don't let me die! Ivan, please! Don't let me die!"*—Felk's world was in ruins because of that bitch.

No, it would not end here. No goddamn way. He would not fail in this critical operation because of a fucking cashier from Queens.

"What do we do, Ivan?"

"We finish her, then we salvage the mission."

"Salvage the mission?"

"We already have more than six million overseas. We offer them the six million, a million per man. They won't turn down six million in cash."

"But there's only the two of us."

"We get our people in Kuwait to hire contractors to join us and then we'll carry out the mission and waste these motherfuckers."

"What about our guys here?"

"When we rescue our people overseas, we'll regroup and devise plans to help our men taken prisoner here. But first—" Felk's eyes blazed at Lisa's car "—first, we're going to collect our payback up there."

50

Lake George, New York

By the time Lisa and the children had reached the turnoff for the cabin, the afternoon sky had dimmed. Rolls of dark, ragged-edged rain clouds gathered above the mountains.

The threat of a storm hung over them as they traveled along a secondary road that wound through sweet-smelling forests for two miles before coming to an intersection. It gave access to the cabins scattered for miles in the vast wooded reaches along Lake George's eastern shore.

The crossroad was marked by Hallick's General Store.

The one-story framed building, with its overflowing flower boxes, was run by Jed and Violet Hallick, who lived thirteen miles away in Southbay. The store had a single gas pump and offered fishing supplies, outdoor gear and groceries in this isolated corner of the region. Their nearly napping dog yawned a welcome from the base of the pay phone on the shaded porch as Lisa and the kids entered.

The bells on the transom rang.

"Mom, can we roast hot dogs on the fire tonight?" Ethan asked.

"If it doesn't rain," Lisa said. "We're going to need buns."

"And chips, too!" Taylor said.

"And a few other things I forgot at home."

While the kids explored the store, Lisa collected her items and put them on the counter where an older man was reading the *New York Times*.

"Hi, Jed." Lisa gave him a bittersweet smile.

Jed Hallick removed his bifocals. He was an understanding man who'd watched Bobby grow up here summer after summer.

"Sorry to hear you sold the place, Lisa."

"It hurts, but I had to do it."

Seeing the sadness behind her eyes, Jed shifted gears as he rang up her purchases. "Vi and the church ladies will be out Tuesday to box up what you want to sell and donate. I'll have Brett get out there with the truck then, too."

He bagged up her items and patted her hand.

"You take care, Lisa. It looks like we're in for a whopper of a storm tonight."

"Jed, you were part of what Bobby loved about this place," Lisa said before she and the kids left. The transom bells rang behind them.

The next stretch from the store to the cabin was just under half a mile, but the old dirt road sliced through forests so thick they blocked the light. In some spots it was treacherously narrow, with sudden valleys and small cliff edges. Leafy branches slapped at Lisa's car while loose gravel popcorned against the undercarriage.

It was as if they'd entered another world.

Lisa stopped at a small, weatherworn sign with the name Palmer hand painted on it. As dust clouds swallowed her car, she inched off the road onto an earthen strip overrun with shrubs.

Through the trees they glimpsed the lake and their cabin.

It was so beautiful here, she thought. They were so lucky to have had this.

The cabin was built in the 1940s with ten-inch hand-hewn pine logs. The lakeside wall was made of floor-to-ceiling glass and offered a sweeping view of the water. French doors opened to the deck, with inviting Adirondack chairs and a path to the dock.

Inside, the cabin had hardwood floors, a stone fireplace, a spacious living room and dining area that flowed to the kitchen. The fridge and stove were powered by batteries and solar panels on an exposed hillside.

At the rear of the main floor were two small bedrooms and a bathroom. The master bedroom was upstairs in the loft. It overlooked the living room area and the lake windows.

No phone, no internet, no TV, a world away from the city.

"Out here you're off the grid," Bobby used to say.

They unloaded the car.

Ethan carried his father's urn and tenderly set it on the hearth before helping carry other things in. After they'd finished, Taylor said she was hungry. So was Ethan.

"Can we roast the hot dogs now?" he asked.

Outside, dusk was approaching, but the rain was holding off.

"Let's go for it," Lisa said.

She went to the fire pit near the deck, heaped some kindling within the circle of stones, piled firewood nearby and got things started. The kids helped bring everything to the picnic table. They each had their own roasting stick. As they cooked their hot dogs, Ethan tried to teach Taylor how to burp.

"Swallow some air, like this."

"Ethan, stop that!" Lisa said before she burped on purpose, making everyone laugh.

After they ate their hot dogs and chips, they toasted marshmallows.

Night fell, but the rain held and they snuggled around the fire in sleeping bags listening to the crackling as the flames painted their faces in yellow and orange light.

"I wish we didn't have to move to California," Taylor said.

"I know," Lisa said. "This is hard and scary for all of us, but I think it's the right thing to do."

"It's okay, Mom," Ethan said. "A lot of good things have happened to us here, but a lot of bad things, too, like Dad, and the new stuff."

"We'll talk—" Lisa swallowed "—we'll talk about it some more tomorrow."

She watched the fire in her children's eyes, thinking how much she needed them and how you can take nothing, not even the next moment in life, for granted.

"Mom," Ethan said. "Tomorrow we're going to put some of Dad's ashes in the lake and around the cabin, right?"

"Yes."

"And that way no matter who owns the cabin, or takes over, it will always belong to Dad and us, sort of, right?"

The flames reflected the tear tracks glistening on Lisa's face.

"Yes, always."

Thunder rolled, splitting the sky.

Lisa felt a raindrop as one sizzled on the fire, then another.

"Okay, time to get inside! Grab what you can!"

The rain came in torrents.

They watched the storm over the lake for half an hour before Lisa got Ethan and Taylor into bed. Then she hauled herself to the loft, exhausted. She had a lot to do in the morning. Jack Gannon was coming to interview her. After that, she needed to start sorting and storing things. Lisa went through a mental checklist as she listened to the rain hissing on the lake.

It was hypnotic.

She felt herself sinking for seconds, minutes, hours, she didn't know how long. She fell asleep unable to stop her thoughts of recent days from assailing her. They replayed over and over again until she was unsure if she was thinking them, or dreaming them, or dreaming about tape.

Duct tape?

Weird.

Its distinctive peel when pulled hard from the roll.

It sounded so real.

Lisa was thinking about it, hearing it.

She woke.

Odd.

Was Ethan playing with duct tape?

It was still storming. Lisa got up and peered down from the loft, her eyes adjusting to the darkness. She saw nothing unusual.

Deciding to check on the kids, she went down the loft stairs, puzzled over what was making that noise.

Lisa switched the light on and froze.

Her stomach contracted.

Ethan's and Taylor's eyes, wide as saucers, pleaded to her.

Duct tape covered their mouths.

Their hands were taped in front of them. Their bodies and legs were bound to the kitchen chairs that were turned from the table. Tears streamed down their faces, snot flowed from their noses. The polished blade of a large hunting knife glinted as it gingerly scraped along Ethan's quivering throat.

Nate Unger was holding the knife. He was wearing latex gloves and watching Lisa.

Ivan Felk was sitting next to Lisa's children, glaring at her.

He was wearing latex gloves and holding a gun.

Oh, Jesus.

Lisa saw the cobra tattoos on their wrists, exactly like the one on the man who had murdered the agent and had held a gun to her head.

"No! Please, no!"

Lisa flew to her children.

Felk smacked Lisa's face, sending her to the floor. Pulling her by her hair, he then hoisted her up as Unger gently brushed his knife over Taylor's neck, her screams muffled by tape.

"God, no! Please don't hurt my kids!"

Felk shoved Lisa into a chair and bound her with tape.

"Please, leave us alone! Please! We've done nothing."

Lisa continued pleading until he pressed a strip over her mouth. Felk nodded, and Unger, who had a holstered gun strapped to his leg, lifted Taylor, chair and all, and carried her to her bedroom.

Lisa began thrashing, screaming under her tape. Unger returned for Ethan and carried him off to his room.

Felk positioned himself in a chair opposite Lisa.

"Here's how this will go," he said. "We'll remove the tape from your mouth, you'll cooperate. We'll finish things and leave. Fair enough?"

Lisa nodded.

Unger ripped the tape from her mouth.

Felk held up her lost supermarket ID.

"You were there, on the floor beside the cop," Felk said. "What did you tell the FBI?"

Seconds ticked by as Lisa grasped the gravity of every aspect; the men had not covered their faces, which meant she could clearly identify them. They wore gloves.

Oh, my God, they're going to kill us!

Her mind spun until Felk yelled at her

"What did you tell the FBI?"

"Your tattoo—I described it—it was all I saw."

"What else?"

"That's it—that's all I saw. Please let my children go."

"What else does the FBI know?"

"I don't know."

"You're lying!"

Felk nodded to the children's rooms.

"Want me to send my friend in there to bring back pieces of your pups? Maybe start with a finger and an ear, the same way the motherfuckers in Afghanistan are doing it to my people?"

"Don't you touch them! I swear I don't know! The FBI didn't tell me anything!"

"Did we leave anything behind?"

"I don't know!"

"How did they get to our people in San Francisco?"

"Please, I don't know."

"DON'T FUCKING LIE TO ME!"

Felk thrust his tattooed wrist to within inches of her face.

"This is the symbol of good men who sacrificed everything for people like you. But now these men are going to die because you, an insignificant piece of nothing from Queens, got in the way."

Felk drew his face to Lisa's.

"I should've fucking wasted you when I had the chance. It's a mistake I won't make twice. You're going to suffer the same agony my men and my brother have suffered, long and slow. This is my vengeance."

51

Lake George, New York

Ethan's fists were clenched in fear.

Stop bawling, he told himself. *Stop shaking.*

From his room where he was bound to the kitchen chair, he heard the creeps yelling at his mom. He squeezed his fists tighter and ordered himself to stop crying.

You have to get free.

He had a plan and the key to it was in his right hand.

Before the creeps had come into his room and grabbed him, they'd made a noise, which woke him. He'd seized his penknife from his nightstand. The creeps never made him open his hands when they taped his wrists in front of him. Guess they figured he was just a scared little kid.

You stupid jerks. I'll show you.

Ethan could feel his knife, the pearl-handled beauty, like it was part of him.

He very carefully moved it around just so and after a couple of tries managed to open the sharp little blade. He regripped the knife and began cutting at the tape around his wrists, forcing them apart until the tape gave way, freeing his hands.

Yes!

He sliced at the rest of his bindings, yanked the tape away, stood up and went to the door. He opened it a crack, saw the creeps swearing at his mom. If Ethan stepped into the hall to free Taylor, they'd see him.

We need help now.

He got dressed so fast, put on his shoes, his jacket, quietly unlatched the big window next to his bed and slipped out.

He gulped air.

The rain drenched him and he headed for the winding dirt road, glancing back at the cabin, his heart wrenching at leaving his mother and sister behind, but a voice told him to run.

He ran as fast as he could, praying a car would come.

Anybody.

He didn't dare stop.

The rain had turned the road to greasy mud. He tried to stay on the shoulder, to get traction from the gravel there, but he fell twice. Soon his legs grew numb from running and falling. His sides and lungs ached. Fear had evaporated all his saliva, and his throat was ragged from panicked breathing.

His prayers for a car were in vain.

No one lived near them. His only hope was to get to Hallick's store.

He slowed to a trot, then walked as fast as he could. Fear compelled him to keep moving until at last he saw a light in the distance and found his second wind. The light got bigger as the store emerged. Its darkened windows signaled it was closed while the sign on the door confirmed it.

He reached the pay phone out of breath.

Doubling over, he waited until he could breathe and talk, then picked up the handset. There was a dial tone. Ethan punched 911.

"Washington County Emergency—" *static* "—your emerg—"

"Hello! I'm at Hallick's store and some bad guys are—hello!"

Static drowned the call.

Ethan hung up and pressed 911 again.

Again static.

Is it the storm doing this?

He tried three more times without success. Tears stung his eyes; he couldn't think until he remembered the card that reporter Jack Gannon had given him. It was in his jeans.

It had a 1-800 number.

Ethan found the card and tried it, not understanding why the line rang clear, but it did, loud and clear.

Static-free.

"World Press Alliance, New York," a night news editor answered.

"My name is Ethan Palmer. I'm ten years old. Some guys are trying to kill my mom and sister right now! I got away and we need help. I need to talk to Jack Gannon."

"Whoa, hold on, son. Where are you? Is there a number, address?"

"At our cabin by Lake George. I'm at the pay phone at Hallick's store."

"Can you give me the number on the pay phone?"

The editor kept Ethan on the line and used other phones to make emergency calls.

52

Some ten miles south from where Ethan stood, Jack Gannon was in the Evergreen Rise Motel making notes on his laptop for his interview with Lisa in the morning.

He'd put on his sweatpants and a T-shirt, and was digging into cream cakes, potato chips and ginger ale as he worked. Junk food was a weakness when he was on the road, or stressed.

Gannon had been delayed leaving Manhattan and was glad he'd checked in just before the storm hit. Funny, he was just now thinking how the motel clerk had told him he was at the edge of the zone for wireless service, when his cell phone rang.

Is that ESP? He shrugged as he answered the call.

"Gannon."

"Jack, its Neal at the night desk. You're not going to believe this."

As the night editor explained, Gannon got up and started fumbling for his clothes, the map to Lisa's cabin and his car keys.

"Christ, I'm fifteen minutes from there. I'm leaving now."

"Be careful. We got the New York State Police and some locals rolling."

"Call Frank Morrow at the FBI. Here's his cell."

Gannon rushed to his Pontiac Vibe and roared off for Hallick's store and Lisa's cabin.

53

Lake George, New York

As Lisa's hopes melted she took stock of her life, all that was good, all that she'd endured and all that she'd dreamed.

It wasn't right. She did not deserve this. Ethan and Taylor did not deserve this.

We've already lost too much.

As Lisa regarded the bastards who wanted to take away everything from her, her fear turned to anger. She had to fight.

Fight for everything that matters.

"Why are you doing this to us?"

"We bled and died for our country overseas, then we went back to hunt terrorists and do dirty, secret jobs for our governments. They betrayed us and left our men to die."

"What's that got to do with me and my kids and the decent people you murdered?"

"Collateral damage. They got in the way of our war on terrorism."

"You're not at war with my children!"

"Shut up!" Unger said.

"You dishonor all the brave people who gave their lives overseas. You're not soldiers!"

"I said, shut the fuck up!" Unger said.

"Soldiers don't terrorize little children. You're criminals, murdering cowards, and you'll burn for what you've done."

Felk left for the door, came back and dropped a shovel on the floor in front of Lisa.

"Time to go, bitch!"

They cut her from her bindings and marched her from the cabin into the woods and rain at gunpoint. Felk held his gun on Lisa. Unger kept his holstered and carried the shovel, guiding her by flashlight. They progressed along through the thick forest until they came to a meadow.

"Dig," Felk said. "About three feet down. We're going to bury you along with your two pups. No witnesses. No trace. No nothing."

Unger tossed the shovel on the ground, stepped back, withdrew his gun and trained it on Lisa. Felk stood opposite, keeping her at gunpoint. Both were just out of reach for her to swing the shovel at them.

Lisa trembled as the shovel's spade bit into the wet earth.

54

Lake George, New York

Gannon's headlights raked through the night rain across the small parking lot at Hallick's General Store and found Ethan huddled in a corner of the porch.

He was sheltered but soaked and shivering.

Gannon hurried him into his car and blasted the heat.

"Are you all right, Ethan?"

He shook his head.

"They're going to hurt my mom and sister."

"Who are they? How many? Do they have guns?"

"Yes, they have guns. I saw two big men. I think they're the same people my mom saw hurt people at the truck stop."

"Okay, listen, we should wait. Help is coming—"

"No! It'll be too late! You have to do something now!"

Gannon rubbed his chin, thinking hard. Could he live with himself if he sat there when he could've helped?

"All right," he said. "You stay here at the store until the police come. Tell them I've gone to the cabin. I'll get as close as I can to see what I can do."

"Drive to the great big round rock, it's like a ball,"

Ethan said. "Then walk from there so they won't see your lights."

Gannon found the round rock and parked. The flashlight in his glove compartment had dead batteries. He got out and started walking through the darkness along the twisting dirt road unable to believe what had unfolded.

He had no idea what he was going to do. He had no weapon; he'd taken a firearms course in Buffalo for a story, but he hated guns. He could be facing two armed men with military training. Murderers. He shoved his concerns aside. Lisa and her eight-year-old daughter were in there and he had to do some—

Gannon stopped dead.

Was that a voice?

Senses heightened, he concentrated on his surroundings, when he saw it—a flash of light in the forest and voices.

Was that it?

He was close enough to the cabin for it to be them. Lisa's directions had said there were no other neighbors nearby.

Gannon strained to see in the rain and darkness. He left the road and inched through the woods toward the light and the voices. He fought to be as careful as possible, not to fall, or make noise. The rush of the downpour helped deaden his advance and he drew close enough to see two men, one holding a flashlight and a gun, the other holding a gun. Between them a woman with a shovel was digging.

Jesus.

It was Lisa.

Gannon took a long deep breath and swallowed hard. He had no time to think.

I've got to do something.

* * *

Lisa had dug an oblong hole well over two feet deep into the soft earth.

Through her prayers, tears and rage, emotions swirled.

God, please don't let the children suffer.

We'll be together soon, Bobby…

"Deep enough." Felk nudged Lisa with his gun. "Get in there and get on your knees."

Lisa sobbed as she got into the hole.

"Don't hurt my children."

"Go get her pups, Nate," Felk said.

Unger tramped off to the cabin, following the path lit by his flashlight, while Felk lowered himself, keeping his gun on Lisa.

"We'll do them in front of you, so it's the last thing you see."

"No, please."

They heard Unger's boots on the cabin's wooden deck, heard the door as he went inside, then rapid movement on the deck again as Unger shouted into the woods.

"The boy's gone!"

"Gone? What the—"

Felk turned from Lisa and a blurred force shot from the darkness, knocking Felk to the ground. Fueled by some overwhelming power and lightning instinct…*fight with all you have*…Lisa seized the shovel and before either man knew what had happened she'd clubbed Felk's head three times, and was moving on the stranger.

"No! Don't! It's me, Jack Gannon!"

She turned the blade of the shovel and again she beat Felk with such frenzy Gannon had to pull her away. He used the flashlight to find the gun and remove all rounds as they saw light flashing as Unger came crashing through the forest.

"Ivan, he's gone!" Unger approached the hole, panting. "I don't know how he got free. I taped—"

Unger's last thought was wondering what caused the explosion of stars before everything went dark—not knowing that the flat steel back of Lisa's shovel had landed full force on his face.

With Unger on the ground, Lisa smashed him with the shovel several more times before Gannon could stop her.

Both men were unconscious and bleeding profusely. Gannon had removed the rounds from Unger's gun.

"It's all right," Gannon told Lisa. "Ethan got away. He got to the store and called for help."

Lisa was sobbing.

"He's safe at the store. Help is coming," Gannon said.

While Gannon gripped the shovel and kept watch on the men, Lisa ran back to the cabin, took care of Taylor and returned with the duct tape. They bound Felk and Unger, who were still bleeding badly but semiconscious.

Lisa, Taylor and Gannon watched over the killers in the rain.

No one spoke. There were no words.

Twenty minutes later, the headlights of the first sheriff's car poked through the trees and Gannon signaled the deputy with the flashlight.

Epilogue

The incident at Lake George was news for weeks.

Press agencies across the United States and around the world reported on it with Canadian, German, British journalists, and those in Afghanistan, Pakistan, Iraq and Kuwait, highlighting local elements.

But the definitive stories came from the World Press Alliance, which produced an exclusive series that dissected Ivan Felk's Operation Retribution and everything it had touched.

Jack Gannon led a team of WPA reporters who examined Ivan Felk and the men behind the attack, chronicling their lives and careers as elite ex-soldiers contracted by shadowy, global security firms for secret missions.

The WPA posted parts of Harlee Shaw's video online and analyzed Red Cobra Team 9's disastrous operation into the forbidden zone. They revealed how it had spawned the 6.3-million-dollar heist in New York and the plot to hit the Federal Reserve in San Francisco before a widowed, single mother of two from Queens brought it all to an end.

Twice, Ivan Felk had held a gun to Lisa Palmer's head, Gannon wrote in his profile of her. The first time was when she'd witnessed the murder of FBI agent Gregory

Dutton; the second time when Felk hunted her down to her family cabin in Upstate New York, where he'd forced her to dig graves for herself and her children in his plan to eliminate her as a witness.

"I shouldn't be alive," Lisa said in the interview. "Something told me to fight, that it wasn't my time."

Gannon detailed how ten-year-old Ethan Palmer used his penknife, a cherished gift from his late father, to escape and call for help, in a story that illustrated her family's refusal to be defeated.

"Everyone faces hardship, but you have to keep going," Lisa said.

Gannon wrote how Lisa had made the heart-wrenching decision to leave Queens with her children and start a new chapter of their lives. He did not disclose the new location in the article.

In the weeks that followed, Gannon learned how authorities had concluded that Lisa would be eligible for the two-hundred-thousand-dollar reward that had been posted in the heist, once the surviving suspects had been convicted of their crimes. Her wish was for the reward to be shared with the families of the guards and agent who had been murdered.

The FBI's ongoing investigation reached around the globe. Working with police in Kuwait and Pakistan, agents made more arrests and were able to recover much of the cash stolen from American Centurion.

The *Times* of London, quoting intelligence sources, broke stories on how shortly after the WPA's news reports had exposed the unsanctioned military action in the forbidden zone, coalition forces launched surgical air strikes against "terrorist strongholds" in the region.

The strikes ensured an end to the hostage ordeal involving Red Cobra Team 9.

No one survived the bombings.

The activities in the disputed territory raised disturbing questions about potentially rogue intelligence operations, which led to a probe by the United Nations, the U.S. Senate Select Committee on Intelligence and calls for congressional hearings.

In New York, there was talk that the WPA's series was a leading contender for a Pulitzer, and Gannon was approached by two publishers to write a book on the case. The morning he went to Lisker to request a leave of absence, he was surprised: Lisker's office had been cleared out.

"When Beland got wind that he was going to take a job with an investment firm, he ordered him to leave forthwith," Carter O'Neill said. "Dolf Lisker was never quite attuned with the craft, Jack. Not like you."

With the case cleared, FBI special agent Frank Morrow took a long lunch one day and walked to Ground Zero, where he looked back on his life. Reflecting on September 11, he was grateful that he was given proper time to say goodbye. He booked a few weeks off, then, with Beth and Hailey, drove south along the East Coast. By the time they'd reached the Keys, Morrow had decided to undergo chemo and take that three percent chance at hope. They spent their days talking and watching the sunset on the Gulf of Mexico.

Some months later, after she'd sold her house, on the day before she was set to leave Queens with her children, Lisa Palmer met Gannon for coffee at one of the outdoor plazas near Penn Station.

"I just wanted to thank you for everything, Jack."

"How are you and the kids doing?"

"Better, with all this behind us." She smiled.

"Listen," he said. "I don't know much about karma, but

with all you've faced so far, I'd say you deserve nothing but the best for the rest of your life."

She kissed his cheek and smiled.

"If you ever get out to California, feel free to stop by."

Lisa Palmer had a nice smile and that's what Gannon remembered long after she left him standing alone on the busy street across from Madison Square Garden.

As he walked back to the office, he accepted what he was: a loner. It took him much of his life to realize that he would always be alone to do what he did best: search for the truth.

He'd searched for the truth where it concerned his sister, Cora, and he searched for it behind every kind of injustice he'd encountered because that's where the story was.

And he would always find the story.

At that moment, near La Guardia's runways in the East River, on Rikers Island, Ivan Felk lay on his cot in his cell.

He was sore, still recovering.

His face was permanently scarred from the beating Lisa Palmer had given him. He was awaiting trial on four first-degree murder charges and a long list of related charges. Under federal law he was likely to receive the death penalty.

Last week, Felk heard how Unger had hung himself in his cell.

This morning, reading an old copy of the *Washington Post* from the library, Felk learned about the air strike.

Forgive me, Clay.

Everybody and everything was gone now.

But it was not the end.

The *Post* also carried one of Jack Gannon's features, the one about Lisa Palmer. Felk stared at her photo for hours, absorbing her, slowly devouring her the way a snake swallows its prey.

No, this was not the end.

Death penalty cases were long, complex. They'd take years, maybe even decades. And in that time, they'd move Felk constantly, to court, to his cell, even to other facilities. And in that time, he'd study, he'd learn.

Then he'd execute his escape.

No, this would never be over.

* * * * *

Acknowledgments
and a Personal Note

The Burning Edge is loosely inspired by a true case, a commando-style armored car heist that I'd covered many years ago while working as a crime reporter. Other aspects of the novel were drawn from real-life situations that I, or others I knew, have experienced. But I won't go into any of it here.

It's too personal.

I want to thank Special Agent Anne Beagan of the FBI's New York Division who patiently suffered many questions from me to ensure my work of fiction rang true. If this story worked for you, it's because of Anne's kind help. If this story fell short for you, then blame me; the mistakes are mine.

Many thanks to Amy Moore-Benson, Miranda Indrigo and to the incredible editorial, marketing, sales and PR teams at Harlequin and MIRA Books in Toronto, New York and around the world.

Wendy Dudley, as always, made this story better.

Very special thanks to Barbara, Laura and Michael.

It's important you know that, in getting this book to you, I benefited from the hard work and generosity of many people, too many to thank individually here. I am indebted to everyone in all stages of production, the sales representatives, librarians and booksellers for putting my work in your hands.

This brings me to what I hold to be the most critical part of the entire enterprise: you, the reader. This aspect has become something of a creed for me, one that bears repeating with each book.

Thank you very much for your time, for without you, a book remains an untold tale. Thank you for setting your life on pause and taking the journey. I deeply appreciate my growing audience around the world and those who've been with me since the beginning who keep in touch. Thank you all for your very kind words. I hope you enjoyed the ride and will check out my earlier books while watching for my next one. I welcome your feedback. Drop by at www.rickmofina.com, subscribe to my newsletter and send me a note.

Rick Mofina

Laurel, Montana

Flames licked the night sky as the house burned.

Neighbors could see the woman trapped upstairs, banging her hands against her bedroom window. Two men were working in vain with garden hoses when the first engine arrived with Jeff Griffin's crew.

They laid lines, started attacking the blaze from two points and extended the aerial. Jeff, a thirty-four-year-old firefighter with the Laurel Volunteer Fire Department, charged up the ladder with an ax in his hand and a sixty-pound tank on his back.

He had seconds to get the woman out.

Glass exploded from the window of the adjoining room, pelting him with shards and debris as flames roared. The woman's eyes widened with terror. The room was aglow behind her. She had to be eighty. He smashed her window, unleashing blast-furnace heat. As he seized the woman's hand, she was swallowed by acrid smoke and he lost his grip, lost sight of her.

Jeff didn't have time to think of his wife, Sarah, their new baby, Lee Ann, their son, Cole, or his own safety.

Hell, he wasn't even paid to put his life on the line.

But he climbed into the room.

Blind, he reached into the churning clouds, feeling around, finding her hand, just when a great whip-crack collapsed half the back roof. The woman was trembling. He hoisted her to the sill as part of the floor gave way to the inferno below. Jeff straddled the sill with the woman in his arms. The skeletal remains of the upper house yawed as he got his boots on the ladder. Jeff felt the building shift as he got the woman across his chest. Putting his hands through her arms and legs, he descended the ladder.

She was losing consciousness.

He got her down to the lawn, got the oxygen flowing into her until the paramedics took over. Her signs were good. No one else was in the building. As crews battled the fire, Jeff remained kneeling beside her. Amid the flashing lights, sirens and growling pumper, he yanked off his helmet and took her hand in his.

She smelled of soap and ash. She was wearing a cotton nightgown printed with tiny roses. Her bare feet were in tattered slippers. The oxygen mask covering her face underscored a long, hard life. Jeff figured her to be a woman with pioneer blood; a woman whose family had endured every tribulation. He saw it written in her violet eyes as they found his.

He held her in his gaze, his body still pulsing with adrenaline.

He saw her wedding ring. Was she someone's mother, someone's grandmother? He didn't know her, which was rare in Laurel, a suburb of 7,000, southwest of Billings. In Laurel, almost everyone pretty much knew everybody, or darned near.

This woman was a stranger to him.

Yet in the brief moment he held her hand, something happened between them. In the ripples of the averted tragedy, Jeff felt a fresh stab of unease. It was in the way she was looking at him, with mounting intensity.

As if she was reading a sign of something to come.

A portent.

As the paramedics loaded her, it dawned on Jeff that the fear rising in her eyes was not for her.

It was for him.

MIRAEXP313014

RICK MOFINA

32948	IN DESPERATION	___ $9.99 U.S.	___ $11.99 CAN.
32901	SIX SECONDS	___ $7.99 U.S.	___ $9.99 CAN.
32794	THE PANIC ZONE	___ $9.99 U.S.	___ $11.99 CAN.
32638	VENGEANCE ROAD	___ $7.99 U.S.	___ $8.99 CAN.

(limited quantities available)

TOTAL AMOUNT	$ _____
POSTAGE & HANDLING	$ _____
($1.00 for 1 book, 50¢ for each additional)	
APPLICABLE TAXES*	$ _____
TOTAL PAYABLE ·	$ _____

(check or money order—please do not send cash)

To order, complete this form and send it, along with a check or money order for the total above, payable to MIRA Books, to: **In the U.S.:** 3010 Walden Avenue, P.O. Box 9077, Buffalo, NY 14269-9077; **In Canada:** P.O. Box 636, Fort Erie, Ontario, L2A 5X3.

Name: _____
Address: _____ City: _____
State/Prov.: _____ Zip/Postal Code: _____
Account Number (if applicable): _____

075 CSAS

*New York residents remit applicable sales taxes.
*Canadian residents remit applicable GST and provincial taxes.

MIRA | **H HARLEQUIN®**
™ www.Harlequin.com

MRM0112BL